The Freebooters
A Story Of The Texan War

By

Gustave Aimard

Double 9
BOOKS

The Freebooters
A Story Of The Texan War
by Gustave Aimard

Copyright © 2024

ISBN: 978-93-62203-52-6

Published by

DOUBLE 9 BOOKS

2/13-B, Ansari Road
Daryaganj, New Delhi – 110002
info@double9books.com
www.double9books.com
Tel. 011-40042856

ABOUT THE AUTHOR

Gustave Aimard wrote multiple volumes about Latin America and the American frontier. Oliver Aimard was born in Paris. As he previously stated, he was the offspring of two married individuals, "but not to each other". His father, François Sébastiani de la Porta (1775-1851), was a commander in Napoleon's army and a representative of the Louis Philippe government. Sebastiani was married to the Duchess of Coigny. In 1806, the couple had a daughter, Alatrice-Rosalba Fanny. The mother died shortly after she was born. Fanny was reared by her grandmother, Duchess of Coigny. Aimard was placed as a baby with a family that were paid to raise him. By the age of nine or twelve, he was sent off on a herring boat. Later, about 1838, he served briefly with the French Navy. After one more trip to America (when he claims he was adopted into a Comanche tribe), Aimard returned to Paris in 1847, the same year his half-sister, Duchess de Choiseul-Pralin, was cruelly killed by her noble husband. Reconciliation or acknowledgement by his biological family did not occur. After serving briefly in the Garde Mobil, Aimard returned to the Americas.

CONTENTS

PREFACE

Apart from the thrilling interest of Aimard's new story, which I herewith offer to English readers, I think it will be accepted with greater satisfaction, as being an historical record of the last great contest in which the North Americans were engaged. As at the present moment everything is eagerly devoured that may tend to throw light on the impending struggle between North and South, I believe that the story of "THE FREEBOOTERS," which is rigorously true in its details, will enable my readers to form a correct opinion of the character of the Southerners.

The series, of which this volume forms a second link, will be completed in a third volume, to be called "THE WHITE SCALPER," which contains an elaborate account of the liberation of Texas, and the memorable battle of San Jacinto, together with personal adventures of the most extraordinary character.

L.W.

7, DRAYTON TERRACE,

WEST BROMPTON.

CHAPTER I
FRAY ANTONIO

All the wood rangers have noticed, with reference to the immense virgin forests which still cover a considerable extent of the soil of the New World, that, to the man who attempts to penetrate into one of these mysterious retreats which the hand of man has not yet deformed, and which preserve intact the sublime stamp which Deity has imprinted on them, the first steps offer almost insurmountable difficulties, which are gradually smoothed down more and more, and after a little while almost entirely disappear. It is as if Nature had desired to defend by a belt of thorns and spikes the mysterious shades of these aged forests, in which her most secret arcana are carried out.

Many times, during our wanderings in America, we were in a position to appreciate the correctness of the remark we have just made: this singular arrangement of the forests, surrounded, as it were, by a rampart of parasitic plants entangled one in the other, and thrusting in every direction their shoots full of incredible sap, seemed a problem which offered a certain degree of interest from various points of view, and especially from that of science.

It is evident to us that the circulation of the air favours the development of vegetation. The air which circulates freely round a large extent of ground covered with lofty trees, and is driven by the various breezes that agitate the atmosphere, penetrates to a certain depth into the clumps of trees it surrounds, and consequently supplies nourishment to all the parasitical shrubs vegetation presents to it. But, on reaching a certain depth under the covert, the air, less frequently renewed, no longer supplies carbonic acid to all the vegetation that covers the soil, and which, through the absence of that aliment, pines away and dies.

This is so true, that those accidents of soil which permit the air a more active circulation in certain spots, such as the bed of a torrent or a gorge between two eminences, the entrance of which is open to the prevailing wind, favour the development of a more luxuriant vegetation than in flat places.

It is more than probable that Fray Antonio[1] made none of the reflections with which we begin this chapter, while he stepped silently and quietly through the trees, leaving the man who had helped him, and probably saved his life, to struggle as he could with the crowd of Redskins who attacked him, and against whom he would indubitably have great difficulty in defending him.

Fray Antonio was no coward; far from it: in several critical circumstances he had displayed true bravery; but he was a man to whom the existence he led offered enormous advantages and incalculable delights. Life seemed to him good, and he did all in his power to spend it jolly and free from care. Hence, through respect for himself, he was extremely prudent, only facing danger when it was absolutely necessary; but at such times, like all men driven into a corner, he became terrible and really dangerous to those who, in one way or the other, had provoked in him this explosion of passion.

In Mexico, and generally throughout Spanish America, as the clergy are only recruited from the poorest class of the population, their ranks contain men of gross ignorance, and for the most part of more than doubtful morality. The religious orders, which form nearly one-third of the population, living nearly independent of all subjection and control, receive among them people of all sorts, for whom the religious dress they don is a cloak behind which they give way with perfect liberty to their vices, of which the most venial are indubitably indolence, luxury, and intoxication.

Enjoying a great credit with the civilized Indian population, and greatly respected by them, the monks impudently abuse that halo of sanctity which surrounds them, in order to shamefully plunder these poor people under the slightest excuses.

Indeed, blackguardism and demoralisation have attained such a pitch in these unhappy countries, which are old and decrepit without ever having been young, that the conduct of the monks, offensive it may seem in the sight of Europeans, has nothing at all extraordinary for those among whom they live.

Far from us the thought of leading it to be supposed that among the Mexican clergy, and even the monks we have so decried, there are not men worthy of the gown they wear, and convinced of the sanctity of their mission; we have, indeed, known many of that character; but unfortunately they form so insignificant a minority, that they must be regarded as the exception.

Fray Antonio was assuredly no better or worse than the other monks whose gown he wore; but, unluckily for him, for some time past fatality appeared to have vented its spite on him, and mixed him up, despite his firm will, in events, not only opposed to his character but to his habits, which led him into a multitude of tribulations each more disagreeable than the other, and which were beginning to make him consider that life extremely bitter, which he had hitherto found so pleasant.

The atrocious mystification of which John Davis had rendered the poor monk a victim, had especially spread a gloomy haze over his hitherto so gay mind; a sad despondency had seized upon him; and it was with a heavy and uncertain step that he fled through the forest, although, excited by the sounds of combat that still reached his ear, he made haste to get off, through fear of falling into the hands of the Redskins, if they proved the victors.

Night surprised poor Fray Antonio ere he had reached the skirt of this forest, which seemed to him interminable. Naturally anything but hard-working, and not at all used to desert life, the monk found himself greatly embarrassed when he saw the sun disappear on the horizon in a mist of purple and gold, and the darkness almost instantaneously cover the earth. Unarmed, without means of lighting a fire, half-dead with hunger and alarm, the monk took a long glance of despair around him, and fell to the ground, giving vent to a dull groan: he literally did not know to what saint he should appeal.

Still, after a few moments, the instinct of self-preservation gained the mastery over discouragement, and the monk, whose teeth chattered with terror on hearing re-echoed through the forest the lugubrious roaring of the wild beasts, which were beginning to awaken, and greeted in their fashion the longed-for return of gloom—rose with a feverish energy, and suffering from that feverish over-excitement which fear raised to a certain pitch produces, resolved to profit by the fugitive rays that still crossed the glade, to secure himself a shelter for the night.

Opposite to him grew a majestic mahogany tree, whose interlaced branches and dense foliage seemed to offer him a secure retreat against the probable attack of the gloomy denizens of the forest.

Assuredly, under any other circumstances than those in which he found himself, the bare idea of escalading this immense forest would have appeared to the monk the height of folly and mental aberration, owing first to his paunch, and next to his awkwardness, of which he felt intimately convinced.

But it was a critical point: at each instant the situation grew more dangerous; the howling came nearer in a most alarming manner; there was no time to hesitate; and Fray Antonio did not do so. After walking once or twice round the tree, in order to discover the spot which offered him the greatest facility for his ascent, he gave vent to a sigh, embraced the enormous and rugged trunk with his arms and knees, and painfully commenced his attempted climb.

But it was no easy matter, especially for a plump monk, to mount the tree, and Fray Antonio soon perceived this fact at his own expense; for each time that, after extraordinary efforts, he managed to raise himself a few inches from the ground, his strength suddenly failed him, and he fell back on the ground with lacerated hands and torn clothes.

Ten times already had he renewed his efforts, with the desperation produced by despair, without seeing them crowned with success; the perspiration poured down his face; his chest panted; he was in a state to produce pity even in his most obstinate enemy.

"I shall never succeed in mounting it," he muttered sadly; "and if I remain here, I am a lost man, for within an hour I shall be infallibly devoured by some tiger in search of its supper."

This final reflection, which was incontestably true, restored a fresh ardour to the monk, who resolved to make a new and supreme attempt But this time he wished to take all his precautions; consequently, he began collecting the dead wood round him and piling it at the foot of the tree, so as to form a scaffolding high enough for him to reach, without any great difficulty, a branch sufficiently low for him, while careful to remain awake, to hope to spend the night without fear of being devoured—an alternative for which the worthy monk did not feel the slightest inclination.

Soon, thanks to the vivacity of his movements, Fray Antonio had a considerable heap of wood piled up around him. A smile of satisfaction lit up his wide face, and he breathed again, while wiping away the perspiration that poured down his face.

"This time," he muttered, calculating with a glance the space he had to cover, "if I do not succeed, I shall be preciously clumsy."

In the meanwhile the last gleams of twilight, so useful to the monk, had entirely disappeared; the absence of the stars, which had not yet shown themselves, left a profound obscurity in the sky, which was even more obscure under the covert; all was beginning to be blotted out, only allowing here and there a few clumps of trees to be distinguished, as they designed their gloomy masses in the night, or a few patches of water, the result of the last storm, which studded the forest with paler spots. The evening breeze had risen, and could be heard soughing through the foliage with a sad and melancholy plaintiveness.

The dangerous denizens of the forest had quitted their lurking places, and crushed the dead wood, as they eagerly came on, amid a deafening current of catlike howls. The monk had not an instant to lose, if he did not wish to be attacked on all sides at once by the wild beasts, whom a lengthened fast rendered more terrible still.

After taking a searching glance around him in order to assure himself that no pressing danger threatened him, the monk devotedly crossed himself, fervently recommended himself to Heaven with a sincerity he had probably never evinced before, and then, suddenly making up his mind, began resolutely climbing up the pile of wood. After several unsuccessful attempts, he at last reached the top of this fictitious mount.

He then stopped for a minute to draw breath; indeed, thanks to his ingenious ideas, Fray Antonio was now nearly ten feet from the ground. It is true that any animal could easily have overthrown this obstacle; but for all that, this beginning of success revived the monk's courage, the more so because, on raising his eyes he saw a few paces above him, the blessed branch toward which he had so long extended his arms in vain.

"Come!" he said, hopefully.

He embraced the tree once more, and recommenced his fatiguing clambering. Either through skill or accident Fray Antonio at length managed to seize the branch with both hands, and clung to it with all his strength. The rest was as nothing. The monk assembled by a supreme effort all the vigour his previous attempts had left him, and raising himself by his arms, tried to get astride on the branch. Owing to his energetic perseverances, he had raised his head and shoulders above the branch, when all at once he felt a hand or a claw fasten round his right leg, and squeeze it as in a vice. A shudder of terror ran over the monk's body: his blood stood still in his veins; an icy perspiration beaded on his temples, and his teeth chattered fit to break.

"Mercy!" he exclaimed in a choking voice, "I am dead. Holy virgin, have pity on me."

His strength, paralyzed by terror, deserted him, his hands let loose the protecting branch, and he fell in a lump at the foot of the tree. Fortunately for Fray Antonio, the care he had taken in piling up the dead wood to a considerable extent broke his fall, otherwise it would probably have been mortal: but the shock he experienced was so great that he completely lost his senses. The monk's fainting fit was long: when he returned to life and opened his eyes again, he took a frightened glance around, and fancied he must be suffering from a horrible nightmare.

He had not stirred from the spot, so to speak: he still found himself by the tree, which he had tried so long to climb up in vain, but he was lying close to an enormous fire, over which half a deer was roasting, and around him were some twenty Indians, crouching on their heels, silently smoking their pipes, while their horses, picketed a few yards off, and ready to mount, were eating their provender.

Fray Antonio had seen Indians several times before, and had stood on such intimate terms, indeed, with them, as to be able to recognize them. His new friends were clothed in their war garb, and from their hair drawn off their foreheads, and their long barbed lances, it was easy to recognize them as Apaches.

The monk's blood ran cold, for the Apaches are notorious for their cruelty and roguery. Poor Fray Antonio had fallen from Charybdis into Scylla; he had only escaped from the jaws of the wild beasts in order to be in all probability martyred by the Redskins. It was a sad prospect which furnished the unlucky monk with ample material for thoughts, each more gloomy than the other, for he had often listened with a shudder to the hunters' stories about the atrocious tortures the Apaches take a delight in inflicting on their prisoners with unexampled barbarity.

Still, the Indians went on smoking silently, and did not appear to perceive that their captive had regained his senses. For his part, the monk hermetically closed his eyes, and anxiously preserved the most perfect tranquillity, in order to leave his dangerous companions, so long as he could, in ignorance of the state in which he was.

At length the Indians left off smoking, and after shaking the ash out of their calumets, passed them again through their girdle; a Redskin removed from the fire the half deer which was perfectly roasted, laid it in abanijo leaves in front of his comrades, and each drawing his scalping knife, prepared for a vigorous attack on the venison, which exhaled an appetizing odour, especially for the nostrils of a man who, during the whole past day, had been condemned to an absolute fast.

At this moment the monk felt a heavy hand laid on his chest, while a voice said to him with a guttural accent, which, however, had nothing menacing about it.

"The father of prayer can open his eyes now, for the venison is smoking, and his share is cut off."

The monk, perceiving that his stratagem was discovered, and excited by the smell of the meat, having made up his mind, opened his eyes, and sat up.

"Och!" the man who had before spoken said, "My father can eat; he must be hungry, and has slept enough."

The monk attempted to smile, but only made a frightful grimace, so alarmed did he feel. As however, he was really hungry as a wolf, he followed the example offered him by the Indians, who had already commenced their meal, and set to work eating the lump of venison which they had the politeness to set before him. The meal did not take long; still it lasted long enough to restore a little courage to the monk, and make him regard his position from a less gloomy side than he had hitherto done.

In truth, the behaviour of the Apaches toward him had nothing hostile about it; on the contrary, they were most attentive in serving him with what he needed, giving him more food so soon as they perceived that he had nothing before him: they even carried their politeness so far as to give him a few mouthfuls of spirit, an extremely precious liquid, of which they are most greedy, even for their own use, owing to the difficulty they experience in obtaining it.

When he had ended his meal, the monk, who was almost fully reassured as to the amicable temper of his new friends, on seeing them light their pipes, took from his pocket tobacco and an Indian corn leaf, and after rolling a *pajillo* with the skill which the men of Spanish race possess, he conscientiously enjoyed the bluish smoke of his excellent Havana tobacco, *costa abajo*.

A considerable space of time elapsed thus, and not a syllable was exchanged among them. By degrees the ranks of the Redskins thinned: one after the other, at short intervals, rolled themselves in their blankets, lay down with their feet to the fire, and went to sleep almost immediately. Fray Antonio, crushed by the poignant emotions of the day, and the enormous fatigue he had experienced, would gladly have imitated the Indians, had he dared, for he felt his eyes close involuntarily, and found immense difficulty in contending against the sleep that overpowered him. At last the Indian who hitherto had alone spoken, perceiving his state of somnolency, took pity on him. He rose, fetched a horsecloth, and brought it to the monk.

"My father will wrap himself in this fressada,[2]" he said, employing the bad Spanish in which he had hitherto spoken; "the nights are cold, and my father needs sleep greatly, he will, therefore, feel warmed with this. Tomorrow, a Chief will smoke the calumet with my father in council. Blue-fox desires to have a serious conversation with the father of prayer of the Palefaces."

Fray Antonio gratefully accepted the horsecloth so graciously offered by the Chief, and without attempting to prolong the conversation, he wrapped himself up carefully, and lay down by the fire so as to absorb the largest amount of caloric possible. Still the Indian's words did not fail to cause the monk a certain degree of anxiety.

"Hum!" he muttered to himself, "That is the reverse of the medal. What can this Pagan have to say to me? He does not mean to ask me to christen him, I suppose? especially as his name appears to be Blue-fox, a nice savage name, that. Well, heaven will not abandon me, and it will be day tomorrow. So now for a snooze."

And with this consolatory reflection the monk closed his eyes: two minutes later he slept as if never going to wake again.

Blue-fox, for it was really into the hands of that Chief the monk had so unexpectedly fallen, remained crouched over the fire the whole night, plunged in gloomy thought, and watching, alone of his comrades, over the common safety: at times, his eyes were fixed with a strange expression on the monk who was fast asleep, and far from suspecting that the Apache Chief was so obstinately engaged with him.

At sunrise Blue-fox was still awake: he had remained the whole night without once changing his position, and sleep had not once weighed down his eyelids.

[1] See "Border Rifles," same publishers.

[2] "frazada."

CHAPTER II
INDIAN DIPLOMACY

The night passed calm and peaceful. At the moment when the sun appeared on the horizon, saluted by the deafening concert of the birds, hidden beneath the foliage, Blue-fox, who had hitherto remained motionless, extended his right arm in the direction of the monk, who was lying by his side, and gently touched him with his hand. This touch, slight as it was, sufficed, however, to arouse Fray Antonio.

There are moments in life when, although the body reposes, the mind retains all its delicate perceptions and vigilance; the monk was in a similar situation. The gentleness the Apaches displayed towards him on the previous night was so extraordinary, and opposed to their usual habit of treating white men, their inveterate foes, that the monk, despite the coolness which formed the basis of his character, understood that the strange conduct of the men into whose power he had fallen must result from very powerful motives, and that, in spite of the pretended friendship they showed him, he would do well to keep on his guard, in order to be able to make head against the storm, from whatever quarter it might come.

In consequence of this reasoning, while taking advantage of the friendly feeling of the Indians, he craftily watched their movements, only yielded to sleep with great circumspection, and then slept with one eye open, to employ the vulgar expression. Hence at the first signal he was ready to respond to the Indian's summons with a vivacity that brought an equivocal smile upon the latter's stern features. The Redskins are physiognomists by nature; and, in spite of the tranquillity the monk affected, Blue-fox had, from certain signs that never deceive, guessed the secret alarm that internally devoured him.

"Has my brother slept well?" the Indian asked in his hoarse voice; "The Wacondah loves him, has watched over his sleep, and kept Nyang, the genius of evil, away from his dreams."

"I have, indeed, slept well, Chief, and I thank you for the cordial hospitality you have been pleased to grant me."

A smile played round the Indian's lips, as he continued:—

"My father is one of the Chiefs of prayer of his nation, the God of the Palefaces is powerful, He protects those who devote themselves to His service."

As this remark required no answer, the monk contented himself by bowing in the affirmative. Still, his anxiety increased; beneath the Chiefs gentle words he fancied he could hear the hoarse voice of the tiger, which licks its lips ere devouring the booty it holds gasping in its terrible claws.

Fray Antonio had not even the resource of pretending not to understand the dangerous speaker, for the Chief expressed himself in bad Spanish, a language all the Indian tribes understand, and which, despite their repugnance to use it, they still employ in their dealings with the white men.

The morning was magnificent; the trees, with their dew-laden leaves, seemed greener than usual; a slight mist, impregnated with the soft matutinal odours, rose from the ground, and was sucked up by the sunbeams, which with each moment grew warmer. The whole camp was still sunk in sleep; the Chief and the monk were alone awake. After a moment's silence, Blue-fox continued:—

"My father will listen," he said; "a Chief is about to speak; Blue-fox is a Sachem, his tongue is not forked, the words his chest breathes are inspired by the Great Spirit."

"I am listening," Fray Antonio replied.

"Blue-fox is not an Apache, although he wears their costumes, and leads one of their most powerful tribes on the war trail; Blue-fox is a Snake Pawnee, his nation is as numerous as the grains of sand on the borders of the great lake. Many moons ago, Blue-fox left the hunting grounds of his nation, never to return to them, and became an adopted son of the Apaches; why did Blue-fox act thus?"

The Chief interrupted himself. The monk was on the point of answering that he did not know the fact, and cared very little about learning it, but a moment's reflection made him understand the danger of such an answer to a man so irritable as the one he was now talking with.

"The brothers of the Chief were ungrateful to him," he replied with feigned interest, "and the Sachem left them; after shaking off his moccasins at the entrance of their village."

The Chief shook his head in negation.

"No," he answered, "the brothers of Blue-fox loved him, they still weep for his absence; but the Chief was sad, a friend had abandoned him, and took away his heart."

"Ah!" said the monk, not at all understanding.

"Yes," the Indian continued; "Blue-fox could not endure the absence of his friend, and left his brothers to go in search of him."

"Of course you have found the person again, Chief, to whom you devoted yourself?"

"For a long time Blue-fox sought, but did not succeed in obtaining any news of him; but one day he at length saw him again."

"Good, and now you are re-united?"

"My father does not understand," the Indian answered drily.

This was perfectly correct. The monk did not understand a syllable of what it pleased the Chief to tell him—the more so, as this obscure narrative interested him but very slightly; and while the Apache was speaking, he was cudgelling his brains to discover the motives for this confidence. The consequence was that most of the words uttered by the Chief struck his ear, but only produced an empty sound, whose meaning did not reach his mind; but the peremptory accent with which Blue-fox uttered the last sentence, aroused him, and while recalling him to a feeling of his present position, made him comprehend the danger of not seeming to take an interest in the conversation.

"Pardon me, Chief," he eagerly answered; "on the contrary, I perfectly understand; but I am subject to a certain absence of mind completely independent of my will, which I hope you will not feel offended at, for I assure you it is no fault of mine."

"Good, my father is like all the Chiefs of Prayer of the Palefaces, his thoughts are constantly directed to the Wacondah."

"So it is, Chief," the monk exclaimed, delighted at the way in which his apology was accepted; "continue your narrative, I beg, for I am now most anxious to listen to it."

"Wah! My father constantly traverses the prairies of the Palefaces."

"Yes, for the duties of my office oblige me to—"

Blue-fox quickly interrupted him.

"My father knows the pale hunters of these prairies?"

"Nearly all."

"Very good; one of these hunters is the friend so deeply regretted by Blue-fox."

"Who is he?" the monk asked.

The Indian did not seem to hear the question, for he went on—

"Very often the Redskin warrior has been led a short distance from his friend by the incidents of the chase, but never near enough to make himself known."

"That is unfortunate."

"The Chief would like to see his friend, and smoke the calumet of peace with him at the council fire, while conversing about old times, and the period when, as children of the same tribe, they traversed together the hunting grounds of the Sachem's terrible nation."

"Then the hunter is an Indian?"

"No, he is a Paleface; but if his skin is white, the Great Spirit has placed an Indian heart in his bosom."

"But why does not the Chief frankly go and join his friend, if he knows where he is? He would be probably delighted to see him again."

At this insinuation, which he was far from anticipating, the Chief frowned, and a cloud momentarily crossed his face; but the monk was too little of an observer to remark this emotion: he had asked the question, as he would have done any other, unmeaningly, and simply to show the Chief by replying that he was an attentive listener. After a few seconds, the Indian reassumed that apathy which the Redskins rarely put off, and only when taken by surprise, and continued—

"Blue-fox does not go to meet his friend, because the latter is not alone, and has with him enemies of your Chief."

"That is different, and I can understand your prudence."

"Good," the Indian added, with a sardonic smile, "wisdom speaks by the mouth of my rather; he is certainly a Chief of prayer, and his lips distil the purest honey."

Fray Antonio drew himself up, and his alarm was beginning to be dissipated; he saw vaguely that the Redskin wished to ask something of him—in short, that he wanted his help. This thought restored his courage, and he tried to complete the effect he fancied he had produced on his Machiavellian questioner.

"What my brother is unable to do, I can undertake," he said, in an insinuating voice.

The Apache gave him a piercing glance.

"Wah!" he replied, "Then my father knows where to find the Chiefs friend?"

"How should I know it?" the monk objected; "You have not told me his name yet."

"That is true; my father is good, he will forgive me. So he does not yet know who the Pale hunter is?"

"I know him, perhaps, but up to the present I am ignorant whom the Chief alludes to."

"Blue-fox is rich; he has numerous horses; he can assemble round his totem one hundred warriors, and ten times, twenty times more. If my father is willing to serve the Sachem, he will find him grateful."

"I ask nothing better than to be agreeable to you. Chief, if it lies in my power; but you must explain: clearly what I have to do, in order that I may make no mistake."

"Good; the Sachem will explain everything to his father."

"In that way, nothing will be easier."

"Does my father believe so?"

"Well, I do not see what can prevent it."

"Then my father will listen. Among all the Pale hunters, whose moccasins trample the prairie grass in all directions, there is one who is braver and more terrible than the rest; the tigers and jaguars fly at his approach, and the Indian warriors themselves are afraid to cope with him. This hunter is no effeminate Yori; the blood of the Gachupinos does not flow in his veins; he is the son of a colder land, and his ancestors fought for a lengthened period with the Long Knives of the East."

"Good," the monk said; "from what the Chief tells me, I see that this man is a Canadian."

"That is the name given, I think, to the nation of my friend."

"But among all the hunters I am acquainted with, there is only one who is a Canadian."

"Wah!" said the Chief, "Only one?"

"Yes; his name is Tranquil, I think, and he is attached to the Larch-tree hacienda."

"Wah! That is the very man. Does my father know him?"

"Not much, I confess, but still sufficiently to present myself to him."

"Very good."

"Still, I warn you, Chief, that this man, like all his fellows, leads an extremely vagabond life, being here today and gone tomorrow; so that I am in great doubt as to where I should seek him."

"Wah! my father need not trouble himself about that; the Sachem will lead him to the camp of the Tiger killer."

"In that case, very good; I will undertake the rest."

"My father must carefully retain in his heart the words of Blue-fox. The warriors are awaking; they must know nothing. When the hour arrives, the Chief will tell my father what he wants of him."

"As you please, Chief."

The conversation broke off here. The warriors were really awaking, and the camp, so quiet a few moments previously, had now the aspect of a hive, when the bees prepare at sunrise to go in search of their daily crop. At a sign from the Chief, the hachesto, or public crier, mounted a fallen tree, and twice uttered a shrill cry. At this appeal all the warriors, even those still lying on the ground, hastened to range themselves behind the Chief. A deep silence then prevailed for several minutes; all the Indians, with their arms folded on their chest, and their faces turned to the rising sun, awaited what the Sachem was about to do.

The latter took a calabash full of water, which the hachesto handed him, and in which was a spray of wormwood. Then raising his voice, he sprinkled toward the four cardinal points, saying—

"Wacondah, Wacondah! Thou unknown and omnipotent spirit, whose universe is the temple, Master of the life of man, protect thy children!"

"Master of the life of man, protect thy children!" the Apaches repeated in chorus, respectfully bowing.

"Creator of the great sacred Tortoise, whose skill supports the world, keep far from us Nyang, the genius of evil! Deliver our enemies to us, and give us their scalps. Wacondah! Wacondah! Protect thy children!"

"Wacondah! Wacondah! Protect thy children!" the warriors repeated.

The Sachem then bowed to the sun, and then towards the contents of the calabash, saying—

"And thou, sublime star, visible representative of the omnipotent and invincible Creator, continue to pour thy vivifying heat on the hunting grounds of thy Red Sons, and intercede for them with the Master of life. May this clear water I offer thee be grateful. Wacondah! Wacondah! Protect thy children!"

"Wacondah! Wacondah! Protect thy children!" the Apaches repeated, and followed their Chief's example by kneeling reverently. The latter then took a medicine rod from the hachesto, and waved it several times over his head, while shouting in a loud voice—

"Nyang, spirit of evil, rebel against the Master of life; we brave and despise thy power, for the Wacondah protects us!"

All the congregation uttered a loud yell, and rose. When the morning prayer had been said, and the rites performed, each man began attending to his daily duties.

Fray Antonio had witnessed with extreme astonishment this sacred and affecting ceremony, whose details, however, escaped his notice, for the words uttered by the Chief had been in the dialect of his nation, and consequently incomprehensible to the monk. Still, he experienced a certain delight on seeing that these men, whom he regarded as barbarians, were not entirely devoid of better feelings, and religious faith.

The expiring campfires were rekindled, in order to prepare the morning meal, while scouts started in every direction, to assure themselves that the road was free, and no enemy on the watch. The monk, being now completely reassured, and beginning to grow accustomed to his new position, ate with good appetite the provisions offered him, and made no objection to mount the horse the Chief indicated to him, when they prepared to set out on the termination of the meal.

Fray Antonio was beginning to find that the savages, who had been represented to him in such gloomy colours, were not so wicked as they were said to be, and he was almost inclined to believe that they had been calumniated. In truth, their hospitality had never once been in default; on the contrary, they had apparently studied to please him.

They rode on for several hours along tracks marked by the wild beasts, forced, through the narrowness of the paths, to go in Indian file, that is to say, one behind the other; and although the monk perceived that the Sachem constantly kept by his side, he did not feel at all alarmed by it, remembering the conversation they had in the morning.

A little before midday the band halted on the bank of a small stream, shadowed by lofty trees, where they intended to wait till the great heat had passed over. The monk was not at all vexed at this delay, which enabled him to rest in the cool. During the halt Blue-fox did not once address him, and the monk made no attempt to bring on a conversation, as he much preferred enjoying a siesta.

At about four P.M. the band mounted, and set out again; but this time, instead of going at a walking pace, they galloped. The Indians, by the way, only recognize these two paces; they consider trotting an absurdity, and we confess that we are somewhat of their opinion. The ride was long; the sun had set for more than two hours, and still the Indians galloped. At length, at a signal from their Chief, they halted. Blue-fox then went up to the monk, and drew him a little aside.

"We shall separate here," he said; "it would not be prudent for the Apaches to go further: my father will continue his journey alone."

"I?" the monk said, in surprise; "You are jesting, Chief—I prefer remaining with you."

"That cannot be," the Indian said, in a peremptory voice.

"Where the deuce would you have me go at this hour, and in this darkness?"

"My father will look," the Chief continued, stretching out his arm to the south-west, "does he see that reddish light scarce rising above the horizon?"

Fray Antonio looked attentively in the direction indicated. "Yes," he said, presently, "I do see it."

"Very good; that flame is produced by a campfire of the Palefaces."

"Oh, oh! are you sure of that?"

"Yes; but my father must listen; the Palefaces will receive my father kindly."

"I understand; then I will tell Tranquil that his friend Blue-fox desires to speak with him, point out where he is, and—"

"The magpie is a chattering and brainless bird, which gabbles like an old squaw," the Chief roughly interrupted him; "my father will say nothing."

"Oh!" the monk said, in confusion.

"My father will be careful to do what I order him, if he does not wish his scalp to dry on the lance of a Chief."

Fray Antonio shuddered at this menace.

"I swear it, Chief," he said.

"A man does not swear," the Chief remarked, brutally; "he says yes or no. When my father reaches the camp of the Palefaces, he will not allude to the Apaches; but when the Pale hunters are asleep, my father will leave the camp and come to warn Blue-fox."

"But where shall I find you?" the monk asked, piteously, beginning to perceive that he was destined to act as the spy of the savages in one of their diabolical machinations.

"My father need not trouble himself about that, for I shall manage to find him."

"Very good."

"If my father is faithful, Blue-fox will give him a buffalo skin full of gold dust; if not, he must not hope to escape the Chief; the Apaches are crafty, the scalp of a Chief of prayer will adorn the lance of a Chief; I have spoken."

"You have no further orders to give me?"

"No."

"Good-bye, then." "Till we meet again," the Apache said, with a grin.

Fray Antonio made no reply, but uttered a deep sigh, and pushed on in the direction of the camp. The nearer he drew to it, the more difficult did it appear to him to accomplish the sinister mission with which the Apache Chief had intrusted him; twice or thrice the idea of flight crossed his mind, but whither could he go? And then it was probable that the Indians placed but slight confidence in him, and carefully watched him in the gloom.

At length the camp appeared before the monk's startled eyes, as he could not draw back, for the hunters had doubtless perceived him already; he decided on pushing forward, while desperately muttering—

"The Lord have mercy upon me!"

CHAPTER III
DOWN THE PRECIPICE

The romancer has an incontestable advantage over the historian. Not being obliged to restrict himself to historical documents, he bases his work chiefly on tradition, and revels in those incidents of private life disdained by cold and severe history, which is constrained to describe only great events, and is not permitted to descend to the frequently trivial causes which not only prepared, but actually brought them about.

Frequently, after a long journey, the traveller, fatigued by the vast horizons incessantly unrolled before him, and rendered giddy by the sharp air of the elevations along which he has been riding, looks down on the plain, and his eye rests with indescribable pleasure on those modest points in the landscape which at the outset he despised. In the same way the romancer halts at the familiar episodes of the great poem, and listens to the simple stories told him by those who were actors in the scenes merely indicated by history. Such stories complete the dry and stern narrative of great wars, but historians dare not transcribe them.

It is true that in these stories ignorance is nearly always perceptible, and prejudice very frequently; but life is found in them, for if the narrators tell inexactly what happened, they at any rate say frankly how they felt, what they heard and saw themselves, and the errors they sometimes involuntarily make are not falsehoods, but relative truths, which it is the duty of the romancer to classify and put in their proper place.

We have several times visited the narrow defile where the Border Rifles and the Mexicans fought the action we described in a previous volume. [1] Bending over the precipice, with our eyes fixed on the yawning abyss beneath us, we heard the narrative of the strange incidents of that battle of giants, and if we had not been certain of the veracity of the narrator, we should certainly have not only doubted but completely denied the possibility of certain facts which are, however, rigorously true, and which we are now about to impart to the reader.

The Border Rifles saw with a shriek of horror the two men, intertwined like serpents, roll together over the precipice; the flashes of the fire, which was beginning to die out for want of nourishment, after devastating the crests of the hills, threw at intervals a lurid light over this scene, and gave it a striking aspect.

The first moment of stupor past, John Davis, mastering with difficulty the emotion that agitated him, sought to restore courage, if not hope, to all these men who were crushed by the terrible catastrophe. John Davis enjoyed, and justly so, a great reputation among the Borderers. All know the close friendship which attached the Americans to their chief: in several serious affairs he had displayed a coolness and intelligence which gained him the respect and admiration of these men: hence they immediately responded to his appeal, by grouping silently round him, for they understood intuitively that there was only one man among them worthy of succeeding the Jaguar, and that he was the North American.

John Davis had guessed the feelings that agitated them, but did not allow it to be seen: his face was pale, his appearance sad: he bent a thoughtful glance on the rude, determined men who, leaning on their rifles, gazed at him mournfully, and seemed already tacitly to recognize the authority with which he was, probably, about to invest himself.

Their expectations were deceived, at least, temporarily. Davis, at this moment, had no intention of making the Borderers elect him as their chief: the fate of his friend entirely absorbed him, and all other considerations disappeared in the presence of the one idea.

"Caballeros," he said, in a melancholy tone, "a terrible misfortune has struck us. Under such circumstances, we must summon up all our courage and resignation, for women weep, but men revenge themselves. The death of the Jaguar is not only an immense loss for ourselves, but also for the cause we have sworn to defend, and to which he has already given such great proof of devotion. But, before bewailing our chief, so worthy in every respect of the sorrow which we shall feel for him, we have one duty to accomplish—a duty which, if we neglect it, will cause us piercing remorse at a later date."

"Speak, speak, John Davis, we are ready to do anything you order us," the Borderers exclaimed unanimously.

"I thank you," the American continued, "for the enthusiasm with which you have replied to me: I cannot believe that an intellect so vast, a heart so noble, as that of our beloved Chief can be thus destroyed. God, I feel convinced, would not thus have broken a cause for which we have so long been struggling with such devotion and self-denial. Heaven will have performed a miracle in favour of our Chief, and we shall see him reappear among us safe and sound! But whatsoever may happen, should this last hope be denied us, at any rate, we must not abandon like cowards, without attempting to save him, the man who twenty times braved death for each of us. For my part, I swear by all that is most sacred in the world, that I will not leave this spot till I have assured myself whether the Jaguar be dead or alive."

At these words a buzz of assent ran along his hearers, and John Davis continued, "Who knows whether our unhappy Chief is not lying crushed, but still breathing, at the foot of this accursed abyss, and reproaching us for our cowardly desertion of him?"

The Border Rifles declared, with the most energetic oaths, that they would find their Chief again, dead or alive.

"Good, my friends," the American exclaimed; "if he be unhappily dead, we will place his body in the ground and protect his remains, so dear to us on many accounts, from the insults of wild beasts: but, I repeat to you, one of those presentiments which never deceive, because they come from God, tells me that he is still alive."

"May Heaven hear you, John Davis," the Borderers shouted, "and restore us our Chief."

"I am going to descend the precipice," the American said; "I will inspect its most secret recesses, and before sunrise we shall know what we have to hope or fear."

This proposal of John Davis' was greeted as it deserved, by enthusiastic shouts. When the excitement of the hearers had slightly calmed, the American prepared to carry out his design.

"Permit me a remark," said an old wood ranger.

"Speak, Ruperto, what is it?" Davis answered.

"I have known the spot where we now are for a long time, and have often hunted deer and antelopes here."

"Come to facts, my friend."

"You can act as you please, John Davis, on the information I am about to give you; by turning to the right, after marching for about three miles, you get round the hills, and what appears to us from here a precipice, is, in fact, only a plain, very enclosed, I allow, but easy to traverse on horseback."

"Ah, ah," John said thoughtfully, "and what do you conclude from that, Ruperto?"

"That it would be, perhaps, better to mount and skirt the hills."

"Yes, yes, that is a good idea, and we will take advantage of it; take twenty men with you, Ruperto, and proceed at full speed to the plain you allude to, for we must not throw away any chance; the rest of the band will remain here to watch the environs, while I effect the descent of the barranca."

"You still adhere to your idea, then?"

"More than ever."

"As you please, John Davis, as you please, though you risk your bones on such a black night as this."

"I trust in Heaven, and I hope it will protect me."

"I hope so too for your sake; but I must be off—here's luck."

"Thanks, the same to you."

Red Ruperto then went off, followed by twenty borderers, who spontaneously offered to accompany him, and soon disappeared in the darkness. The descent John Davis was preparing to make, was anything but easy. The American was too experienced a wood ranger not to know, and hence took all proper precautions. He placed in his belt next his knife a wide and strong axe, and fastened round his waist a rope formed of several *reatas*. Three men seized the end of the rope, which they turned round the stem of a tree, so as to let it out without a shock, whenever the American desired it. As a final precaution, he lit a branch of ocote wood, which was to serve as his guide during his perilous descent, for the sky was perfectly black, which rendered the gloom so thick that it was impossible to see anything two paces away. His last measures taken with the coolness that distinguishes men of his race, the North American pressed the hands held out to him, tried once again to restore hope to his comrades by a few hearty words, and kneeling on the brink of the abyss, began slowly descending.

John Davis was a man of tried courage, his life had been one continued struggle, in which he had only triumphed through his strength of will and energy; still, when he began descending into the barranca, he felt chilled to the heart, and could not repress a slight start of terror, which ran over all his limbs like an electric flash. Still, he fought against this emotion, which is nothing but that instinct of self-preservation which duty has placed in the heart of every man, the bravest as the most cowardly, and continued his descent.

Although he was fastened round the waist, it was no easy task to go down this almost perpendicular wall, to which he was compelled to cling like a reptile, clutching at every tuft of grass or shrub he came across, or else he had been carried away by the wind, which blew furiously, and would have crushed him like a nutshell against the sides of the abyss.

The first minutes were the most terrible to the bold adventurer; the feet and hands must grow accustomed to the rude task imposed on them, and they only gradually learn to find, as it were instinctively, their resting places; and this remark, which may appear erroneous to certain persons, who, fortunately for themselves, have never been obliged to try the experiment, will be recognized as rigorously true by all travellers who have been compelled to ascend or descend mountains. After a few minutes, when the mind remains at liberty, the body assumes of its own accord the necessary equilibrium, the feet find secure resting places, and the hands settle unhesitatingly on the grass or roots which offer them the indispensable degree of resistance.

John Davis had hardly gone ten yards down, ere he found himself on a wide ledge covered with thick shrubs; hitherto the descent had been extremely rapid. Lighting himself by the torch, the American traversed in every direction this species of esplanade, which was about a dozen paces in circumference; and, on carefully examining the thick shrubs which covered it, the adventurer perceived that the tops had been broken as if they had received a tremendous blow.

Davis looked around him. He soon concluded that this enormous gap could only have been made by the fall of two bodies: this remark gave him good hope, for at so slight a distance from the mouth of the abyss, the two enemies must have been full of life; the rapidity of their fall must have naturally been arrested by the shrubs; they might have met at various distances similar obstacles, and consequently have undergone several comparatively harmless falls. This hypothesis, erroneous though it was, still might be true.

John Davis continued his descent; the slope became constantly less abrupt, and the adventurer met within his passage, not merely shrubs, but clumps of trees, grouped here and there. Still, as John Davis found no further traces, a fear fell upon him, and painfully contracted his heart; he was afraid lest the shrubs, through their elasticity, might have hurled the two unhappy men into space, instead of letting them follow the slope of the precipice. This thought so powerfully occupied the American's mind, that a deep discouragement seized upon him, and for some moments he remained without strength or will, crouching sadly on the ground.

But Davis was a man of too stern a character, and endowed with such an energetic will, to give way for any length of time to despair: he soon raised his head, and looked boldly around him.

"I must go on," he said in a firm voice. But, at the moment when he prepared to continue his descent, he suddenly gave a start of surprise, and uttered a cry as he rushed quickly toward a black mass, to which he had hitherto paid but slight attention.

We once again ask our readers' pardon for the improbability of the following detail; but we repeat that we are not explaining, but narrating, confining ourselves to telling the truth, without pretending to discuss the greater or less possibility of facts, which, however extraordinary they may appear, are exactly true.

The white-headed eagle, the most powerful and the best provided of the birds, ordinarily builds its nest on the sides of barrancas, at the top of the loftiest trees, and chiefly those denuded of branches to a considerable height, but they are never found on rocks. This nest, strongly built, is composed of sticks from three to five feet in length, fastened together and covered with Spanish braid, a species of cryptogamic plant of the lichen family, wild grass, and large patches of turf. When the nest is completed, it ordinarily measures from six to seven feet in diameter, and at times the accumulation of materials there is so considerable—for the same nest is frequently occupied for a number of years, and receives augmentations each season—that its depth equals its diameter. As the nest of the white-headed eagle is very heavy, it is generally placed in the centre of a fork formed by the fortuitous meeting of several large branches.

John Davis, by the help of his torch, had just discovered a few yards from him, and almost on a level with the spot where he was standing, an eagle's nest, built on the top of an immense tree, whose trunk descended for a considerable depth in the precipice.

Two human bodies were lying stretched across this nest, and the American only required one glance to assure himself that they were those of the Jaguar and the Mexican Captain. They were perfectly motionless, and still fast locked in each other's arms.

It was not at all an easy undertaking to reach this nest, which was nearly ten yards from the sides of the precipice; but John Davis did not give in on that account; now that he had found the body of his Chief again, he was determined to learn, at all risks, whether he were alive or dead. But what means was he to employ to acquire this certainty? How reach the tree, which oscillated violently with every gust? After ripe reflection, the American recognized the fact that he could never climb the tree alone; he therefore placed his hands funnel-wise to his month, and gave the shout agreed on with his comrades. The latter drew up the reata, and after half an hour of unheard of fatigue, Davis found himself again among his comrades.

The Border Rifles crowded round him eagerly to ask the details of his expedition, which he hastened to give them, and which were received with shouts of joy by all. Then happened a thing which proves how great was the affection all these men bore their Chief; without exchanging a word, or coming to any agreement, all procured torches, and, as if obeying the same impulse, began descending the abyss.

Through the multiplicity of torches, which spread abroad sufficient light, and, before all, the skill of these men, accustomed since childhood to run about the forests, and clamber up rocks and precipices in sport, this descent was effected without any further misfortunes to deplore, and the whole band was soon assembled at the spot whence the American had first discovered the nest of the white-headed eagle.

All was in the same state as Davis left it: the two bodies were still motionless, and still intertwined. Were they dead, or only in a faint? Such was the question all persons asked themselves, and no one could answer it. All at once a loud noise was heard, and the bottom of the barranca was illumined by a number of torches. Ruperto's party had arrived. Guided by the flashes they saw running along the sides of the precipice, the latter soon discovered the nest, and the truth was revealed to them.

The arrival of Ruperto and his comrades was a great comfort to the Americans, for now nothing would be more easy than to reach the nest. Four powerful adventurers, armed with axes, glided along the side of the precipice to the foot of the tree, which they began felling with hurried strokes, while John Davis, and the men with him, threw their reatas round the top branches of the tree, and gradually drew it towards them. The tree began gracefully bending, and at length lay on the side of the barranca, without receiving any very serious shock.

John Davis immediately entered the nest, and drawing his knife from his belt, bent over the body of the Jaguar, and put the blade to the young man's lips. There was a moment of profound anxiety for these men; their silence was so complete, that the beating of their hearts might be heard. They stood with their eyes obstinately fixed on the American, daring scarcely to breathe, and, as it were, hanging on his lips. At length John rose, and placed the knife near a torch; the blade was slightly tarnished.

"He lives, brothers, he lives!" he shouted.

At these news the Border Rifles broke out into such a howl of joy and happiness, that the nightbirds, startled in their gloomy hiding places, rose on all sides, and began flying heavily backwards and forwards, while uttering discordant and deafening cries. But this was not all: the next point was to get the Jaguar out of the precipice, and let him down into the gorge. We have said that the two bodies were closely intertwined. The adventurers felt but slender sympathy for Captain Melendez, the primary cause of the catastrophe, which had so nearly proved fatal to the Jaguar; hence they were not at all eager to assure themselves whether he were dead or alive; and when the moment arrived to find means for conveying the body of their Chief into the barranca, a very serious and stormy discussion arose on the subject of the Mexican officer. The majority of the adventurers were of opinion that the easiest way of separating the two bodies was by cutting off the Captain's arms, and throwing his body into the abyss, to serve as food for wild beasts. Those who were more excited talked about stabbing him at once, so as to make quite sure that he did not recover. Some even had seized their knives and machetes to carry out this resolution, but John Davis suddenly interfered.

"Stop!" he shouted, eagerly, "the Jaguar lives; he is still your Chief, so leave him to treat this man as he thinks proper. Who knows whether the life of this officer may not be more valuable to us than his death?"

The adventurers were not easily induced to spare the Captain, and adhered for a while to their proposal of stabbing him, after cutting off his arms. Still, owing to the influence he enjoyed with the band, Davis succeeded in making them listen to reason, and they began arranging how to get the bodies down.

[1] See Border Rifles, same Publishers.

CHAPTER IV
TWO ENEMIES

In the great work of creation, God indubitably most profoundly set the seal of his omnipotence in the heart of forests. The ocean, despite its immense extent, offers sailors only a despairing monotony, or sudden upheavals, which fill the mind with a secret and invincible terror. The mountains which stud the globe, and elevate to immense heights their serrated peaks, covered with eternal snow, only inspire terror, and represent to the astonished eyes of the tourist a terrific maze of chaos and travailing nature.

But when you reach the verge of one of those splendid oases of verdure which are called virgin forests, you undergo involuntarily an impression of religious contemplation and gentle melancholy at the sight of these thousand arches of foliage, intertwined like the ceiling of an old Gothic church, in which the moss-clad trunks of centennial oaks represent the clustered columns, rising at one spot only a few feet from the ground, at others soaring to the skies.

Then, animated by the purer air, breathing with the full power of the lungs, attracted and fascinated by the mobile and infinite perspectives that open out on all sides—feeling the movement easier on the soft carpet of soil and dust accumulated by departed ages, the traveller's step grows freer, his glance more piercing, and his hand more firm, and he begins sighing for the hazardous and masculine life of the desert. The further he proceeds beneath these shifting shadows, while life is as noisy all around as a rising tide, the more does the freshness which circulates through the foliage purify the blood, and strengthen the limbs; and he comprehends more and more the irresistible attractions of the forest, and the religious love the wood rangers have for it.

Men habituated to a desert life are never willing to quit it again; for they understand all its voices, have sounded all its mysteries, and to them the forest is a world which they love much as the sailor does the sea. When a glowing sun enlivens the wild and picturesque landscape, when the glistening snow on the far-off peaks stands out like a silver ribbon above the masses of verdure, when the birds twitter among the leaves, the insects buzz on the grass, and the wild beasts in their unknown lairs, add their solemn sounds to the concert;—at such a moment all invites reverie and contemplation, and the wood rangers feel themselves the nearer to God, because they are the further from man.

These bold explorers of the desert are picked men, and powerfully built, kept constantly in movement, and forced each second into a contest with the obstacles that incessantly arise before them. No danger terrifies them, no difficulty arrests them; perils they brave, difficulties they surmount as if in sport; for, hurled by the divine will beyond the pale of common law, their existence is only a succession of strange incidents and feverish adventures, which cause them to live a century in a few moments.

The hesitation of the Border Rifles was short; for these half-savage men, an obstacle to be overcome could only prove a stimulus for their minds, so fertile in resources.

The two wounded men, securely fastened on cross pieces of wood by reatas, were let down in turn to the bottom of the precipice, and laid on the bank of a small stream, which ran noiselessly through this plain, forming the most capricious windings. John Davis, fearing some outbreak on the part of his angry comrades, himself undertook to let the Captain down, in order to be certain that no accident would happen to him.

When the wounded men had been removed from the eagle's nest, which had so miraculously saved them, the adventurers glided along the cliff with singular address and rapidity, and the whole band was soon collected on the bank of the stream. As is frequently the case in a mountainous country, the bottom of the barranca was a rather wide prairie, sheltered between two lofty hills, which enclosed it on the right and left, thus forming a species of gorge, which, at the spot where the fight took place, was really a gulf of great depth.

John Davis, without losing a moment, lavished on the Jaguar all the attention his state demanded; while Ruperto, though much against the grain, did the same for the Mexican Captain, by the American's peremptory orders.

During the various events we have described, the whole night had slipped away, and the sun rose at the moment the adventurers completed their perilous descent. The country then resumed its real aspect, and what had appeared by the flickering light of the torches a desolate and arid desert, became a charming and smiling landscape.

The sun has enormous power over the human organisation: it not only dispels those sombre phantoms which are produced by the darkness, but also revives the mind and restores to the body its elasticity and vigour, which have been neutralised by the piercing cold of night. With day, hope and joy returned to the heart of the adventurers; a joy rendered more lively still by the sight of the cases hurled over the previous night by the Mexicans, and which, though crushed by their fall, had lost none of their precious contents. Hence, the heroic courage and devotion of the Mexicans had no other result than allowing them to die bravely at their posts, for their sacrifice had not obtained the anticipated result.

The prairie soon assumed a lively aspect, to which it certainly was not accustomed; the adventurers lit fires, erected jacals, and the camp was formed in a few minutes. For a very lengthened period Davis' efforts to bring his friend to life remained sterile; still, the Jaguar had received no wound; he did not seem to have a limb broken; his syncope resulted solely from the moral effect of his horrible fall.

For all that, the American, far from giving in, redoubled his care and attention, and at length, saw his efforts crowned with success. The Jaguar made a weak movement, his lips parted as if he were about to speak, he raised his hand to his brow, gave a deep sigh, and partly opened his eyes, but closed them instantly, probably dazzled by the brilliant sunlight.

"At length he is saved!" the American exclaimed, joyously.

The adventurers surrounded their Chief, anxiously watching his every movement. The young man soon opened his eyes again, and, helped by Davis, managed to sit up. A slight patch of red was visible on his cheekbones, but the rest of his face retained an ashen and cadaverous hue. He looked slowly round him, and the absent expression of his glance gradually changed into a gleam of intelligence. "Drink!" he muttered in a hollow and inarticulate voice.

John Davis uncorked his flask, bent over the wounded man, and placed it to his lips. The latter drank eagerly for two or three minutes, and then stopped with a sigh of relief.

"I fancied I was dead," he said.

"By Heaven!" John Davis remarked, "It was a close shave."

"Is Captain Melendez still alive?"

"Yes."

"What state is he in?"

"No worse than your own."

"All the better."

"Shall we hang him?" Ruperto remarked, still adhering to his notion.

The Jaguar started, frowned, and then shouted with greater strength than he might be supposed to possess—

"On your life, not a hair of his head must fall; you answer for him to me body for body."

And he added in a low voice, unintelligible by the hearers, "I swore it—"

"'Tis a pity," Ruperto went on. "I am certain that hanging a Mexican Captain would have produced an excellent effect through the country."

The Jaguar made a sign.

"All right, all right," the adventurer continued; "if it is not pleasant to you, we will say no more about it. No matter, that is a funny notion of yours."

"Enough," the young man said; "I have given my orders."

So soon as he was alone. Captain Melendez let his head fall on his hands, and tried to re-establish the balance in his mind and arrange his ideas, which the shock he had received had utterly disordered. Still he gradually yielded to a species of lethargy, the natural result of his fall, and soon fell into a deep sleep.

He slept peacefully for several hours, nothing happening to disturb his repose; and when he awoke he found himself quite a new man; the restorative sleep he had enjoyed had completely rested his nervous system, his strength had returned, and it was with an indescribable feeling of joy that he rose and walked a few steps on the prairie. With calmness of mind courage returned, and he was ready to recommence the contest. He noticed, too, with a certain degree of pleasure, that the adventurers left him at perfect liberty, and did not appear to pay any attention to him.

Ruperto returned, but this time he had put off his mocking air, and carried some provisions in a basket. The adventurer offered them to the Captain with rough politeness, in which, however, the desire to be agreeable was perceptible. The Captain readily accepted the food, and ate with an appetite that surprised himself after so serious a fall.

"Well," Ruperto remarked, "did I not tell you that you would be soon cured? It is just the same with the Captain—he is as fresh as a floripondio, and was never better in his life."

"Tell me, my friend," Don Juan answered, "may I be allowed to speak with the Chief?"

"Very easily—the more so, as it seems that he has something to say to you."

"Indeed."

"Yes, and he even ordered me to ask you if you would allow him an interview after dinner."

"Most heartily; I am entirely at his orders; especially," the Captain added, with a smile, "since I am his prisoner."

"That is true; well, eat quietly, and while you are doing so I will convey your message."

Hereupon Ruperto left the Captain, who did not require the invitation to be repeated, but vigorously attacked the provisions placed before him. His meal was soon over, and he had been walking up and down for some time, when he saw the Jaguar approach. The two men bowed ceremoniously, and examined each other for some moments with the greatest attention.

Up to this moment they had hardly seen one another; their interview of the previous evening had taken place in the darkness, and then fought obstinately; but they had found no time to form mutual opinions as they now did with the infallible glance of men who are accustomed to judge in a second, persons with whom they have dealings. The Jaguar was the first to break the silence.

"You will excuse, Caballero," he said, "the rusticity of my reception: banished men have no other palace save the dome of the forests that shelter them."

The Captain bowed.

"I was far from expecting," he said, "so much courtesy from—"

He stopped, not daring to utter the word that rose to his lips, through fear of offending the other.

"From bandits, I suppose, Captain?" the Jaguar replied, with a smile. "Oh, no denial, I know what we are called at Mexico. Yes, Caballero, at the present day we are outlaws, border ruffians, freebooters; tomorrow, perhaps, we shall be heroes and saviours of a people; but so the world goes; but let us leave that. You wished to speak to me, I heard."

"Did you not also evince a desire, Caballero, to have an interview with me?"

"I did, Captain; I have only one question to ask you, though—will you promise me to answer it?"

"On my honour, if it be possible."

The Jaguar reflected for a moment, and then continued—

"You hate me, I suppose?"

"What makes you imagine that?"

"How do I know?" the Jaguar replied, with embarrassment; "a thousand reasons, as, for instance, the obstinacy with which you sought to take my life a few hours agone."

The Captain drew himself up, and his face assumed a stern expression which it had not worn hitherto.

"I pledge you my word to be frank with you, Caballero," he said.

"I thank you beforehand."

"Between yourself and me, personally, no hatred can exist—at any rate, not on my side; I do not know you, I only saw you yesterday for the first time; never, to my cognizance, have you come across my path before, hence I have no reason to hate you. But beside the man there is the soldier; as an officer in the Mexican army—"

"Enough, Captain," the young man sharply interrupted him; "you have told me all I desired to know; political hatreds, however terrible they may be, are not eternal. You do your duty as I believe I do mine—that is to say, as well as you possibly can, and to that I have no objection. Unfortunately, instead of fighting side by side, we are in opposite camps; fatality decrees it so; perhaps, some day these unhappy dissensions will cease, and then, who knows whether we may not be friends?"

"We are so already, Caballero," the Captain said, warmly, as he held out his hand to the Jaguar.

The latter pressed it vigorously.

"Let us each follow the road traced for us," he said; "but if we defend a different cause, let us maintain, when the contest is raging, that esteem and friendship which two loyal enemies ought to feel, who have measured their swords and found them of equal length."

"Agreed," said the Captain.

"One word more," the Jaguar continued. "I must respond to your frankness by equal frankness."

"Speak."

"I presume that the question I asked surprised you?"

"I confess it."

"Well, I will tell you why I asked it."

"What good will that do?"

"I must; between us two henceforth there must be nothing hidden. In spite of the hatred I ought to feel for you, I feel myself attracted to you by a secret sympathy, which I cannot explain, but which urges me to reveal to you a secret on which the happiness of my life depends."

"I do not understand you, Caballero; the language seems strange to me. Explain yourself, in Heaven's name."

A feverish flush suddenly covered the Jaguar's face.

"Listen, Captain, if you only know me today for the first time, your name has been ringing in my ears for many months past."

The officer fixed an inquiring glance on the young man.

"Yes, yes," the latter continued, with increasing animation, "she ever has your name on her lips—she only speaks of you. Only a few days back—but why recall that? Suffice it for you to know that I love her to distraction."

"Carmela?" the Captain muttered.

"Yes," the Jaguar exclaimed, "you love her too!"

"I do," the Captain replied, simply, as he looked on the ground with an air of embarrassment.

There was a lengthened silence between the two men. It was easy to discover that each of them was having an internal fight; at length the Jaguar managed to quell the storm that growled in his heart, and went on, in a firm voice—

"Thanks for your loyal answer, Captain; in loving Carmela you take advantage of your good right, just as I do; let this love, instead of separating, form a stronger link between us. Carmela is worthy of the love of an honourable man; let us each love her, and carry on an open warfare, without treachery or trickery; all the better for the man she may prefer. She alone must be judge between us; let her follow her heart, for she is too pure and good to deceive herself and make a bad choice."

"Good!" the Captain exclaimed, enthusiastically; "You are a man after my own heart, Jaguar, and whatever may happen, I shall always think with gladness that I have pressed your honest hand, and am worthy of being counted among your friends. Yes, I have a deep and sincere love for Carmela; for a smile from her rosy lips I would joyfully lay down my life; but I swear that I will follow the noble example you give me, and the struggle shall be as honourable on my side as on yours."

"Viva Cristo!" the young man said with frank and simple delight, "I was sure we should end by coming to an understanding."

"To produce that," the Captain remarked, with a smile, "we only needed the opportunity for an explanation."

"Canarios, I trust that it will not be repeated under similar conditions, for it is a perfect miracle that we are still alive."

"I am not at all anxious to repeat the experiment."

"Nor I either, I swear to you. But the sun is rapidly declining on the horizon: I need not tell you that you are free, and at liberty to go wherever you please, if it is not your intention to remain any length of time with us: I have had a horse got ready which you will permit me to offer you."

"I gladly accept it: I do not wish to have any false pride with you, and afoot in these regions, which are quite strange to me, I should feel greatly embarrassed."

"That need not trouble you, for I will give you a guide to accompany you, till you get in the right road."

"A thousand thanks."

"Where do you propose going? Of course, if my question be indiscreet, I do not expect you to answer it."

"I have nothing to hide from you; I intend joining General Rubio as quickly as possible, to whom I must report the accident that has happened to the conducta de plata, and the terrible catastrophe of which I have been the victim."

"It is the fortune of war, Captain."

"I do not reproach you; I merely say it was an unfortunate affair."

"Had it been possible to save the conducta by courage and devotion, you would have doubtless done it, for you performed your duty worthily."

"I thank you for this praise."

"It will be easy for you to reach General Rubio's camp before sunset."

"Do you think so?"

"I am sure of it, for you are only three leagues at the most from it."

"So near as that? Had I but known it," the Captain said in a tone of regret.

"Yes, but you were ignorant of the fact. But, nonsense, what good is it returning to that, you will take your revenge some day or the other."

"You are right; what is done cannot be undone, so I will be off."

"Already?"

"I must."

"That is true."

The Jaguar made a signal to a borderer standing a short distance off.

"The Captain's horse," he said.

Five minutes later, this borderer, who was no other than Ruperto, reappeared, leading two horses, one of which was a magnificent mustang, with delicate limbs, and flashing eye. The Captain reached the saddle at one leap, and Ruperto was already mounted. The two enemies, henceforth friends, shook hands for the last time, and after an affectionate parting, the Captain let his horse go.

"Mind, no tricks, Ruperto!" the Jaguar said in a peremptory voice to the adventurer.

"All right, all right!" the latter growled in reply.

The horsemen left the prairie. The Jaguar looked after them as long as he could see them, and then returned thoughtfully to the jacal, which served as his tent.

CHAPTER V
GENERAL RUBIO

As the opportunity offers itself, let us say a few words about the military organization of the United States of Mexico, an organization as singular as all the rest of the machinery by means of which the strange government of this eccentric Republic does its work.

A military uniform generally pleases the masses; a soldier's life has something in it so independent of ordinary life, that all nations more or less allow themselves to be carried away and seduced by the glitter of embroidery and epaulettes, the rolling of drums, and the shrill notes of the bugles. Young nations, especially, like to play at soldiering, to make standards flutter, horses curvet, and mighty sabres flash.

The struggle of Mexico with Spain lasted ten years, constant, feverish, and obstinate: it was fertile in terrible events and striking incidents. The Mexicans, held by their oppressors in the most complete subjection, were as simple at the beginning of the revolution as at the period of the conquest: the majority did not know how to load a gun, and none of them had ever had firearms in their hands. Still, excited by the ardent desire for liberty which boiled in their hearts, their progress in military tactics was rapid, and the Spaniards soon learned at their own expense that these wretched guerillas, commanded by priests and curates, who at the outset were only armed with lances and arrows, became at length capable of responding to their platoon fire, dying bravely without yielding an inch, and inflicting terrible defeats upon them. The enthusiasm and hatred of the oppressors had made soldiers of all the men capable of bearing arms.

When the independence was proclaimed and the war ended, the part played by the army was at an end in a country which, without immediate neighbours, had no foreign intervention to apprehend in its internal affairs and had no invasion to fear. The army, therefore, ought to have laid down the arms which had so valiantly achieved the liberty of the country, and returned peaceably home. Such was its duty, and such was expected; but this was a great mistake. The army felt itself strong and feared; hence it wished to keep the place it had assumed, and, impose conditions in its turn.

Having no longer enemies to combat, the Mexican army constituted itself, or its private authority, the arbiter of the destinies of the country it had been called out to defend: in order to secure promotion among the officers, the army made revolutions. Then commenced that era of pronunciamentos, in which Mexico is fatally ensnared, and which is leading it irresistibly to that gulf in which its independence, so dearly acquired, and even its nationality, will be finally wrecked.

From the sub-lieutenant to the general of division, each officer made a stepping stone of a pronunciamento to gain a step—the lieutenant to become captain; the captain, colonel; the colonel, general; and the general, president of the Mexican Republic. There are generally three to four presidents at once; often enough there are five, or even six; a single president would be regarded as an extraordinary phenomenon—a *rara avis*. We believe that since the proclamation of Independence no single president has governed the country for six consecutive months. The result of this state of things is, that the army has fallen into extreme discredit; and while the profession of arms was honourable at the period of the struggle against the Spaniards, it is exactly the reverse now. The army is, therefore, necessarily recruited from the lowest classes of society, that is to say, from bandits, leperos, and even the villains condemned for robbery or assassination.

All these men, on reaching certain grades, merely change their uniform, while retaining in the new rank where accident places them their vices and low habits; hence young men of good family are not at all inclined to accept an epaulette, and despise a profession regarded with so little honour by the respectable classes of society. In a corps so badly organised, where discipline does not exist, and military education is a nullity, any *esprit de corps* must be unknown, and that is the case. And yet this army has been good, and it counts magnificent exploits on its books; its soldiers and officers displayed great bravery in the critical phases of the War of Independence.

But at the present day everything is dead, the feeling of duty is despised, and honour—that powerful stimulus to the soldier—is trampled under foot. Duelling, that necessary evil to a certain point to make the soldier respect the cloth he wears, is forbidden under the severest penalties; and if you horsewhip a Mexican officer, or call him a coward or a scoundrel, the only risk you run is of being treacherously assassinated.

It needs a lengthened apprenticeship to become a soldier and obtain the proper spirit; it is only after long and serious study, when he has suffered great privations, and looked death several times in the face, that a man acquires that knowledge and coolness which enable him to sacrifice his life without calculation, and fulfil the duties of a true soldier.

Most of the Mexican generals would blush at their ignorance if they found themselves face to face with the lowest non-commissioned officer of our army; for they know absolutely nothing, and have not the least idea of their art. With Mexican officers all is reduced to this: changing the scarf. The colonel wears a red one, the brigadier-general's is green, and that of the general of division white. It is for the purpose of obtaining the last colour that all the pronunciamentos are made.

Badly clothed, badly fed, and badly paid, the Mexican troops are a scourge to the civilian population, whom they shamelessly and pitilessly squeeze upon the slightest pretext. From what we have written, it is easy to see how an armed corps thus disorganised must be dangerous to everybody, for it knows no restraint, and lives beyond the law which it despises. The present state of Mexico proves the incontestable truth of our assertions.

We have not wished to enter into personalities, but treated the question generally, seeking to show what it is really. There are, we allow, some officers of merit—a few truly honourable men—in this unhappy army; but they are pearls lost in the mud, and the number is so limited, that if we quoted all their names, we should not reach a hundred. This is the more sad, because the further Mexico goes, the nearer it approaches the catastrophe; and, ere long, the evil that undermines this fair country will be incurable, and it will sink for ever—not under the blows of strangers, but assassinated by its own children.

General Don José Maria Rubio was in no way distinguished from the herd of Mexican officers, but he possessed over those who surrounded him the immense advantage of being a soldier of the war of Independence, and in him experience amply compensated for his lack of education. His history was simple, and may be told in a few words.

Son of an evangelista or public writer at Tampico, he had with great difficulty learned a little reading and writing under the auspices of his father; this pretence at education, slight as it was, was destined to be of great utility to him at a later date. The great uprising, of which the celebrated Fray Hidalgo was the promoter, and which inaugurated the revolution, found young José Maria wandering about the neighbourhood of Tampico, where he gained a livelihood by the most heterogeneous trades. The young man—a little bit of a muleteer, a little bit of a fisherman, and a good deal of a smuggler—intoxicated by the smell of gunpowder, and fascinated by the omnipotent influence Hidalgo exercised over all those who approached him, threw his gun over his shoulder, mounted the first horse he came across, and gaily followed the revolutionary band. From that moment his life was only one long succession of combats.

He became in a short time, thanks to his courage, energy, and presence of mind, one of the guerillas most feared by the Spaniards; always the first in attack, the last to retreat. Chief of a cuadrilla composed of picked men, to whom the most daring and wild expeditions appeared but child's play, and favoured by constant good luck, for fortune ever loves the rash, José Maria soon became a terror to the Spaniards, and his mere name inspired them with indescribable terror. After serving in turn under all the heroes of the Mexican war of Independence, and fighting bravely by their side, peace found him a brigadier-general.

General Rubio was not ambitious; he was a brave and honest soldier, who loved his profession passionately, and who needed to render him happy the roll of the drum, the lustre of arms, and military life in its fullest extent. When he fought, the idea never occurred to him that the war would end some day or other; and hence he was quite surprised and perfectly demoralised when peace was made and independence proclaimed.

The worthy General looked round him. Everybody was preparing to retire to the bosom of his family, and enjoy a repose do dearly purchased. Don José Maria might perhaps have desired nothing better than to follow the example; but his family was the army, and he had, or at least was acquainted with, no other. During the ten years' fighting which had just elapsed, the General had completely lost out of sight all the relations he possessed. His father, whose death he learned accidentally, was the sole person whose influence might have brought him to abandon a military career, but the paternal hearth was cold. Nothing attracted him to the province, and he therefore remained under the banner, though not through ambition. We repeat that the worthy soldier did himself justice, and recognised the fact that he had attained a position far superior to any he might ever have dared to desire; but he could not live alone or abandon old friends with whom he had so long suffered, combated—in a word, shared good and evil fortune.

The different Chiefs, who immediately began coveting power, and succeeded each other in the presidential chair, far from fearing the general, whose simple and honest character was known to them, on the contrary sought his friendship, and lavished on him proofs of the most frank and real protection; for they felt convinced that he would never abuse their confidence in him.

At the period when the Texans began agitating and claiming their independence, the Mexican Government, deceived at the outset by the agents appointed to watch that state, sent insufficient forces to re-establish order, and crush the insurgents: but the movement soon assumed such a distinctly revolutionary character, that the President found it urgent to make an effective demonstration. Unfortunately it was too late; the dissatisfaction had spread: it was no longer a question of suppressing a revolt, but stifling a revolution, which is not at all the same thing.

The President of the Mexican Republic then learned at his own cost that, in every human question, there is something more powerful than the brute force of bayonets: it is the idea whose time has come and hour struck. The troops sent to Texas were beaten and driven back on all sides; in short, they were compelled to treat with the insurgents, and withdraw ignominiously.

The government could not, and would not, accept such a dishonouring check inflicted by badly-armed and undisciplined bands, and they resolved to make a last and decisive effort. Numerous troops were massed on the Texan frontiers; and to terrify the insurgents, and finish with them at one blow, a grand military demonstration was made.

But the war then changed its character: the Texans, nearly all North Americans, skilful hunters, indefatigable marchers, and marksmen of proverbial reputation, broke up into small bands, and instead of offering the Mexican troops a front, which would have enabled them to outmanoeuvre and crush them, they began a hedge war, full of tricks and ambushes, after the manner of the Vendeans, the first result of which was to enormously fatigue the soldiers by compelling them to make continual marches and counter-marches, and produced among them discouragement and demoralization, by compelling to fight against a shifting foe, whom they knew to be everywhere, and yet could never seize.

The position became more and more critical. These outlaws, branded with the epithets of bandits, border ruffians, and freebooters, whom they affected to confound with the villains who congregate in these countries, and whom they obstinately treated as such by granting them no quarter, and shooting them without trial wherever they were captured: these men, now disciplined, hardened, and strong in the moral support of their fellow citizens, who applauded their successes, and put up vows for them, had boldly raised the flag of Texan independence, and after several engagements, in which they decimated the troops sent against them, compelled the latter to recognize them as the avowed defenders of an honourable cause.

Among the numerous generals of the republic, the president at length chose the only man capable of repairing the successive disasters undergone by the government. General Don José Maria Rubio was invested with the supreme command of the troops detached to act against Texas. This choice was most lucky; the general, an honest man and brave soldier, was incapable of selling himself, however great the price offered. Hence there was no reason to fear treachery from him, from which others, less susceptible or more avaricious than he was, had not recoiled. As an old soldier of the war of Independence, and ex-guerilla, Don José Maria was thoroughly conversant with all the tricks, and was the very man to fight with advantage against the foes that awaited him.

Unfortunately, this selection was made very late. Still, the General, while perfectly comprehending the immense responsibility he assumed, accepted without a murmur the rude task imposed on him. Certain men have the incontestable privilege of being born for the positions they occupy; their intellect seems to grow with the situation; made for great things, they ever remain on a level with events, whatever the nature of the latter may be. The General possessed this precious faculty; at the first glance he judged his enemies with that coolness which renders old soldiers so strong, and his plan was formed in a few minutes.

He immediately changed the tactics employed by his predecessors, and adopted a system diametrically opposite. Instead of fatiguing his troops by purposeless marches which had no result, he seized on the strongest positions, scattered his troops through cantonments, where they supported each other, and in case of need could all he assembled under his orders within four-and-twenty hours.

When these precautions were taken, still keeping his forces in hand, he prudently remained on the defensive, and instead of marching forward, watched with indefatigable patience for the opportunity to fall on the enemy suddenly and crush him.

The Texan Chiefs soon comprehended all the danger of these new and skilful tactics. In fact, they had changed parts; instead of being attacked, the insurgents were obliged to become the assailants, which made them lose all the advantages of their position, by compelling them to concentrate their troops, and make a demonstration of strength, contrary to their usual habits of fighting.

To the young officers who murmured at the plan adopted by the general, and made sarcastic remarks on his prudence, the latter replied with a smile that there was no hurry, that war was a game of skill in which the cleverest man won; and that he must not, for the sake of little lustre, let himself be led away to compromise the success of an enterprise which, with a little patience, must lead to certain success. The result proved that the general reasoned correctly, and that his plan was good.

The insurgents, reduced to inactivity by the system the new Chief of the Mexican army adopted, tried several times to attack his entrenchments, and draw him out; but the general contented himself with killing as many of them as he could, and would not move a step forward.

The conducta de plata intrusted to Captain Melendez had an immense importance in the eyes of the needy government at the capital; the dollars must at all hazards reach Mexico in safety; the more so, because for some time past the arrival of coin from Texas had become desperately irregular, and threatened to leave off altogether ere long.

General Rubio found himself reluctantly compelled to modify temporarily the line he had traced; he did not doubt that the insurgents, advised of the passage of the conducta, would make the greatest efforts to intercept and seize it, for they also suffered from a great want of money, and the millions sent to Mexico were of the utmost importance to them. Hence their plans must be foiled, and the conducta saved. For this purpose the General collected a large body of troops, placed himself at their head, and advanced by forced marches to the entrance of the defile, where, from the reports of his spies, he knew that the insurgents were ambuscaded; then, as we have seen, he sent off a sure man (or whom he supposed to be) to Captain Melendez, to warn him of his approach, and put him on his guard.

We have narrated in the "Border Rifles" what took place, and how truly worthy the General's express was of the confidence placed in him.

The Mexican camp stood in the centre of a beautiful plain, facing the defile through which the conducta must pass, according to the General's instructions. It was evening, and the sun had set for about an hour. Don José Maria, rendered anxious by the Captain's delay, and beginning to suspect a mishap, had sent off scouts in different directions to bring him news, and a prey to an agitation, which each moment that passed augmented, was walking anxiously about his tent, cursing and swearing in a low voice, frowning and stopping every now and then to listen to those thousand noises which arise at night without apparent cause, and pass as if borne on the wings of the Djinns.

General Don José Maria Rubio was still a young man; he was about forty-two, though he seemed older, through the fatigues of a military life, which had left rude marks on his martial and open countenance; he was tall and well-built; his muscular limbs, his wide and projecting chest denoted great vigour; and though his close-shaven hair was beginning to turn grey, his black eye had a brilliancy full of youth and intelligence.

Contrary to the habits of Mexican general officers, who, under all circumstances, make a great display of embroidery, and are gilded and plumed like charlatans, his uniform had a simplicity and severity which added to his military appearance, and gave him that aspect of reflection and majesty which is so befitting the chief of an army.

A sabre and a pair of holster pistols were carelessly thrown across a map on the table in the centre of the room, over which the General frequently bent in his agitated walk. The gallop of a horse, at first distant, but which rapidly drew nearer, was heard. The sentinel outside the tent challenged, "Who goes there?"

The horseman stopped, leapt to the ground, and a moment later the curtain of the tent was thrust aside, and a man appeared.

It was Captain Don Juan Melendez.

"Here you are, at last!" the General exclaimed, as his countenance grew brighter.

But on noticing the impression of sorrow spread over the officer's features, the General, who had walked two steps toward him, stopped, and his face again assumed an anxious look.

"Oh, oh!" he said, "What can have happened? Captain, has any mishap occurred to the conducta?"

The officer bowed his head.

"What is the meaning of this, Caballero?" the General continued, angrily; "Have you suddenly grown dumb?"

The Captain made an effort. "No, General," he answered.

"The conducta! Where is the conducta?" he went on, violently.

"Captured!" Don Juan replied, in a hollow voice.

"Viva Dios!" the General shouted, as he gave him a terrible glance, and stamped his foot: "The conducta captured, and yourself alive to bring me the news?"

"I could not get myself killed."

"I really believe, Heaven pardon me!" the General said, ironically, "that you have not even received a scratch."

"It is true."

The General walked up and down the tent in the utmost agitation. "And your soldiers, Caballero," he went on, a minute later, stopping before the officer, "I suppose they fled at the first shot?"

"My soldiers are dead, General."

"What do you say?"

"I say, General, that my soldiers fell to the last man defending the trust confided to their honour."

"Hum, hum!" the General remarked, "Are they all dead?"

"Yes, General, all lie in a bloody grave; I am the only survivor of fifty brave and devoted men."

There was a second silence. The General knew the Captain too well to doubt his courage and honour. He began to suspect a mystery.

"But I sent you a guide," he at length said.

"Yes, General, and it was that guide who led us into the trap laid by the insurgents."

"A thousand demons! If the scoundrel——"

"He is dead," the Captain interrupted him, "I killed him."

"Good. But there is something about the affair I cannot understand."

"General," the young man exclaimed, with some animation, "though the conducta is lost, the fight was glorious for the Mexican name. Our honour has not suffered; we were crushed by numbers."

"Come, Captain, you are one of those men above suspicion, whom not the slightest stain can affect. If necessary, I would give bail for your loyalty and bravery before the world. Report to me frankly, and without any beating round the bush, all that has happened, and I will believe you; give me the fullest details about this action, in order that I may know whether I have to pity or punish you."

"Listen, then, General. But I swear to you that if after my report the slightest doubt remains in your heart as to my honour and the devotion of my soldiers, I will blow out my brains in your presence."

"Speak first, Caballero, we will see afterwards what your best course should be."

The Captain bowed, and began an exact report of what had taken place.

CHAPTER VI
THE HUNTER'S COUNCIL

We will now return to Tranquil, whom we have too long neglected. The Canadian had left his friends two musket shots from the Texan encampment, intending, were it required, to call in Carmela: but that was not necessary; the young man, though unwillingly, had consented to all the Canadian asked of him, with which the latter was delighted, for without knowing exactly why, he would have been sorry to facilitate an interview between the young people.

Immediately after his conversation with the leader of the Freebooters, the hunter rose, and, in spite of the Jaguar's efforts to retain him, left the camp. He then remounted his horse, and, only half satisfied by his conversation with the Jaguar, returned thoughtfully to the spot where his friends were camping. The latter were awaiting him anxiously, and Carmela especially was suffering from a terrible uneasiness.

It was a strange fact, which women alone can explain, that the maiden, perhaps unconsciously, entertained toward the Jaguar and Captain Melendez feelings which she was afraid to analyze, but which led her to take an equal interest in the fate of those two men, and fear a collision between them, whatever the result might have proved. But for all that, it is certain that if she had been obliged to explain the reason which impelled her to act thus, she would have been unable to answer; and had anybody told her that she loved one or the other, she would have energetically protested; under the honest conviction that she spoke the truth.

Still, she felt herself, perhaps from different motives, irresistibly attracted toward them. She started at their approach; the sound of their voices caused her an internal thrill of happiness; if she remained long without news of them, she grew sad, pensive, and anxious; their presence restored her all her gaiety and birdlike freedom.

Was it friendship, or was it love? Who can answer?

Tranquil found his friends comfortably located in a narrow clearing, near a fire, over which their next meal was cooking. Carmela, a little apart, questioned with an impatient glance the path by which she knew the hunter must arrive. So soon as she perceived him, she uttered a suppressed cry of delight, and made a movement to run and meet him; but she checked herself with a flush, let her head droop, and concealed herself timidly behind a clump of floripondios.

Tranquil peacefully dismounted, took the bridle off his horse, which he sent with a friendly slap on the croup to join its comrades, and then sat down by the side of Loyal Heart.

"Ouf!" he said, "Here I am, back again, and not without difficulty."

"Did you run any dangers?" Loyal Heart asked, eagerly.

"Not at all; on the contrary, the Jaguar received me, as he was bound to do, that is, as a friend; and I have only to complain of his courtesy; besides, we have known each other too long for it to be otherwise."

Carmela had softly come up to the hunter; she suddenly bent her graceful head down to him, and offered him her forehead to kiss.

"Good day, father," she said, demurely, "you have already returned?"

"Already!" Tranquil answered, as he kissed her and laughed, "Hang it, girl, it seems as if my absence did not appear to you long."

"Pardon me, father, I did not mean that," she said, in great confusion.

"What did you mean, then, my child?"

"Oh, nothing."

"Yes you did, you little rogue! But you cannot deceive me, with all your tricks; I am too old a fox to be taken in by a girl."

"You are unkind, father," she answered, with a pout, "you always give a false meaning to what I say."

"Only think of that, señorita! Well, do not be in a passion, I have brought you good news."

"Do you mean it?" she said, clasping her hands joyfully.

"Would you doubt my word?"

"Oh, no, father."

"Very good, so now sit down by my side and listen."

"Speak, speak, father," she exclaimed eagerly, as she took the seat allotted her.

"You seem to take great interest in Captain Melendez, my child?"

"I, father!" she exclaimed with a start of surprise.

"Hang it! I fancy a young lady must feel a lively interest in a person, to take such a step for his sake as you have done."

The maiden became serious.

"Father," she said a moment later with that little, resolute tone spoilt children know so well how to assume; "I could not tell you why I acted as I did; I swear that it was against my will, I was mad; the thought that the Captain and the Jaguar were about to engage in a mortal combat, made me chill at heart; and yet I assure you, now that I am cool, I question myself in vain to discover the reason which urged me to intercede with you to prevent that combat."

The hunter shook his head.

"All that is not clear, Niña," he replied; "I do not at all understand your arguments. Hang it! I am only a poor woodranger, possessing no more learning than I have drawn from the great scenes of nature I constantly have before my eyes, and a woman's heart is to me a closed book, in which I could not decipher a line. Still, girl, believe me, take care, and do not play imprudently with weapons whose strength and mechanism you are ignorant of; though the antelope be so light and active when it is leaping from rock to rock on the verge of precipices, the moment arrives when it grows giddy, its head turns, and it rolls into the abyss—I have often seen similar catastrophes in the forests. Take care, my girl, take care, and believe in the old hunter's experience."

Carmela pensively leant her blushing brow on the Canadian's shoulder, and lifted to him her large blue eyes full of tears.

"I am suffering, father," she murmured sadly.

"Good Heavens! My child, you are suffering, and did not tell me—are you ill?" he exclaimed anxiously; "How imprudent it was of you to be out in the desert by night."

"You are mistaken, father," she replied with a faint smile; "I am not ill, it is not that."

"What is it then?"

"I do not know, but my heart is contracted, my bosom is oppressed. Oh, I am very unhappy!"

And hiding her head in her hands, she burst into tears. Tranquil looked at her for a moment with an astonishment mingled with terror.

"You, unhappy!" he at length exclaimed as he smote his head passionately. "Oh, whatever has been done to her, that she should weep thus!"

There was a silence of some minutes' duration, when the conversation seemed to take a confidential turn. Loyal Heart and Lanzi rose quietly, and soon disappeared in the chaparral. Tranquil and the maiden were hence alone. The hunter was suffering from one of those cold fits of passion which are so terrible because so concentrated; adoring the girl, he fancied in his simple ignorance that it was he who, without suspecting it, through the coarseness and frivolity of his manner, rendered her unhappy, and he accused himself in his heart for not having secured her that calm and pleasant life he had dreamed for her.

"Forgive me, my child," he said to her with emotion; "forgive me for being the involuntary cause of your suffering. You must not be angry with me, for really it is no fault of mine, I have always lived alone in the desert, and never learned how to treat natures so frail as those of women; but henceforth I will watch myself. You will have no reason to reproach me again. I promise you I will do all you wish, my darling child—well, does that satisfy you?"

By a sudden reaction, the maiden wiped away her tears, and bursting into a joyous laugh, threw her arms round the hunter's neck, and kissed him repeatedly.

"It is you who should pardon me, father," she said in her wheedling voice, "for I seem to take pleasure in tormenting you, who are so kind to me; I did not know what I was saying just now; I am not unhappy, I do not suffer, I am quite happy, and love you dearly, my good father; I only love you."

Tranquil looked at her in alarm; he could not understand these sudden changes of humour, whose cause escaped him.

"Good Heavens!" he exclaimed, clasping his hands in terror; "My daughter is mad!"

At this exclamation, the laughing girl's gaiety was augmented. The silvery sound of her laugh would have made a nightingale die of envy.

"I am not mad, father," she said, "I was so just now when I spoke to you in the way I did, but now the crisis has past; forgive me, and think no more about it."

"Hum!" the hunter muttered, as he raised his eyes to Heaven in great embarrassment; "I desire nothing more, Niña; but I am no further on than I was before, and on my word I understand nothing of what is passing through your mind."

"What matter, so long as I love you, father? All girls are so, and no importance must be attached to their caprices."

"Good, good, it must be so since you say it, little one. But for all that, I suffered terribly, your words rent my heart."

Carmela lovingly kissed him.

"And the Jaguar?" she asked.

"All is arranged; the Captain has nothing to fear from him."

"Oh, the Jaguar has a noble heart; if he has pledged his word, he may be trusted."

"He has given it to me."

"Thanks, father. Well, now that all is arranged according to our wishes—"

"Your wishes?" the hunter interrupted.

"Mine or yours, father—is that not the same thing?"

"That is true, I was wrong—go on."

"Well, I say, call your friends, who are walking about close by, I suppose, and let me eat, for I am dying of hunger."

"Are you?" he said eagerly.

"Indeed, I am; but I was ashamed to tell you."

"In that case you will not have long to wait."

The Canadian whistled; and the two men, who probably only awaited this signal, made their appearance at once. The venison was removed from the fire, laid on a leaf, and all seated themselves comfortably.

"Hilloh!" Tranquil said all at once, "Why, where is Quoniam?"

"He left us shortly after your departure," Loyal Heart made answer "to go to the Larch-tree hacienda, as he told us."

"All right, I did not think of that; I am not anxious about my old comrade, for he will manage to find us again."

Each then began eating with good appetite, and troubled themselves no further about the Negro's absence. It is a noteworthy fact, that men whom the life they lead compels to a continual employment of their physical faculties, whatever may be the circumstances in which they are, or the dangers that surround them—always eat with a good appetite, and sleep soundly, so indispensable for them is the satisfaction of these two material wants, in order that they may successfully resist the incessant incidents of their existence, which is so varied, and full of accidents of every description.

During the hunter's meal, the sun had set, and night invaded the forest. Carmela, exhausted by the various events of this day, retired almost immediately to a light jacal of leaves which Loyal Heart had built for her. The maiden needed to restore order in her ideas, and take a few hours' rest, the privation from which had over-excited her nervous system, and caused the crisis which had fallen on her a few hours previously.

When they were alone, the hunters laid in a stock of dead wood, which would keep the fire in all night then, after throwing on some handfuls of dry branches, they sat down in Indian fashion, that is to say, with their back to the flame, so that their eyes might not be dazzled by the light, and they could distinguish in the gloom the arrival of any unwelcome guest, man or wild beast. When this precaution had been taken, and the rifles laid within hand reach, they lit their pipes and smoked silently.

It is specially at night, when the sounds of day die out to make room for the mysterious rumours of the darkness, that the desert assumes a grand and imposing appearance, which affects the mind, and leads it into those gentle and melancholy reveries which are so full of charm. The purer night air refreshed by the breeze which passes through the branches and gently agitates them; the murmuring of the water among the lilies; the confused buzz of myriads of invisible insects; the silence of the desert interrupted by the melodious and animated sounds; and that busy hum of the great flood of life which comes from God and passes away incessantly to be constantly renewed — all these things plunge the strong-hearted man involuntarily into a religious contemplation, which those to whom the grand scenes of nature are unknown, cannot imagine.

The night was cold and clear; a profusion of light flashed from the millions of stars that studded the dark olive sky, and the moon poured on the earth her silvery rays which imparted a fantastic appearance to objects. — The atmosphere was so pure and transparent that the eye could distinguish, as in bright day, the surrounding landscape. Several hours passed thus, and one of the three men, seduced as they were by the splendour of the night, thought of taking that rest which, however, was so necessary after the fatigues of the day.

"Who will keep watch tonight?" Lanzi at length asked, as he passed the stem of his pipe through his belt; "We are surrounded by people amongst whom it is wise to take precautions."

"That is true," said Loyal Heart; "do you sleep, and I will watch for all."

"One moment," the Canadian said; "if sleep does not too greatly overpower you. Lanzi, we will profit by Carmela's absence to hold a council. The situation in which we are is intolerable for a girl, and we must make up our minds to some course at once. Unluckily, I know not what to do, and your ideas will hardly suffice, I fear, to get me out of my embarrassment."

CHAPTER VII
AN OLD FRIEND

Tranquil was too old and too crafty a wood ranger to let himself be surprised. With his eyes obstinately fixed on the spot whence the sound that had aroused him came, he tried to pierce the darkness, and distinguish any movement in the chaparral which would permit him to form probable conjectures as to the visitors who were arriving.

For a long period the noise he had heard was not repeated, and the desert had fallen back into silence. But the Canadian did not deceive himself. Up to all Indian tricks, and knowing the unbounded patience of the Redskins, he continued to keep on his guard; still, as he suspected that in the darkness searching glances were fixed on him and spying his slightest movements, Tranquil yawned twice or thrice, as if overcome by sleep, drew back the hand he had laid on his rifle barrel, and pretending to be unable to resist sleep any longer, he let his head sink on his chest with a natural movement.

Nothing stirred. An hour elapsed ere the slightest rumour disturbed the silence of the forest. Still, Tranquil felt confident that he had not deceived himself. The sky grew gradually brighter, the last star had disappeared, the horizon was assuming those fiery red tints which immediately precede the appearance of the sun: the Canadian, weary of this long watching, and not knowing to what he should attribute this inaction on the part of the Redskins, resolved at last to obtain the solution of the enigma. He therefore started suddenly to his feet and took up his rifle.

At the moment he prepared to go on the discovery, a noise of footsteps near him, mingled with the rustling of leaves, and the breaking of dry branches, smote his ear.

"Ah, ah!" the Canadian muttered, "It seems they have made up their mind at last; let us see who these troublesome neighbours are."

At the same instant, a clear feminine voice rose harmoniously and sonorously in the silence. Tranquil stopped with a start of surprise. This voice was singing an Indian melody, of which this was the first verse—

"I confide my heart to thee in the name of the Omnipotent.
I am unhappy, and no one takes pity on me;
Still God is great in my eyes."

"Oh!" the hunter muttered, with a nervous quivering, "I know that song, it is that of the betrothed of the Snake-Pawnees. How is it that these words strike my ear so far from their hunting grounds? Can a detachment of Pawnees be wandering in the neighbourhood? Oh, no! That is impossible. I will see who this singer is who has awaked with the sun."

Without further hesitation, the hunter walked hurriedly toward the thicket, from the centre of which the melody had been audible. But at the moment he was about to enter it, the shrubs were quickly parted, and two Redskins entered the clearing, to the amazement of the Canadian.

On coming within ten paces of the hunter the Indians stopped, and stretched their arms out in front of them, with fingers parted in sign of peace; then, crossing their arms on their chest, they waited. At this manifestation of the peaceful sentiments of the newcomers, the Canadian rested the butt of his rifle on the ground, and examined the Indians with rapid glance.

The first was a man of lofty stature, with intelligent features and open countenance; as far as it was possible to judge the age of an Indian, this man seemed to have passed the middle stage of life. He was dressed in his full warpaint, and the condor plume, fastened above his right ear, indicated that he held the rank of a Sachem in his tribe.

The other Redskin was not a man, but a woman, twenty years of age at the most; she was slim, active, and elegant, and her dress was decorated in accordance with the rules of Indian coquetry: still, her worn features, on which only the fugitive traces of a prematurely vanished beauty were visible, shewed that, like all Indian squaws, she had been pitilessly compelled to do all those rude household tasks, the whole weight of which the men lay on them, regarding it as beneath their dignity to interfere.

At the sight of these two persons, the hunter involuntarily felt an emotion, for which he could not account; the more he regarded the warrior standing before him, the more he seemed to find again in this martial countenance the distant memory of the features of a man he had formerly known, though it was impossible for him to recall how or where this intimacy had existed; but overcoming his feelings, and comprehending that his lengthened silence must appear extraordinary to the persons who had been waiting so long for him to address to them the compliments of welcome, which Indian etiquette demands, he at length decided on speaking.

"The Sachem can approach without fear and take his seat by the fire of a friend," he said.

"The voice of the Pale hunter rejoices the heart of the Chief," the warrior answered; "his invitation pleases him; he will smoke the calumet of friendship with the Pale hunter."

The Canadian bowed politely; the Sachem gave his squaw a sign to follow him, and he crouched on his heels in front of the fire, where Loyal Heart and Lanzi were still asleep. Tranquil and the warrior then began smoking silently, while the young Indian squaw was busily engaged with the household duties and preparing the morning meal. The two men allowed her to do so, not noticing apparently the trouble she took.

There was a lengthened silence. The hunter was reflecting, while the Indian was apparently completely absorbed by his pipe. At last he shook the ash out of the calumet, thrust the stem through his belt, and turned to his host—

"The Walkon and the Maukawis," he said, "always sing the same song; the man who has heard them during the moons of spring recognizes them in the moons of winter, it is not the same with man; he forgets quickly; his heart does not bound at the recollection of a friend; and if he meet him again after many moons, his eyes do not see him."

"What does the Chief mean?" the Canadian asked, astonished at these words, which seemed to convey a reproach.

"The Wacondah is powerful," the Indian continued; "it is he who dictates the words my breast breathes; the sturdy oak forgets that he has been a frail sapling."

"Explain yourself, Chief," the hunter said, with great agitation; "the sound of your voice causes me singular emotion; your features are not unknown to me; speak, who are you?"

"Singing-bird," the Indian said, addressing the young woman, "you are the *cihuatl* of a Sachem; ask the great Pale hunter why he has forgotten his friend—the man who, in happier times, was his brother?"

"I will obey," she answered, in a melodious voice; "but the Chief is deceived; the great Pale hunter has not forgotten the Wah-rush-a-menec of the Snake Pawnees."

"Oh!" Tranquil exclaimed, warmly, "Are you really Black-deer, my brother? My heart warned me secretly of your presence, and though your features had almost faded from my memory, I expected to find a friend again."

"Wah! is the Paleface speaking the truth?" the Chief said, with an emotion he could not quite conceal; "Has he really retained the memory of his brother, Black-deer?"

"Ah, Chief," the hunter said, sadly; "to doubt any longer would be an insult to me; how could I suppose I should ever meet you here, at so considerable a distance from the wigwams of your nation?"

"That is true?" the Indian remarked, thoughtfully; "my brother will forgive me."

"What!" Tranquil exclaimed, "Is that charming squaw I see there, the Singing-bird, that frail child whom I so often tossed on my knee?"

"Singing-bird is the wife of a Chief," the Indian answered, flattered by the compliment; "at the next fall of the leaves forty-five moons will have passed since Black-deer bought her of her father for two mustangs and a panther skin quiver."

Singing-bird smiled gracefully at the hunter, and went on with her duties.

"Will the Chief permit me to ask him a question?" Tranquil went on.

"My brother can speak, the ears of a friend are open."

"How did the Sachem learn that he would find me here?"

"Black-deer was ignorant of it: he was not seeking the great Pale hunter; the Wacondah has permitted him to find a friend again, and he is grateful."

Tranquil looked at the warrior in surprise. He smiled.

"Black-deer has no secret from his brother," he said, softly; "the Pale hunter will wait; soon he shall know all."

"My brother is free to speak or be silent; I will wait."

The conversation ceased here. The Sachem had wrapped himself in his buffalo robe, and did not appear disposed, to give any further explanation at present. Tranquil, restrained by the duties of hospitality, which in the desert prohibit any interrogation of a guest; imitated the Chiefs reserve; but the silence had lasted but a few minutes, when the hunter felt a light hand laid on his shoulder, while a soft and affectionate voice murmured in his ear:—"Good morning, father."

And a kiss completed the silence.

"Good-morning, little one," the hunter replied, with a smile; "did you sleep well?"

"Splendidly, father."

"And you have rested?"

"I no longer feel fatigued."

"Good; that is how I like to see you, my darling girl."

"Father," the inquisitive maiden said, as she looked around, "have visitors arrived?"

"As you see."

"Strangers?"

"No, old friends, who, I hope, will soon be yours."

"Redskins?" she asked with an instinctive start of terror.

"All of them are not wicked," he answered with a smile: "these are kind." Then, turning to the Indian woman, who had fixed her black velvet looking eyes on Carmela with simple admiration, he called out, "Singing-bird!"

The squaw bounded up like a young antelope. "What does my father want?" she asked, bowing gently.

"Singing-bird," the hunter continued, "this girl is my daughter, Carmela," and taking in his bony hand those of the two women, he clasped them together, adding with emotion, "Love one another like sisters."

"Singing-bird will feel very happy to be loved by the White lily," the Indian squaw replied; "for her heart has already flown towards me."

Carmela, charmed at the name which the squaw with her simple poesy had given her, bent down affectionately to her and kissed her forehead.

"I love you already, sister," she said to her, and holding her by the hand, they went off together twittering like two nightingales. Tranquil looked after them with a tender glance. Black-deer had witnessed this little scene with that Indian phlegm which nothing even disturbs: still, when he found himself alone with the hunter, he bent over to him, and said in a slightly shaking voice,—

"Wah! my brother has not changed: the moons of winter have scattered snow over his scalp, but his heart has remained as good as when it was young."

At this moment the sleeper awoke.

"Hilloh!" Loyal Heart said gaily, as he looked up at the sun, "I have had a long sleep."

"To tell you the truth," Lanzi observed, "I am not an early bird either: but nonsense! I will make up for it. The poor beasts of horses must be thirsty, so I will give them water."

"Very good!" said Tranquil; "By the time you have done that, breakfast will be ready."

Lanzi rose, leaped on his horse, and seizing the lasso of the others, went off in the direction of the stream without asking questions relative to the strangers. On the prairie it is so: a priest is an envoy of God, whose presence must arouse no curiosity. In the meanwhile Loyal Heart had also risen: suddenly his glance fell on the Indian Chief, whose cold eye was fixed on him: the young man suddenly turned pale as a corpse, and hurriedly approached the Chief.

"My mother!" he exclaimed in a voice quivering with emotion, "my mother—"

He could say no more. The Pawnee bowed peacefully to him.

"My brother's mother is still the cherished child of the Wacondah," he answered in a gentle voice; "her heart only suffers from the absence of her son."

"Thanks, Chief," the young man said with a sigh of relief; "forgive this start of terror which I could not overcome, but on perceiving you I feared lest some misfortune bad happened."

"A son must love his mother: my brother's feeling is natural; it comes from the Wacondah. When I left the Village of Flowers, the old greyhead, the companion of my brother's mother, wished to start with me."

"Poor ño Eusabio," the young man muttered, "he is so devoted to us."

"The Sachems would not consent; greyhead is necessary to my brother's mother."

"They were right, Chief; I thank them for retaining him. Have you followed my trail from the village?"

"I did."

"Why did you not awake me on your arrival?"

"Loyal Heart was asleep. Black-deer did not wish to trouble his sleep: he waited."

"Good! my brother is a Chief; he acted as he thought advisable."

"Black-deer is intrusted with a message from the Sachems to Loyal Heart. He wishes to smoke the calumet in council with him."

"Are the reasons that have brought my brother here urgent?"

"They are."

"Good! my brother can speak, I am listening."

Tranquil rose, and threw his rifle over his shoulder.

"Where is the hunter going?" the Indian asked.

"While you tell Loyal Heart the message I will take a stroll in the forest."

"The white hunter will remain; the heart of Black-deer has nothing hidden from him. The wisdom of my brother is great; he was brought up by the Redskins; his place is marked out at the council fire."

"But perhaps you have things to tell Loyal Heart which only concern yourselves."

"I have nothing to say which my brother should not hear; my brother will disoblige me by withdrawing."

"I will remain, then, Chief, since such is the case."

While saying these words, the hunter resumed his seat, and said: "Speak, Chief, I am listening."

The methodical Indian drew out his calumet, and, to display the importance of the commission with which he was entrusted, instead of filling it with ordinary tobacco, he placed in it *morhichee*, or sacred tobacco, which he produced from a little parchment bag he took from the pouch all Indians wear when travelling, and which contains their medicine bag, and the few articles indispensable for a long journey. When the calumet was filled, he lit it from a coal he moved from the fire by the aid of a medicine rod, decorated with feathers and bills.

These extraordinary preparations led the hunters to suppose that Black-deer was really the bearer of important news, and they prepared to listen to him with all proper gravity. The Sachem inhaled two or three whiffs of smoke, then passed the calumet to Tranquil, who, after performing the same operation, handed it to Loyal Heart. The calumet went the round thus, until all the tobacco was consumed.

During this ceremony, which is indispensable at every Indian council, the three men remained silent. When the pipe was out, the Chief emptied the ash into the fire, while muttering a few unintelligible words, which, however, were probably an invocation to the Great Spirit; he then thrust the pipe in his girdle, and after reflecting for some moments, rose and began speaking.

"Loyal Heart," he said, "you left the Village of Flowers to follow the hunting path at daybreak of the third sun of the moon of the falling leaves; thirty suns have passed since that period, and we are hardly at the beginning of the moon of the passing game. Well, during so short a period many things have occurred, which demand your immediate presence, in the tribe of which you are one of the adopted sons. The war hatchet, so deeply buried for ten moons between the prairie Comanches and the Buffalo Apaches, has suddenly been dug up in full council, and the Apaches are preparing to follow the war trail, under the orders of the wisest and most experienced Chiefs of the nation. Shall I tell you the new insults the Apaches have dared to offer your Comanche fathers? What good would it be? Your heart is strong, you will obey the orders of your fathers, and fight for them."

Loyal Heart bowed his head in assent.

"No one doubted you," the Chief continued; "still, for a war against the Apaches, the Sachems would not have claimed your help; the Apaches are chattering old women, whom Comanche children can drive off with their dog-whips; but the situation has all at once become complicated, and it is more your presence at the council of the nation than the aid of your arm, though you are a terrible warrior, which your fathers desire. The Long knives of the East and the Yoris have also dug up the hatchet, and both have offered to treat with the Comanches. An alliance with the Palefaces is not very agreeable to Redskins; still, their anxiety is great, as they do not know which side to take, or which party to protect."

Black-deer was silent.

"The situation is, indeed, grave," Loyal Heart answered; "it is even critical."

"The Chiefs, divided in opinion, and not knowing which is the better," Black-deer continued, "sent me off in all haste to find my brother, whose wisdom they are aware of, and promise to follow his advice."

"I am very young," Loyal Heart answered, "to venture to give my advice in such a matter, and settle so arduous a question. The Comanche nation is the queen of the prairies; its Chiefs are all experienced warriors; they will know better than I how to form a decision which will at once protect the interests and honour of the nation."

"My brother is young, but wisdom speaks by his mouth. The Wacondah breathes in his heart the words his lips utter; all the Chiefs feel for him the respect he deserves."

The young man shook his head, as if protesting against such a mark of deference. "Since you insist," he said, "I will speak; but I will not give my opinion till I have heard that of this hunter, who is better acquainted with the desert than I am."

"Wah!" said Black-deer, "the Pale hunter is wise; his advice must be good; a Chief is listening to him."

Thus compelled to explain his views, Tranquil had involuntarily to take part in the discussion; but he did not feel at all inclined to take on himself the responsibility of the heavy burden which Loyal Heart tried to throw off his own shoulders. Still, he was too thoroughly a man of the desert to refuse giving his opinion in council, especially upon so important a question. After reflecting for some moments, he therefore at length decided on speaking.

"The Comanches are the most terrible warriors of the prairie," he said, "no one must try to invade their hunting grounds; if they make war with the Apaches, who are vagabond and cowardly thieves, they are in the right to do so; but for what good object would they interfere in the quarrels of the Palefaces? Whether Yoris or Long knives, the Whites have ever been, at all times, and under all circumstances, the obstinate enemies of the Redskins, killing them wherever they may find them, under the most futile pretexts, and for the most time simply because they are Indians. When the coyotes are tearing each other asunder on the prairie, do the Indians try to separate them? No. They say, let them fight it out—the more that fall, the fewer thieves and plunderers will there be in the desert. To the Redskins the Palefaces are coyotes thirsting for blood. The Comanches should leave them to devour each other; whichever party triumph, those who have been killed will be so many enemies the fewer for the Indians. This war between the Palefaces has been going on for two years, implacably and obstinately. Up to the present the Comanches have remained neutral; why should they interfere now? However great the advantages offered them may be, they will not be equivalent to a neutrality, which will render them stronger and more dangerous in the sight of the Whites. I have spoken."

"Yes," Loyal Heart said, "you have spoken well, Tranquil. The opinion you have offered is the only one the Comanches ought to follow, an interference on their part would be an act of deplorable folly, which the Sachems would soon regret having committed."

Black-deer had carefully listened to the Canadian's speech, and it appeared to have produced a certain impression on him; he listened in the same way to Loyal Heart, and when the latter had ceased speaking, the Chief remained thoughtful for a while, and then replied—

"I am pleased with the words of my brothers, for they prove to me that I regarded the situation correctly. I gave the council of the Chiefs the same advice my brothers just offered. My brothers have spoken like wise men, I thank them."

"I am ready to support in council," Loyal Heart remarked, "the opinions the white hunter has offered, for they are the only ones which should prevail."

"I think so too. Loyal Heart will accompany the Chief to the callis of the nation?"

"It is my intention to start on my return tomorrow; if my brother can wait till then, we will start together."

"I will wait."

"Good; tomorrow at daybreak we will follow the return trail in company."

The council was over, yet Tranquil tried vainly to explain to himself how it was that Black-deer, whom he had left among the Snake Pawnees, could now be an influential Chief of the Comanche nation; and the connection between Loyal Heart and the Chief perplexed him not a bit less. All these ideas troubled the hunter's head, and he promised himself on the first opportunity to ask Black-deer for the history of his life since their separation.

As soon as Lanzi returned with the horses, the hunters and Carmela sat down to breakfast, waited on by Singing-bird, who performed her duties with extreme grace.

CHAPTER VIII
QUONIAM'S RETURN

The meal did not take long; each of the guests, busied with secret thoughts, ate quietly and silently. Tranquil, though he did not dare ask any questions of Black-deer or Loyal Heart, for all that, burned to learn by what concourse of extraordinary events these two men, who had started from diametrically opposite points, had eventually grown into such close intimacy.

Nor did he understand any better how a white man of a pure race, young, and who appeared to have received a certain education, had so completely given up relations with men of his ideas, to adopt, as Loyal Heart had done, the mode of life of the Redskins, and become, as it were, a part of one of these nations.

But the tiger killer was too well acquainted with prairie manners to try and lead the conversation to a topic which might perhaps have displeased his comrades, and which, at any rate, would have displayed a curiosity on his part unworthy of an old wood ranger; he therefore contented himself with cudgelling his brains to try and strike a spark which might guide him to the discovery of the truth, without permitting himself the slightest allusion to a subject which he longed to know all about.

Carmela felt a great friendship for Singing-bird, and so soon as the meal was ended, led her off to the jacal, where both began chattering. In accordance with the arrangements the hunters had made, Loyal Heart and Tranquil took their rifles, and entered the forest on opposite sides, to go in quest of game. Black-deer and Lanzi remained behind to protect the women in the slightly probable event of an attack.

The two men, lying on the ground side by side, slept or smoked with that apathy and careless indolence peculiar to men who despise talking for the sake of talking, and thus expending energy which they may require at any moment. Several hours passed away thus, nothing occurring to trouble the calmness and silence that reigned over the bivouac, except at intervals the joyous laughter of the two young women, which vibrated harmoniously on the ears of the hunters, and brought a slight smile to their lips.

A little before sunset the hunters returned, almost simultaneously, bending beneath the weight of the game they had killed. Loyal Heart, moreover, had lassoed a horse, which he brought in for Black-deer, who had not one. The sight of this animal caused the adventurers some alarm, and numerous conjectures. It was not at all wild; it had allowed Loyal Heart to approach it without difficulty, who made a prisoner of it almost without opposition. Moreover, and this increased the restlessness of its new owners, it was completely equipped in the Mexican fashion.

Tranquil concluded from this, after reflecting for a moment, that the freebooters had attacked the conducta de plata, and the animal, whose rider had probably been killed, had escaped during the action. But which side had gained the day, no one was able to conjecture.

After a rather lengthy discussion, it was at last agreed that so soon as night had completely set in, Black-deer should go reconnoitring, while those who remained in the camp redoubled their vigilance, through fear of a surprise, either from the border ruffians or the Mexican soldiers; for although the adventurers were known to both parties, they justly feared the excesses to which they might give way in the intoxication of victory.

This fear, correct perchance as far as the troops were concerned, was not at all so with the men commanded by the Jaguar, and merely proved that the worst, and at the same time most erroneous opinion was entertained of them.

The sun was just disappearing behind the dense mass of lofty mountains that marked the horizon, when the hurried paces of a horse were heard a short distance off. The hunters seized their weapons, and posted themselves behind the enormous boles of the sumach trees that surrounded them, in order to be ready for any event. At this moment the cry of the blue jay was repeated twice.

"Take your places again at the fire," Tranquil said, "'tis a friend."

In fact, a few moments later, the branches cracked, the shrubs were smartly thrust aside, and Quoniam made his appearance. After nodding to the company, he dismounted, and sat down by the side of the Panther-killer.

"Well, gossip," the latter asked him at once; "what news have you?"

"Plenty," he answered.

"Then, I suppose, you have been reconnoitring?"

"I did not have the trouble to ask questions; I only required to listen in order to learn in an hour more news than I could have discovered in a year."

"Oh, oh," the Canadian said, "eat something, compadre, and when your appetite is satisfied, you will tell us all you have learnt."

"I wish for nothing better, especially as there are sundry matters it is as well for you to know."

"Eat then without further delay, that you may be able to talk to us all the sooner."

The Negro did not let the invitation be repeated, and began vigorously attacking the provisions which Tranquil had put aside, and which Loyal Heart now spread on the ground. The hunters were eager to hear the news of which Quoniam stated himself to be the bearer; after all they had been able to see during the past few days, they must possess considerable importance. Still, however great their curiosity might be, they succeeded in hiding it, and patiently waited till the Negro had finished his meal. The latter, who suspected what thoughts were crossing their minds, did not put their patience to a long trial; he ate with the proverbial rapidity of hunters, and had finished in a twinkling.

"Now I am quite at your service," he said, as he wiped his mouth on the skirt of his hunting shirt, "and ready to answer all your questions."

"We have none to ask you," Tranquil said; "we wish you, gossip, to give us a short narrative of all that has happened to you."

"Yes, I fancy that will be the best; in that way it will be clearer and more easy for you to show the conclusions you think the most suitable."

"Excellently reasoned, my friend; we are listening to you."

"Do you know why I left you?" Quoniam began.

"Yes, I was told, and approved of it highly."

"All the better, because I fancied for a moment that I did wrong in going without informing you, and I was on the point of returning."

"You would have done wrong."

"At present I am convinced of that, and congratulate myself on having pushed forward. It is not a long ride from here to the Larch-tree hacienda in a straight line; my horse is good; I went straight ahead, and covered the distance in eight hours."

"That was good riding."

"Was it not? But I was in a hurry to join you again, and most anxious not to lose any time on the road. When I reached the Larch-tree, there was a great confusion at the hacienda. The peons and vaqueros collected in the patio were talking and shouting all together, while the Capataz, the Major-domo, and even the Signor Haciendero himself, pale and alarmed, were distributing arms, raising barricades before the gates, placing cannon on their carriages—in short, taking all the precautions of men who expect an attack at any moment. It was impossible for me to make myself heard at first, for everybody was speaking at once—women crying, children screaming, and men swearing. I might have fancied myself in a madhouse, so noisy and terrified did I find everybody; at length, however, by going from one to the other, questioning this man, and bullying that one, I learned the following, which enabled me to comprehend the general terror; the affair, I swear to you, was worth the trouble."

"Out with it, friend," Loyal Heart exclaimed, with ill-restrained impatience.

Quoniam had never during life raised any pretensions to be an orator. The worthy Negro, who was naturally very modest, even experienced a certain difficulty in speaking at all. The hunter's unexpected interruption troubled him so that he stopped short, and was unable to find a single word. Tranquil, who had so long known his comrade, hastily interposed.

"Let him tell his story in his own way," he said to Loyal Heart; "if not, it will be impossible for him to reach the end. Quoniam has a way of telling things peculiar to himself; if interrupted, he loses the thread of his ideas, and then he grows confused."

"That is true," said the Negro; "I do not know whence it comes, but it is stronger than I: when I am stopped, it is all up with me, and I get in such a tangle that I cannot find my way out."

"That arises from your modesty, my friend."

"Do you think so?"

"I am sure of it, so do not alarm yourself any more, but go on in the full confidence that you will meet with no further interruption."

"I am most ready to go on, but I have forgotten where I left off."

"At the information you had succeeded in obtaining," Tranquil said, giving Loyal Heart a look which the latter understood.

"That is true: this, then, is what I learned:—The conducta de plata, escorted by Captain Melendez, was attacked by the Border Rifles, or the Freebooters as they are now called, and after a desperate fight, all the Mexicans were killed."

"Ah!" Tranquil exclaimed, in stupor.

"All," Quoniam repeated; "not one escaped; it must have been a frightful butchery."

"Speak lower, my friend," the hunter remarked, as he looked in the direction of the jacal, "Carmela might hear you."

The Negro gave a nod of assent.

"But," he continued, in a lower key, "this victory was not very productive to the Borderers, for the Mexicans had been careful to hurl the gold they carried into a barranca, whence it was impossible to get it out."

"Well played, by Heaven!" the Canadian exclaimed; "The Captain is a brave fellow."

"Was so, you mean," said Quoniam.

"That is true," the Canadian remarked, sadly; "but go on, my friend."

"This victory fired the mine; the whole of Texas has risen; the towns and pueblos are in full revolt, and the Mexicans are pursued like wild beasts."

"Is it so serious as that?"

"Much more than you suppose. The Jaguar is at this moment at the head of a real army; he has hoisted the flag of Texan independence, and sworn that he will not lay down arms till he has restored liberty to his country, and driven the last Mexican beyond the frontier."

There was a moment of stupor among his audience.

"Is that all?" Tranquil at length asked.

"Not yet," Quoniam made answer.

"Have you further bad news to tell us?"

"You shall judge for yourself, my friend, when I have told you all I know."

"Speak, then, in heaven's name!"

"This is the information I have picked up. Considering that you would not be sorry to hear these important news as speedily as possible, I hastened to finish my business with the Capataz. I had some difficulty in finding him, as he was so busy; so soon as I got hold of him, instead of giving me the money I asked him for, he answered me that I must be off at once, and tell you to come to the hacienda as soon as you could, for, under the circumstances, your presence there was indispensable."

"Hum!" said Tranquil, without any further explanation of his thoughts.

"Seeing," Quoniam went on, "that there was nothing more to expect of the Capataz, I took leave of him and remounted my horse; but just as I was leaving, a great noise was heard outside, and everybody rushed to the gates, uttering shouts of joy. It seems that General Don José Maria Rubio, who commands the province, considers that the position of the hacienda is a very important point to defend."

"Of course," Tranquil said; "the Larch-tree commands the entrance of the valley, and as long as it remains in the power of the Mexicans, insures the entry of their troops into the state."

"That is it, though I do not remember the term they employed."

"Was it, strategetical position?"

"The very thing."

"Yes, the hacienda, built at the period of the conquest, is a perfect fortress; its thick, battlemented walls, its situation on an elevation which cannot be commanded, and which on one side holds under its guns the mountain passes, and on the other the valley de los Almendrales, render it a point of the utmost importance, which can only be carried by a regular seige."

"That is what everybody said down there; it seems, too, that such is General Rubio's opinion, for the cause of all the disturbance I heard was the arrival of a large body of troops commanded by a Lieutenant Colonel, who had orders to shut himself up in the hacienda, and defend it to the last extremity."

"In that case war is declared?"

"Of course."

"Civil war," Tranquil continued, mournfully, "that is to say, the most odious and horrible of all; a war in which fathers fight against sons, brothers against brothers, in which friend and foe speak the same tongue, issue from the same stem, have the same blood in their veins, and through that very reason are the more inveterate and rend each other with greater animosity and rage; civil war, the most horrible scourge that can crush a people! May God grant in his mercy that it be short; but, since divine patience is at length wearied, and the Omnipotent has permitted this fratricidal struggle, let us hope that right and justice may remain victorious, and that the oppressors, who are the cause of all these misfortunes, may be for ever expelled from a territory which they have too long sullied by their unworthy and odious presence."

"May God grant it!" his hearers replied, in a deep voice.

"But how did you succeed in escaping from the hacienda after the arrival of the troops, Quoniam?" Tranquil continued.

"I saw that, if I amused myself by admiring the uniform and fine appearance of the troops, when order was slightly restored, the gates would be closed, and my hopes of escaping foiled for a long time. Without saying a word, I dismounted, and leading my horse by the bridle, glided through the mob so cleverly, that I at length found myself outside. I then leaped into the saddle, and pushed straight ahead. I was only just in time, I declare, for five minutes later all the gates were closed."

"And then you came straight here?"

Quoniam smiled cunningly. "Do you think so?" he said.

"Hang it! I suppose so, at least."

"Well, you are mistaken, gossip; I did not return straight here: and yet it was not my inclination that prevented it, I assure you."

"What happened, then?"

"You will see, for I have not finished yet."

"Go on, then; but be brief, if that is possible."

"Every man does what he can, and you have no right to ask more of him."

"That is true, speak as you think proper."

"Never," the Negro continued, "did I gallop in such good spirits; my horse stretched out, so that it was a pleasure to see; and it seemed as if the poor brute understood my impatience to get away from the hacienda, so fast did it race. This ride lasted thus, without interruption, for nearly five hours; at the end of that period I thought it advisable to grant my horse a few minutes' rest, that it might regain its breath, for animals are like men precisely—if you overwork them, they break down all at once; and that would have happened to me had I not been careful to stop in time. I therefore allowed my horse to rest for two hours; then, after rubbing it down, I started again, but had not yet reached the end of my adventures. I had scarce galloped an hour longer ere I fell into a large party of horsemen, armed to the teeth, who suddenly emerged from a ravine, and surrounded me ere I had even time enough to notice them. The meeting was anything but agreeable—the more so, as they did not appear at all well disposed toward me; and I do not exactly know how I should have got out of the hobble, had not one of the men thought proper to recognize me, though I do not remember ever to have met him before, and burst out, 'Why, it is a friend; 'tis Quoniam, Tranquil's comrade!' I confess that this exclamation pleased me; a man may be brave, but there are circumstances in which he feels frightened, and this is what happened to me at that moment."

The hunters smiled at the Negro's simple frankness, but were careful not to interrupt him, as they felt instinctively that he had reached the most interesting point of his long and prolix narration.

"At once," the latter continued, "the manner of these men changed entirely; they became most polite and attentive, in proportion as they had been, previously brutal. 'Lead him to the commandant,' said one of them the others approved, and I gave in, because resistance would have been folly. I followed without any remark, the man who led me to their Chief, though inwardly cursing the wasps' nest into which I had fallen. Fortunately I had not far to go. Can you guess, Tranquil, who this Chief was to whom I was led?"

"The Jaguar," the hunter answered.

"What!" the Negro exclaimed, in amazement, "Have you guessed it? Well! I swear to you that I did not suspect it in the least, and was greatly surprised at seeing him. But I must do him the justice of saying that he received me very well; he questioned me about a good many matters, which I answered as well as I could—where I came from, what was doing at the hacienda, where I was going, and so on. In short, he conversed with me for more than an hour; then, doubtless, satisfied with the information I had given him, he left me free to continue my journey, and began his own. It seems that he is going straight to the Larch-tree hacienda."

"Does he intend to lay siege to it?"

"That is his intention, I believe; but, although he is at the head of nearly twelve hundred determined bandits, I do not think his nails, and those of his comrades, will be hard enough to dig a hole in such stout walls."

"That is in God's hands. Have you finished your narrative?"

"Very soon."

"Go on, then."

"Before restoring me to liberty, the Jaguar inquired after you and Doña Carmela with considerable interest. Then he wrote a few words on a piece of paper, which he handed me, with a recommendation to be sure and give it you so soon as I rejoined you."

"Good Heaven!" Tranquil exclaimed, in agitation, "And you have delayed so long in executing your commission!"

"Was I not obliged to tell you first what had happened to me? But there is no time lost, for here is the paper."

While saying this, Quoniam drew a paper from his pocket, and offered it to Tranquil, who almost tore it out of his hands. The Negro, convinced that he had carried out his commission excellently, did not at all comprehend the hunter's impatience; he looked at him for a moment with an air of amazement, then shrugged his shoulders almost imperceptibly, filled his pipe, and began smoking, not troubling himself further about what was going on around him.

The hunter quickly unfolded the paper; he turned it over and over in his hands with an air of embarrassment, taking a side glance every now and then at Loyal Heart, who had drawn a burning log from the fire, and now held it within reading distance, for night had completely set in. This went on for some minutes; at length, Loyal Heart, understanding the reason of the hunter's hesitation, resolved on speaking to him.

"Well," he said, with a smile, "what does your friend Jaguar write?"

"Hum!" said the hunter.

"Perhaps," the other continued, "it is so badly written that you cannot make out his scrawl. If you permit me, I will try."

The Canadian looked at him. The young man's face was calm; nothing evidenced that he had a thought of making fun of the hunter. The latter shook his head several times, and then burst into a hearty laugh.

"Deuce take all false shame!" he said, as he gave him the letter. "Why should I not confess that I cannot read? A man whose life has been spent in the desert ought not to fear confessing an ignorance which can have nothing dishonouring for him. Read, read, my lad, and let us know What our doubtful friend wishes."

And he took the log from the young man's hands.

Loyal Heart took a rapid glance at the paper. "The letter is laconic," he said, "but explicit. Listen:

"'The Jaguar has kept his word. Of all the Mexicans who accompanied the conducta, only one is alive free and unwounded—Captain Don Juan Melendez de Gongora. Will the friends of the Jaguar have a better opinion of him?'"

"Is that all?" Tranquil asked.

"Yes."

"Well," the hunter exclaimed, "people may say as they please, but, by Heavens! The Jaguar is a fine fellow."

"Is he not, father?" a gentle voice murmured in his ear.

Tranquil started at this remark, and turned sharply round. Carmela was by his side, calm and smiling.

CHAPTER IX
HOSPITALITY

We have said that night had fallen for some time past, and it was quite dark under covert. In the black sky a chaos of clouds, laden with the electric fluid, rolled heavily along. Not a star glistened in the vault of heaven; an autumnal breeze whistled gustily through the trees, and at each blast covered the ground with a shower of dead leaves.

In the distance could be heard the dull and mournful appeals of the wild beasts proceeding to the drinking place, and the snapping bark of the coyotes, whose ardent eyes at intervals gleamed like incandescent coals amid the shrubs. At times lights flashed in the forest and ran along the fine marsh grass like will-o'-the-wisps. Large dried up sumach trees stood at the corners of the clearing, in which the bivouac was established, and in the fantastic gleams of the fire waved like phantoms their winding sheets of moss and lianas. A thousand sounds passed through the air; nameless cries escaped from invisible lairs, hollowed beneath the roots of the aged trees; stifled cries descended from the crests of the quebradas, and our adventurers felt an unknown world living around them, whose proximity froze the soul with a secret terror.

Nature was sad and melancholy, as when she is in travail with one of those terrible overthrows so frequent in these regions. In spite of themselves, the hunters underwent the influence of this discomfort of the desert. There are black hours in life, in which, either through the action of external objects, or the common and mysterious disposition of the inner being, that *me* which cannot be defined, the strongest men feel unconsciously mastered by a strange contagion of sadness which they seem to breathe in the air, and which overpowers them without power of defence. The news brought by Quoniam had further augmented this tendency of the hunters to melancholy; hence the conversation round the fire, ordinarily gay and careless, was sad and short. Everyone yielded to the flood of gloomy thoughts that contracted his heart, and the few words exchanged at lengthened intervals between the hunters generally remained unanswered.

Carmela alone, lively as a nightingale, continued in a low voice her conversation with Singing-bird, while warming herself, for the night was cold, and not noticing the anxious sideglances which the Canadian at times gave her. At the moment when Lanzi and Quoniam were preparing to go to sleep, a slight crackling was heard in the shrubs. The hunters, suddenly torn from their secret thoughts, raised their heads quickly. The horses had stopped eating, and with their heads turned to the thicket, and ears laid back, appeared to be listening.

In the desert, everything has a reason; the wood rangers, accustomed to analyse all the rumours of the prairie, know and explain them without ever making a mistake; the rustling of the branch on which the hand rests, the noise of the leaf falling on the ground, the murmur of the water over the pebbles—nothing escapes the marvellous sagacity of these men, whose senses have acquired an extraordinary delicacy.

"Someone is prowling round us," Loyal Heart muttered in a voice not above a breath.

"A spy, of course," said Lanzi.

"Spy or no, the man who is approaching is certainly a white," said Tranquil, as he stretched out his arm to clutch the rifle lying by his side.

"Stay, father," Carmela said eagerly, as she seized his arm; "perhaps it is a poor wretch lost in the desert, who needs help."

"It may be so," Tranquil replied after a moment's reflection; "at any rate, we shall soon know."

"What do you intend doing?" the girl exclaimed, terrified at seeing him rise.

"Go and meet the man, and ask him what he wants, that is all."

"Take care, father."

"Of what, my child?"

"Suppose this man were one of the bandits who traverse the desert?"

"Well, what then?"

"And he were to kill you?"

The Canadian shrugged his shoulders.

"Kill me, girl, nonsense! Reassure yourself, my child, whoever the man may be, he will not see me unless I deem it necessary. So let me alone."

The maiden tried once more to prevent his departure, but the Canadian would listen to nothing. Freeing himself gently from Carmela's affectionate clutch, he picked up his rifle and disappeared in the chaparral with so light and well-measured a step, that he seemed rather to be gliding on a cloud, than walking on the grass of the clearing.

So soon as he reached the centre of the thicket, from which the ill-omened sound he had heard came, the hunter, ignorant as he was as to how many enemies he had to deal with, redoubled his prudence and precautions: after a hesitation which lasted only a few seconds, he lay down on the ground, and began gently crawling through the grass, without producing the slightest rustling sound.

We will now return to the monk, whom we left proceeding toward the hunters' bivouac, accompanied by Blue-fox. The Apache Chief, after giving him the instructions he thought best adapted to inspire him with a wholesome terror, and compel him to serve his plans, left him alone, and disappeared so suddenly, that the monk could not guess in what direction he had gone. When he was alone, Fray Antonio took a timid glance around him; his mind was perplexed, for he could not conceal from himself how delicate and difficult of accomplishment was the mission with which the Chief had entrusted him, especially when dealing with a man so clever and well versed in Indian tricks as the tiger killer.

More than once the monk cursed the malignity of his planet which led him into such traps, and seemed to take a delight in accumulating on his head all the annoyances and tribulations possible. For a moment, he thought of flight, but he reflected that he was doubtless carefully watched, and that at the slightest suspicious movement he attempted, the invisible guardians who were watching him would suddenly appear before him, and compel him to carry out the adventure to the end.

Fortunately for himself, the monk belonged to that privileged class of men whom even the greatest annoyances but slightly affect, and who, after feeling wretched for a few moments, frankly make up their minds, saying to themselves that when the moment arrives in which they run a risk, an accident will perhaps draw them from their trouble, and turn matters to their advantage, in lieu of crushing them.

This reasoning, false though it be, is employed more frequently than may be supposed by a number of people, who, after saying to themselves "when it comes, we shall see," push boldly onwards, and, extraordinary to say, generally succeed in getting out of the hobble, without the loss of too many feathers, and without themselves knowing what they did to have so lucky an escape.

The monk, therefore, resolutely entered the covert, guiding himself by the light of the fire as a beacon. For some minutes he went on at a tolerable pace, but gradually as he approached, his alarm returned; he remembered the rough correction Captain Melendez had administered to him, and this time he feared even worse.

Still, he was now so near the bivouac that any backsliding would be useless. For the purpose of granting himself a few minutes' further respite, he dismounted, and fastened his horse to a tree with extreme slowness: then, having no further plausible pretext to offer himself for delaying his arrival among the hunters, he decided on starting again, employing the most minute precautions not to be perceived too soon, through fear of receiving a bullet in his chest, before he had time to have an explanation with the persons he visited at so awkward an hour.

But Fray Antonio, unluckily for himself, was extremely obese; he walked heavily, and like a man accustomed to tread the pavement of a town; moreover, the night was extremely dark, which prevented him seeing two yards ahead, and he could only progress with outstretched hands, tottering at each step, and running against every obstacle that came across his path.

Hence he did not go far, ere he aroused the persons he desired so much to surprise, and whose practised ear, constantly on the watch, had at once noticed the unusual sound which he had himself not noticed. Fray Antonio, extremely satisfied with his manner of progression, and congratulating himself in his heart at having succeeded so well in concealing himself, grew bolder and bolder, and began to feel almost entirely reassured, when suddenly he uttered a slight cry of terror, and stopped as if his feet had been rooted in the ground. He had felt a heavy hand laid on his shoulder.

The monk began trembling all over, though not daring to turn his head to the right or left, for he was persuaded in his heart that his last hour had arrived.

"Hilloh, Señor Padre, what are you doing in the forest at such an hour?" a hoarse voice then said to him.

But Fray Antonio was unable to answer; terror had rendered him deaf and blind.

"Are you dumb?" the voice went on a minute after in a friendly voice. "Come, come, it is not wise to traverse the desert at so late an hour."

The monk did not reply.

"Deuce take me," the other exclaimed, "if terror has not rendered him idiotic. Come, bestir yourself, canarios."

And he began shaking him vigorously.

"Eh, what?" the monk said, in whom a species of reaction was beginning to take place.

"Come, there is some progress, you speak, hence you are not dead," Tranquil went on joyously, for it was he who had so cruelly frightened the monk; "follow me, you must be frozen, don't let us remain here."

And passing his arm through the monk's, he led him away; the latter followed him passively and mechanically, not able yet to understand what was happening to him, but still beginning to regain a small amount of courage. In a few minutes, they reached the clearing.

"Ah!" Carmela exclaimed in surprise; "Fray Antonio! By what accident is he here, when he started with the conducta de plata?"

This remark made the hunter prick his ears; he examined the monk attentively, and then compelled him to sit down by the fire.

"I trust that the good father will explain to us what has happened to him," he muttered.

Everything, however, has an end in this world; and the monk for some time past had seemed destined to pass, with the greatest rapidity and almost without transition, from the extremest terror to the most complete security. When he was a little warmed, the confusion produced in his ideas by the sudden meeting with the hunter gradually yielded to the cordial reception given him; and Carmela's gentle voice breaking pleasantly on his ear, completely re-established the balance of his mind, and dismissed the mournful apprehensions that tormented him.

"Do you feel better, holy Father?" Carmela asked him, with much sympathy.

"Yes," he said, "I thank you, I am now quite comfortable."

"All the better. Will you eat? Would you like to take any refreshment?"

"Nothing at all, I thank you, for I have not the least appetite."

"Perhaps you are thirsty, Fray Antonio; if so, here is a bota of refino," said Lanzi, as he offered him a skin more than half full of the comforting liquid.

The monk permitted himself to be persuaded sufficiently to prove that he was no lover of ardent spirits; then he allowed himself to be convinced, and seizing the bota, drank a hearty draught of the generous fluid. This libation restored him all his coolness and presence of mind.

"Then," he said, as he turned the bota to the half-breed, and gave vent to a sigh of relief, "Heaven preserve me; were the Evil One to come now in person, I feel capable of holding my own against him."

"Ah, ah!" said Tranquil, "It seems, my good father, as if you were now completely restored to the possession of your intellectual faculties."

"Yes, and I will give you the proof whenever you like."

"Hang it! You challenge me. I did not dare cross-question you before; but, as it is so, I will no longer hesitate."

"What do you wish to know?"

"A very simple matter: how it is that a monk finds himself at such an hour alone in the heart of the desert?"

"Nonsense," Fray Antonio said, gaily. "Who told you that I was alone?"

"Nobody; but I suppose so."

"Do not make any suppositions, brother, for you would be mistaken."

"Indeed!"

"Yes, as I have the honour of telling you."

"Still, when I met you, you were alone."

"Granted."

"Well?"

"The others were further off, that's all."

"What others?"

"The persons who accompanied me."

"Ah! And who are they?"

"That is the question——Nonsense," he said, a minute after, as if holding a conversation with himself, "the most disadvantageous reports are current about me. I am accused of a number of bad actions; suppose I were to try and do a good one, that might change my luck. Who knows whether I may not be rewarded at a later date? At any rate, here goes."

Tranquil and his comrades listened in extreme surprise to the monologue of the monk, not knowing exactly what to think of this man, and half inclined to deem him mad. The latter perceived the impression he produced on his hearers.

"Listen," he said, in a stern voice, and with a slight frown, "form what opinion of me you like, that is a matter of indifference to me; still I do not wish it to be said, that I requited your cordial hospitality by odious treachery."

"What do you mean?" Tranquil exclaimed.

"Listen to me. I uttered the word treachery, and perhaps I was wrong, for nothing proves to me that it is so; still, all sorts of reasons lead me to suppose that it is nothing else persons tried to force me into committing for your injury."

"Explain yourself, in Heaven's name; you speak in enigmas, and it is impossible to understand you."

"You are right, so I will be clear: which of you gentlemen bears the name of Tranquil?"

"It is I."

"Very good. Owing to certain circumstances, the recital of which would not at all interest you, I unluckily fell into the hands of the Apaches."

"Apaches!" Tranquil exclaimed, in surprise.

"Good Lord, yes," the monk continued; "and I assure you that when I found myself in their power, I did not feel at all comfortable. Still, I was wrong to be alarmed; far from inventing for me one of those atrocious tortures which they mercilessly inflict on the whites who are so unhappy as to become their prisoners, they treated me, on the contrary, with extreme gentleness."

Tranquil fixed a scrutinising glance on the monk's placid face.

"For what purpose did they that?" he asked, with a suspicious accent.

"Ah," Fray Antonio went on, "that I could not comprehend, though I am perhaps beginning to suspect it."

The hearers bent toward the speaker with an expression of impatient curiosity.

"This evening," the monk went on, "the Chief of the Redskins himself accompanied me to within a short distance of your bivouac; on coming in sight of your fire he pointed it out to me, saying, 'Go and sit down at that brasero. You will tell the great Pale hunter that one of his oldest and dearest friends desires to see him.' Then he left me, after making the most horrible threats if I did not obey him at once. You know the rest."

Tranquil and his comrades regarded each other in amazement, but without exchanging a word. There was a rather long silence; but Tranquil at length took on himself to express aloud the thought each had in his heart.

"'Tis a trap," he said.

"Yes," Loyal Heart remarked; "but for what purpose?"

"How do I know?" the Canadian muttered.

"You said, Fray Antonio," the young man continued, addressing the monk, "that you suspected the motives of the Apaches' extraordinary treatment of you?"

"I did say so," he replied.

"Let us know that suspicion."

"It was suggested to me by the conduct of the pagans, and by the clumsy snare they laid for you; it is evident to me that the Apache Chief hopes, if you consent to grant the interview he asks, to profit by your absence to carry off Doña Carmela."

"Carry me off!" the maiden exclaimed, with a start of horror, surprised and alarmed at once by this conclusion, which she was far from anticipating.

"The Redskins are very fond of white women," the monk continued, coolly; "most of the incursions they make into our territory are undertaken for the purpose of carrying off captives of that colour."

"Oh!" Carmela exclaimed, with an accent of indomitable resolution, "I would sooner die than become the slave of one of those ferocious demons."

Tranquil shook his head sadly. "The monk's supposition appears to me correct," he said.

"The more so," Fray Antonio confirmed him, "because the Apaches who made me prisoner are the same that attacked the Venta del Potrero."

"Oh, oh," said Lanzi, "in that case I know their Chief, and his name; he is one of the most implacable enemies of the white men. It is very unlucky that I did not succeed in burying him under the ruins of the venta, for Heaven is my witness that such was my intention."

"What is the fellow's name?" the hunter asked, sharply, evidently annoyed at his verbiage.

"Blue-fox!" said Lanzi.

"Ah," Tranquil said, ironically and with a dark frown, "I have known Blue-fox for many years, and you, Chief?" he added, turning to Black-deer.

The name of the Apache Sachem had produced such an impression on the Pawnee, that the hunter was startled by it. The Indians retain under all circumstances an apathetic mask, which they consider it an honour not to remove, whatever may happen; but the mere name of Blue-fox, pronounced as if by accident, was sufficient to melt that indifference, and cause Black-deer to forget Indian etiquette.

"Blue-fox is a dog, the son of a coyote," he said, as he spat on the ground disdainfully; "the gypaètes would refuse to devour his unclean carcase."

"These two men must have a mortal hatred for each other," the Canadian muttered, as he took a sideglance at the inflamed features and sparkling eyes of the Indian Chief.

"Will my brother kill Blue-fox?" the Pawnee asked.

"It is probable," Tranquil answered; "but in the first place, let us try to play this master rogue a trick, who fancies us stupid enough to be caught in the clumsy snares he lays in our path. Be frank, monk, have you told us the truth?"

"On my honour."

"I should prefer any other oath," the Canadian said ironically, in a low voice. "Can you be trusted?"

"Yes."

"Is what you said to us about your return to honest courses sincere?"

"Put me on my trial."

"That is what I intend to do; but reflect ere answering. Do you really intend to be of service to us?"

"I do."

"Whatever may happen?"

"Whatever may happen, and whatever the consequence may be of what you ask of me."

"That will do. I warn you that, in all probability, you will be exposed to serious perils."

"I have told you that my resolution is formed; speak, therefore, without further hesitation."

"Listen to me, then."

"I am doing so. Have no fear of finding me recoil, so cut it short."

"I will try to do so."

CHAPTER X
THE LARCH-TREE HACIENDA

Though the report made by Quoniam was in every respect true, the Negro was ignorant of certain details of which we will now inform the reader, because these events are closely connected with our story, and clearness renders it indispensable that they should be made known. We will, therefore, return to the Larch-tree hacienda.

But, in the first place, let us explain the meaning of this word "hacienda," which we have employed several times in the course of this narrative, and which several authors have employed before us, without understanding its significance.

In Sonora, Texas, and all the old Spanish colonies generally, where the land is, as it were, left to anyone who likes to take possession of it and cultivate it, there may be found at immense distances, and broadcast like almost imperceptible dots over the waste lands, vast agricultural establishments, each as large as one of our counties. These establishments are called haciendas, a word we improperly translate by farm, which has not at all the same meaning.

Immediately after the conquest, the Cortez, Pizarros, Almagros, and other leaders of adventurers hastened to repay their comrades by dividing among them the lands of the conquered, following, perhaps without suspecting it, the example which had been given them a few centuries previously by the leaders of the Barbarians, after the break-up and dismemberment of the Roman Empire.

The conquerors were few in number, the shares were large; and the majority of these ragged conquerors, who in their own country had not even a roof to shelter their heads, found themselves all at once masters of immense domains, which they immediately set to work turning to account, laying down the sword without regret to take the pick, that is to say, compelling the Indians who had become their slaves to clear for them the land they had stolen.

The first care of the new possessors of the soil was to erect, in positions easy to defend, houses, whose lofty, thick, and embattled walls rendered them thorough fortresses, behind which they could easily defy any attempted revolt on the part of their slaves. The inhabitants had been allotted like the ground; each Spanish soldier received a considerable number as his share; arms cost nothing. There was no lack of stone, and hence the buildings were constructed of vast proportions, and of such extreme strength, that even at the present day, after the lapse of several centuries, these haciendas are an object of admiration to the traveller.

Slaves alone, for whom the measure of time no longer exists, and whose only hope is death, can undertake and complete these Cyclopean buildings, of which we, men of another age, cannot understand the existence on the globe, where they stand at various spots, like dumb and touching protests.

At the haciendas, in addition to agriculture, which, especially at the present day, has greatly fallen off, owing to the incessant invasions of the Indian bravos, the breeding of cattle and horses is carried on to a considerable extent. Hence, each of these farms contains an infinity of servants of all descriptions, peons, vaqueros, etc., and resembles a small town.

The owners of these establishments are consequently men belonging to the highest society, and the richest and most intelligent class in the country. The majority prefer residing in the cities, and visit only at long intervals their haciendas, the management of which they entrust to the major-domo and capataz, who are themselves semi-savages, whose life is spent in riding constantly from one end to the other of the hacienda.

The Larch-tree hacienda, but a short distance from the mountains whose passes it commanded, was therefore of great strategetical value to both the parties now disputing the possession of Texas. The insurgent chiefs understood this as well as the Mexican generals did.

After the total destruction of the detachment commanded by Captain Melendez, General Rubio hastened to throw a powerful garrison into the Larch-tree. As an old soldier of the Independence, accustomed to the incessant struggles of a people that desires to be free, he had divined the revolution behind the insurrection, on seeing that for ten years past these insurgents, though incessantly conquered, seemed to grow from their ashes again to return more obstinate and powerful than before, and expose their chests to the pitiless bullets of their oppressors.

He was aware that the inhabitants only awaited the announcement of a success, even though problematical, to rise to a man, and make common cause with the daring partisans, branded by their enemies with the name of Border ruffians, but who in reality were only the forlorn hope of a revolution, and apostles acting under a holy and noble idea. Far from offering Captain Melendez reproaches, which he knew that the latter did not deserve, the General pitied and consoled him.

"You have your revenge to take, Colonel," he said to him, for this grade, long deserved by the young officer, had just been given him by the President of the Republic; "your new epaulettes have not yet smelt powder. I propose giving you a splendid opportunity for christening them."

"You will fulfil my wishes, General," the young officer replied, "by entrusting me with a perilous enterprise, my success in which will serve to wipe out the shame of my defeat."

"There is no shame, Colonel," the General replied, kindly, "in being conquered as you were. War is only a game like any other, in which chance often declares for the weaker side; let us not despond at an insignificant check, but try, on the contrary, to cut the comb of these cocks who, pluming themselves on their ephemeral triumph, doubtless imagine that we are terrified and demoralised by their victory."

"Be assured, General, that I will help you to the best of my ability. Whatever be the post you confide to me, I will die at it before surrendering."

"An officer, my friend, must put off that impetuosity which so well becomes the soldier, but it is a grave fault in a Chief trusted with the lives of his fellow men. Do not forget that you are a head, and not an arm."

"I will be prudent, General, as far as the care for my honour will permit me."

"That will do, Colonel—I ask no more."

Don Juan merely bowed in response.

"By-the-bye," said the General, presently, "have these partisans any capable men at their head?"

"Very capable, General; thoroughly acquainted with guerilla fighting, and possessing a bravery and coolness beyond all praise."

"All the better, for in that case we shall reap more glory in conquering them. Unfortunately, they are said to wage war like perfect savages, pitilessly massacring the soldiers that fall into their hands; indeed, what has happened to you is a proof of it."

"You are mistaken, General. Whatever these men may be, and the cause for which they fight, it is my duty to enlighten and disabuse you, for they have been strangely calumniated; it was only after my repeated refusals to surrender that the action began. Their Chief even offered me my life at the moment when I hurled myself with him into the yawning abyss at our feet. When I became their prisoner they restored me my sword, gave me a horse and a guide, who brought me within musket shot of your outposts: is that the conduct of cruel men?"

"Certainly not, and I am pleased to see you thus do justice to your enemies."

"I merely declare a fact."

"Yes, and an unlucky one for us; these men must consider themselves very strong to act thus. This clemency of theirs will attract a great number of partisans to their ranks."

"I fear it."

"And I too. No matter, the moment has arrived to act with vigour; for, if we do not take care, within a week the very stones of this country, of which we are still the masters, will rise to expel us, and the ground will grow so hot under our feet, that we shall be compelled to fly before these undisciplined masses of badly armed *guasos*, who harass us like swarms of mosquitoes."

"I await your orders, General."

"Do you feel strong enough to mount again?"

"Perfectly."

"Very good, then. I have prepared three hundred men, cavalry and infantry; the latter will mount behind the horsemen, in order not to delay the march, which must be rapid, for my object is that you should reach the hacienda before the insurgents; and fortify yourself there."

"I will reach it."

"I count on you. Two mountain guns will follow your detachment, and will prove sufficient; for, if I am rightly informed, the hacienda has six in good condition. Still, as ammunition may run short, you will take sufficient with you to last for a fortnight. At all risks, the hacienda must hold out for that period against all the attacks the insurgents may make."

"It shall hold out, I swear it to you, General."

"I trust entirely to you."

The General walked to the entrance of the tent and raised the curtain.

"Summon the officers told off for the expedition," he said.

Five minutes later the officers appeared; nine in number—two captains of cavalry, two of infantry, two lieutenants, and two alferez or second lieutenants, and a captain, lieutenant, and alferez of artillery. The General looked for a moment searchingly at these men, who stood serious and motionless before him.

"Caballeros," he at length said, "I have carefully chosen you from the officers of my army, because I know that you are brave and experienced;

you are about to carry out, under Colonel Don Juan Melendez de Gongora, a confidential mission, which I would not have given to others whose devotion to their country was less known to me. This mission is most perilous. I hope that you will accomplish it like brave men, and return here with glory."

The officers bowed their thanks.

"Do not forget," the General continued, "that you owe your soldiers an example of subordination and discipline; obey the Colonel as myself in all he may order for the good of the service and the success of your enterprise."

"We cannot desire a better Chief than the one your Excellency has selected to lead us," one of the Captains answered; "under his orders we are certain of performing prodigies."

The General smiled graciously.

"I count on your zeal and bravery. Now, to horse without further delay, for you must have left the camp within ten minutes."

The officers bowed and retired. Don Juan prepared to follow them.

"Stay," the General said to him; "I have one final recommendation to give you."

The young man walked up to him.

"Shut yourself up carefully in the place," the General went on. "If you are invested, do not attempt any of those sallies, which often compromise the fate of a garrison, without positive advantage. Content yourself with vigorously repulsing attacks, sparing the blood of your soldiers, and not expending your ammunition needlessly. So soon as my final arrangements are made, I will march in person to your help; but you *must* resist till then, at any cost."

"I have already told you I will do so, General."

"I know that you will. Now, my friend, to horse, and may you be fortunate."

"Thanks, General."

The Colonel bowed, and immediately withdrew to place himself at the head of the small band, which, collected a short distance off, only awaited his arrival to start. The General was standing in the doorway of his tent to witness their departure. Don Juan mounted, drew his sabre, and turned toward the motionless detachment.

"Forward!" he commanded.

The squadrons at once started, and began drawing out in the darkness like the black folds of an ill-omened serpent. The General remained in the doorway of his tent for some time, and when the last sound had died away in the night, he pensively re-entered the tent, and let the curtain fall behind him, muttering in a low and sad voice—

"I have sent them to death, for Heaven fights on the side of our adversaries."

And, after shaking his head several times with an air of discouragement, the old soldier of the war of Independence fell into an equipal, hid his face in his hands, and plunged into serious reflections.

In the meanwhile, the detachment rapidly continued its march. Thanks to the Mexican fashion of mounting infantry *en croupe*, the troops carried out their movements with a rapidity that seemed almost prodigious, the more so as American horses go very quickly, and endure great fatigue without injury.

The Americans of the South are generally very harsh to their horses, to which they pay no attention. Never in the interior does a horse pass the night, whatever the weather may be, otherwise than in the open air. Every morning it receives its ration for the whole day, marching frequently fourteen, or even sixteen hours, without stopping or drinking; when evening arrives, the harness is removed, and it is left to find its food where it can. On the Indian border, where there is much to fear from the Redskins, who are great admirers of horses, and display admirable skill in stealing them, certain precautions are used at night; the horses are picquetted in the interior of the bivouac, and feed on the pea vines, the young tree shoots, and a few measures of maize or other corn, which is given with extreme parsimony. Still, in spite of the careless way in which they are treated, we repeat that these horses are very handsome, vigorous, remarkably docile, and of great speed.

Colonel Melendez arrived at an early hour in sight of the hacienda, for his troops had made a forced march through the night. With a rapid glance the experienced Chief of the Mexicans examined the neighbourhood, but the plain was deserted.

The Larch-tree hacienda stood like an eagle's nest on the top of a hillock, whose abrupt sides had never been smoothed, as the steepness of their ascent was regarded as a means of defence in the event of an attack. Thick walls turned yellow by time, at each angle of which could be seen the threatening muzzles of two guns peering out, gave this strongly-built house the appearance of a real fortress.

The Mexicans increased their already rapid pace, in order to reach the hacienda before the gates were opened, and the ganado let out. The scene presented by this magnificent plain at sunrise, had something imposing about it. The hacienda, whose roof was still veiled in mist; the gloomy forests in the distance, which ran with almost imperceptible undulations along the spurs of the sierra; the silvery thread of a small stream, which wound with capricious meanderings through the plain, and whose waters sparkled in the hot sunbeams; the dumps of larches, sumachs, and Peru trees, which rose here and there from amid the tall grass, and agreeably broke the monotony of the plain, while from the thickets rose the joyous song of the birds saluting the return of day—in a word, all seemed to breathe repose and happiness in this abode momentarily so tranquil.

The Mexicans reached the hacienda, whose gates were not opened till the inhabitants were well assured that the newcomers were really friends. They had already heard of the general insurrection occasioned by the surprise of the conducta de plata, and hence the Major-domo, who commanded in the absence of Don Felipe de Valreal, proprietor of the hacienda, kept on his guard.

This Major-domo, whose name was Don Felix Paz, was a man of about five-and-forty at the most, tall, well-built, and powerful; he had, in truth, the appearance of a perfect *hombre de a caballo*, an essential condition for fulfilling his onerous duties. This Major-domo came in person to receive the Mexican detachment at the gate of the hacienda. After congratulating the Colonel, he informed him that so soon as he received the news of the general revolt of the province, he had brought all his cattle in, armed the servants, and rendered the guns on the platform serviceable.

The Colonel complimented him on his diligence, established his troops in the outhouses destined for the peons and vaqueros, took military possession of all the posts, and, accompanied by the Major-domo, made a strict inspection of the interior of the fortress. Don Juan Melendez, being well acquainted with the carelessness and sloth of his fellow countrymen, expected to find the hacienda in a wretched state, but was agreeably deceived. This large estate, situated on the limits of the desert, as it were between civilisation and barbarism, was too exposed to the unforeseen attacks of Redskins and bandits of every description who congregate on the border, for its owner not to watch with the utmost care over its defence. This wise foresight was at this moment of a great utility for the siege which, in all probability, they would have to withstand ere long.

The Colonel found but very little to alter in the arrangements made by the Major-domo; he contented himself with cutting down several clumps of trees which, being situated too near the hacienda, might shelter sharpshooters, who could annoy their artillery men. At each entrance of the hacienda barricades were erected by his orders, composed of branches interlaced, and outside the walls the arms of all the healthy men were called into requisition, to dig a deep and wide trench, the earth from which, thrown up on the side of the hacienda, formed a breast-work, behind which the best shots in the garrison were placed. The two mountain guns brought by the Colonel remained horsed, so that they might be transported to the point of danger. Finally, the Mexican flag was haughtily hoisted on the top of the hacienda.

Counting the servants, to whom Don Felix had distributed arms, the garrison amounted to nearly four hundred men, a sufficient force to resist a coup de main, especially in so good a position as this; there was plenty of ammunition and food; the Mexicans were animated by the best spirit, and the Colonel, therefore, felt certain of being able to hold out for a fortnight against troops more numerous and experienced than those the insurgents had at their disposal.

The works of fortification were carried on with such great activity, that they were completed within twenty-four hours of the Colonel's arrival at the hacienda. The scouts, sent out in all directions, came back without any fresh news of the insurgents, whose movements were so cleverly veiled, that, since the affair of the conducta, they seemed to have disappeared without leaving a trace, and buried themselves in the bowels of the earth.

This complete want of news, far from reassuring the Colonel, on the contrary, augmented his anxiety. This factitious tranquillity, this gloomy silence of the landscape, seemed to him more menacing than if he had heard of the approach of the enemy, whose masses, however, he felt, by a species of secret intuition, were gradually drawing in round the post he had been selected to defend.

It was the second day after the arrival of the Mexicans at the Larch-tree; the sun was disappearing behind the mountains in masses of gold; night would soon set in. Colonel Melendez and the Major-domo, leaning on one of the battlements of the platform, were absently gazing out on the immense landscape unrolled at their feet, while conversing together. Don Juan had in a few minutes appreciated the loyalty and intelligence of the Major-domo; hence these two men, who thoroughly understood each other, had become friends.

"Another day past," said the Colonel, "and it has been impossible for us yet to learn the movements of the insurgents. Does not that appear extraordinary to you, Don Felix?"

The Major-domo sent forth a cloud of smoke from his mouth and nostril, took his husk cigarette from his mouth, and quietly flipped away the ash.

"Very extraordinary," he said, without turning his head, and continuing to look fixedly at the sky.

"What a singular man you are! Nothing disturbs you," Don Juan went on half angrily, "Have all our scouts returned?"

"All."

"And still brought no news?"

"None."

"By Heaven! Your coolness would make a saint swear! What are you looking at so fixedly in the sky? Do you fancy you can find the information we require there?"

"Perhaps so," the Major-domo replied seriously. Then extending his hand in a north-east direction, he said—

"Look there."

"Well?" the Colonel said looking in the direction indicated.

"Do you see nothing?"

"On my honour, no."

"Not even those flocks of herons and flamingos flying in large circles, and uttering shrill cries which you can hear from here?"

"Certainly I see birds; but what have they in common——?"

"Colonel," the Major-domo interrupted him, turning and drawing himself up to his full height; "prepare to defend yourself; the enemy is there."

"What—the enemy? you are mad, Don Felix; look out in the last gleams of day, the plain is deserted."

"Colonel, before becoming Major-domo at the Larch-tree hacienda, I was a wood ranger for fifteen years; the desert is to me a book, every page of which I can peruse. Watch the timid flight of those birds, notice the numberless flocks which are constantly joining those we first perceived; those birds, driven from their nests, are flying haphazard before an enemy who will soon appear. That enemy is the insurgent army, whose masses will soon be visible to us, probably preceded by fire."

"Rayo de Dios, Don Felix," the Colonel suddenly exclaimed; "you are right, look there!"

A red line, momentarily growing wider, suddenly appeared on the extreme verge of the horizon.

"Did the flight of the birds deceive us?" the Major-domo asked.

"Forgive me, friend, a very excusable ignorance, but we have not a moment to lose."

They went down at once; five minutes later the defenders of the hacienda lined the tops of the walls, and ambushed themselves behind the exterior intrenchments. The Texan army, now perfectly visible, was deploying on the plains in heavy columns.

CHAPTER XI
A METAMORPHOSIS

We must now go back for some days, and return to the encampment of the hunters, whom we left in a most awkward position, watched by the vigilant eye of the Apaches, and compelled to trust temporarily to Fray Antonio, that is to say, to a man for whom, in his heart, not one of them felt the slightest sympathy. Still, had it been possible to read the monk's mind, their opinion about him would probably have been completely changed.

A revolution had taken place in this man's mind, and he had been unconsciously overcome by that influence which upright natures ever exert over those which have not yet been entirely spoiled. However, whatever was the cause of the change which had taken place almost suddenly in the monk's ideas, we are bound to state that it was sincere, and that Fray Antonio really intended to serve his new friends, whatever the consequences might be to himself.

Tranquil, accustomed, through the desert life he led, to discover with a certain degree of skill the true feelings of persons with whom accident brought him in contact, thought it his duty to appear to trust, under present circumstances, entirely on the monk, though he might not give perfect credence to his protestations of devotion.

"Are you brave?" he asked him, continuing the conversation.

Fray Antonio, surprised by the sudden question, hesitated for a moment.

"That depends," he said.

"Good; that is the answer of a sensible man. There are moments when the bravest is afraid, and no man can answer for his courage."

The monk gave a sign of assent.

"We have," Tranquil continued, "to cheat the cheater, and play at diamond cut diamond with him; you understand me?"

"Perfectly. Go on."

"Very good. Return to Blue-fox,"

"What?"

"Are you afraid?"

"Not exactly; but I fancy he may proceed to extremities with me."

"That is a risk to be run."

"Well, be it so," he exclaimed resolutely, "I will run it."

The Canadian looked fixedly at him.

"That will do," he said to him. "Here, take these, and, at any rate, if you are attacked, you will not die unavenged."

And he put a brace of pistols in his hand. The monk examined them attentively for a moment, turning them over so as to assure himself that they were in good state, then he hid them under his gown with a start of joy.

"I fear nothing now," he said; "I am going."

"Still I must explain to you— —"

"For what good purpose?" the monk interrupted him. "I will tell Blue-fox that you consent to have an interview with him; but, as you do not care to go alone to his camp, you prefer seeing him without witnesses in the middle of the prairie."

"That will do, and you will bring him with you to the spot where I shall be waiting."

"I will try, at any rate."

"That is what I mean."

"But where will you wait for him?"

"On the skirt of the forest."

"All right."

"One parting hint."

"Out with it."

"Keep a few paces from the Chief, not before or behind, but on his right hand, if possible."

"Very good; I understand."

"Well, I trust you will succeed."

"Oh, now I fear nothing, as I am armed."

After uttering these words, the monk rose and walked away with a quick and firm step. The Canadian looked after him for some time.

"Is he a traitor?" he muttered.

"I do not think so," Loyal Heart answered.

"May Heaven grant it!"

"What is your plan?"

"It is simple: we can only triumph over the enemies who surround us by stratagem; hence, that is the only thing I intend employing. We must escape from these red demons at all hazards."

"That is true. But, when we have succeeded in throwing them out, where shall we go?"

"We must not dream, in the present excited state of the country, of making a long journey across the desert with two females; it would be running certain ruin."

"That is true; but what can we do?"

"It is my intention to proceed to the Larch-tree hacienda. There, I fancy, my daughter will obtain the best protection for the present."

"Permit me to remind you that yourself refused to have recourse to that."

"That is true; hence I only resolve on it when in a fix. As for you——"

"Oh, I will accompany you," Loyal Heart quickly interrupted him.

"Thanks," the Canadian exclaimed, warmly. "Still, in spite of all the pleasure your generous offer occasions me, I cannot accept it."

"Why not?"

"Because the nation which had adopted you claims your help, and you cannot refuse it."

"It will wait; besides, Black-deer will make my excuses."

"No," the Chief said, distinctly; "I will not leave my Pale friends in danger."

"By Jove!" Tranquil exclaimed joyously, "As it is so, we shall have some fun; hang it all, if five resolute and well-armed men cannot get the best of a hundred Apaches. Listen to me, comrades: while I go ostensibly to the meeting I have granted Blue-fox, follow me in Indian file, and be ready to appear directly I give you the signal by imitating the cry of the mockingbird."

"All right."

"You, Lanzi and Quoniam, will watch over Carmela."

"We will all watch over her, friend, trust to us," said Loyal Heart.

Tranquil gave his comrades a parting farewell, threw his rifle over his shoulder, and left the encampment. He had hardly disappeared ere the hunters lay down on the ground, and crawled on his trail, Carmela guided by Singing-bird forming the rearguard. The maiden felt an involuntary shudder run over her limbs as she entered the forest. This night march, whose issue might prove so fatal, terrified her, and suggested gloomy forebodings, which she feared to see realised at every step.

In the meanwhile Fray Antonio continued his journey, and soon emerged from the forest. Far from his resolution being shaken, the nearer he drew to the Apaches he felt it, on the contrary, become firmer. The monk was eager to prove to the hunters that he was worthy the confidence they placed in him; and if at times the thought of the dangers to which he exposed himself crossed his mind, he drove it off, being determined to risk his life, if needed, in saving Doña Carmela, and preventing her falling into the hands of the cruel enemies who were preparing to seize her.

Fray Antonio had gone hardly five hundred yards from the forest, when a man suddenly emerged from a thicket and barred his passage. The monk suppressed with difficulty a cry of terror at this unexpected apparition, and started back. But immediately regaining his coolness, he prepared to sustain the terrible contest that doubtless menaced him, for he had recognised Blue-fox at the first glance. The Chief examined him in silence, fixing on him his deep black eye with an expression of suspicion which did not escape the monk.

"My father has been a long time," he at length said, harshly.

"I could not be any quicker," the monk answered.

"Wah! My father returns alone; the great Pale warrior was afraid; he did not accompany my father."

"You are mistaken, Chief; the man you call the great Pale hunter, and whom I call Tranquil, was not afraid, and did not refuse to accompany me."

"Och! Blue-fox is a Sachem; his eye pierces the thickest darkness; though he may look he sees nothing."

"That is probably because you do not look in the right direction, that's all."

"My father will explain. Blue-fox desires to know how his Pale friend carried out the mission the Sachem confided to him."

"I took the best advantage possible of my meeting with the hunter, in order to carry out the orders I had received."

"My father will pardon me, I am only a poor Indian without brains; things must be repeated to me several times before I can understand them. Will the great Pale hunter come?"

"Yes."

"When?"

"At once."

"Where is he then?"

"I left him over there, at the verge of the forest. He is waiting for the Chief."

Blue-fox started at this remark, and fixed on the monk a glance which seemed trying to read the most secret thoughts of his heart.

"Why did he not accompany my father here?" he said.

The monk assumed the most simple look possible.

"On my faith, I do not know," he answered; "but of what consequence is it?"

"It is pleasanter to converse on the prairie."

"Do you think so? Well, it is possible. For my part I do not see any difference between here and there."

This was said with such apparent carelessness, that, in spite of all his craft, the Chief was deceived.

"Has the great Pale hunter come alone?"

"No," Fray Antonio replied, boldly.

"If that be so, Blue-fox will not go."

"The Chief will reflect."

"What is the use of reflecting? The father has deceived his Red friend."

"The hunter could not come alone."

"Why not?"

"Because he did not wish to leave in the forest the girl who accompanies him."

The Indian's face suddenly brightened, and assumed an expression of extraordinary cunning.

"Wah!" he said, "And no other person but the young Pale virgin accompanies the hunter?"

"No. It seems that the other white warriors who were with him left him at daybreak."

"Does my father know where they are gone?"

"I did not inquire. That does not concern me. Every man has enough business of his own without troubling himself about that of others."

"My father is a wise man."

The monk made no reply to this compliment.

These words were rapidly exchanged between the two men. Fray Antonio had answered so naturally, and with such well-played frankness, that the Indian, whose secret thoughts the Mexican's answers flattered, felt all his suspicions vanish, and went, head down, into the snare so adroitly laid for him.

"Och!" he said, "Blue-fox will see his friend."

"The father can return to the camp of the Apache warriors."

"No, thank you, Chief," the monk answered, resolutely, "I prefer remaining with people of my own colour."

Blue-fox reflected for an instant, and then replied, with an ironical smile playing round his thin lips—

"Good; my father is right. He can follow me, then."

"It is evident," the monk thought to himself, "that this accursed pagan is devising some treachery. But I will watch him, and at the slightest suspicious movement I will blow out his brains like the dog he is."

But he kept these reflections to himself, and followed the Chief with an easy and perfectly indifferent air. In the moonbeams, which allowed objects to be distinguished for a considerable distance, they soon perceived, on the extreme verge of the forest, the dark outline of a man leaning on a rifle.

"Ah," the Chief said, "we must make ourselves known."

"That need not trouble you. I take it on myself to warn the hunter when the time arrives."

"Good," the Indian muttered, and they continued to advance.

Blue-fox, though he placed confidence in his companion, only advanced, however, with extreme caution and prudence, examining the shrubs, and even the smallest tufts of grass, as if assuring himself that they concealed no enemy. But, with the exception of the man they perceived before them, the place seemed plunged in profound solitude; all was calm and motionless; no unusual sound troubled the silence.

"Let us stop here," said Fray Antonio, "it would be imprudent for us to advance further without announcing ourselves, although the hunter has probably recognized us already; for, as you perceive, Chief, he has not made the slightest move."

"That is true, but it is as well to be cautious," the other replied.

They stopped at about twenty yards from the covert, where Fray Antonio placed his hands funnel-wise on either side his mouth, and shouted at the full extent of his lungs—

"Hilloh! Tranquil, is that you?"

"Who calls me?" the latter immediately answered.

"I—Fray Antonio. I am accompanied by the person you are expecting."

"Advance without fear," Tranquil replied. "Those who seek me without any intention of treachery have nothing to fear from me."

The monk turned to the Apache Chief. "What shall we do?" he asked him.

"Go on," the latter replied, laconically.

The distance which separated them from the hunter was soon covered; and the Mexican becoming an impromptu master of the ceremonies, presented the two men to each other. The Sachem took a searching glance around him.

"I do not see the young Pale girl," he said.

"Did you wish to speak to her or to me?" the Canadian answered, drily. "I am ready to listen to you. What have you to say to me?"

The Indian frowned; his suspicions were returning; he gave a menacing glance at the monk, who, obeying the advice given him, had insensibly withdrawn a few steps, and was preparing to be an apparently calm witness of the coming scene. Still, after an internal conflict of some seconds, the Sachem succeeded in mastering the wrath that agitated him, and assumed an affable and confiding countenance.

"I only wished to speak to my brother," he replied, in an insinuating voice; "Blue-fox has for many moons desired to see again the face of a friend."

"If it were really as the Chief says," the hunter continued, "nothing could have been more easy. Many days have succeeded one to the other; many years have been swallowed up in the immense gulf of the past, since the period when, young and full of faith, I called Blue-fox my friend. At that period he had a Pawnee heart; but now that he has plucked it from his bosom, to exchange it for an Apache heart, I know him no longer."

"The great hunter of the Palefaces is severe to his Red brother," the Indian answered, with feigned humility, "What matter the days that have passed, if the hunter finds again his friend of the olden time?"

The Canadian smiled disdainfully as he shrugged his shoulders.

"Am I an old woman, to be deceived by the smooth words of a forked tongue?" he said. "Blue-fox is dead; my eyes only see here an Apache Chief, that is to say, an enemy."

"Let my brother remove the skin from his heart, he will recognise a friend," the Indian continued, still in a honeyed voice.

Tranquil involuntarily felt impatient at such cynical impudence.

"A truce to fine speeches, whose sincerity I do not believe in," he said. "Was he my friend who a few days ago tried to carry off my daughter, and at the head of his warriors attacked the calli in which she dwelt, and which is now reduced to ashes?"

"My brother has heard the mockingbird whisper in his ear, and put faith in its falsehoods; the mocker is a chattering and lying bird."

"You are more chattering and lying than the mocker," Tranquil exclaimed, as he violently stamped the butt of his rifle on the ground. "For the last time I repeat to you that I regard you not as a friend, but as an enemy. Now, we have nothing more to say to one another, so let us separate, for this unpleasant conference has already lasted too long."

The Indian took a piercing glance around him, and his eye sparkled ferociously.

"We will not part thus," he said, as he walked two or three steps nearer the hunter, who still remained motionless. The latter attentively followed his every movement, while affecting the most perfect confidence.

As for Fray Antonio, through certain signs that do not deceive men accustomed to Indian tricks, he understood that the moment for acting vigorously was fast approaching, and while continuing to feign the most perfect indifference to the interview of which he was witness, he had quietly drawn the pistols from under his gown, and held them cocked in his hand, ready to employ them at the first alarm. The situation was growing most awkward between the two speakers: each was preparing for the struggle, although the faces were still calm and their voices gentle.

"Yes," Tranquil continued, without displaying the slightest emotion, "we will part thus, Chief, and may Heaven grant that we may never find ourselves face to face again."

"Before separating, the hunter will answer one question."

"I will not, for this conversation has lasted too long already. Farewell!"

And he fell back a pace. The Sachem stretched forth his arm to stop him.

"One word!"

"I will not," the Canadian replied.

"Then die, miserable dog of a Paleface," the Chief exclaimed, at length throwing off the mask and brandishing his tomahawk with extreme rapidity.

But at the same instant a man rose like a black phantom behind the Apache Chief, threw his arms round his body, and lifting him with wondrous strength, hurled him to the ground, and placed his knee on his chest, ere the Sachem, surprised and alarmed by this sudden attack, had attempted to defend himself.

At the yell uttered by Blue-fox, some fifty Apache warriors appeared as if by enchantment, but almost at the same moment the hunter's comrades, who, although invisible, had attentively followed the incidents of this scene, stood by the Canadian's side. Fray Antonio, from whom they were far from expecting such resolution, brought down two Apaches with his pistols, and rejoined the Whites.

Two groups of implacable enemies were thus opposed; unfortunately, the hunters were very weak against the numerous foes that surrounded them on all sides. Still, their firm demeanour and flashing eyes evidenced their unbending resolution to let themselves be killed to the last man, sooner than surrender to the Redskins.

It was an imposing spectacle offered by this handful of men surrounded by implacable foes, and who yet seemed as calm as if they were peaceably seated round their campfire. Carmela and Singing-bird, suffering from sharp pangs of terror, pressed all in a tremor to the side of their friends.

Blue-fox still lay on the ground, held down by Black-deer, whose knee compressed his chest, and neutralised all the tremendous efforts he made to rise. The Apaches, with their long barbed arrows pointed at the hunters, only awaited a word or a sign to begin the attack. A silence of death brooded over the prairie: it seemed as if these men, before tearing each other to pieces, were collecting all their strength to bound forward and rush on each other. Black-deer was the first to break the silence.

"Wah!" he shouted, in a voice rendered hoarse with passion, as he brandished over his enemy's head his scalping knife, whose blade emitted sinister gleams; "at length I meet thee, dog, thief, chicken heart; I hold my vengeance in my hands; at last thy scalp will adorn my horse's mane."

"Thou art but a chattering old woman; thy insults cannot affect me, so try something else. Blue-fox laughs at thee; thou can'st not compel him to utter a cry of pain or make a complaint."

"I will follow thy advice," Black-deer shouted, passionately, and seized his enemy's scalp lock.

"Stop, I insist," the Canadian shouted, in a thundering voice, as he seized the arm of the vindictive Chief.

The latter obeyed.

"Let that man rise," Tranquil continued.

Black-deer gave him a ferocious glance, but made no reply.

"It must be so," the hunter said.

The Comanche Chief bent his head, restored his enemy to liberty, and fell back a pace. With one bound Blue-fox sprang up; but, instead of attempting flight, he crossed his arms on his chest, resumed that mask of impenetrable stoicism which Indians so rarely doff, and waited. Tranquil regarded him for a moment with a singular expression, and then said —-

"I was wrong just now, and my brother must pardon me. No, the memories of youth are not effaced like clouds which the wind bears away. When I saw the terrible danger that menaced Blue-fox, my heart was affected, and I remembered that we had been for a long time friends. I trembled to see his blood flow before me. Blue-fox is a great Chief, he must die as a warrior in the sunshine, he is free to rejoin his friends; he can go."

The Chief raised his head.

"On what conditions?" he said, drily.

"On none. If the Apache warriors attack us, we will fight them; if not, we will continue our journey peacefully. The Chief must, decide, for events depend on his will."

Tranquil, in acting as he had done, had furnished an evident proof of the profound knowledge he possessed of the character of the Redskins, among whom any heroic action is immediately appreciated at its full value. It was a dangerous game to play, but the situation of the hunters was desperate, despite their courage; if the fight had begun, they must have been naturally crushed by numbers, and pitilessly massacred. For the success of his plan the Canadian could only calculate on a good feeling on the part of Blue-fox, and he had staked his all.

After carefully listening to Tranquil's remarks, Blue-fox remained silent for some minutes, during which a violent combat went on in his heart; he felt that he was the dupe of the snare into which he had tried to draw the hunter by reminding him of their old friendship; but the murmurs of admiration, which his warriors were unable to suppress, on seeing the Canadian's noble deed, warned him that he must dissimulate, and feign a gratitude which he was far from experiencing.

The power of an Indian Chief is always very precarious; and he is often constrained, in spite of himself, to bow before the demands of his subordinates, if he does not wish to be overthrown and have a new Chief set up immediately in his place. Blue-fox, therefore, slowly drew his scalping knife from his belt, and let it fall at the hunter's feet.

"The great White hunter and his brothers can continue to follow their path," he said; "the eyes of the Apache warriors are closed, they will not see them. The Palefaces can depart, they will find no one on their road till the second moon from this; but then they must take care; an Apache Chief will set himself on their trail, in order to ask back from them the knife he leaves them, and which he will require."

The Canadian stooped down and picked up the knife, which he passed through his belt.

"When Blue-fox asks me for it, he will find it there," he said, as he pointed to it.

"Och! I will manage to take it again. Now, we are even. Farewell!"

The Chief then bowed courteously to his enemies, made a prodigious bound back, and disappeared in the lofty grass. The Apache warriors uttered their war yell twice, and almost immediately their black outlines disappeared in the gloom. Tranquil waited for a few minutes, and then turned to his comrades.

"Now, we will set out," he said; "the road is free."

"You got out of the scrape cleverly," Loyal Heart said to him; "but it was a terrible risk."

The Canadian smiled, but made no further reply. Then they started.

CHAPTER XII
THE SUMMONS

Europeans, accustomed to the gigantic wars of the Old World, in which enormous masses of two to three hundred thousand men on both sides come into collision on the battle field, where armies have divisions of thirty or forty thousand men, a cavalry often of sixty to eighty thousand sabres, and in which the guns are counted by hundreds, have a difficulty in forming an idea of the way in which war is waged in certain parts of America, as well as the component strength of the armies of the New World.

In Mexico, a population of several millions can hardly collect ten thousand men under arms, an enormous number in those countries. The various republics which were formed on the dismemberment of the Spanish colonies, such as Peru, Chile, New Granada, Bolivia, Paraguay, &c., cannot succeed in assembling more than two or three thousand men under their banners, and that, too, with immense sacrifices; for these countries, which, territorially speaking, are each far larger than England, are nearly deserted, being incessantly decimated by civil war, which gnaws at them like a hideous leprosy, and left almost uninhabitable by the neglect of the various governments, which succeed each other with a giddy and almost fabulous rapidity.

These governments, submitted to rather than accepted by these unfortunate nations, although powerless for good, owing to their precarious duration, are omnipotent for evil, and profit by it to plunder the people, and load their creatures with riches, not troubling themselves about the abyss they are opening beneath their feet, and which, daily growing deeper, will eventually swallow up all these accidental nationalities, which will be dead almost ere they are born, and have only known liberty by name, though never in a position to appreciate its blessings.

Texas, at the period when it claimed its independence, in a contest of ten years, so obstinately, counted over its entire territory only a population of six hundred thousand—a very weak and modest amount, when compared with the seven million of the Mexican confederation. Still, as we have remarked in a preceding chapter, the Texan population was composed, in a great measure, of North Americans—energetic, enterprising men, of known courage, who, annoyed by the long lasting tyranny the Federal government exercised over them, through jealousy and narrowness of views, had sworn to be free at any price, and took up arms in order to guarantee the possession of their estates, and their personal security.

The combat had been going on for ten years; at first timid and secret, it had gradually widened, holding in check the Mexican power, and at length attained that final and supreme period when the alternative is victory or death.

The surprise of the conducta, so skilfully managed by the Jaguar, had been the electric spark destined to definitively galvanize the country, and make it rise as one man for this modern Thermopylae. The independent chiefs, who were fighting all along the border, had, at the unexpected news of the decisive success obtained by the Jaguar, assembled their *cuadrillas*, and, by common agreement, and through an heroic impulse, ranged themselves under the banners of the youthful chieftain, and pledged him obedience, in order to carry through the liberation of their country.

Thanks to the generous assistance on the part of all the Guerilla leaders, the Jaguar suddenly found himself at the head of imposing forces, that is to say, he collected an army of about eleven hundred men. Our readers must not smile at the name of army given to what would represent a regiment with us. Never before had Texas collected so many fighting men under one Chief. And then, after all, everything is relative in this world, and the greatest masses do not accomplish the most brilliant exploits. Did we not see, a few years back, in Sonora, the heroic and unfortunate Count de Raousset Bourbon, at the head of only two hundred and fifty ragged Frenchmen, half dead with hunger and fatigue, attack Hermosillo, a town of fifteen thousand souls, enclosed with walls, and defended by twelve thousand regulars and six thousand Indians, carry it *in an hour*, and enter it, sword in hand, at the head of his soldiers, who did not themselves dare to believe in their heroism?[1]

The Jaguar's army was composed of men hardened by lengthened fighting, who burned to cope with the Mexicans, and who, before all, wished to be free! No more was needed for them to accomplish miracles. The Jaguar was thoroughly acquainted with the character of his soldiers; he knew that he must only ask one thing of them—an impossibility—and this he had, consequently, determined to attempt.

Through the wish of the new commander-in-chief, all the captains of cuadrillas assembled in a council of war, in order to draw up a plan of campaign. Each party gave his opinion. The debate was short, for all entertained the same idea—and that was, to seize on the Larch-tree hacienda, in order to cut off the communications of the Mexican army, prevent it from receiving reinforcements from the other states of the confederation; and, once masters of the fortress, to defeat in detail the different Mexican detachments scattered over Texan territory. As this plan was remarkably simple, the Jaguar resolved to carry it out immediately. After leaving a detachment of five hundred horseman to cover his rear, and avoid any surprise, he advanced with his main body by forced marches on the Larch-tree, with the intention of investing and carrying it by assault ere the Mexicans had found time to put a garrison in it and throw up intrenchments.

Unfortunately, despite all the diligence the Jaguar had displayed in the execution of his plan, the Mexicans, owing to the lengthened experience and infallible glance of General Rubio, had been more prompt than he, and the place had been in a perfect state of defence two days ere the Texan army appeared at the foot of its walls.

This disappointment greatly annoyed the Jaguar, but did not discourage him; he saw that he would have to lay siege to the Larch-tree, and bravely made his preparations. The Americans dug up the soil with wondrous rapidity, and a night was sufficient for them to finish the preparatory works, and make breast-works and parapets. The Mexicans gave no signs of life, and allowed the insurgents to establish themselves in their lines without opposition; by sunrise all was finished.

It was a strange spectacle offered by this handful of men, who, without artillery or siege material of any description, boldly traced lines round a stoutly-built fortress, admirably situated for resistance, and defended by a numerous garrison, which was determined not to surrender. But what in this heroic madness produced admiration, and almost stupor, was the conviction these men had that they would eventually take the place. This persuasion, by doubling the strength of the insurgents, rendered them capable of accomplishing the greatest things.

As they arrived after sunset, when the night had all but set in, the Texans had formed an imperfect idea of the defensive state of the place which they proposed to besiege; hence, when day broke, they eagerly proceeded to see what enemy they would have to deal with. The surprise was anything but agreeable to them, and they were compelled to confess to themselves in their hearts that the job would be a tough one, and that the intrenchments they proposed to carry had a formidable appearance. This surprise was changed almost into discouragement when the fortress haughtily hoisted the Mexican flag, saluting it with several rounds of grapeshot, which fell into the centre of the camp, and killed and wounded some fifteen men.

But this movement of weakness was but short; a reaction speedily took place in these energetic men, and it was with hurrahs and shouts of joy that they displayed the colours of Texan independence. For valid reasons they did not accompany the hoisting of their flag by cannon shots, but they saluted it with salvos of musquetry, whose well-sustained fire gave back to the besieged the death they had scattered through the camp.

The Jaguar, after attentively examining the fortifications, resolved to proceed according to rule, and summon the place to surrender before beginning the siege seriously. Consequently, he hoisted a white flag on the top of the entrenchments, and waited; a few moments later, a flag of the same colour appeared on the breastwork thrown up outside the place.

The Jaguar, preceded by a trumpeter, followed by two or three officers, left the camp and climbed up the hill on which the hacienda was situated. A number of officers equal to his own had left the place and advanced to meet him. On arriving at about an equal distance from the two lines, the Jaguar halted, and in a few minutes the Mexican officers, commanded by Don Felix Paz, joined him. After the usual compliments had been exchanged with extreme politeness, the Major-domo asked—

"With whom have I the honour of speaking?"

"With the Commander-in-Chief of the Texan army," the Jaguar answered.

"We do not recognise any Texan army," the Major-domo said drily. "Texas forms an integral portion of Mexico; her army, the only one she ought to possess, is Mexican."

"If you do not know the one I have the honour of commanding," the Jaguar said with a smile of superb irony, "ere long, please Heaven, it will have made so much noise, that you will be compelled to recognise it."

"That is possible; but for the present we do not know it."

"Then, you do not wish to parley?"

"With whom?"

"Come, Caballero, suppose we are frank with one another—are you willing?"

"I wish for nothing better."

"You know as well as I do that we are fighting for our independence."

"Very good. In that case you are insurgents?"

"Certainly, and feel proud of the title."

"Hum! We do not treat with insurgents, who are placed beyond the pale of the law, and who, as such, cannot offer us any serious guarantee."

"Caballero," the Jaguar exclaimed with ill-disguised impatience, "I have the honour of remarking that you insult me."

"I am very sorry for it; but what other answer than that can I give you?"

There was a momentary silence; the vigorous resistance offered him made the Jaguar feel seriously alarmed.

"Are you the Fort-Commandant?" he asked.

"No."

"Why did you come, then?"

"Because I was ordered to do so."

"Hum! And who is the Governor of the place?"

"A Colonel."

"Why did he not come in person to meet me?"

"Because he probably did not think it worth while to put himself out of the way."

"Hum! That way of behaving seems to me rather lax, for war has laws which every man is bound to follow."

"Maybe, but it is not war in this case, that must not be let out of sight."

"What is it then, in your opinion?"

"Insurrection."

"Well, I wish to speak with your Commandant, for I can only treat with him. Are you disposed to let me see him?"

"That does not depend on me, but on him."

"Very good. Can I trust to your delivering my message to him?"

"I do not see why I should not."

"Be kind enough, then, to return at once to him, and I will wait for you here, unless you permit me to enter the fortress."

"That is impossible."

"As you please; I will, therefore, await your reply here."

"Very well."

The two men bowed courteously, and took leave of each other. Don Felix Paz re-entered the fortress, while the Jaguar, sitting on the trunk of a felled tree, examined with the greatest attention the fortifications of the hacienda, the details of which he could easily survey from the spot where he now was. The young man leaned his elbow on his knee, and let his head rest on his hand; his eyes wandered over the surrounding objects with an expression of indefinable melancholy; gradually a gloomy sadness seized on his mind; while indulging in his thoughts, external objects disappeared from his sight, and isolating himself completely, he gave way to the flood of bitter recollections which rose from his heart to his brain, and removed him from the preoccupations of his present situation.

For a long time he had been plunged in this species of prostration, when a friendly voice smote his ear. The Jaguar, suddenly drawn from his reverie by the sound of a voice which he fancied he recognised, threw up his head sharply, and gave a start of surprise on recognising Don Juan Melendez de Gongora, for it was really the Colonel who was now addressing him. The Texan Chief rose, and spoke to his officers.

"Back, Caballeros," he said; "this gentleman and myself have matters to talk about which no one must hear."

The Texans withdrew out of earshot. The Colonel was alone, for on recognising the Jaguar, he had ordered his escort to await him at the base of the intrenchments.

"I meet you here again then, my friend," the Jaguar said sadly.

"Yes," the young officer answered; "fatality seems determined to keep us in constant opposition."

"On examining the height and strength of your walls," the Independent continued, "I had already recognized the difficulties of the task forced on me; these difficulties have now grown almost into impossibilities."

"Alas, my friend, fate wills it so, we are forced to submit to its caprices; and while in my heart deploring what takes place, I am yet resolved to do my duty as a man of honour, and die in the breach, with my breast turned toward you."

"I know it, brother, and cannot feel angry with you; for I too am resolved to carry out the difficult task imposed on me."

"Such are the terrible exigencies of civil war, that the men most inclined to esteem and love one another, are compelled to be foes."

"God and our country will judge us, friend, and our consciences will absolve us; men are not combating, but principles fatally placed in opposition."

"I was not aware that you were the Chief of the insurrectionary bands that have invested the place, although a secret foreboding warned me of your presence."

"That is strange," the Jaguar muttered, "for I also felt the foreboding to which you allude; that is why I so strongly insisted on having an interview with the Commandant of the hacienda."

"The same reason urged me, on the contrary, not to show myself; but I thought I must yield to your entreaty, and hence here I am; I swear to you that I should have wished to avoid this interview, which is so painful to both of us, in consequence of our mutual feelings."

"It is better that it should have taken place; now that we have had a frank explanation, we shall be better fitted to do our duty."

"You are right, friend; it is perhaps better that it should be so; let me press your honest hand for the last time, and then each of us will resume his part."

"Here is my hand, friend," the young Chief made answer.

The two men heartily shook hands, and then fell back a few paces, making a signal to their respective escorts to rejoin them. When the officers were ranged behind the Chiefs, the Jaguar ordered his bugler to sound the summons; the latter obeyed, and the Mexican trumpet immediately replied. The Jaguar then advanced two paces, and courteously took off his hat to the Colonel.

"With whom have I the honour of speaking?" he asked.

"I am," the officer replied, returning the salute, "Colonel Don Juan Melendez de Gongora, invested by General Don José Maria Rubio, Commander-in-Chief of the Mexican forces in Texas, with the military government of the Larch-tree hacienda, which present circumstances have raised to the rank of a first class fortress; and who may you be, Caballero?"

"I," the Jaguar answered, as he drew himself up, and placed his hat again on his head, "am the Supreme Chief of the Confederated Army of Texas."

"The men who take that name, and the person who commands them, can only be regarded by me as traitors and fosterers of rebellion."

"We care little, Colonel, what name you give us, or the manner in which you regard our acts. We have taken up arms to render our country independent, and shall not lay them down till that noble task is accomplished. These are the proposals I think it my duty to make you."

"I cannot and will not treat with rebels," the Colonel said, clearly and distinctly.

"You will act as you please, Colonel; but humanity orders you to avoid bloodshed, if possible, and your duty imperiously commands you to listen to what I have to say to you."

"Be it so, Caballero, I will listen to you, and then will see what answer I have to give you; but I must ask you to be brief."

The Jaguar leaned the point of his sabre on the ground, and giving a clear and piercing glance at the Mexican staff, he continued, in a loud, firm, and accentuated voice—

"I, the Commander-in-Chief of the Liberating Army of Texas, summon you, a Colonel in the service of the Mexican Republic, whose sovereignty we no longer recognise, to surrender to us this Larch-tree hacienda, of which you entitle yourself the Governor, and which you hold without right or reason. If, within twenty-four hours, the said hacienda is put into our hands, with all it contains, guns, ammunition, material of war, and otherwise, the garrison will quit the place with the honours of war, under arms, with drums and fifes playing. Then, after laying down their arms, the garrison will be free to retire to the interior of Texas, after making oath that during a year and a day they will not serve in Texas against the Liberating Army."

"Have you ended?" the Colonel asked, with ill-disguised impatience.

"Not yet," the Jaguar coldly answered.

"I must ask you to make haste."

On seeing these two men exchange savage glances, and placed in such a hostile position face to face, no one would have supposed that they were fond of each other, and groaned in their hearts at the painful part fate compelled them to play against their will. The truth was, that in one military fanaticism, in the other an ardent love of his country, had imposed silence on every other feeling, and only permitted them to listen to one, the most imperious of all—the sentiment of duty. The Jaguar, perfectly calm and firm, continued in the same resolute accent—

"If, against my expectations, these conditions are refused, and the place obstinately defends itself, the Army of Liberation will immediately invest it, carry on the siege with all the vigour of which it is capable, and when the hacienda is captured, it will undergo the fate of towns taken by assault; the garrison will be decimated, and remain prisoners till the end of the war."

"Very good," the Colonel replied, ironically; "however harsh these conditions may be, we prefer them to the former; and if the fate of arms betray us, we will endure without complaint the law of the conquerors."

The Jaguar bowed ceremoniously.

"I have only to withdraw," he said.

"One moment," the Colonel said, "You have explained to me your conditions, so it is now your turn to hear mine."

"What conditions can you have to offer us, since you refuse to surrender?"

"You shall hear."

The Colonel looked round him with a glance of assurance; then, crossing his arms on his chest, and drawing himself up with the air of sovereign contempt for those who surrounded him, began speaking in a sharp and sarcastic voice—

"I," he said, "Don Juan de Melendez de Gongora, Colonel in the service of the Mexican Republic, considering that the majority of the individuals assembled at this moment at the foot of my walls are poor, ignorant men, whom bad example and bad counsel have led into a revolt, which they detest in their hearts—for I know that the Mexican Government has ever been just, kind, and paternal to them; considering, moreover, that possibly the fear of the severe chastisement which they have deserved by their culpable conduct keeps them, against their desire and will, in the ranks of the rebels; employing the prerogative given me by my title of governor of a first class fortress, and a field officer in the Mexican army, I promise them, that if they immediately lay down their arms, and, as a proof of sincere repentance, surrender to me the Chiefs who deceived them and led them into revolt—I promise them, I repeat, a complete pardon and oblivion of the faults they may have committed up to today, but only on this condition. They have till sunset of the present day to make their submission; when that period is passed, they will be regarded as inveterate rebels, and treated as such—-that is to say, hanged without trial, after their identity has been proved, and deprived in their last moments of the consolations of religion, as being unworthy of them. As for the Chiefs, as traitors, they will be shot in the back, and their bodies fastened by the feet on gibbets, where they will remain as food for birds of prey, and serve as an example to those who may venture in their track. Reflect, then, and repent, for such are the sole conditions you will obtain of me. And now, Caballeros," he said, turning to his officers, "we will return to the fort, as we have nothing more to do here."

His hearers had listened with increasing surprise to this strange address, uttered in a tone of sarcasm and haughty contempt, which had filled the hearts of the Jaguar's comrades with gall, while the Mexican officers looked at each other with a laugh. By a sign, the Jaguar imposed silence on his comrades, and bowed respectfully to the Colonel.

"Your will be done," he said to him. "God will judge between us; the bloodshed will fall on your head."

"I accept the responsibility," the Commandant remarked, disdainfully.

"Then, the words you have just uttered are serious?"

"They are."

"You are quite resolved on opposing us?"

"Of course."

"Your resolution will not change?"

"It is immovable."

"We will fight, then," the Jaguar exclaimed, enthusiastically. "*Viva la patria, viva la Independencia!*"

This cry, repeated by his comrades, was heard in the camp, and taken up with extraordinary enthusiasm by his comrades.

"*Viva Mejico!*" the Colonel said.

He then retired, followed by his officers. On his side, the Jaguar returned to his camp, resolved to attempt a vigorous hand stroke on the place. On both sides preparations were made for the implacable struggle that was about to begin between members of the same family and children of the same soil; a homicidal and fearful struggle, a hundredfold more horrible than a foreign war!

[1] See the "Gold-Seekers," same publishers.

CHAPTER XIII
THE SIEGE

While all this was going on, the hunters, as we mentioned before, resumed their journey, so soon as the Apaches disappeared. The night was clear, and the hunters marched in Indian file, that is to say, one after the other; still, through a prudential motive, Carmela was placed pillion-wise behind Tranquil, while Singing-bird rode with Black-deer.

The Canadian had whispered a few words to Lanzi and Quoniam, upon which the two men, without replying, dug their spurs in, and started at a gallop.

"When you have ladies with you," Tranquil said, with a laugh to Loyal Heart, "it is necessary to take precautions."

The hunter, however, did not ask him for any explanation, and the four men continued their march in silence. During the whole night nothing occurred to disturb their journey; the Apaches kept their word faithfully, and had really withdrawn. Tranquil had not for a moment doubted their promise. At times the hunter turned to the maiden, and asked her with ill-disguised anxiety if she felt fatigued, but Carmela constantly replied in the negative. A few minutes before sunrise, he bent down to her for the last time.

"Courage," he said, "we shall soon arrive."

The girl attempted to smile, but this long night spent on horseback had crushed her; she could not even find the courage to answer, so annihilated was she, and Tranquil, anxious for his daughter, hurried on. Still in the sunbeams, whose warmth caressed her, the maiden felt newborn, her courage returned, and she drew herself up with a sigh of relief. The journey, then, became more gay; for each, on this much desired appearance of day, had forgotten his fatigue and the emotions of the past night. Two hours later they reached the base of a hill, halfway up which was a natural grotto.

"Our friends are expecting us there," said Tranquil.

A few moments later, the little band entered the grotto on horseback, without leaving any traces of its passage. This grotto, like many others in that country, possessed several entrances, and through this peculiarity it often served as a refuge to the wood rangers, who, being thoroughly conversant with all its windings, could easily escape from the search of any enemies who might have followed their trail. It was divided into several compartments, without visible communication with each other, and formed a species of maze, which ran with inextricable windings under the whole of the hill. On the prairie the name of the Jaguar's grotto had been given it.

The two hunters, sent forward by the Canadian, were seated by an enormous fire of heather, and quietly roasting a magnificent haunch of venison, as they silently smoked their pipes. Although they must have been waiting a long time for their friends, on the arrival of Tranquil and his comrades they contented themselves with a slight bow, and did not evince the slightest desire to know what had occurred since their departure, for these men had lived so long on the desert, that they had grown to assume all the Indian habits. Tranquil led the two females into a grotto a considerable distance from the principal one.

"Here," he said in a gentle whisper, "you must speak as little as possible, and as low as you can, for you never know what neighbours you may have; pay great attention to this piece of advice, for your safety depends on it. If you require me, or have an inclination to join us, you know where we are, and it is an easy matter for you to come; good-bye."

His daughter caught him by the arm for a moment, and whispered in his ear. He bowed in reply, and went out. When the two females found themselves alone, their first impulse was to fall into each other's arms. This first emotion past, they lay on the ground with that feeling of comfort which is experienced when you have sighed during a long period for a rest, the want of which you greatly feel. At the expiration of about an hour, Tranquil returned.

"Are we going to start again?" Carmela asked hurriedly, with an ill-disguised agitation.

"On the contrary, I expect to remain here till sunset."

"Heaven be praised!" the maiden exclaimed.

"I have come to tell you that breakfast is ready, and that we are only awaiting your presence to begin our meal."

"Eat without us, my dear papa," Carmela answered; "at this moment we have more need of sleep than anything else."

"Sleep if you like; I have brought you, however, male clothing, which I must ask you to put on."

"What, father, dress ourselves as men?" Carmela said in surprise, and with a slight repugnance.

"You must, child—it is indispensable."

"In that case I will obey you, father."

"Thank you, my daughter."

The hunter withdrew, and the two young women soon fell asleep. Their sleep lasted a long time, for the sun was beginning to sink beneath the horizon, when they awoke, completely recovered from their fatigue. Carmela, fresh and rosy, felt no effects of the long sleeplessness of the preceding night; and the Indian girl, stronger, or more hardened, had not suffered so much as her companion. The two girls then began, while chattering and laughing, to prepare everything necessary for the disguise the hunter had recommended them.

"Let us begin our toilette," Carmela said gaily to Singing-bird.

At the moment when they were removing their dresses, they heard the noise of footsteps near them, and turned like two startled fawns, thinking that Tranquil was coming to see whether they were awake yet; but a couple of words distinctly pronounced, caused them to listen, and stand quivering with emotion, surprise, and curiosity.

"My brother has been a long time," the voice had said, which seemed to belong to a man standing scarce three paces from them; "I have been expecting him for two hours."

"By Heaven, Chief, your remark is perfectly correct; but it was impossible for me to come sooner," another person immediately answered, whose strongly pronounced accent proved to be a foreigner.

"My brother will speak without loss of tune."

"That is what I intend doing,"

At this moment Tranquil came up. The young women laid the forefinger on their lips, recommending silence; the hunter understood what this meant, and advanced on tiptoe to listen.

"The Jaguar," the second speaker continued, "desires most eagerly that, in accordance with the promise you made him, you should join his army with your warriors."

"Up to the present that has been impossible."

"Blue-fox!" Tranquil muttered.

"I warn you that he accuses you of breach of faith."

"The Pale Chief is wrong; a Sachem is not a chattering old woman who knows not what he says. This evening I shall join him with two hundred picked warriors."

"We shall see, Chief."

"At the first song of the mankawis, the Apache warriors will enter the camp."

"All the better. The Jaguar is preparing a general assault on the fort, and only awaits your arrival to give the signal of attack."

"I repeat to my brother that the Apaches will not fail."

"Those confounded Mexicans fight like demons; the man who commands them seems to have galvanized them, they second him so well. There was only one good officer in the Mexican army, and we are obliged to fight against him. It is really most unlucky."

"The Chief of the Yoris is not invulnerable. The arrows of the Apaches are long—they will kill him."

"Nonsense," the other said ill-temperedly; "this man seems to have a charm that protects him. Our Kentuckian rifles are wonderfully true, and our marksmen possess a far from common skill; but no bullet can hit him."

"While coming to this grotto, Blue-fox raised the scalp of a Chief of the Yoris."

"Ah!" the first speaker observed with indifference.

"Here it is; this man was the bearer of a necklace."

"A letter, by Heavens!" the other exclaimed anxiously; "What have you done with it? You have not destroyed it, I trust?"

"No, the Chief has kept it."

"You did well. Show it to me, perhaps it is important."

"Wah! It is some medicine of the Palefaces; a Chief does not want it; my brother can take it."

"Thanks!"

There was a moment's silence, during which the hearts of the three hearers might have been heard beating in unison, so great was their anxiety.

"By Jove!" the white man suddenly burst out; "A letter addressed to Colonel Don Juan Melendez de Gongora, Commandant of the Larch-tree, by General Rubio. You were in luck's way, Chief. Are you sure that the bearer of this letter is dead?"

"It was Blue-fox who killed him."

"In that case I feel confident, for I can trust to you. Now, this is what you must do: so soon as——"

But while speaking thus, the two men had withdrawn, and the sound of their voices was lost in the distance, so that it was impossible to hear the termination of the sentence, or guess its purport.

The two women turned round. Tranquil had disappeared, and they were again alone. Carmela, after listening to this strange conversation, of which accident allowed her to catch a few fragments, had fallen into a profound reverie, which her companion, with that sense of propriety innate in Indians, was careful not to disturb.

In the meanwhile, time slipped away, the gloom grew denser in the grotto, for night had set in; the two young women, afraid to remain alone in the obscurity, were preparing to rejoin their companions, when they heard the sound of footsteps, and Tranquil entered.

"What!" he said to them, "Not ready yet? Make haste to put on your masculine attire, for every minute is an age."

The girls did not allow this to be repeated; they disappeared in an adjoining compartment, and returned a few minutes later, entirely disguised.

"Good," the Canadian said, after examining them for a moment; "we are going to try and enter the Larch-tree hacienda. Now follow me, and be prudent."

The eight persons left the grotto, gliding along in the darkness like phantoms.

No one, unless he has tried the experiment, can imagine what a night march on the desert is, when you are afraid each moment of falling into the hands of invisible enemies, who watch you behind every bush. Tranquil had placed himself at the head of the little party, who marched in Indian file, at times stooping to the ground, going on his hands and knees, or crawling on his stomach so as to avoid notice.

Doña Carmela, in spite of the extraordinary difficulties she had to surmount, advanced with admirable courage, never complaining, and enduring, without seeming to notice them, the scratches of the roots and brambles, which lacerated her hands, and caused her atrocious suffering. After three hours of gigantic effort in following Tranquil's trail, the latter stopped, and had them look around them. They raised their heads, and found themselves in the camp of the Texan insurgents. All around them, in the moonbeams, they could see the elongated shadows of Indian sentries, leaning on their long lances, motionless as equestrian statues, who were watching over the safety of their Paleface brothers. The young women felt a thrill of terror run over their persons at this sight, which was not of a nature to reassure them.

Fortunately for them, the Indians keep very bad guard, and most generally only place sentries to frighten the enemy. On this occasion, as they knew very well, they had no sortie to apprehend on the part of the Larch-tree garrison, the sentinels were nearly all asleep; but the slightest badly-calculated move, the merest false step, might arouse them, for these men, who are habituated in keeping their senses alive, can hardly ever be taken unawares.

At about two hundred yards at the most from the adventurers were the advanced works of the Larch-tree, gloomy, silent, and apparently, at least, abandoned or plunged in sleep. Tranquil had only stopped to let his comrades fully understand the imminent danger to which they were exposed, and urge them to redouble their caution, for, at the slightest weakness, they would be lost. After this they started again. They advanced thus for one hundred yards, or about half the distance separating them from the Larch-tree, when suddenly, at the moment when Tranquil stretched out his arms to shelter himself behind a sandhill, several men, crawling in the opposite direction found themselves face to face with him. There was a second of terrible anxiety.

"Who goes there?" a low and menacing voice asked.

"Oh!" he said; "We are saved! It is I—Tranquil the Tigrero."

"Who are the persons with you?"

"Wood rangers, for whom I answer."

"Very good; pass on."

The two parties separated, and crawled in opposite directions. The band with which the hunters exchanged these few words was commanded by Don Felix Paz, who, more vigilant than the Texans, was making a round of the glacis to assure himself that all was quiet, and no surprise need be feared. It was very lucky for Tranquil and his companions that the Jaguar, in order to do honour to Blue-fox, had this night intrusted the camp guard to his warriors, and that, confiding in the Redskins, the Texans had gone to sleep, with that carelessness characteristic of Americans; for, with other sentries than those through whom they had glided unseen, the adventurers must infallibly have been captured.

Ten minutes after their encounter with Don Felix, which might have turned out so fatally for them, the hunters reached the gates, and at the mention of Tranquil's name a passage was at once granted them. They were at length in safety within the hacienda, and it was high time that they should arrive; a few minutes longer and, Carmela and her companion would have fallen by the wayside. In spite of all their courage and goodwill, the girls could no longer keep up, their strength was exhausted. Hence, so soon as the danger had passed, and the nervous excitement, which alone sustained them, ceased, they fell down unconscious.

Tranquil raised Carmela in his arms, and carried her to the interior of the hacienda; while Black-deer, who, in spite of his apparent insensibility, adored his squaw, hurried up to restore her to life.

The unexpected arrival of Tranquil caused a general joy among the inhabitants of the hacienda, who all had a deep friendship for this man, whose glorious character they had had so many opportunities of appreciating. The hunter was still busied with his daughter, who was just beginning to recover her senses, when Don Felix Paz, who had finished his rounds, entered the cuarto, with a message from the Colonel to the Canadian, begging the latter to come to him at once.

Tranquil obeyed, for Doña Carmela no longer required his assistance—the maiden had scarce regained her senses, ere she fell into a deep sleep, the natural result of the enormous fatigue she had endured during several days. While proceeding to the Colonel's apartments, Tranquil questioned the major-domo, with whom he had been connected for several years, and who had no scruples about answering the hunter's queries.

Matters were far from being well at the Larch-tree; the siege was carried on with an extraordinary obstinacy on both sides, and with many strange interludes. The insurgents, greatly annoyed by the artillery of the fort, which killed a great many of them, and to which they could not reply, owing to their absolute want of cannon, had adopted a system of reprisals, which caused the besieged considerable injury. This simple system was as follows: The insurgents, who were mostly hunters, were exceedingly skilful marksmen, and renowned as such in a country where the science of firing is carried to its extreme limits. A certain number of these marksmen sheltered themselves behind the epaulments of the camp; and each time a gunner attempted to load a piece, they infallibly shot away his hands.

This had been carried so far, that nearly all the gunners were *hors de combat*, and it was only at very long intervals that a gun was fired from the fort. This isolated shot, badly aimed, owing to the precipitancy with which the men laid the gun, through their fear of being mutilated, caused but insignificant damage to the insurgents, who applauded, with reason, the good result of their scheme.

On the other hand, the fort was so closely invested, and watched with such care, that no one could enter or quit it. It was impossible for those in the fort to understand how it was that the adventurers had managed to slip in after traversing the whole length of the enemy's camp. We must state, too, in order to treat everybody with justice, that the adventurers understood it less than anybody.

The garrison of the hacienda lived, then, as if they had been roughly cut off from the world, for no sound transpired without, and no news reached them. This situation was extremely disagreeable to the Mexicans; unfortunately for them, it was daily aggravated, and threatened to become, ere long, completely intolerable. Colonel Melendez, since the beginning of the siege, had proved himself what he was, that is to say, an officer of rare merit, with a vigilance nothing could foil, and a trustworthy bravery. Seeing his gunners so cruelly decimated by the Texan bullets, he undertook to take their place, loading the guns at his own peril, and firing them at the insurgents.

Such courage struck the Texans with so great admiration, that although it would several times have been easy for them to kill their daring foe, their rifles had constantly turned away from this man, who seemed to find a delight in braving death at every moment. The Jaguar, while closely investing the fort, and eagerly desiring to carry it, had given peremptory orders to spare the life of his friend, whom he could not refrain from pitying and admiring, as much for his courage as for his devotion to the cause he served.

Although it was near midnight, the Colonel was still up; at the moment when the hunter was brought to him, he was walking thoughtfully up and down his bedroom, consulting from time to time a detailed plan, of the fortifications that lay open on a table.

Tranquil's arrival caused him great satisfaction, for he hoped to obtain from him news from without. Unfortunately, the hunter did not know much about the political state of the country, owing to the isolated life he led in the forests. Still, he answered with the greatest frankness all the questions the Colonel thought proper to ask him, and gave him the little information he had been enabled to collect; then he told him the various incidents of his own journey. At the name of Carmela the young officer was slightly troubled, and a vivid flush suffused his face; but he recovered, and listened attentively to the hunter's story. When the latter came to the incident in the grotto, and the fragment of conversation he had overheard between the

Apache Chief and the Texan, his interest was greatly excited, and he made him repeat the story.

"Oh, that letter," he muttered several times, "that letter; what would I not give to know its contents!"

Unhappily, that was impossible. After a moment, the Colonel begged Tranquil to continue his story. The hunter then told him in what way he had managed to cross the enemy's lines and introduce himself into the fort. This bold action greatly struck the Colonel.

"You were more fortunate than prudent," he said, "in thus venturing into the midst of your enemies."

The hunter smiled good-temperedly.

"I was almost certain of succeeding," he said.

"How so?"

"I have had a long experience of Indian habits, which enables me to make nearly certain with them."

"Granted; but in this case you had not Indians to deal with."

"Pardon me, Colonel."

"I do not understand you, so be kind enough to explain."

"That is an easy matter. Blue-fox entered the Texan camp this evening, at the head of two hundred warriors."

"I was not aware of it," the Colonel said, in surprise.

"The Jaguar, to do honour to his terrible allies, confided to them the camp guard for this night."

"Hence?"

"Hence, Colonel, all the Texans are sleeping soundly at this moment, while the Apaches are watching, or, at least, ought to be watching over the safety of their lives."

"What do you mean by ought to be watching?"

"I mean that the Redskins do not at all understand our manner of carrying on war, are not accustomed to sentinel duty, and so everybody is asleep in the camp."

"Ah!" said the Colonel, as he began once more, with a thoughtful air, the promenade he had interrupted to listen to the hunter's story.

The latter waited, taking an interrogative glance at Don Felix, who had remained in the room till it pleased the Commandant to dismiss him. A few minutes passed, and not a syllable was exchanged; Don Juan seemed to be plunged in serious thought. All at once he stopped before the hunter, and looked him full in the face.

"I have known you for a long time by reputation," he said, sharply. "You pass for an honest man, who can be trusted."

The Canadian bowed, not understanding to what these preliminaries tended.

"I think you said the enemy's camp was plunged in sleep?" the Colonel continued.

"That is my conviction," Tranquil answered; "we crossed their lines too easily for it to be otherwise."

Don Felix drew nearer.

"Yes," the young officer muttered, "we might give them a lesson."

"A lesson they greatly need," the Major-domo added.

"Ah, ah!" the Colonel said, with a smile; "Then you understand me, Don Felix?"

"Of course."

"And you approve?"

"Perfectly."

"It is one in the morning," the Colonel went on, as he looked at a clock standing on a console; "at this moment sleep is the deepest. Well, we will attempt a sortie; have the officers of the garrison aroused."

The Major-domo went out: five minutes later the officers, still half-asleep, obeyed their Chief's orders.

"Caballeros," the latter said to them, so soon as he saw them all collected round him, "I have resolved to make a sortie against the rebels, surprise them, and fire their camp, if it be possible. Select from your soldiers one hundred and fifty men, in whom you can trust; supply them with inflammable matters, and in five minutes let them be drawn up in the Patio. Go; and before all, I recommend you the deepest silence."

The officers bowed, and at once left the room. The Colonel then turned to Tranquil.

"Are you tired?" he asked him.

"I am never so."

"You are skilful?"

"So they say."

"Very good. You will serve as our guide; unfortunately, I want two others."

"I can procure them for your Excellency."

"You?"

"Yes, a wood ranger and a Comanche Chief, who entered the fort with me, and for whom I answer with my life; Loyal Heart and Black-deer."

"Warn them, then, and all three wait for me in the Patio."

Tranquil hastened to call his friends.

"If that hunter has spoken the truth, and I believe he has," the Colonel continued, addressing the Major-domo, "I am convinced we shall have an excellent opportunity for repaying the rebels a hundredfold the harm they have done us. Do you accompany me, Don Felix?"

"I would not for a fortune leave you one inch, under such circumstances."

"Come, then, for the detachment must be ready by this time."

They went out.

CHAPTER XIV
THE PROPOSAL

On the same night, almost at the same hour, the Jaguar, seated on a modest oak equipal in his tent, with his elbow leaning on the table and his head on his hand, was reading, by the light of a candle that emitted but a dubious light, important despatches he had just received. Absorbed in the perusal, the young Commander of the insurgents paid no attention to the noises without, when suddenly a rather sharp puff of wind caused the flame of the candle to flicker, and the shadow of a man was darkly defined on the canvas of the tent.

The young man, annoyed at being disturbed, raised his head angrily, and looked toward the entrance of the tent, with a frown that promised nothing very pleasant for his inopportune intruder. But at the sight of the man who stood in the door-way, leaning on a long rifle, and fixing on him eyes that sparkled like carbuncles, the Jaguar restrained with difficulty a cry of surprise, and made a move to seize the pistols placed within reach on the table.

This man, whom we have already had occasion to present to the reader under very grave circumstances, had nothing, we must confess, in his appearance that spoke greatly in his favour. His stern glance, his harsh face, rendered still harsher by his long white beard, his tall stature and strange attire, all about him, in a word, inspired repulsion and almost terror. The Jaguar's movement produced a sinister smile on his pale lips.

"Why take up your weapons?" he said, in a hoarse voice, as he struck the palm of his hand against his rifle barrel; "had I intended to kill you, you would have been dead long ago."

The young man wheeled round his equipal, which brought him face to face with the stranger. The two men examined each other for a moment with the most minute attention.

"Have you looked at me enough?" the stranger at length asked.

"Yes," the Jaguar answered; "now tell me who you are, what brings you here, and how you reached me."

"Those are a good many questions at once, still I will try to answer them. Who am I? No one knows, and there are moments when I am myself ignorant; I am an accursed, and a reprobate, prowling about the desert like a wild beast in search of prey; the Redskins, whose implacable enemy I am, and in whom I inspire a superstitious terror, call me the Klein Stoman; is this information sufficient for you?"

"What?" the young man exclaimed utterly astounded, "The White Scalper!"

"I am the man," the stranger quietly answered; "I am also known at times by the name of the Pitiless."

All this had been said by the old man in that monotonous and hoarse voice peculiar to men who, deprived for a long time of the society of their fellow men, have been restricted to a forced silence, and hence speaking has become almost a labour to them. The Jaguar gave a start of repulsion at the sight of this sinister man, whose mournful reputation had reached him with all its horrors. His memory immediately recalled all the traits of ferocity and cruelty imputed to this man, and it was under the impression of this recollection that he said to him with an accent of disgust he did not wish to conceal—

"What is there in common between you and me?"

The old man smiled sarcastically.

"God," he answered, "connects all men to each other by invisible bonds which render them responsible one for the other; He willed it so, in His supreme omniscience, in order to render society possible."

On hearing this wild, solitary man pronounce the name of Deity, and utter so strange an argument, the Jaguar felt his surprise redoubled.

"I will not discuss the point with you," he said; "everyone in life follows the path destiny has traced for him, and it does not belong to me to judge you either favourably or unfavourably; still, I have the right of denying any connection with you, whatever may be your feelings toward me, or the motives that brought you hither; up to the present, we have been strangers to each other, and I desire to remain so for the future."

"What do you know of it? What certainty have you that this is the first time we have been face to face? Man can no more answer for the past than for the future; both are in the hands of One more powerful than him, of Him who judges of actions immediately, and for whom there is only one weight and one measure."

"I am astonished," the Jaguar answered, involuntarily interested, "that the name of Deity should be so often on your lips."

"Because it is deeply engraved on my heart," the old man said with an accent of gloomy sorrow which spread a veil of melancholy over his austere features. "You said yourself that you would not judge me; retain, if you will, the evil impression which the probable false statements of others have made on you. I care little for the opinion of men, for I recognise no other judge of my actions but my conscience."

"Be it so; but permit me to remark that time is rapidly slipping away, night is advancing. I have serious business to attend to, and need to be alone."

"In a word, you show me the door; unluckily, I am not disposed, for the present, to accede to your request, or, if you prefer it, obey your orders; I wish first to answer all your questions, and then, if you still insist on it, I will retire."

"Take care, for this obstinacy on your part may lead to dangerous consequences for you."

"Why threaten a man who does not insult you?" the old man replied with undiminished coolness; "Do you fancy that I put myself out of the way for nothing? No, no, serious motives bring me to you; and if I am not mistaken, ere long you will allow that the time you are unwilling to grant me, could not be better employed than in listening to me."

The Jaguar shrugged his shoulders impatiently; he felt a repugnance to employ violence against a man who, after all, had in no way infringed on the laws of politeness, and, spite of himself, a species of secret presentiment warned him that the visit of this singular old man would be useful to him.

"Speak then," he said a moment after, in the tone of a man who resigns himself to endure a thing that displeases him, but which he cannot elude; "but pray be brief."

"I am not so used to speaking as to find pleasure in making long harangues," the Scalper replied; "I will only say things strictly indispensable to be properly understood by you."

"Do so then without further preamble."

"Be it so. I now return to the second question you asked me: What reason brought me here? I will tell you presently, but first answer your third question—How I got here?"

"In truth," the Jaguar exclaimed, "that seems to me extraordinary."

"Not so extraordinary as you suppose; I might tell you that I am too old a hand on the prairies not to foil the most vigilant sentries; but I prefer confessing the truth, as it will be more profitable to you. You have this night confided the guard of the camp to Apache dogs, who, instead of watching, as they pledged themselves to do, are asleep on their posts, so thoroughly that the first comer can enter your lines as he thinks proper; and this is so true, that scarce two hours back a party of eight went through the whole length of your camp, and entered the hacienda, without encountering opposition from anyone."

"Viva Dios!" the Jaguar exclaimed, turning livid with passion; "Can it possibly be so?"

"I am the proof of it, I fancy," the old man answered simply.

The young Chief seized his pistols, and made a hurried movement to rush out, but the stranger restrained him.

"What good will it do," he said, "to pick a quarrel with your allies? It is an accomplished fact, so it is better to undergo the consequences. Still, let it serve you as a lesson to take better precautions another time."

"But these men who crossed the camp?" the Jaguar said sharply.

"You have nothing to fear from them; they are poor devils of hunters, who were probably seeking a refuge for the two women they brought with them."

"Two women?"

"Yes, a white and an Indian; although they were dressed in male attire, I recognized them the more easily, because I have been watching them for a long time."

"Ah," said the Jaguar thoughtfully, "do you know any of these hunters?"

"Only one, who is, I believe, tigrero to the hacienda."

"Tranquil!" the Jaguar exclaimed with aft expression impossible to render.

"Yes."

"In that case, one of the females is his daughter Carmela'"

"Probably."

"She is now, then, at the Larch-tree?"

"Yes."

"Oh," he burst out, "I must at all hazards carry that accursed hacienda."

"That is exactly what I came to propose to you," the Scalper said quietly.

The young man advanced a step.

"What do you say?" he asked.

"I say," the old man replied in the same tone, "that I have come to propose to you the capture of the hacienda."

"You! It is impossible."

"Why so?"

"Because," the Jaguar went on with agitation, "the hacienda is well fortified: it is defended by a numerous and brave garrison, commanded by one of the best officers of the Mexican army, and for the seventeen days I have been investing these accursed walls, I have been unable, despite all my efforts, to take one forward step."

"All that is correct."

"Well?"

"I repeat my proposition."

"But how will you effect it?"

"That is my business."

"That is not an answer."

"I can give you no other."

"Still?"

"When force does not avail, stratagem must be employed; is not that your opinion?"

"Yes; but one must have the necessary means in his hands."

"Well, I have them."

"To seize the hacienda?"

"I will introduce you into the interior—the rest is your affair."

"Oh, once inside, I will not leave it again."

"Then, you accept?"

"One moment."

"Do you hesitate?"

"I do."

"When I offer you an unexpected success?"

"For that very reason."

"I do not understand you."

"I will explain myself."

"Do so."

"It is not admissible that you have come to make such a proposal for my sake, or that of the cause I serve."

"Perhaps not."

"Let us deal frankly. Whatever your character may be, you have a manner of looking at things which renders you perfectly indifferent to the chances, good or bad, of the struggle going on at this moment in this unhappy country."

"You are quite correct."

"Am I not? You care little whether Texas be free or in slavery?"

"I admit it."

"You have, then, a reason for acting as you are now doing?"

"A man always has a reason."

"Very good; well, I wish to know that reason."

"And suppose I refuse to tell it to you?"

"I shall not accept your proposition."

"You will be wrong."

"That is possible."

"Reflect."

"I have reflected."

There was a moment's silence, which the old man interrupted—

"You are a suspicious and headstrong boy," he said to him, "who, through a false feeling of honour, risk losing an opportunity which you will probably never find again."

"I will run the risk; I wish to be frank with you; I only know you from very ill reports; your reputation is execrable, and nothing proves to me that, under the pretext of serving me, you may not be laying a snare for me."

The old man's pale face was covered by a sudden flush at these rude words, a nervous tremor agitated all his limbs; but, by a violent effort, he succeeded in mastering the emotion he experienced, and after a few minutes, he replied in a calm voice, in which, however, there remained some traces of the tempest that growled hoarsely in his heart—

"I forgive you," he said; "you had a right to speak to me as you did, and I cannot be angry with you. Time is slipping away, it is nearly one in the morning; it will soon be too late to execute the bold plan I have formed; I will therefore only add one word—reflect before answering me, for on that answer my resolution, depends. The motive that urges me to offer to introduce you to the hacienda is quite personal, and in no way affects or concerns you."

"But what guarantee can you offer me on the sincerity of your intentions?"

The old man walked a step forward, drew himself up to his full height, stamped with an accent of supreme majesty—

"My word, the word of a man who, whatever may be said about him, has never failed in what he owes himself; I swear to you on my honour, before that God in whose presence you and I will probably soon appear, that my intentions are pure and loyal, without any thought of treachery. Now, answer, what is your resolve?"

While uttering these words, the old man's attitude, gestures, and race were imprinted with such nobility and grandeur, that he seemed transfigured. In spite of himself, the Jaguar was affected: he felt himself led away by this accent, which seemed to him to come straight from the heart.

"I accept," he said in a firm voice.

"I expected it," the old man replied; "in young and generous natures good feelings always find an echo. You will not repent the confidence you give me."

"Here is my hand," the young man said passionately; "press it without fear, for it is that of a friend."

"Thanks," the old man said, as a burning tear beaded on his eyelashes; "that word repays me for much suffering and sorrow."

"Now, explain your plan to me."

"I will do so in two words; but, ere we discuss the plan we shall adopt, collect noiselessly three or four hundred men, so that we may be able to start immediately we have come to an understanding."

"You are right."

"I need not advise you to be prudent; your men must assemble in the utmost silence. Take no Redskins with you, for they would be more injurious than useful. I am not desirous to be seen by them, for you know that I am their enemy."

"Do not trouble yourself, I will act as you wish."

The Jaguar went out, and remained away for about a quarter of an hour; during that time the White Scalper remained motionless in the centre of the tent, leaning pensively on his rifle barrel, the butt of which rested on the ground. Soon could be heard outside something like the imperceptible buzzing of bees in a hive. It was the camp awakening. The Jaguar came in again.

"Now," he said, "the order is given; within a quarter of an hour, four hundred men will be under arms."

"That is a longer period than I need for what I have to say to you; my plan is most simple, and if you follow it point for point, we shall enter the hacienda without striking a blow; listen to me attentively."

"Speak."

The old man drew an equipal up to the table at which the Jaguar was standing, sat down, placed his rifle between his legs, and began—

"For very many years I have known the Larch-tree hacienda. Owing to events too long to tell you, and which would but slightly interest you, I was resident in it for nearly a year as Major-domo. At that period the father of the present owner was still living, and for sundry reasons had the greatest confidence in me. You are aware that at the period of the conquest, when the Spaniards built these haciendas, they made them fortresses rather than farmhouses, as they were compelled to defend themselves nearly daily against the aggressions of the Redskins; now, you must know that in such a fortress there is a masked gate, a secret sally port, which, if necessary, the garrison employ, either to receive reinforcements or provisions, or to evacuate the place, should it be too closely invested."

"Oh," the Jaguar said, smiting his forehead, "can the hacienda have one of these sally ports?"

"Patience, let me go on."

"But look," the young man objected, "here is the detailed plan of the Larch-tree, made by a man whose family have lived there for three generations from father to son, and there is nothing of the sort marked on it."

The old man gave a careless glance at the plan the young man showed him.

"Because," he replied, "the secret is generally known to the owner of the hacienda alone; but let me finish."

"Speak, speak."

"These sally ports, so useful at the time of the conquest, became eventually perfectly neglected, owing to the long peace that reigned in the country; then, by degrees, as they served no purpose, the recollection of them was totally lost, and I am convinced that the majority of the hacienderos at the present day are ignorant of the existence of these secret gates in their habitation; the owner of the Larch-tree is one of the number."

"How do you know? Perhaps the gate is blocked up, or at least defended by a strong detachment."

The old man smiled.

"No," he said, "the gate is not stopped up, nor is it guarded."

"Are you certain?"

"Did I not tell you that I have been prowling about the neighbourhood for some days?"

"I do not remember it."

"I wished to assure myself of the existence of this gate, which an accident led me to discover in former days."

"Well?"

"I have sought it, found it, and opened it."

"Viva Dios!" the Jaguar shouted joyfully; "In that case the hacienda is ours."

"I believe so, unless a fatality or a miracle occur—two things equally improbable."

"But where is this gate situated?"

"As usual, at a spot where it is the most unlikely to suspect its existence. Look," he added, bending over the plan, "the hacienda, being built on a height, runs a risk in the event of a long siege of seeing its wells dry up— does it not?"

"Yes."

"Very good. The river on this side runs along the foot of the rocks on which its walls are built."

"Yes, yes," said the young man, who was eagerly following the indications made by the old man.

"Judging rightly," he went on, "that on this side the hacienda was impregnable, you contented yourself with establishing on the river bank a few outposts, intended to watch the enemy's movements."

"Any flight on that side is impossible—in the first place, owing to the height of the walls; and next, through the river, which forms a natural trench."

"Well, the gate by which we shall enter is among those very rocks, almost on a level with the water; it opens into a natural grotto, the entrance of which is so obstructed by creepers, that from the opposite bank it is impossible to suspect its existence."

"At length," the Jaguar exclaimed, "this redoubt, which has hitherto been one of the links of the heavy chain riveted round Texas, will be tomorrow one of the most solid barriers of her independence. May Heaven be praised for permitting so brilliant a triumph to crown our efforts!"

"I hope to see you master of the place before sunrise."

"May Heaven hear you!"

"Now, we will start whenever you please."

"At once, at once."

They then left the tent. According to the Jaguar's orders, John Davis had roused four hundred men, chosen from the boldest and most skilful fellows of the force. They were drawn up a few paces from the tent, motionless and silent. Their rifles, whose barrels were bronzed lest they might emit any denunciatory gleams in the moonbeams, were piled in front of them.

The officers formed a group apart. They were conversing together in a low voice, with considerable animation, not at all understanding the orders they had received, and not knowing for what reason the Chief had them awakened. The Jaguar advanced toward them, and the officers fell back. The young man, followed by the Scalper, entered the circle, which at once closed up again. John Davis, on perceiving the old man, whom he at once recognised, uttered a stifled cry of surprise.

"Caballeros," the Jaguar said, in a low voice, "we are about to attempt a surprise, which, if it succeed, will render us masters of the hacienda almost without a blow."

A murmur of surprise ran round the circle.

"A person in whom I have the most entire confidence," the Jaguar continued, "has revealed to me the existence of a secret gate, not known to the garrison, which will give us access to the fort. Each of you will now take the command of his men. Our march must be as silent as that of Indian warriors on the war trail. You have understood me fully, so I count on your aid. In the event of separation, the watchword will be *Texas y libertad* To your posts."

The circle was broken up, and each officer placed himself at the head of his men. John Davis then went up to the Jaguar.

"One word," he said to him, bending to his ear to speak. "Do you know who that man is, standing close to you?"

"Yes."

"Are you sure?"

"It is the White Scalper."

"And you trust to him?"

"Entirely."

The American tossed his head.

"Was it he who revealed to you the existence of the sally port by which we are to enter?"

"Yes."

"Take care."

In his turn, the Jaguar shrugged his shoulders.

"You are mad," he said.

"Well, that is possible," John replied; "but for all that, I will watch him."

"As you please."

"Well, let us be off."

The American followed his Chief, casting a parting look of suspicion on the old man. The latter did not seem to trouble himself at all about this aside. Apparently indifferent to what went on around him, he waited, quietly leaning on his rifle, till it pleased the Jaguar to give the command for departure. At length, the word "march" ran from rank to rank, and the column started.

These men, the majority of whom were accustomed to long marches in the desert, placed their feet so softly on the ground, that they seemed to glide along like phantoms, so silent was their march. At this moment, as if the sky wished to be on their side, an immense black cloud spread across the heavens and interrupted the moonbeams, substituting, almost without transition, a deep obscurity for the radiance that previously prevailed, and the column disappeared in the gloom. A few paces ahead of the main body, the Jaguar, White Scalper, and John Davis marched side by side.

"Bravo!" the young man muttered; "Everything favours us."

"Let us wait for the end," the American growled, whose suspicions, far from diminishing, on the contrary were augmented from moment to moment.

Instead of leaving the camp on the aide of the hacienda, whose gloomy outline was designed, sinister and menacing, on the top of the hill, the Scalper made the column take a long circuit, which skirted the rear of the camp. The deepest silence prevailed on the plain, the camp and hacienda seemed asleep, not a light gleamed in the darkness, and it might be fancied, on noticing so profound a calm, that the plain was deserted; but this factitious calm held a terrible tempest, ready to burst forth at the first signal.

These men, who walked on tiptoe, sounding the darkness around them, and with their finger placed on the rifle trigger, felt their hearts beat with impatience to come into collision with their enemies. It was a singular coincidence, a strange fatality, which caused the besiegers and besieged to attempt a double surprise at the same hour, almost at the same moment, and send blindly against each other men who on either side advanced with the hope of certain success, and convinced that they were about to surprise asleep the too confident enemy, whom they burned to massacre.

So soon as they had left the camp, the insurgents drew near the river, whose banks, covered with thick bushes and aquatic plants, would have offered them, even in bright day, a certain shelter from the Mexicans. On coming within about half a league of the entrenchments, the column halted; the Scalper advanced alone a few yards, and then rejoined the Jaguar.

"We shall have to cross the river here," he said; "there is a ford, and the men will only be up to their waists in water."

And, giving the example, the old man stepped into the bed of the river. The others followed immediately, and, as the Scalper had announced, the water was only up to their waists. They passed threes in front, and closing up the ranks, so as to resist the rather strong current, which, without these precautions, might have carried them away. Five minutes later, the whole band was collected in the interior of the grotto, at the end of which was the secret door.

"The moment has arrived," the Jaguar then said, "to redouble our prudence; let us avoid, if it be possible, bloodshed. Not a word must be uttered, or a shot fired, without my orders, under penalty of death." Then, turning to the White Scalper, he said, in a firm voice—"Now, open the door!"

There was a moment of supreme anxiety for the insurgents, who awaited with a quiver of impatience the downfall of the frail obstacle that separated them from their enemies.

CHAPTER XV
A THUNDERBOLT

We will now return to the hacienda.

The Colonel and the Major-domo went down to the Patio, where they found assembled the one hundred and fifty men selected for the execution of the surprise, which the Colonel proposed to attempt on the rebel camp. Tranquil, according to the orders he had received, after assuring himself that Carmela was enjoying a sound and refreshing sleep, hastened to tell Loyal Heart and Black-deer what the Colonel expected from them. The two men immediately followed their friend into the Patio, where the soldiers were already assembled.

The Colonel divided his men into three detachments, each of fifty men: he took the command of the first, keeping the Canadian with him; Don Felix, having Loyal Heart for guide, had the command of the second; and the third, at the head of which was placed a captain, an old soldier of great experience, was directed by Black-deer. These arrangements made, the Colonel gave the order for departure. The detachments at once separated, and left the hacienda by three different gates.

The Colonel's plan was extremely simple; descend unheard to the rebels' camp, enter it, and fire it on three different sides; then, profiting by the disorder and tumult occasioned by this surprise, rush on the rebels with shouts of "Viva Mejico!" prevent them rallying or extinguishing the fire, massacre as many as possible, and afterwards effect an orderly retreat on the hacienda.

At the moment when the Mexicans left the hacienda, the same thing happened to them as to the insurgents, who left their camp at the same moment, that is to say, they were suddenly enveloped in thick darkness. The Colonel bent down to Tranquil, and said to him good-humouredly—

"This is a good omen for the success of our expedition."

The Jaguar was saying the same thing to White Scalper almost simultaneously.

The three detachments silently descended the hill, marching in Indian file, and taking the greatest care to stifle the sound of their footsteps on the ground. On coming within a certain distance of the Texan entrenchments, they halted, with one accord, to take breath, like tigers, which at the moment of leaping on the prey they covet, draw themselves up, in order to take a vigorous impetus. The soldiers wheeled, so as to present a rather extensive line; then each lay down on the sand, and at the signal, muttered in a low voice by the guides, they began crawling like reptiles through the tall grass, cutting passages through the bushes, advancing in a straight line, and clearing obstacles, without thinking of turning them.

We have said that White Scalper, no doubt with the intention of causing the Larch-tree garrison to feel greater security, and persuade them that all was quiet in camp, had objected to the Apache sentries being aroused, for he considered their vigilance quite unnecessary,—not supposing for a moment that the Mexicans would dare to leave their lines of defence and take the initiative in a sally. The direction the old man had given to the detachment he guided, by drawing it away from the approaches of the fortress, had also favoured the Colonel's plans, which, without that, would have been, in all probability, foiled.

Still, the Canadian hunter was too prudent and accustomed to the tricks of Indian war not to assure himself previously that there was no trap to apprehend. Hence, on arriving about fifteen yards from the breastworks, he ordered a halt. Then, gliding like a serpent through the shrubs and dead trees that covered the ground at this spot, he pushed forward a reconnoissance. Loyal Heart and Black-deer, to whom he had given detailed instructions how to act before leaving the hacienda, executed the same manoeuvre. The absence of the scouts was long, or, at least appeared so to all these men, who were so impatient to bound on the enemy and begin the the attack. At length Tranquil returned, but he was anxious and frowning, and a gloomy restlessness seemed to agitate him. These signs did not escape the Colonel's notice.

"What is the matter with you?" he asked him. "Are the rebels alarmed? Have you noticed any signs of agitation in their camp?"

"No," he replied, with his eyes obstinately fixed before him, as if he wished to pierce the gloom and read the mysteries it contained. "I have seen nothing, noticed nothing; the deepest calm, apparently, prevails in the camp."

"Apparently, do you say?"

"Yes; for it is impossible that this calm can be real, for most of the Texan insurgents are old hunters, accustomed to the rude fatigues of a desert life. I can just understand that, during the first part of the night, they might not notice the gross neglect of the Apache sentries; but what I cannot in any way admit is, that during the whole night not one of these partisans, to whom prudence is so imperiously recommended, should have got up to make the rounds and see that all was in order. Above all, I cannot understand this of the Jaguar—that man of iron, who never sleeps, and who, though still very young, possesses all the wisdom and experience which are usually the appanage of men who have passed middle life."

"And you conclude from this?"

"I conclude that we should, perhaps, do better by not continuing this reconnoissance further, but return at full speed to the hacienda; for, unless I am greatly mistaken, this gloomy night covers some sinister mystery which we shall see accomplished ere long, and of which we may fall the victims, unless we take care."

"From what you say to me," the Colonel made answer, "I see that you rather give me the expression of your own personal opinions than the result of important facts you may have seen during your reconnoissance."

"That is true, Colonel; but, if you will permit me to speak so, I would observe that these opinions emanate from a man for whom, thanks to his experience, the desert possesses no secrets, and whom his presentiments rarely deceive."

"Yes, all that is true; and, perhaps, I ought to follow your advice. My resolution has possibly been premature, but now, unfortunately, it is too late to recall it. Withdrawing is an impossibility, for that would prove to my soldiers that I was mistaken, which is not admissible. We must, at any cost, accept the consequences of our imprudence, and push on, no matter what happens. Still, we will redouble our prudence, and try to accomplish our scheme without incurring too great a risk."

"I am at your orders, Colonel, ready to follow you wherever you may please to lead me."

"Forward, then, and may Heaven be favourable to us!" the young officer said, resolutely.

The order was whispered along the line, and the soldiers, whom this long conference had perplexed, and who were afraid they should be obliged to turn back, received it joyfully, and advanced with renewed ardour. The ground that separated them from the breastwork was soon covered, and the entrenchments were escaladed ere a single Apache sentry had given the alarm.

Suddenly, from three different points of the camp an immense flame shot up, and the Mexicans rushed forward, shouting *"Viva Mejico!"* as the insurgents, who, hardly awake yet, ran hither and thither, not understanding these flames which surrounded them, and these terrible yells which sounded in their ears like a funereal knell.

For nearly an hour the contest was a chaos; smoke and noise covered everything else. According to the American custom, most of the insurgents had their wives and children with them: hence, from the first moment the fight assumed gigantic and terrible proportions. The country was covered with a confused medley of startled women, who called to their husbands or brothers, Apache horsemen galloping among the terrified foot soldiers and overthrown tents, from which rose the cries of children and the groans of the wounded. All around the camp an immense line of smoke bordered the flames kindled by the Mexicans, who bounded forward like wild beasts, uttering fearful yells. All these united sounds formed a chorus of inexpressible horror, whose echo extended to the extreme verge of the horizon as sad and mournful as that of the rising tide. Such are the fearful results of civil wars: they let loose and aggravate all the evil passions of man; the latter forget every human feeling in the hope of attaining the object they desire, and incessantly push onward, not caring whether they stumble over ruins or wade through blood.

Still, when the first feeling of surprise had passed, the insurgents began gradually rallying, in spite of the incessant efforts of the Mexicans, and the resistance was organized to a certain extent. Colonel Melendez had gained his object, the success of his plan was complete, the losses of the Texans in men and ammunition were immense; he did not wish, with the few troops he had under him, to advance further into a blazing camp, where they walked under a vault of flames, running the risk of being struck at each moment by the ruins of the powder magazines, which exploded one after the other with a terrible noise.

The Colonel took a triumphant glance at the ruins piled up around him, and then ordered the retreat to be sounded. The Mexicans had allowed their ardour to carry them in every direction; some, in spite of the repeated warnings of their Chief, were already too far off for it to be possible for them to fall in directly. These must be waited for, therefore.

The three detachments formed in a semicircle, firing on the insurgents, who profited by the moment of respite chance afforded them to become constantly more numerous. They then noticed the small strength of their assailants, and rushed resolutely upon them. The Mexicans, now united, wished to effect their retreat, but at each instant their position became more difficult, and threatened to become even critical. The Texans, who were still the more numerous, with rage in their hearts at having allowed themselves to be thus surprised, and burning for vengeance, vigorously pressed the Mexicans, who, compelled to retreat inch by inch, and keep a front constantly to the enemy, were on the point of being outflanked, in spite of the heroic resistance they opposed to the assailants.

Colonel Melendez, seeing the danger of the position, collected forty resolute men, and placing himself at their head, rushed on the insurgents with an irresistible impetuosity. The latter, surprised in their turn by this vigorous attack, which they were far from expecting, recoiled, and at length fell back some hundred yards to reform, closely pursued by the Colonel.

This lucky diversion gave the main body of the Mexicans time to gain ground, and when the Texans returned to the charge with fresh ardour, the propitious moment had passed, and the Mexicans were definitively protected from any assault.

"*Viva Dios!*" the Colonel said, as he rejoined his company; "the affair was hot, but the advantage remains with us."

"I did not see the Jaguar during the whole action," the Canadian muttered.

"That is true," the young man replied, "and is most strange."

"His absence alarms me," the hunter said sadly; "I should have preferred his being there."

"Where can he be?" the Colonel remarked, suddenly turning thoughtful.

"Perhaps we shall learn only too soon," the Canadian replied with a shake of the head, foreboding misfortune.

All at once, and as if chance had wished to justify the hunter's sad forebodings, an immense noise was heard in the hacienda, amid which could be distinguished cries of distress, and a well-sustained musketry fire. Then, a sinister glare rose above the Larch-tree, which it coloured with the hues of fire.

"Forward! Forward!" the Colonel cried; "The enemy have got into the fort!"

At the first glance, the young officer understood what had taken place, and the truth at once struck his mind. All rushed toward the hacienda, inside which an obstinate contest seemed to be raging. They soon reached the gates, which, fortunately for them, still remained in the hands of their comrades, and rushed into the patio, where a horrible spectacle offered itself to their sight. This is what had happened.

At the moment when White Scalper prepared to break in the door with the lever, the clamour made by the Mexicans in firing the camp, reached the ears of the Texans assembled in the grotto.

"*Rayo de Dios!*" the Jaguar shouted; "What is the meaning of that?"

"Probably the Mexicans are attacking your camp," the old man quietly answered.

The young Chief gave him an ugly look.

"We are betrayed," said John Davis, as he cocked a pistol, and pointed it at the old man.

"I am beginning to believe it," the Jaguar muttered, all his suspicions coming back.

"By whom?" the White Scalper asked with a smile of contempt.

"By you, you villain!" the American answered roughly.

"You are mad," the old man said with a disdainful shrug of his shoulders; "if I had betrayed you, should I have led you here?"

"That is true," said the Jaguar; "but it is strange, and the noise is unceasing. The Mexicans are doubtless massacring our companions; we cannot abandon them thus, but must hurry to their assistance."

"Do nothing of the sort," the Scalper sharply exclaimed. "Hasten, on the contrary, to invade the fortress, which I doubt not is abandoned by the greater part of its defenders; your companions, so soon as they have rallied, will be strong enough to repulse their assailants."

The Jaguar hesitated.

"What is to be done?" he muttered with an undecided air, as he bent an enquiring glance on the men as they passed round him.

"Act without loss of a moment," the old man eagerly exclaimed, and with a vigorously dealt stroke he broke in the door, which fell in splinters to the ground; "here is the way open, will you recoil?"

"No! No!" they shouted impetuously, and rushed into the gaping vault before them.

This vault formed a passage wide enough for four persons to march abreast, and of sufficient height for them not to be obliged to stoop; it rose with a gentle incline, and resembled a species of labyrinth, owing to the constant turns it took. The darkness was complete, but the impulse had been given, and no other noise was audible save that of the panting breathing of these men, and their hurried footsteps, which sounded hollow on the damp ground they trod. After a twenty minutes' march, which seemed to last an age, the Scalper's voice rose in the gloom, and uttered the single word, "Halt!" All stopped.

"Here we shall have to make our final arrangements," the Scalper continued; "but in the first place let me procure you a light, so that you may know exactly where you are."

The old man, who seemed gifted with the precious privilege of seeing in the darkness, walked about for some minutes in various directions, doubtless collecting the ingredients necessary for the fire he wished to kindle; then he struck a light, lit a piece of tinder, and almost immediately a brilliant flame seemed to leap forth from the ground, and illumined objects sufficiently for them to be distinguished. The Scalper had simply lighted a fire of dry wood, probably prepared beforehand.

The Texans looked curiously around them, so soon as their eyes, at first dazzled by the bright flames of the fire, had grown accustomed to the light. They found themselves in a very large, almost circular vault, somewhat resembling a crypt; the walls were lofty, and the roof was rounded in the shape of a dome. The ground was composed of a very fine dry sand, as yellow as gold. This room seemed cut out of the rock, for no sign of masonry was visible.

In the background, a staircase of some twenty steps, wide, and without bannister, mounted to the roof, where it terminated, and it was impossible to distinguish whether there were any trapdoor or opening. This trap doubtless existed, but time had covered its openings with the impalpable dust, which it incessantly wears off even the hardest granite. After attentively examining the vault by the aid of a blazing log, the Jaguar returned to the old man, who had remained by the fire.

"Where are we?" he asked him. Each curiously extended his ear to hear the Scalper's answer.

"We are," he said, "exactly under the patio of the hacienda; this staircase ends in an opening I will point out to you, and which leads into a long-deserted corral, in which, if I am not mistaken, the wood stores of the hacienda are now kept."

"Good," the Jaguar answered; "but before venturing into what may be an adroitly laid trap, I should like, myself, to visit the corral of which you speak, in order to see with my own eyes, and assure myself that things are really as you say."

"I ask nothing better than to lead you to it."

"Thank you; but I do not see exactly how we shall manage to open the passage of which you speak, without making a noise, which will immediately bring down on us the whole of the garrison, of which I am excessively afraid, as we are not at all conveniently situated for fighting."

"That need not trouble you; I pledge myself to open the trap without making the slightest noise."

"That is better; but come, time presses."

"That is true. Come."

The two men then proceeded to the flight of stairs. On reaching the top, the White Scalper thrust his head against the ceiling, and after several attempts a slab slowly rose, turned over, and fell noiselessly on its side, leaving a passage large enough for two men to pass together. White Scalper passed through this opening. With one bound the Jaguar stood by his side, pistol in hand, ready to blow out his brains at the first suspicious movement. But he soon perceived that the old man had no intention of betraying him, and, ashamed at the suspicion he had evidenced, he hid his weapon.

As the Scalper had stated, they found themselves in an abandoned corral—a sort of vast stall, open to the sky, in which the Americans keep their horses; but this one was quite empty. The Jaguar went up to a door behind which he heard the sound of footsteps and the clanking of arms, and assured himself that nothing was more easy than to burst this door open.

"Good," he muttered; "you have kept your word; thank you."

The Scalper did not seem to hear him; his eyes were fixed on the door with a strange intensity, and his limbs trembled, as if he had been attacked by ague. Without attempting to discover the cause of his old comrade's extraordinary emotion, the Jaguar ran to the opening, over which he bent down. John Davis was standing on the top step.

"Well?" he asked.

"All goes well. Come up, but do not make any noise."

The four hundred Texans then rose one after the other from the vault. Each, as he came out of the trap, silently fell in. When all had entered the corral, the Jaguar returned the slab to its place. Then, returning to his comrades, said in a low but perfectly distinct voice:

"Our retreat is now cut off; we must either conquer or die."

The insurgents made no reply; but their eyes flashed such fire, that the Jaguar comprehended that they would not give way an inch. It was a moment of terrible suspense while White Scalper was forcing the door.

"Forward!" the Jaguar shouted.

All his comrades rushed after him with the irresistible force of a torrent that is bursting its dykes.

Very different from the Texans, whose camp had so easily been invaded, the Mexicans were not asleep, but perfectly awake. By orders of the Commandant, so soon as he had left the hacienda the whole garrison got under arms, and fell in the patio, ready, if need was, to go immediately to the aid of the expeditionary corps, still, they were so far from expecting an attack, especially in this manner, that the sudden apparition of this band of demons, who seemed to have ascended from the infernal regions, caused them extraordinary surprise and terror, and during some time there was an inextricable confusion.

The Texans, skilfully profiting by the terror their presence caused, redoubled their efforts to render it impossible for their enemies to offer any lengthened resistance. But, shut up as they were in a court without an outlet, the very impossibility of flight gave the Mexicans the necessary courage to rally and fight courageously. Collected round their officers, who encouraged them by voice and example, they resolved to do their duty manly, and the combat began again with fresh obstinacy.

It was at this moment that Colonel Melendez and the soldiers who followed him burst into the patio, and by their presence were on the point of restoring to their party the victory which was slipping from them. Unfortunately, this success arrived too late: the Mexicans, surrounded by the Texans, were compelled, after a desperate resistance and prodigies of valour, to lay down their arms, and surrender at discretion.

For the second time Don Juan Melendez was prisoner to the Jaguar. As on the first occasion, he was compelled to break his sword, conquered by fatality rather than by his fortunate enemy.

The first care of the Jaguar, so soon as he was master of the fort, was to give strict orders that the females should not be insulted. The conditions imposed on the conquered by the Chief of the Texan army were the same as he had offered them at the outset. The Mexicans, persuaded that the Texans were no more than half savage men, were agreeably surprised at this lenity, which they were far from expecting, and pledged themselves without hesitation to observe scrupulously the conditions of the capitulation. The Mexican garrison was to leave the hacienda at daybreak.

The preliminaries of the surrender had scarce been agreed on between the two leaders ere piercing cries were suddenly heard from the building occupied by the women. Almost immediately the White Scalper, who had been lost out of sight during the excitement of the combat, emerged from these buildings bearing across his shoulders a woman whose long hair trailed on the ground. The old man's eyes flashed, and foam came from his mouth. In his right hand he brandished his rifle, which he held by the barrel, and fell back step by step, like a tiger at bay, before those who tried in vain to bar his passage.

"My daughter!" Tranquil shrieked, as he rushed toward him.

He had recognised Carmela; the poor child had fainted, and seemed dead. The Colonel and the Jaguar had also recognised the maiden, and by a common impulse hurried to her aid.

The White Scalper, recoiling step by step before the cloud of enemies that surrounded him, did not reply a word to the insults poured upon him. He laughed a dry and sharp laugh, and whenever an assailant came too near him, he raised his terrible club, and the imprudent man rolled with a fractured skull on the ground.

The hunters and the two young men, recognising the impossibility of striking this man without running the risk of wounding her they wished to save, contented themselves with gradually contracting the circle round him, so as to drive him into a corner of the court, where they would be enabled to seize him. But the ferocious old man foiled their calculations; he suddenly bounded forward, overthrew those who opposed his passage, and climbed with headlong speed up the steps leading to the platform. On reaching the latter, he turned once again to his startled enemies, burst into a hoarse laugh, and leaped over the breastwork into the river, bearing with him the young girl, of whom he had not loosed his hold.

When the witnesses of this extraordinary act of folly had recovered from the stupor into which it threw them, and rushed on the platform, their anxious glances in vain interrogated the river—the waters had reassumed their ordinary limpidness. White Scalper had disappeared with the unhappy victim whom he had so audaciously carried off. To accomplish this unheard-of ravishment he had surrendered the Larch-tree hacienda to the Texan army. What motive had impelled the strange man to this unqualifiable action? The impenetrable mystery that enveloped his life rendered any supposition impossible.

CHAPTER XVI
THE CONSPIRATORS

More fortunate than dramatic authors, the romancers, being bound by no rules of time and place, can, at their pleasure, transport their action and characters from one country to another, and then return to their starting point, not having any account to give of the time that has elapsed, or of the space they have traversed. Employing in our turn this privilege, we will momentarily quit the Indian border, on the skirt of which our story has hitherto passed, and crossing at a leap over about two hundred miles, beg the reader to follow us to Galveston, in the centre of Texas, four months after the events we chronicled in our last chapter.

At the period when our story is laid, that city, in which General Lallemand wished to found the *Champ d'Asyle*—that sublime Utopia of a noble and broken heart—was far from that commercial prosperity which the progress of civilization, successive immigrations, and, most of all, the speculations of bold capitalists, have caused it to attain during the last few years. We shall therefore describe it such as it was during our stay in America, leaving out of sight the enormous transformations it has since undergone.

Galveston is built on the small sandy islet of St. Louis, which almost closes up the mouth of the Rio Trinidad. At that time the houses were low, mostly built of wood, and surrounded by gardens planted with fragrant trees, which impregnated the atmosphere with delicious odours.

Unfortunately there is one thing that cannot alter—the climate and the nature of the soil. The suffocating heat that almost continually prevails in the town corrodes the earth and changes it into an impalpable dust, in which you sink up to the knees, and which, at the least breath of air, penetrates into the eyes, mouth, and nostrils; myriads of mosquitoes, whose stings are extremely painful; and, above all, the bad quality of the water, which the inhabitants collect with great difficulty in plank reservoirs during the rainy season, and which the sun renders boiling—these grievous occurrences, especially for Europeans, render a residence at Galveston insupportable, and even most dangerous.

The Texans themselves so greatly fear the deadly influence of this climate that, during the torrid heat of summer, rich persons emigrate by hundreds to the mainland, so that the town, which becomes almost suddenly deserted by this momentary departure, assumes a look of sad desolation which is painful to behold.

About four in the afternoon, at the moment when the rising sea breeze began to refresh the atmosphere, a little Indian canoe, made of beech bark, left the mainland, and vigorously impelled by two men supplied with wide sculls, proceeded toward the city and pulled alongside the plank quay, which served at that time as the landing place. So soon as the canoe was stationary, a third person, carelessly reclining in the stern sheets, rose, looked round him as if to recognise the spot where he was; then, taking a spring, he landed on the quay. The canoe immediately turned round, though not a syllable had been exchanged between the scullers and the passenger they had brought.

The latter then pulled his hat over his eyes, wrapped himself carefully in the folds of a wide zarapé of Indian fabric and striking colour, and proceeded hastily towards the centre of the city. After a walk of a few minutes the stranger stopped in front of a house, whose comfortable appearance and well-tended garden showed that it belonged to a person who, if not rich, was in easy circumstances. The door was ajar; the stranger pushed it, entered, and closed it after him; then, without any hesitation, like a man sure of what he was about, he crossed the garden, in which he met nobody, entered the passage of the house, turned to the right, and found himself in a room modestly, though comfortably furnished.

On reaching this room the stranger fell into a butaca with the air of a tired man delighted to rest after a long journey, took off his zarapé, which he placed on the equipal, threw his hat upon it, and then, when he had made himself comfortable, he rolled a husk cigarette, struck a light with a gold mechero he took from his pocket, lit his papelito, and was soon surrounded by a dense cloud of bluish and fragant smoke, which rose above his head and formed a species of halo.

The stranger threw his body back, half closed his eyes, and fell into that gentle ecstasy which the Italians call the *dolce far niente*, the Turks, *kief*, and for which we northerns, with our more powerful constitutions, have found no name, for the simple reason that we do not know it.

The stranger had reached about the half of his second cigarette when another person entered the room. This man, who did not appear to take the slightest notice of the previous arrival, behaved, however, precisely as he had done: he also took off his zarapé, reclined on a butaca, and lit up a cigarette. Presently the garden sand creaked beneath the footsteps of a third visitor, followed immediately by a fourth, and then by a fifth; in short, at the end of an hour twenty persons were assembled in this room. They all smoked with apparent carelessness, and since their arrival had not exchanged a syllable.

Six o'clock struck from a clock standing on a sideboard. The last stroke of the hour had scarce ceased vibrating ere the company, as if by common agreement, threw away their cigars, and rose with a vivacity that certainly was little to be expected after their previous carelessness. At the same moment a secret door opened in the wall, and a man appeared on the threshold.

This man was tall, elegant, and aristocratic, and appeared to be young. A half-mask of velvet concealed the upper part of his face; as for his attire, it was exactly similar to that of the other persons in the room, but a brace of long pistols and a dagger were passed through the girdle of red China crape which was wound tightly round his waist. At the appearance of the stranger a quiver ran, like an electric current, through the lines of visitors. The masked man, with head erect, arms crossed on his chest, and body haughtily thrown back, gave his audience a glance, which could be seen flashing through the holes in the velvet.

"It is well," he at length said, in a sonorous voice; "you are faithful to your promise, Caballeros, not one of you have kept us waiting. This is the eighth time I have assembled you during the month, and each time I have found you equally prompt and faithful; thanks, in the name of the country, Caballeros."

His auditors bowed silently, and the stranger continued, after a slight pause—

"Time presses, gentlemen; the situation is growing with each moment more serious; today we have no longer to attempt an adventurous stroke; the hour has arrived to stake our heads resolutely in a glorious and decisive game. Are you ready?"

"We are," they all answered unanimously.

"Reflect once more before pledging yourselves further," the Mask continued, in a thrilling voice: "this time I repeat to you, we shall take the bull by the horns, and have a hand-to-hand fight with it; of one hundred chances, ninety-eight are against us."

"No matter," the person who first entered the room said, haughtily; "if two chances are left us, they will be sufficient."

"I expected no less from you, John Davis," the stranger said, "you have ever been full of devotion and self-denial; but, perhaps, among our comrades some may not think as you do entirely. I do not regard this as a crime, for a man may love his country and yet not consent to sacrifice his life to it without regret; still, I must have perfect confidence in those who follow me; they and I must have but one heart and one thought. Let those, then, who feel a repugnance to share in the task we have to perform tonight withdraw. I know that if prudence urges them to abstain this time, under circumstances less desperate I should find them ready to support me."

There was a lengthened silence, and no one stirred; at length the stranger said, with an expression of joy which he did not try to conceal—

"Come, I was not mistaken; you are brave fellows."

John Davis shrugged his shoulders.

"By heaven!" he said, "The trial was useless; you ought to have known long ago what we are."

"Certainly I knew it, but my honour commanded me to act as I have done. Now, all is said: we shall succeed or perish together."

"Very good, that is what I call speaking," the ex-slave dealer said, with a hearty laugh; "the partisans of Santa Anna must have to hold their own; for, if I am not greatly mistaken, ere long we shall cut them into stirrup leathers."

At this moment a shrill whistle, although rather remote, was heard: a second whistle, still nearer, replied.

"Gentlemen," the stranger said, "we are warned of the approach of an enemy; perhaps it is only a false alarm, still the interest of the cause we defend imperiously ordains prudence. Follow John Davis, while I receive the troublesome fellow who is intruding on us."

"Come," said the American.

The conspirators, for they were no other, displayed some hesitation, for they felt a repugnance to hide themselves.

"Leave me," the stranger went on, "you must."

All bowed and left the room after John Davis by the secret door, which had offered passage to their Chief, and which closed upon them without displaying a sign of its existence, as it was so carefully hidden in the wall. A third whistle, close by, was heard at this moment.

"Yes, yes," the Chief said, with a smile, "whoever you may be, you can come now; if you possessed the craft of the opossum and the eyes of the eagle, I defy you to discover anything suspicious here."

He took off his mask, concealed his weapons, and lay back in a butaca. Almost immediately the doors opened, and a man appeared. It was Lanzi, the half-breed; he was dressed like the sailors of the port, with canvas trousers drawn in round the hips, a white shirt, with a blue turned down collar, with a white edging, and a tarpaulin hat.

"Well," the Chief asked, without turning, "why did you warn us, Lanzi?"

"It is highly necessary," the other answered.

"Is it serious, then?"

"You shall judge for yourself. The governor is coming hither with several officers and a company of soldiers."

"General Rubio?"

"In person."

"Hang it!" the conspirator said, "Are we threatened with a domiciliary visit?"

"You will soon know, for I hear him."

"Very good; we shall see what they want of us. In the meanwhile take this mask and these weapons."

"The weapons too?" the other said in surprise.

"What shall I do with them? That is not the way in which I must fight them at this moment. Be off, here they are!"

The half-breed took the mask and pistols, pressed a spring, and disappeared through the door. The garden gravel could now be heard creaking under the footsteps of several persons. At length the door of the saloon was thrown open, and the General entered, followed by four or five officers, who, like himself, were in full dress. The General stopped on the threshold, and took a piercing glance around; the Chief had risen, and was standing motionless in the centre of the apartment.

General Rubio was a thorough man of the world. He bowed politely, and apologized for having thus entered the house without being announced; but he found all the doors open, and no servant had come up to him.

"These excuses are useless, Caballero," the young man answered; "the Mexican government has for a long time accustomed us to its unceremonious way of behaving toward us; besides, the governor of the city has the right, I presume, to enter any house when he thinks proper, and if he does not find the door open, to have it opened, either with a masterkey or a crowbar."

"Your remarks, Caballero," the General answered, "breathe an irritation that must be regretted. The state of effervescence in which Texas is at this moment would be more than sufficient to justify the unusual step I am taking with you."

"I know not to what you are pleased to allude, Señor General," the young man remarked, coldly; "it is possible that Texas may be in a state of effervescence, and the annoyances the government have put on it would completely justify this; but as concerns myself, personally, I might perhaps have a right to complain of seeing my house invaded by an armed force, without any previous summons, when nothing authorizes such an arbitrary measure."

"Are you quite sure, Caballero, that I have not the right to act as I am doing? Do you consider yourself so free from suspicion that you really consider this measure arbitrary?"

"I repeat to you, Caballero," the young man continued, haughtily, "that I do not at all understand the language you do me the honour of addressing to me. I am a peaceable citizen; nothing in my conduct has, as far as I know, aroused the jealous solicitude of the government; and if it pleases its agents to make me undergo ill-deserved annoyance, it is not in my power to oppose it otherwise than by protesting energetically against the insult offered me. You have force on your side, General, so do as you think proper; I am alone here, and shall not attempt in any way to resist the measures you may think proper to take."

"That language, Caballero, evidently comes from a man assured of his safety."

"You are mistaken, General; it is that of a free man, unjustly insulted."

"It may be so, but I shall not discuss the point with you. You will permit me, however, to remark, that for a man so justly indignant, and apparently solitary, you are very carefully guarded; for, if the house be empty, as you state, the environs are guarded by friends of yours, who, I must allow, perform admirably the commission with which they were intrusted, by warning you sufficiently early of unexpected visits for you to take your precautions in consequence, and render it an easy matter to get rid in a twinkling of persons whose presence here might compromise you."

"Instead of speaking thus in enigmas, General, it would be better, perhaps, to have a clear explanation; then, knowing the charge brought against me, I might attempt to defend myself."

"Nothing is more easy, Caballero; still, you will allow me to remark that we have been talking together for some time, and you have not yet offered me a chair."

The young chieftain gave the General an ironical glance.

"Why should I employ toward you those conventional forms of politeness, General? From the moment when, without my authority, and against my will, you introduced yourself into this house, you should have considered yourself as quite at home. It is I, then, who am the stranger here, and in that position I am no longer permitted to do the honours of this house."

"Caballero," the General answered, with a movement of impatience, "I am grieved to find in you this stiffness and determination to quarrel. When I entered this house, my intentions with respect to you were, perhaps, not so hostile as you suppose; but, since you force me to a clear and categorical explanation, I am prepared to satisfy you, and prove to you that I am acquainted not only with your conduct, but with the plans you entertain and are carrying out, with a tenacity and boldness which, if I did not take, would lead inevitably to their speedy realization."

The young man started, and a flash burst from his wild eye at this direct insinuation, which revealed to him the danger with which he was menaced; but immediately regaining his presence of mind, and extinguishing the fire of his glance, he replied, coolly —

"I am listening to you, General."

The latter turned to his officers.

"Do as I do, señores," he said, as he sat down; "take seats, as this caballero refuses to offer them to us. As this friendly conversation may be prolonged for some time yet, it is unnecessary that you should fatigue yourselves by listening to it standing."

The officers bowed, and seated themselves comfortably on the butacas with which the apartment was furnished. The General continued, after a few moments of reflection, during which the young man looked at him carelessly, while rolling a husk cigarette:

"And in the first place, to proceed regularly, and prove to you that I am well-informed of all that concerns you," he said, purposely laying a stress on the words, "I will begin by telling you your name."

"In truth, General, you should have begun with that," the young man said, negligently.

"You are," the General went on, quietly, "the famous Chief whom the insurgents and Freebooters have christened the Jaguar."

"Ah, ah!" he remarked, ironically, "So you know that, Señor Governor?"

"And a good many more things, as you shall see."

"Go on," he said, as he threw himself back with the graceful negligence of a friend on a visit.

"After giving a powerful organization to your revolt on the Indian border by seizing the Larch-tree hacienda, and allying yourself with certain Comanche and Apache tribes, you understood that, to succeed, you must give up that guerilla warfare, which I confess you had carried on for some time with considerable success." "Thanks," said the Jaguar, with an ironical bow.

"You therefore entrust the temporary command of your bands to one of your comrades, and yourself come into the heart of Texas, with your most faithful associates, in order to revolutionize the coast, and deal a great blow by seizing a seaport. Galveston, by its position at the mouth of the Trinidad river, is a strategical point of the utmost importance for your plans. For two months past you have been concealed in this house, which you have made the headquarters of your insurrection, and where you are making all the preparations for the audacious enterprise you wish to attempt. You have at your disposal numerous emissaries and faithful conspirators; the government of the United States supply you with abundance of arms and ammunition, which you think you will soon have need of. Your measures have been so well taken, and your machinations carried on with such great skill; you fancy yourself so nearly on the point of success, that hardly an hour back you convened here the principal members of your party, in order to give them their final instructions. Is it so? Am I correctly informed? Answer me, Caballero."

"What would you have me answer, Caballero," the young man said, with a delightful smile, "since you know all?"

"Then, you confess that you are the Jaguar, the Chief of the Freebooters!"

"Canarios, I should think so."

"You also allow that you came here with the intention of seizing the city?"

"Incontestably," the other said, with an air of mockery; "it does not allow the shadow of a doubt."

"Take care," the General remarked drily; "it is a much more serious matter than you seem to think."

"What the deuce would you have me do General? It is not my fault. You enter my house, without giving me notice, with a crowd of officers and soldiers; you surround my residence, carry it by storm, and when you have finished this pretty job worthy of an alguazil, without showing me the slightest scrap of paper authorising you to act in that way, you tell me to my face that I am the Chief of the bandits, a conspirator, and Lord knows what; and then you request me to prove it. On my faith! Any other in my place would act as I am doing; like me, he would bow to the weight of so great a military force and such an entire conviction. All this seems to me so extraordinary and novel, that I am beginning to doubt my own identity, and I ask myself if I have not been hitherto deceived in believing myself, Martin Gutierrez, the ranchero of Santa Aldegonida, in the State of Sonora, and if I am not, on the contrary, the ferocious Jaguar, of whom you speak to me, and for whom you do me the honour of taking me. I confess to you, General, that all this perplexes me in the highest degree, and I should feel greatly obliged if you would kindly bring me to some settled conviction."

"Then, Caballero, up to the present you have been jesting!" the General said hastily.

The Jaguar began laughing.

"*Cuerpo de Cristo,*" he replied. "I should think so. What else could I do in the face of such accusations? Discuss them with you? You know as well as I do, General, that it is useless to attempt to overthrow a conviction. Instead of telling me that I am the Jaguar, prove it to me, and then I will bow to the truth. That is very simple, it appears to me."

"Very simple, indeed, Caballero; I hope to be able soon to give you that certainty."

"Very good; but till then, I would observe that you entered my house in a way contrary to law, that the domicile of a citizen is inviolable, and that what you have done today, only a juez de letras, armed with a legal warrant, was empowered to do."

"You would possibly be correct, Caballero, if we lived in ordinary times; but at this moment such is no longer the case; the State is in a state of siege, the military power has taken the place of the civil authority, and alone has the right to command and have carried out those measures that relate to the maintenance of order."

The young man, while the General was speaking, had taken a side glance at the clock. When the governor ceased he rose, and bowing ceremoniously, said:

"To be brief, be kind enough, then, to explain to me categorically, and without further circumlocution, the motives for your presence in my house; we have been talking a long time and I have not yet been able to read your intentions. I should, therefore, feel obliged by your making them known to me without delay, as important business claims my presence abroad; and if you insist on staying here, I shall be compelled to leave you to yourselves."

"Oh, oh! You change your tone, I fancy, Caballero," the General said, with a little irony. "I will tell you the motives you desire to learn; as for your leaving the house without me or my sanction, which is the same thing, I fancy you would find it rather difficult."

"Which means, I presume, that you look upon me as a prisoner, General?"

"Nearly so, Caballero. When your house has been carefully searched, and we are convinced there is nothing suspicious in it, I may, perhaps, permit you to be put aboard a ship which will carry you far away from the territory of the Mexican Confederation."

"What! Without a warrant, by your mere will?"

"By my mere will: yes, Caballero."

"*Canarios*, Señor General, I see that your government has preserved the healthy Spanish traditions, and is deliciously arbitrary," the Jaguar said, mockingly; "the only question is whether I shall voluntarily submit to such treatment."

"You must have already perceived that force is not on your side, at least for the present."

"Oh, General, when a man has right on his side, force can soon be found."

"Try it, then, Caballero; but I warn you that it will be at your own risk and peril."

"Then you will employ force to coerce a single, unarmed man in his own house?"

"That is my intention."

"Oh! If that be so, I thank you, for you leave me free to act."

"What do you mean by that remark, Caballero?" the General asked, with a frown.

"What do you mean by yours, Señor Governor? I consider that all means are good to escape an arbitrary arrest, and that I shall employ them without the slightest hesitation."

"Try it," the officer said, ironically,

"When the moment for action arrives, I shall not wait for your permission to do so, General," the Jaguar replied, with equal sarcasm.

Although this was the first time General Rubio and the Jaguar had met, the Governor of Galveston had long been acquainted with the reputation of the man with whom he had to deal; he knew how fertile in resources his mind was, and the audacious temerity that formed the basis of his character; personally he owed him a grudge for carrying off the conducta de plata, and capturing the Larch-tree, hence he entertained a lively desire to take an exemplary revenge on his bold adventurer.

The tone in which the Jaguar uttered the last words caused the General a moment's anxiety; but after taking a glance round him, he was reassured. In fact, owing to the precautions taken by the old soldier, it seemed materially impossible that his prisoner could escape, for he was alone, unarmed, in a house surrounded by soldiers, and watched by several resolute officers; he, therefore, regarded his answer as bravado, and took no further notice of it.

"I absolve you beforehand," he said disdainfully, "for any efforts you may make to escape."

"I thank you, General," the Jaguar answered, with a ceremonious bow. "I expected nothing else from your courtesy; I make a note of your promise."

"Be it so. Now, with your permission we are about to commence our domiciliary visit."

"Do so, General, pray do so; if you desire it, I will myself act as your guide."

"In my turn I thank you for this obliging offer, but I do not wish to put your kindness to a trial; the more so, as I am thoroughly acquainted with this house."

"Do you think so, General?"

"Judge for yourself."

The Jaguar bowed without replying, and carelessly leant his elbow on the couch upon which the clock stood.

"We will first begin with this saloon," the General continued.

"You mean that you will finish with it," the young man remarked, with an ironical smile.

"Let us look first at the secret door in that wall."

"What! You know it then?"

"It seems so."

"Hang it all! You are better informed than I supposed."

"You do not know all yet."

"I hope so; judging from the commencement, I expect some extraordinary discoveries."

"Perhaps so. Will you make the spring work yourself, Caballero, or would you prefer my doing it?"

"On my word, General, I confess that all this interests me so hugely that, until fresh orders, I desire to remain a simple spectator, in order not to trouble my pleasure."

This continued irony produced an involuntary impression on the General; the calm and coldly mocking attitude of the young man troubled him in his heart; he feared a snare, without knowing when or how it would reveal itself.

"Pay attention, Caballero," he said in a menacing tone to the Jaguar; "I know for a fact that when I arrived you had a large party assembled here; on my entrance, your comrades fled by that door."

"That is true," the young man said with a nod of assent.

"Take care," the General continued, "that if assassins are hidden behind that door, the blood shed will fall on your head."

"General," the Jaguar said seriously, "press the spring, the passage is empty; I require no aid but my own to deliver myself from your clutches when I think proper."

The Governor no longer hesitated; he walked resolutely to the wall, and pressed the spring; his officers had followed him, ready to aid him if any danger presented itself. The Jaguar did not stir. The door opened, and displayed a long and completely deserted corridor.

"Well, General, have I kept my word?" the Jaguar said.

"Yes, Señor, I must concede it. Now, Caballeros," the General continued, addressing his officers, "draw swords, and forward!"

"One moment, if you please," said the Jaguar.

"What do you want, Señor?"

"You will remember that I warned you you would end your domiciliary visit with this room?"

"Well?"

"I will keep that second promise as I did the first."

At the same instant, and ere the General and his officers could account for what was happening, they felt the flooring give way beneath their feet, and they rolled to the bottom of a vault, of slight depth, it is true, but buried in the most intense gloom.

"A pleasant journey!" the Jaguar said with a laugh, as he closed the trap again.

CHAPTER XVII
THE SPY

While these events were occurring, the sun had set, and night almost immediately succeeded day. So soon as the Jaguar had closed the trap on his prisoners, he proceeded toward the masked door to rejoin his comrades; but a sound of footsteps he heard outside, made him change his plans; he shut the door again, and returned to his old position to await the newcomer. The latter did not delay long. Although the night was too dark to allow the Jaguar to recognise his features, by the sparkling of his gold lace, and the clank of his spurs and steel scabbard on the pavement, he saw that he was once more in the presence of a Mexican officer high in command. At the end of a moment, however, the Jaguar's eyes, gifted possibly with that precious quality possessed by animals of the feline race to see through the darkness, appeared to have recognised the stranger. The young man frowned, and gave a start of disappointment.

"Is there no one here?" the officer asked, as he stopped in the doorway with very excusable hesitation.

"Who are you, and what do you want?" the Jaguar answered, disguising his voice.

"That is a curious question," the officer continued, as he stepped forward with his hand on his sabre hilt; "first have this room lighted up, which looks like a cut-throat's den, and then we will talk."

"It is not necessary for what we have to say to each other, you can leave your sabre at rest; although this house is dark, it is no cut-throat den, as you seem to believe."

"What has become of General Rubio and the officers who accompanied him?"

"Am I their keeper, Colonel Melendez?" the Jaguar asked in a sarcastic tone.

"Who are you, who appear to know me and answer so strangely?"

"Perhaps a friend, vexed at seeing you here, and who would be glad were you elsewhere."

"A friend would not hide himself as you are doing."

"Why not, if circumstances compel him?"

"A truce to this exchange of puerile speeches; will you answer my question, yes or no?"

"Which question?"

"The one I asked you about the General."

"Suppose I refuse?"

"I shall know how to compel you."

"That is haughty language, Colonel."

"Which I shall support by deeds."

"I do not think so: not that I doubt your courage, Heaven forbid, for I have long known it."

"Well! What will prevent me?"

"You have not the means to carry out your wishes."

"They are easily found."

"Try it."

While speaking, the Colonel had mechanically taken a couple of steps into the room.

"I shall soon return," he said, as he laid his hand on the door latch.

The Jaguar only answered by a hoarse laugh. The door was closed, in vain did the Colonel try to open it; it resisted all his efforts.

"I am your prisoner, then?" he said, addressing the young man.

"Perhaps so; it will depend on yourself."

"You wish me to fall into the same snare into which the General and his officers probably fell before me. Try it, Señor; still I warn you that I am on my guard, and will defend myself."

"Your words are harsh, Colonel. You gratuitously insult a man of whom, up to the present, you have no cause to complain, and whom you will regret having attacked when you know him."

"Tell me the fate of my companions, and what your intentions are with regard to myself."

"My intentions are better than yours, Colonel; for, if you had me in your power, as I have you in mine, it is probable that your General, if not yourself, would make me pay dearly for the imprudence I have committed;

but enough of this, we have lost too much time already. General Rubio and his officers are my prisoners, and you feel in your heart that I can do what I please with you; withdraw the soldiers who surround my house, pledge me your word of honour that no attempt shall be made on me by the Mexican Government for four-and-twenty hours, and I will immediately restore you all to liberty."

"I know not who you are, Señor; the conditions you wish to impose on me are those a conqueror would offer to enemies reduced to impotence."

"What else are you at this moment?" the young man interrupted violently.

"Be it so; but I cannot take it on myself to accept or decline these conditions, as the General alone has the right to form a determination and pledge his word."

"Then, ask himself what his intentions are, and he will answer you."

"Is he here, then?" the Colonel exclaimed eagerly, as he moved a step forward.

"It is of little consequence to you where he is, provided he hear and answer you; do not stir from where you are; one step further, and you are a dead man; what is your resolve?"

"I accept."

"In that case speak to him."

The Jaguar worked the spring that opened the trap, and displayed the entrance of the vault into which the Mexican officers had been so suddenly hurled; but the darkness was so intense, that the Colonel could perceive nothing, in spite of his efforts to try and distinguish a gleam; he merely heard a slight sound produced by the grating of the trap in its groove. The Colonel understood that he must get out of the difficulty as well as he could.

"General," he said raising his voice, "can you hear me?"

"Who speaks?" the General answered immediately.

"I, Colonel Melendez de Gongora."

"Heaven be praised!" the General shouted; "in that case all goes well."

"On the contrary, all goes ill."

"What do you mean?"

"That, like yourself, I am in the hands of the accursed insurgents who have captured you."

"Mil Demonios!" the old soldier shouted angrily.

"Are you all right?"

"Bodily, yes; my officers and myself have received no wounds; I must confess that the demon who played us this trick was so far civil."

"Thanks, General," the Jaguar said in a tone of mockery.

"Ah, Salteador," the General exclaimed in a rage; "I swear by Heaven that we shall settle our accounts some day."

"I hope so too, General; but for the present, believe me, you had better listen to what Colonel Melendez has to say to you."

"I suppose I must," the Governor muttered. "Speak, Colonel," he added aloud.

"General, we are offered our liberty on condition," the Colonel immediately replied, "that we pledge our word of honour to attempt nothing against the man whose prisoner we are."

"Or against his adherents, whoever they may be," the Jaguar interrupted.

"Be it so, or against his adherents, during the next twenty-four hours, and that the house shall be left free."

"Hum:" said the General, "that requires reflection."

"I give you five minutes."

"Demonios! That is very short; you are not at all generous."

"It is impossible for me to grant a longer period."

"And suppose I refuse?"

"You will not do so,"

"For what reason?"

"Because you are furious with me, and hope to avenge yourself some day."

"Excellently reasoned; but supposing I *do* refuse?"

"In that case, I will treat you and yours exactly as you intended to treat me and mine."

"That is to say?"

"You will be all shot within a quarter of an hour."

There was a mournful silence. No other sound could be heard but the dry and monotonous one produced by the escapement of the clock. These men, collected without seeing each other, in so narrow a space, felt their hearts beat as if to burst their chests; they trembled with impotent rage, for they recognised that they were really in the hands of an implacable foe, against whom any struggle was mad, if not impossible.

"Viva Dios!" the Colonel shouted; "better to die than surrender thus!"

And he rushed forward with uplifted sabre. Suddenly a hand of iron clutched him, threw him down, and he felt the point of his own sword, which he had let fall, slightly prick his throat.

"Surrender, or you are a dead man," a rough voice shouted in his ear.

"No; mil Demonios!" the Colonel said, furiously; "I will not surrender to a bandit; kill me."

"Stop," the Jaguar said, "I insist."

The man who held the Colonel down left him at liberty, and the latter rose, ashamed and partly stunned.

"Well," the young man continued, "do you accept, General?"

"Yes, demon," the latter replied passionately; "but I shall revenge myself."

"Then, you give me your word as a soldier that the conditions I impose on you will be legally carried out by you?"

"I give it; but who guarantees me that you will act honourably on your side?"

"My honour, Señor General," the Jaguar answered, proudly; "my honour, which, as you know, is as unsullied as your own."

"Very good, Señor, I trust to you as you do to me. Must we surrender our swords?"

"General," the Jaguar answered nobly, "a brave soldier never separates from his weapons; I should blush to deprive you of yours. Your companions, like yourself, can keep their swords."

"Thanks for that courtesy, Caballero, for it proves to me that every good feeling is not dead in your heart. Now I am waiting for you to supply me with the means for leaving the place into which you made me fall so skilfully."

"You shall be satisfied, Señor General. As for you, Colonel, you can retire, for the door is now open."

"Not before I have seen you," the officer answered.

"What good would that do, since you have not recognised me?" the young man said, reassuming his natural voice.

"The Jaguar!" the Colonel ejaculated in surprise.

"Ah! I might have expected that; I shall certainly remain now," he added, with a singular inflection in his voice.

"Very good," said the Chief, "remain."

He clapped his hands, and four peons entered with lighted candelabra. So soon as the saloon was lit up, the young officer perceived the General and his aides-de-camp standing up in the vault. A criado brought a ladder to the trap, and the Mexicans ascended—half-pleased, half-ashamed.

"Gentlemen," the insurgent continued, "you are free. Any other in my place would, doubtless, have profited by the bad position in which you were, to impose on you conditions far harder than those I demanded of you; but I only understand a fair fight, steel against steel, chest against chest. Go in peace, but take care, for hostilities have begun between us, and the war will be rude."

"One word before separating," said the General.

"I listen, Caballero."

"Whatever may be the circumstances under which we may meet at a later date, I shall not forget your conduct of this day."

"I dispense you from any gratitude on that account, General; the more so, because if I acted thus it was for reasons entirely strange to you."

"Whatever be the motive of your conduct, my honour urges me to remember your conduct."

"As you please; I only ask you to remember our conditions."

"They shall be punctually carried out."

The Jaguar, upon this, bowed to the General; the latter returned his salute, and, making a sign to his officers to follow him, left the room. The young Chief listened attentively to the sound of the retiring footsteps, and then drew himself up.

"What!" he exclaimed with surprise, on perceiving the Colonel, "are you still here, Señor Don Juan?"

"Yes, brother," the latter answered, in a sad voice, "I am still here."

The Jaguar walked rapidly up to him, and took his hand.

"What have you to say to me, brother?—have you a fresh misfortune to announce?"

"Alas, friend, what greater misfortune could I tell you of than that which, by ruining our dearest hopes, has plunged us into despair?"

"Have you received news of our friends?"

"None."

"Tranquil?"

"I know not what has become of him."

"Loyal Heart?"

"Has also disappeared."

"Listen, brother, this situation cannot endure long; whatever happens, it must cease. Time fails me at this moment to explain to you certain matters you ought to know; but we will meet tomorrow."

"Where, and at what hour?"

"At the Salto del Frayle, at two in the afternoon."

"Why so far and so late, brother?"

"Because between this and then something will happen, which I cannot tell you at present, but which will doubtless oblige me to cross the bay and seek shelter on the mainland."

"I have no right to ask you for an explanation, brother; but take care. Whatever you may attempt, you will have to deal with a rude adversary; the General is furious against you; he has his revenge to take; and if you furnish him with the opportunity, he will not let it slip."

"I am convinced of it, friend, but the die is cast; unfortunately, we follow different roads. Heaven will help the good cause. Your hand once more, and good-bye."

"Good-bye, brother, and it is settled that we meet tomorrow."

"Death alone can prevent me being at the place of meeting I have selected."

The two political enemies, so cordially attached, shook hands and separated. The Colonel wrapped himself in his cloak, and immediately left the room and the house. The General, as he went away, had given the company posted round the mansion orders to follow him, and the street was completely deserted. The Jaguar was so intimately convinced of the fidelity with which General Rubio would fulfil his engagements, that he did not even take the trouble to assure himself of the fact.

So soon as he was alone he closed the trapdoor, touched the spring of the secret door, and left the saloon in his turn, to enter the dark corridor through which, on the General's entrance, his friends had disappeared at the heels of John Davis. This passage, after several turnings, opened into a rather large room, in which all the conspirators were assembled, silent and gloomy, waiting, with their hands on their weapons, till the Chief claimed their assistance.

Lanzi was standing sentry in the doorway, to prevent any surprise: the Jaguar resumed his mask, thrust his pistols in his girdle, and entered. On seeing him, the conspirators gave a start of joy, which was immediately suppressed, however, at a signal from the young man.

"My comrades," he said, in a saddened voice, "I have evil tidings to communicate to you. Had not my measures been so well taken, we should all have been prisoners at this moment. A traitor has slipped in among us, and this man has given the Governor the most detailed and positive information about our projects. A miracle has alone saved us."

A shudder of indignation ran through the ranks of the conspirators; by an instinctive movement they separated, giving each other sinister glances, and laying their hands on their weapons. The vast hall, only lighted by a smoky lamp, whose reddish light threw strange reflections at each breath of air on the energetic faces of the conspirators, had a mournful, and yet striking aspect. After a moment's silence the Chief went on, in a firm and marked voice—

"What matter, comrades, if a cowardly spy has stepped in among us; the hour of fear and hesitation has passed away, and we shall now go to work in the sight of all. No more secret meetings, no more masks," he added, violently tearing off his own and trampling it under foot; "our enemies must know us at length, and learn that we are really the apostles of that liberty which is about to gleam like a brilliant beacon over our country."

"Long live the Jaguar!" the conspirators shouted as they rushed joyfully towards him.

"Yes, the Jaguar," he continued in a thundering voice, "the Chief of the Freebooters, the first man in Texas who dared to rise against our oppressors; the Jaguar, who has sworn to make you free, and who will keep his oath, unless death prevent him; now let the coward who has sold us complete his work by revealing my name to the Governor, who has already almost divined it, and will be happy to acquire the certainty at last. This final denunciation will assuredly be paid highly, but he must make haste, for tomorrow will be too late."

At this moment a man burst through the conspirators, thrusting back right and left those who barred his passage, and placed himself opposite the young Chief.

"Listen," he said, turning to his comrades, "and let what you are about to hear form a profitable lesson to you: — The man who revealed the secret of your meetings to the Governor, the man who sold you, the man, in a word, who wished to give you up, I know!"

"His name, his name!" all the conspirators shouted, brandishing their weapons passionately.

"Silence!" the Jaguar ordered, "allow our comrade to speak."

"Do not give me that name, Jaguar, for I am not your comrade, and never was such. I am your enemy, not your personal enemy, for I do not know you; but the enemy of every man who tries to tear from the Mexican Republic that Texas where I was born, and which is the most brilliant gem of the union. It was I, I alone who sold you, I, Lopez Hidalgo D'Avila, but not in the cowardly way you suppose, for when the moment arrived for me to make myself known to you, I had sworn to do so; now you know all, and I am in your power. There are my weapons," he added, as he threw them disdainfully on the ground; "I shall not resist, and you can do with me as you please."

After uttering these words with a haughty accent impossible to render, Don Lopez Hidalgo proudly crossed his arms on his chest, drew up his head, and waited. The conspirators had listened to this strange revelation with an indignation and rage that attained such a pitch of violence that their will was, so to speak, paralyzed, and in spite of themselves they remained motionless. But so soon as Don Lopez had finished speaking, their feelings suddenly burst out, and they rushed upon him with tiger yells.

"Stay, stay!" the Jaguar shouted, as he rushed forward and made of his own person a rampart for the man on whom twenty daggers were lifted; "Stay, brothers; as this man has said, he is in our power, and cannot escape us; although his blood be that of a traitor, let us not commit an assassination, but try him."

"Yes, yes," the conspirators yelled, "let us try him."

"Silence," the Jaguar ordered, and then turning to Don Lopez Hidalgo, who during their proceedings had remained as calm and quiet as if he were a stranger to what was going on; "will you answer frankly the questions I ask you?" he inquired.

"Yes," Don Lopez simply replied.

"Was it pure love of your country, as you call it, that urged you to pretend to be one of us in order to betray us more securely, or was it not rather the hope of a rich reward that impelled you to the infamous action of which you have been guilty?"

The Mexican shrugged his shoulders with disdain.

"I am as rich as the whole of you put together," he replied; "who does not know the wealthy Don Lopez Hidalgo d'Avila?"

"That is true," one of the company remarked; "this man, I am bound to allow, for I have been acquainted with him for many years, does not know the amount of his fortune."

The Jaguar's forehead was wrinkled by the effect of a little thought.

"Then, that noble and revered feeling, the love of one's country, instead of elevating your soul and making generous feeling spring up in it," he continued, "has made you a coward. Instead of fighting honestly and loyally in the daylight against us, you followed the gloomy path of espial to betray us, and assumed the mask of friendship to sell us."

"I only picked up the weapon yourselves offered me. Did you fight, pray, in the open day? No, you conspired craftily in the darkness; like the mole, you dug the underground mine that was to swallow us up, and I countermined you. But what use is discussion? for you will no more comprehend my assertions than I can yours. Now to the business, for I am convinced that is the only point on which we shall agree."

"One moment, Don Lopez; explain to me the reason why, when no suspicion pointed to you, when no one thought of asking you to account for your actions, you denounced yourself and trusted to our mercy:"

"Although unseen, I overheard what passed between you and your Governor," the Mexican coldly answered; "I saw in what way the perilous position in which I had succeeded in placing you turned to your advantage; I understood that all was lost, and did not wish to survive our defeat."

"Then you know the conditions I imposed on General Rubio?"

"And which he was constrained to accept. Yes, I know them; I am aware, also, that you are too clever and determined a man not to profit by the twenty-four hours' respite which you have so adroitly gained; then I despaired of the cause I was defending."

"Good! Don Lopez, that is all I wished to know. When you entered our association you accepted all the laws?"

"I did so."

"You are aware that you have deserved death?"

"I know it and desire it."

The Jaguar turned to the conspirators, who had listened, panting with fury and impatience, to this singular dialogue.

"Brothers," he said, "you have heard all that passed between Don Lopez Hidalgo d'Avila and myself?"

"Yes," they answered.

"On your soul and conscience, is this man guilty?"

"He is guilty," they burst forth.

"What punishment does he deserve?"

"Death!"

"You hear, Don Lopez; your brethren condemn you to die."

"I thank them; that favour is the only one I hoped and desired to receive from them."

There was a moment of supreme silence; all eyes were fixed on the Jaguar, who, with his head hanging on his breast, and frowning brows, seemed plunged in serious thought. Suddenly the young man raised his head; a lightning glance flashed from his eyes, a strange smile curled his lip, and he said, with a tone of bitter irony —

"Your brethren have condemned you to die; well, I, their Chief, condemn you to live!"

Don Lopez, despite all his courage, felt himself turn pale at these cutting words; he instinctively stooped to pick up the weapons he had previously hurled at his feet; but the Jaguar guessed his thoughts.

"Seize that man!" he shouted.

John Davis and two or three other conspirators rushed on the Mexican, and, in spite of his active resistance, soon rendered him powerless.

"Bind him," the Jaguar next ordered.

This command was immediately carried out.

"Now, listen to me, brothers," the Jaguar continued, in a loud voice — "the task we have taken on ourselves is immense, and studded with perils and difficulties of every description; we are no longer men but lions, and those who fall into our power must eternally bear the mark of our powerful claws. What this man has done for an object honourable in his eyes, another might be tempted to do to satisfy a sordid passion. Death is only the end of life, a moment to endure; many men desire it, through weariness or disgust. Don Lopez has himself told us that he wished to give us a profitable lesson; and he is not mistaken, for we shall profit by it. In killing him we should but accomplish his dearest wish, as himself said: let him live, as we desire to punish him, but let that life he retains be such a burden to him, and so miserable, that he may for ever regret not having fallen beneath our daggers; this man is young, handsome, rich, and honoured by his fellow citizens; let us deprive him, not of his riches, for that is not in our power, but of his beauty, that flower of youth of which he is so proud, and make him the most wretched and despicable being in creation. In that way our vengeance will be complete; we shall have attained our object by imprinting a just terror on the hearts of those who may be tempted hereafter to follow his example."

The conspirators, despite all their resolution and ferocity, experienced a secret terror on hearing the savage words of their chief, whose gloomy countenance reflected a terrible energy.

"Don Lopez Hidalgo d'Avila," the Jaguar continued, in a hollow voice, "traitor to your brothers, your false tongue will be plucked out and your ears cut off. Such is the sentence which I, the Chief of the Freebooters, pass on you; and in order that everybody may know that you are a traitor, a T will be cut on your forehead between your eyebrows."

This sentence caused a momentary stupor among the company; but soon a tiger-like yell burst from all their panting chests, and it was with a tremor of ferocious joy that these men prepared to carry out the atrocious sentence pronounced by their Chief. The prisoner struggled in vain to burst the bonds that held him. In vain he demanded death with loud cries. As the Jaguar had said, the lion's paw was on him; the conspirators were inexorable, and the sentence was carried, out in all its rigour.

An hour later, Don Lopcz Hidalgo d'Avila, bleeding and mutilated, was deposited at the door of the Governor's palace. On his chest was fastened a large placard, on which were written in blood the two words:

COBARDE! TRAIDOR!

After this fearful execution, the conspirators continued their meeting as if nothing extraordinary had interrupted them. But the Jaguar's revenge was foiled—at least partially; for when the unhappy victim was picked up at daybreak he was dead. Don Lopez had found the strength and courage to dash out his brains against the wall of the house near which he had been thrown as an unclean animal.

CHAPTER XVIII
THE PULQUERIA

The same day on which we resume our narrative, on the firing of the cannon from the fort that commands the entrance to the port of Galveston, to announce the setting of the sun, whose glowing disk had just disappeared in the sea, colouring the horizon with a ruddy hue for a long distance, the town, which had, during the day, been plunged into a mournful torpor owing to the heat, woke up all at once with lengthened and joyous clamour.

The streets, hitherto solitary, were peopled as if by enchantment by an immense crowd, which emerged in disorder from all the houses, so eager were they to breathe the fresh air of evening which the sea breeze brought up on its humid wing; the shops were opened, and lit up with an infinite number of coloured paper lamps. Ere long there was in this town, where, scarce an hour earlier, such silence and solitude prevailed, a medley of individuals of all classes and countries—English, Spaniards, Americans, Mexicans, French, Russians, Chinese—all dressed in their national costume: women, coquettishly wrapped in their rebozos, darting to the right and left provocative glances; perambulating tradesmen vaunting their merchandise, and serenos, armed to the teeth, trying to maintain good order. And all this crowd came and went, and stopped,—pushing and elbowing and laughing, singing, shouting, and quarrelling, making the dogs bark and the children cry.

Two young gentlemen, dressed in the simple but graceful uniform of officers of the United States Navy, who were coming from the interior of the town, forced their way with some difficulty through the crowd that impeded their every step on the port, as they proceeded toward the pier, where a large number of boats of all shapes and sizes were tied up. They had scarce reached the landing place ere they were surrounded by some twenty boatmen, who offered their services, while exaggerating in their praiseworthy fashion the surprising qualities and unparalleled speed of their boats, doing so in the bastard patois which belongs to no language, but is formed of words culled haphazard from all, and by means of which, in every seaport, the people of the country and strangers contrive to understand each other, and which is called in the Scales of the Levant the linguafranca.

After giving a careless glance at the numerous skiffs dancing before them, the officers abruptly dismissed the boatmen by peremptorily declining their services; but they did not get rid of them till they had told them they had a boat of their own, and scattered some small change among them. The boatmen withdrew, half vexed, half satisfied, and the officers were at length left alone on the jetty.

We have said that the sun had set for some time, and hence the night was gloomy. Still, the two officers, in order, doubtless, to assure themselves that the darkness concealed no spy, walked several times up and down the jetty, while conversing together in a low voice, and examining with the most scrupulous attention those spots which might have afforded shelter to anyone. They were certainly alone. One of them then drew from his breast one of those silver whistles, such as boatswains employ on board ships, and then produced a soft and prolonged note thrice repeated. A few moments passed, and nothing proved to the officers that their signal had been heard. At last, a soft whistle traversed the air and expired on the ears of the two men who were listening, with bodies bent forward and faces turned to the sea.

"They are coming," said one.

"We will wait," his comrade answered laconically.

They carefully wrapped themselves in their cloaks to guard themselves against the damp sea breeze; they leant against an old gun that served to tie boats up, and remained motionless as statues, without exchanging a syllable. A few minutes passed thus; the darkness grew gradually denser; the noises of the town insensibly died out, and the promenaders, driven away by the coolness of the night, quitted the seashore for the interior of the town. The beach was soon completely deserted—the two officers alone remained leaning against the gun.

At length a remote sound, scarcely perceptible, but which practised ears could recognise, rose from the sea. This sound became gradually more and more distinct; and it was easy, especially for sailors, to recognise the sharp and cadenced sound of oars striking against the tholes and dipping into the sea; although these oars, judging from the sound, were muffled, and employed with the utmost caution.

In fact, the boat itself ere long became visible. Its long black outline stood out in the luminous line traced by the moon on the waves, as it approached the jetty at great speed. The two officers had bent forward curiously, but did not leave the post of observation they had selected. On coming within pistol-shot, the boat stopped. Suddenly, a rough voice, lowered prudently, however, rose in the silence, singing the first verse of a song well known in these parts:

> ¿Qué rumor
> Lejos suena,
> Qué el silencio
> En la serena
> Negra noche interrumpió?[1]

The man who was singing had scarce finished these five lines ere one of the officers took up the song in a sonorous voice; doubtless, replying to the signal made him by the steerer of the boat:

> ¿Es del caballo la veloz carrera,
> Tendido en el escape volador,
> O el aspero rugir de hambrienta fiera,
> O el silbido tal vez del aquilon?[2]

There was a delay of a few seconds, during which no other sound was audible save the monotonous break of the waves as they died away on the beach, or the distant twanging of some jarabés or vihuelas, playing those seguedillas and tyranas so dear to all peoples of the Spanish race. At length, the voice which first struck up the song continued, but this time with an intonation approaching to a threat, although the man who spoke did not appear to be addressing anyone in particular.

"The night is dark, it is imprudent to wander haphazard on the seashore."

"Yes, when a man is alone, and feels his heart die out in his bosom," the officer who had sung answered immediately.

"Who can flatter himself with possessing a firm heart?" the voice went on.

"The man whose arm is ever ready to support his words for the defence of a good cause," the other at once replied.

"Come, come," the sailor exclaimed, gaily, addressing his companions this time; "lay on your oars, lads, the Jaguars are out hunting."

"Take care of the coyotes," the officer said again.

The boat pulled up alongside the jetty; the officers had by this time left their place of shelter, and hurried to the end of the jetty. There a man, dressed in sailor's garb, with an oilskin souwester, whose large brim concealed his features, was standing motionless, with a pistol in either hand.

"Patria!" he said, sharply, when the officers were only two paces from him.

"Libertad!" they answered, without hesitation.

"Viva Dios!" the sailor said, as he returned his pistols to the leather belt that passed round his hips; "It is a good wind that brings you, Don Serapio, and you too, Don Cristoval."

"All the better, Ramirez," said the officer addressed as Serapio.

"Have you any news, then?" his comrade asked, curiously.

"Excellent, Don Cristoval, excellent," Ramirez answered, as he rubbed his hands gleefully.

"Oh, oh!" the two officers muttered, as they exchanged a glance of satisfaction; "Tell us it, then, Ramirez."

The latter took a suspicious glance around.

"I should like to do so," he said, "but the place where we are does not seem at all propitious for a conversation of the nature of the one we have before us."

"That is true," said Don Serapio; "but what prevents us getting into your boat? There we can talk at ease."

But Ramirez shook his head.

"Yes," he said; "but then we should have to push off; and I am no more anxious than I presume you to be, to be discovered and hailed by some guard boat."

"That is true," Don Cristoval objected; "we must find other and less perilous means for conversing, without fear of indiscreet ears."

"What o'clock is it?" Ramirez asked.

Don Serapio struck his repeater.

"Just ten," he answered.

"Good: in that case we have time, since the affair does not come off till midnight. Follow me. I know a pulqueria where we shall be as safe as on the top of the Coffre de Perote."

"But the boat?" Don Cristoval objected.

"Be at your ease—it is commanded by Lucas. However clever the Mexicans may be, he is the man to play at hide and seek with them for the entire night; besides, he has my instructions."

The officers bowed, but made no further remark. The three men then set out, Ramirez walking a few paces in advance of his companions. Although the night was so dark that it was impossible to distinguish objects ten paces off, the sailor proceeded through the narrow and winding streets of the town with as much certainty and ease as if traversing it in broad daylight, in the bright sunshine.

Close to the Cabildo, at the corner of the Plaza Mayor, stood a species of cabin, built of ships' planks, clumsily nailed together, which offered, in the stifling midday hours, a precarious shelter to the leperos and idlers of all sorts, who collected there to smoke, drink mezcal, or play at monte, that game so beloved by Spanish-Americans of all classes.

The interior of this suspicious rancho, honoured with the name of pulqueria, corresponded perfectly with the miserable aspect of the exterior. In a large room, only lighted by the dubious gleam of a smoky candle, a number of individuals, with ferocious countenances, dressed in filthy rags, and armed to the teeth, were collected round a few planks laid across empty barrels, and serving as a table. These men were drinking, and playing with that Mexican coolness which no event, however serious it may be, succeeds in disturbing, and staking piles of gold, which they drew from their patched calzoneras.

It was in front of this unclean pothouse, from the broken door of which escaped a reddish steam, laden with pestilential emanations, that Ramirez stopped.

"Where the deuce are you taking us?" Don Serapio asked him, with an expression of disgust he could not master at the repulsive appearance of this den.

The sailor laid a finger on his lip.

"Silence!" he said, "You shall know. Wait for me here an instant, but be careful to keep in the shade, so as not to be seen; the customers of this honest establishment have such numerous reasons to distrust spies, that if they saw you suddenly appear among them, they might be capable of playing you a trick."

"Why enter such a den as this?"

Ramirez smiled craftily.

"Do you fancy, then," he said, "that if I had only some news to tell you, I should have brought you here?"

"Why else, then?"

"You will soon know; but I can tell you nothing at this moment."

"Go on, then, as it is so; still, I beg you not to keep us too long at the door of this disgusting house."

"All right, I will only go in and come out again."

Then, after again recommending the officers to be prudent, he pushed the door of the pulqueria, which at once opened, and he went in. In the darkest corner of the room two men, almost completely hidden by the dense cloud of smoke that rose over the heads of the gamblers, carefully wrapped in their zarapés of Indian manufacture, with the brim of their hats pulled down over their eyes (a very needless precaution in the darkness where they were), and leaning on their long rifles, whose butts rested on the floor of the room, were whispering in each other's ear, while taking, at intervals, anxious glances at the leperos assembled a few paces from them.

The gamblers, fully engaged, did not dream of watching the strangers, who, however, from their martial demeanour, and the cleanliness of their attire, formed a striking contrast to them, and evidently did not belong to the company that usually assembled at this rancho; hence the strangers had very unnecessarily taken their precautions to escape from inquisitive looks, supposing such were their object.

Eleven o'clock struck from the Cabildo; at the same moment a form appeared in the doorway. This man stopped, took a sharp glance round the room, and then, after a slight hesitation, doubtless caused by the difficulty of recognizing in the crowd the persons he wished to see, he entered the rancho, and walked hastily toward the strangers. The latter turned at the sound of his footsteps, and gave a start of joy on recognizing him. We need hardly say that it was Ramirez. The three men shook hands with an expression of pleasure which proved that with them it was not a mere act of politeness, such as are so greatly abused in what is called the civilized life of towns.

"Well," Ramirez asked, "what have you done?"

"Nothing," one of the men answered, "we were waiting for you."

"And those scoundrels?"

"Are already more than three parts ruined,"

"All the better; they will march with greater impetuosity."

"They must soon see the bottom of their purses."

"Do you think so?"

"I am sure of it; they have been playing since eight in the morning, so the pulquero says."

"Without leaving off?" the sailor said, in surprise.

"They have not ceased for an instant."

"All the better."

"By the bye," one of the strangers remarked, "have you come alone? Where are the men you promised to bring?"

"They are here, and you will see them in a moment."

"Very good. Then it is still for this night?"

"You must know that better than I."

"On my honour, no."

"Then you have not seen him?"

"Seen who?"

"Why, *him*."

"No."

"Hang it all! That is annoying,"

"I did not require to see him,"

"But it is different with me."

"Why so?"

"Because I have executed his orders, as they are with me."

"That is true."

"Viva Dios! I was obliged to employ stratagem to induce them to follow me here."

"Why did you not bring them in at once?"

"I should be very sorry to do so, at least for the present. They are cool and steady naval officers, whose smile, under all circumstances, resembles a grimace, so close do they keep their lips. The free-and-easy manner of our worthy associates," he added, "might possibly displease them."

"But when the master arrives?"

"Oh, then the affair will rest with him alone."

At the same moment a sharp whistle was heard outside, and the gamblers sprang up as if they had received an electric shock. Ramirez bent down to the two men.

"Here he is," he said; "I shall be back directly."

"Where are you going?" one of the strangers asked, sharply.

"To join those who are waiting for me."

And winding through the groups, the sailor left the pulqueria unnoticed. Ramirez had hardly left the room, ere the door was burst open by a violent blow, and a man rushed in. All present took off their hats, as if by common agreement, and bowed respectfully.

We will give, in a few words, a portrait of this new personage, who is destined to play a most important part in this narrative. The stranger seemed to be twenty, or two-and-twenty at the most, though he was probably older; he was slim and delicate, but perfectly proportioned, and all his movements were marked by indescribable grace and nobility. His beardless face was surrounded by magnificent black ringlets, which escaped in profusion from under his hat, and fell in large clusters on his shoulders.

This man had a lofty and wide forehead, intelligent and pensive, and a deep and well-opened eye, an aquiline nose with flexible nostrils, and a disdainful and mocking lip. All his features made up a strange, but commanding countenance. He might be loved, but he must be feared. His feet and hands were small, and evidenced good breeding. Dressed in the picturesque costume of Mexican campesinos, he wore his rich clothes with inimitable grace and ease.

Who was he?

His best friends, and he counted many such among the men in whose midst he had suddenly appeared, could not say.

In America, especially at the period when our story is laid, it was the easiest thing in the world to conceal one's private existence: an intelligent man suddenly revealed himself, no one caring, whence he came or whither he went—a brilliant meteor, he traced a luminous line on the chaos of the revolutionary struggle, which he illumined by the strange flashes of his extraordinary deeds. Then this man—this unknown hero disappeared as suddenly as he had arisen: night closed in round him, the darkness grew denser and denser, and an impenetrable mystery brooded over his birth and his grave.

The stranger was one of these men. He and the Jaguar were thus placed in an identical situation in the eyes of their partisans; but men live so quickly when the hour for the supreme struggle has struck, that no one attempted to pierce the gloom, and obtain the secret of these two young Chieftains.

The man with whom we are now engaged was commonly called El Alferez by his friends and enemies. This word, which in Spanish literally signifies sub-lieutenant, had become the name of this singular person, which he had accepted, and to which he answered.

Why had this strangely selected title been given him? This question, or any other, it is impossible for us to answer—at any rate, for the present.

After taking a haughty and assured glance at the persons collected in disorderly groups around him, the young man leant against a barrel, and, with affected carelessness, said to the individuals who surrounded him— "Well, my scamps, have you amused yourselves properly?"

A murmur of general satisfaction ran along the ranks.

"Good, my coyotes," he continued, with the same mocking tone; "now, I suppose, you would like to smell a little blood?"

"Yes," these sinister persons answered unanimously.

"Well, console yourselves; I will let you smell it ere long, and in a satisfactory manner. But I do not see Ramirez among you; can he have been so awkward as to get himself hung? Although he has deserved it a long time. I do not think him such a fool as to let himself be apprehended by the spies of the Mexican Government."

These words were uttered in a soft voice, harmoniously modulated, but at the same time sharp and rather shrill.

"I heard my name," said Ramirez, as he appeared in the doorway.

"Yes, I mentioned it. Well, are you alone?"

"No."

"Are they both here?"

"Both."

"That is excellent. Now, if the Jaguar be as true to his word as I am to mine, I answer for success."

"I hold your promise, Señor Alferez," said a man who had entered the room some moments previously.

"Rayo de Dios! You and your comrades are welcome; for, of course, you are not alone."

"I have twenty men, worth a hundred."

"Bravo! I recognise the Jaguar in that."

The latter began laughing.

"They only await a signal from me to come in."

"Let them come, let them come; time is precious, so let us not waste it in trifling."

The Jaguar walked to the door, and threw away the lighted cigarette he held in his hand. The twenty conspirators entered, and ranged themselves silently behind their Chief. Ramirez came in immediately after, followed by the two naval officers.

"All is clearly understood between us, Jaguar?"

"All."

"We act toward each other with all frankness and honesty of purpose?"

"Yes."

"You swear it?"

"Without hesitation, I swear it."

"Thanks, my friend. On my side I swear to be a faithful comrade."

"How many men have you?"

"As you see, thirty."

"Who, added to the twenty I bring, give the respectable amount of fifty men; if the affair be properly managed, they are more than we require."

"Now, let us divide our parts."

"Nothing is changed, I think; I will surprise the fort, while you board the corvette."

"Agreed; where are the guides?"

"Here," the two men said, with whom Ramirez conversed when he entered the pulqueria the first time. El Alferez examined them attentively for some minutes, and then turned to the Jaguar.

"You can start, I fancy."

"How many men do you keep with you?"

"Take them all; I will only keep Ramirez and the two persons to whom he has to introduce me."

"That is true," said the sailor.

"Come, my coyotes," El Alferez continued, "follow your new Chief. I place you temporarily under the orders of the Jaguar, to whom I surrender all my claims upon you."

The men bowed, but made no reply.

"And now, brothers," the young man continued, "remember that you are about to fight for the liberty of your country, and that the man who commands you will not grudge his life for the success of the daring stroke he is about to attempt with your aid; that ought to render you invincible. Go."

"Do not forget the signal—one rocket, if we fail."

"Three, if we succeed; and we shall do so, brother."

"May Heaven grant it."

"Till we meet again."

The two men shook hands, and the Jaguar quitted the pulqueria, followed by these savage men, who marched silently behind him, like wild beasts going in quest of prey. Ere long, none remained in the room but the two naval officers, Ramirez, and the pulquero, who, with eyes dilated by terror, looked at and listened to all this, without understanding anything. El Alferez remained motionless, with his body bent forward, so long as it was possible for him to hear the slightest sound of retiring footsteps; when all had become silent again, he drew himself up, and turned to his comrades, who were as attentive as himself.

"May Heaven favour us!" he said, as he piously crossed himself. "Now, Caballeros, it is our turn."

"We are ready," the three men answered.

El Alferez took a rapid glance round the room. The pulquero, either through curiosity, want of occupation, or some other cause, was standing motionless in a distant corner of the room, following with an attentive glance the movements of his singular customers.

"Hilloh!" El Alferez said to him, "come hither."

The pulquero obsequiously doffed his straw hat, and hastened to obey this injunction, which admitted of no reply.

"What do you desire, Excellency?" he asked.

"To ask you a question."

"Pray do so."

"Are you fond of money?

"Well, tolerably so, Excellency," he replied, with a crafty grimace, which doubtless had pretensions to be a smile.

"Very good, here is an onza: when we go away, we will give you a second; but bear in mind that you must be deaf and blind."

"That is easy," he replied, as he pocketed the gold coin, and drew aside.

Since the Jaguar's departure, the two officers had been suffering from an anxiety they did not attempt to conceal, but which El Alferez did not appear to notice, for his face was quite radiant. In fact, the expedition they were going to attempt in the company of the daring partisan seemed to them not only rash but mad, especially since El Alferez had so cavalierly given up to the Jaguar the thirty resolute men, whose support they considered indispensable.

"Come, come, Señors," the young man said, with a smile, after attentively watching them for some moments, "regain your courage; hang it all, you look as if you had been buried and dug up again; and we are not dead yet, I suppose."

"That is true; but we are not much better," Don Serapio said significantly.

El Alferez frowned. "Can you be frightened?" he said, haughtily.

"We are not afraid of dying, but only of failing."

"That is my business: I answer for success on my head."

"We are perfectly aware of what you are capable, Señor; but we are only four men, and after all— —"

"And the boat's crew?"

"That is true; but they are only sixteen men."

"They will be enough."

"I wish it, but can hardly reckon on it."

"Well, say whether you are resolved to obey me at all hazards?"

"We have made the sacrifice of our lives."

"Then, whatever happens, you will act?"

"Whatever happens."

"It is well—"

El Alferez appeared to reflect for a moment, and then addressed the pulquero, who was standing anxiously near him—"Has anything been left with you for me?" he asked him.

"Yes, Excellency; this evening at Oración a man brought a trunk on his shoulders."

"Where is it?"

"As the man assured me that it contained articles of considerable value, I had the chest placed in my bedroom, in order that it might be in safety."

"Lead me to your room."

"Whenever you please, Excellency."

"Señors," El Alferez said, addressing the two naval officers and Ramirez, "wait for me in this room; in ten minutes I will join you again."

And without awaiting a reply, he made a sign to the pulquero to lead the way, and left the room with a rapid step. There was a momentary silence with the three men; they seemed to be engaged in sad thoughts, and looked anxiously around them. Time, which never stands still, had rapidly advanced during the course of the events we have narrated. Nearly the whole night had passed away, the first gleams of dawn were beginning to whiten the smoky walls of the pulqueria, and already some inhabitants, who had risen earlier than the others, were venturing into the streets; ere long the sun would make its appearance.

"Day will soon be here," Don Serapio remarked, as he shook his head anxiously.

"What matter?" Ramirez answered.

"What matter, do you say?" Don Serapio replied in amazement; "but it seems to me that one of the most important conditions for the enterprise we are about to attempt, is darkness."

"Certainly," Don Cristoval supported him, "if we wait till the sun has risen, any surprise will be impossible."

Ramirez shrugged his shoulders.

"You do not know the man under whose orders you have voluntarily placed yourselves," he answered; "impossible things are those he prefers attempting."

"You know him better than we do then, as you speak thus of him?"

"Better than you or anyone," the sailor said with considerable animation; "I have the greatest faith in him; for ten years I have lived by his side, and have many times been able to appreciate all the nobility and generosity that exist in his heart."

"Ah," the two officers said, walking quickly up to him, "who is he, then?"

An ironical smile curled Ramirez's delicate lip.

"You know as well as I do: a warm patriot, and one of the most renowned Chiefs of the revolutionary movement."

"Hum!" Don Sandoval remarked, "that is not what we want to know."

"What then?" he asked with almost imperceptible irony.

"Hang it, you say that you have lived ten years with this man," Don Serapio went on; "you must know certain peculiarities about him which no one else is acquainted with, and which we should not be sorry to know."

"That is possible; unfortunately, I am utterly unable to satisfy your curiosity on that point; if El Alferez has not thought proper to give you certain intimate details about his private life, it is not my place to reveal them to you."

Don Serapio was about to reply rather sharply to the sailor, when the door opened through which Don Alferez had gone out, and the pulquero entered, followed by a lady. The two officers could scarce refrain from a cry of surprise on recognising beneath this dress El Alferez himself. The young Chief wore feminine attire with considerable grace and reality; he walked with such ease, and appeared so accustomed to the thousand knick-nacks of a lady's dress—in a word, the metamorphosis was so complete, that, had it not been for the eye whose strange lustre the young man had not quite succeeded in subduing, the three men could have sworn that this singular being was really a woman.

The costume of El Alferez, though not rich, was elegant, and in good taste; his face, half concealed beneath the silken folds of his rebozo, partly hid his haughty expression; in his right hand he held a pretty sandalwood fan, with which he played with that graceful nonchalance so full of skill which is only possessed by Spanish women and their American daughters.

"Well, Caballeros," the young man said mincingly, in a sweet and harmonious voice; "do you not recognize me? I am the daughter of your friend Doña Leonora Salcedo, Doña Mencia."

The three men bowed respectfully.

"Pardon me, Señorita," Don Serapio replied as he gravely kissed the tips of El Alferez's fingers; "we know you perfectly well, but were so far from anticipating the happiness of meeting you here, that——"

"Even at this moment, after hearing you speak, we dare not yet believe in the reality of what we see."

The pulquero looked in alarm from one to the other. The worthy man understood nothing of what was going on, and he asked himself confidentially were he asleep or awake. In fact, he was not far from believing himself under a spell.

"I do not understand your surprise, Caballeros," the feigned Doña Mencia said with a stress on her words; "was it not arranged some days back between yourselves, my mother, and my husband, that we should go this morning and breakfast with Commandant Rodriguez, on board the *Libertad* corvette?"

"Of course," Don Serapio quickly exclaimed; "excuse me, Señorita, but I really do not know where my head is. How could I have forgotten that?"

"I will excuse you," El Alferez replied with a smile, "but on condition that you repair your inexplicable forgetfulness, and rather ungallant behaviour, by offering me your arm to go on board the corvette at once."

"The more so," Don Cristoval added, "as we have rather a long distance to go, and I have no doubt the Commandant is expecting us."

"Canarios! I should think he was," Ramirez ejaculated; "why, Señor, he sent me with a boat to take you aboard."

"Since that is the case, I think we shall do well by starting without further delay."

"We are at your orders, Señorita."

"Stay, my good man," El Alferez added in a soft voice, and addressing the pulquero, "take this in recollection of me."

The good man, half stunned by what he saw, mechanically held out his right hand, into which the mysterious adventurer carelessly let a gold onza fall; then, taking Don Serapio's arm, he went out, preceded by Don Cristoval and Ramirez, who hurried to get the boat ready. The pulquero stood in his doorway, and looked after the strange visitors who had spent the whole night in his house, as long as he could see them; then he went in again, shaking his head thoughtfully, and muttering, as he jingled the coin he had received—"All this is not clear; a man who is a woman, friends who do not recognize each other after two hours' conversation, that is preciously queer; I am certain something is going to happen. But hang me if I mix myself up in it; it is well, in certain circumstances, to know how to hold one's tongue; besides, it is no business of mine; the money they gave me is good, and I have no right to look further."

Strengthened by this philosophic reasoning, and filled with prudence, the pulquero closed his door, and went to bed in order to fetch up by day the sleep his singular curiosities had made him lose during the night.

[1] What rumour resounds in the distance which interrupts the placid silence of the dark night?

[2] Can it be the rapid gallop of a horse urged along a narrow road—or the ferocious howling of a starving beast of prey—or, perchance, the whistling of the north-west wind?

CHAPTER XIX
AT SEA

It was about four in the morning; the dawn was beginning to mark the horizon with wide white bands; on the extreme line of the water, a bright red reflection, the harbinger of sunrise, announced that the sun would soon appear. At this moment a light brig gradually emerged from the dense fog that hid it, and could be seen sailing close to the wind along the dangerous and rugged coast which forms the entrance of Galveston Bay, at the mouth of the Rio Trinidad.

It was a neat vessel of three hundred tons at the most, with a gracefully-built hull, and its tall masts coquettishly raking. The rigging was carefully painted and tarred, the yards symmetrically square, and more than all, the menacing muzzles of four eight-pounder carronades which peered out of the bulwarks on either side, and the long thirty-two pounder swivel in the bows, indicated that, although a man-of-war pennant might not be flying from the mainmast, it was not the less resolved, in case of necessity, to fight energetically against the cruisers that might attempt to check its progress.

At the moment when we first notice the brig, with the exception of the man at the wheel, and an individual walking up and down the poop smoking his pipe, at the first glance the brig's deck seemed deserted; still, on examining it carefully, fifteen men constituting the watch might have been seen sleeping in the bows, whom the slightest signal would be sufficient to awaken.

"Halloh!" the walker said suddenly, as he halted near the binnacle, and addressed the helmsman; "I fancy the wind is shifting."

"Yes, Master Lovel," the sailor answered, as he raised his hand to his woollen cap; "it has veered round two points."

As the individual who answered to the pleasant name of Lovel is destined to play a certain part in the scenes we have undertaken to describe, we ask our readers' permission to draw his portrait. Physically, he was a man of about fifty, nearly as broad as he was tall, and bearing a striking resemblance to a barrel mounted on feet, but for all that gifted with far from common strength and activity; his violet nose, his thick lips, and highly-coloured face, with large red whiskers, gave him a jovial appearance, to which, however, two small grey and deep-set eyes, full of fire and resolution, imparted something skeptical and mocking.

Morally, he was an honest, worthy man, open-hearted and loyal, an excellent sailor, and loving only two things, or rather beings, in the world: his Captain, who had brought him up, and, as he often said, had taught him to make his first splice by administering tobacco to him, and his ship, which he had seen built, which he had gone aboard when ready for sea, and had never quitted since.

Master Lovel had never known either father or mother; hence he had made the brig and his Captain his family. All his loving faculties, a long time driven back and slumbering in his heart, were so fully concentrated on them, that what he felt for both went beyond the limits of a reasonable affection, and had acquired the veritable proportions of a gigantic fanaticism. However, the Captain, of whom we shall soon speak, amply requited the old sailor's friendship.

"By the way, Lieutenant, I ask your pardon," the helmsman continued, doubtless encouraged by the manner in which his officer had spoken to him; "do you know that we have been making a precious queer navigation the last few days?"

"Do you think so, lad?"

"Hang it, sir, these continued tacks, and that boat we sent ashore yesterday, and has not yet returned—all that is rather singular."

"Hum!" the officer said, without any other expression of his opinion.

"Where may we be going, Lieutenant?" the sailor went on.

"Are you very anxious to know?" Lovel asked him, with a half-sweet, half-bitter tone.

"Well," the other said, as he turned his quid in his mouth, and sent forth a stream of blackish saliva, "I confess that I should not be sorry to know."

"Really now?—well, my boy," the old sailor said, with a crafty smile, "if you are asked, you will answer that you do not know; in that way you are certain of not compromising, and, before all, of not deceiving, yourself."

Then, after looking for an instant at the helmsman's downcast face on receiving this strange answer, he added—"Strike eight bells, my dear; there is the sun rising over there behind the mountains: we will call the watch."

And, after restoring his pipe to the corner of his mouth, he resumed his walk. The sailor seized the cord fastened to the clapper of the bell, and struck four double strokes. At this signal they knew so well, the men lying in the forecastle sprang up tumultuously, and rushed to the hatchway, shouting—

"Up with you, starboard watch; up, up, it is four o'clock. Starboard watch, ahoy!"

So soon as the watch was changed, the master gave the necessary orders to dress the vessel. Then, as the sun was beginning to rise above the horizon in a flood of ruddy vapour, which gradually dispersed the dense fog, that had enveloped the brig throughout the night, like a winding-sheet, he set a man to the foretop to look seaward, and examine the coast they were sailing along. When all these various duties had been discharged, the old sailor resumed his walk, taking a look every now and then at the masts, and muttering between his teeth—"Where can we be going? He would be very kind, if he would tell me: we are making a regular blind man's traverse, and we shall be very lucky if we get out of it safe and sound."

All at once his face brightened, and a glad smile spread over it. The Captain had just left his cabin and come upon deck. Captain Johnson was at this period a man of hardly three-and-thirty years of age, above the middle height; his gestures were simple, graceful, and full of natural elegance; his features were masculine and marked, and his black eyes, in which intelligence sparkled, gave his countenance an expression of grandeur, strength, and loyalty.

"Good morning, father," he said to Master Lovel, as he cordially offered him his hand.

"Good morning, lad," the latter replied; "did you sleep well?"

"Very well, thank you, father. Is there anything new?"

At this question, apparently so simple, the lieutenant drew himself up, raised his hand to his hat, and answered deferentially—

"Captain, there is nothing new on board. I tacked at three o'clock, and, according to your orders, we have been sailing as close to the wind as we could, at a rate of six three-quarter knots an hour, under foretop sails, and always keeping Galveston Point on the larboard quarter."

"That is well," the Captain answered, as he took a glance at the compass and the sails.

In all matters connected with duty, Master Lovel, in spite of the reiterated remarks of his Chief, constantly maintained toward the latter the tone and manner of a subordinate to his superior. The Captain, seeing that the old sailor could not be turned from this, ended by paying no attention to it, and left him free to speak as he thought proper.

"By the way, Captain," the Lieutenant continued, with some hesitation, "we are drawing near the gut; do you intend to pass through it?"

"I do."

"But we shall be sunk."

"Not such fools."

"Hum! I do not see how we shall escape it."

"You will see; besides, must we not go and pick up our boat, which has not yet returned?"

"That is true; I did not think of it."

"Well, you see; and our passengers?"

"I have not seen them yet this morning."

"They will soon come on deck."

"A ship in sight," the watch shouted.

"That is what I was waiting for," said the Captain.

"To tack?"

"On the contrary, to pass without a shot in front of the fort that commands the entrance of the bay."

"I do not understand."

"All right; you soon will."

And speaking to the look-out man, he said —

"In what direction is that ship?"

"To starboard, to windward of us; it is coming out of a creek, in which it was hidden, and steering straight down on the brig."

"Very good," the Captain answered; then, turning to Lovel, he continued: "This ship is chasing us; we shall, by constant short tacks, pass the fort and the battery which crosses fire with it. The Mexicans, who are watching us, feeling convinced that we cannot escape their cruiser, will not take the trouble to fire at us, but let us pass through without offering any obstacle."

And, leaving his lieutenant astounded at this singular line of argument, which he did not at all comprehend, the Captain went on the quarterdeck, and leaning over the gangway, began carefully watching the movements of the ship signalled by the lookout. An hour passed thus, without producing any change in the respective position of the two ships; but the brig, which had no intention of getting too far away from the cruiser, did not carry half the sail it could.

The men had been quietly beaten to quarters, and thirty powerful sailors, armed to the teeth, were holding the running rigging, ready to obey the slightest signal from their Captain. For more than an hour the brig had been approaching the coast, and the Captain, being now compelled to skirt a submarine reef, whose situation was not positively known to him, ordered sail to be reduced, and advanced, sounding lead in hand. The cruiser, on the contrary, was literally covered with canvas, and grew momentarily larger, while assuming the imposing proportions of a first class corvette; its black hull could be clearly distinguished, along which ran a long white stripe, containing sixteen portholes, through which passed the muzzles of her Paixhan guns. On the shore, to which the brig was now close, could be seen a great number of persons of both sexes, who, shouting, yelling, and clapping their hands, eagerly followed the incidents of this strange chase. Suddenly a light cloud of smoke rose from the bow of the corvette, the sound of a gun was dully heard, and a Mexican flag was hoisted at the peak.

"Ah, ah," Captain Johnson said, as he mechanically chumped the end of a cigarette held between his teeth, "she has at length decided on throwing off her incognito. Come, lieutenant, politeness deserves the same; show her our colours; hang it all, they are worth showing."

A minute later, a large star-spangled flag was majestically fluttering at the stern of the brig. At the appearance of the United States colours, so audaciously hoisted, a shout of fury was raised aboard the Mexican corvette, which was taken up by the crowd assembled at the point, though it was impossible to tell, owing to the distance, whether they were shouts of joy or anger.

In the meanwhile the sun was beginning to rise, the morning was growing apace, and there must be an end to the affair, especially as the corvette, confiding in her strength, and now almost within gunshot, would not fail to open fire on the American vessel. Strange to say, the garrisons of the fort and the battery, as the Captain had foreseen, had allowed the brig to double the point without trying to stop it, which it would have been most easy for them to do, owing to the crossfire.

The Captain gave his lieutenant a sign to come to him, and bending down to his ear, whispered something in it.

"Eh, eh!" the lieutenant said with a hearty laugh, "That is an idea! By Jove! We may have some fun."

And, without saying another word, he proceeded forwards. On reaching the swivel gun he had it unlashed and carefully loaded, adding a ball and a grape shot to the ordinary charge. Bending over the sight he seized the screw placed under the breech, then making a sign to the men who stood on either side with handspikes, he began laying the gun slowly and with the utmost precaution, scrupulously calculating the distance that separated the two ships, and the deviation caused by the rolling. At length, when he believed he had attained the desired result, he seized the lanyard, fell back, and made a signal to the Captain, who was impatiently awaiting the termination of his proceedings.

"Attention!" the latter shouted; "Stand by, all."

There was a moment of supreme expectation.

"Is all clear?"

"Yes," the lieutenant replied.

"Ready about," the Captain ordered; "down with the helm! Ease off the jib sheets! Sheet home top sails! Sheet home lower sails! Haul the bowlines taut!"

The sailors hurried to the running rigging, and the ship, obedient to the impulse given it, majestically swung round. At the moment when it fell, and had its bows turned toward the broadside of the corvette, Master Lovel, who was watching for a favourable opportunity to carry out the orders he had received, sharply pulled the lanyard and fired. The Mexicans, confounded by this sudden aggression, which they were far from anticipating from an enemy apparently so weak, replied furiously, and a shower of iron and lead hurtled over the deck and through the rigging of the American ship. The fort and battery continued to preserve the strictest neutrality, and Captain Johnson did not take the trouble to reply.

"Brace up closer to the wind!" he shouted. "Haul down the sheets! We have had fun enough, lads."

The brig continued its course, and when the smoke had dispersed the Mexican corvette could be perceived in a pitiable condition. The shot fired by Master Lovel had carried away her bowsprit close by the head, which naturally entailed the fall of the foremast, and the poor corvette, half rendered unserviceable, and unable longer to pursue its audacious enemy, bore up to repair hastily the worst of the damage.

On board the brig, owing to the hurry in which the Mexicans had returned the fire, only one man had been killed and three slightly wounded. As for the damage, it was trifling; only a few ropes were cut, that was all.

"Now," the Captain said, as he came down from the quarterdeck, "in ten minutes, father, you will tack, and when we are abreast of the fort you will lie to, let down a boat, and let me know."

"What!" the lieutenant could not refrain from saying, "You mean to go ashore?"

"Hang it," said the Captain; "why, I only came here for that purpose."

"Are you going to the fort?"

"Yes. Still, as it is always as well to be on the right side, you will send into the boat the ten most resolute men of the crew, with axes, cutlasses, muskets, and pistols. Let all be in order, and ready for fighting."

"I fancy those precautions will be unnecessary," said a man who had just come on deck and walked up to the spectators.

"Ah! it is you, Master Tranquil," the Captain replied, as he shook hands with the old hunter; for it was he who had so unexpectedly interfered in the conversation. "What do you say?"

"I say," the Canadian replied, in his calm voice, "that your precautions will probably be unnecessary."

"Why so?"

"Hang it! I don't know, for I am not a sailor. But look for yourself. Do you not think as I do—that something extraordinary is taking place on board the corvette?"

The Captain quickly opened his telescope, and fixed it on the Mexican ship.

"It is true," he said, a moment later. "Oh, oh! Can our audacious attempt have proved successful?"

"All leads to the supposition," said the hunter, with his old stoicism.

"By Heavens! I will ascertain."

"What will you do?"

"By Jupiter! Convince myself of what is taking place."

"As you please."

"Bear up!" the Captain ordered.

The manoeuvre was executed. The sheets were let go, and the brig, catching more wind in its sails, advanced rapidly toward the corvette, on board which a strange scene was taking place at this moment, which must interest Captain Johnson in the highest degree. But, in order to make the reader thoroughly understand this scene, we must now return to El Alferez and his comrades, whom we left at their departure from the pulqueria.

At the moment when the four men reached the jetty, although it was about seven in the morning, the beach was nearly deserted; only a few ships' boats were fastened up, and landing the men who were going to buy provisions. It was, therefore, an easy matter for the conspirators to, embark without attracting attention to their movements. At a signal given by Ramirez, the boat which had been pulling back and forwards during the night, came nearer land, and when the four men were seated in the stern sheets, and Ramirez had taken the tiller, the boat started for a small creek situated a little distance beyond the roadstead.

The breeze, which during the night had been rather weak, had gradually risen; the boat was easily got out to sea, sail was hoisted, and it soon entered the creek, where the *Libertad* was riding gently on her anchors. Still, it was easy for a sailor to see that this ship, apparently so quiet, was ready to slip out at a moment's notice. The sails, though furled, were cast off, and the anchor, apeak, only needed a turn of the capstan to be tripped. Posted craftily in this creek, like a bird of prey in the hollow of a rock, the corvette could easily expand its sails, and dart on any suspicious vessel signalled by the lookout. Without uttering a syllable our friends exchanged a significant glance; they understood one another's manoeuvring.

The boat had scarce come within hail ere a sentry, standing in the starboard gangway, hailed it in Spanish. Ramirez replied, and, leaning on the tiller, made the boat describe a graceful curve, and brought her up to the starboard accommodation ladder. The officer of the watch was standing at the top to receive the visitors. On perceiving a lady, he hurried down the ladder to offer his hand, and do her the honours of the ship she was about to enter.

To the right and left of the entrance, sailors, drawn up in file, saluted by raising their hands to their caps, while a boatswain gave the accustomed whistle. As we have already mentioned, the *Libertad* was a first class corvette. Don Manuel Rodriguez, her commandant, was an old sailor, brought up in the Spanish Navy, and had retained its healthy traditions: hence, his ship was kept with great care and coquettishness. Don Serapio and Don Cristoval, themselves naval officers, could not refrain from expressing to the officer of the watch the satisfaction they experienced at seeing a vessel in such splendid order.

Commandant Rodriguez, called by a midshipman, hastened on deck to receive his guests; the boat was fastened astern of the corvette, while its crew went forward with the sailors of the vessel.

Like the other Spanish American Republics, the Mexican Confederation has but few vessels; its navy is composed of but a dozen ships at the most—consisting of corvettes, brigs, and schooners. The gravity of the events taking place in Texas had induced the Mexican Government to send a corvette there, in order to render themselves masters of the sea, and prevent the United States, whose sympathies with the Texan Revolution were notorious, from giving the insurgents help in arms, men, or money.

Commandant Rodriguez, an energetic man, and excellent sailor, had been chosen to carry out this dangerous mission; for two months he had been cruising off the coast of Texas, where he had established a rigorous blockade, and owing to his intelligent arrangements, he had managed, up to the period we have arrived at, to stop or turn back all vessels sent from the United States to the help of the insurgents. The latter, reduced to their own resources, and understanding that the decisive hour would soon strike for them, had resolved to get rid of this corvette, which did them enormous injury, and seize it at all risks.

The Chiefs of the insurgents had formed their plans to this effect. During Commandant Rodriguez's rare visits to Galveston, he was adroitly surrounded by persons who ostensibly professed a deep hatred for the revolution, while in secret they were the active and devoted agents of the insurgent Chiefs. Almost involuntarily the Commandant had been induced to invite several persons to visit his corvette, and breakfast on board; but the old sailor was a true Mexican, that is to say, accustomed to all the tricks and treachery of a country where revolutions have been counted by hundreds during the twenty years since it proclaimed its so-called independence, and his prudence did not fail him under the circumstances. Being not at all anxious to run the risk of seeing his ship boarded, he left the roads, and anchored in a solitary creek, in order to have his elbows at liberty; and then, instead of inviting many persons at the same time, he merely requested Doña Mencia, her father, and two of her cousins, officers in the United States' service, to pay him a visit. We know now who the persons really were who accepted the invitation.

The Captain frowned on seeing the number of the boat's crew; but, reflecting that he had two hundred and fifty men aboard, he did not think for a moment that sixteen men, apparently unarmed, would try to seize his ship, and it was with the most smiling and affectionate air that he received Doña Mencia and the persons who accompanied her.

After showing them all over the corvette, he led his guests to the stern gallery, where a table had been laid, and a magnificent breakfast awaited them. Only five persons sat down, the supposed young lady, her pretended cousins, the commandant, and his first lieutenant, an old sailor like himself, full of experience and bravery. The breakfast began in the most cordial and frank manner; the Commandant regretted that Doña Mencia's father had been unable to accompany her, as he had promised, and a most gallant conversation went on. Presently, a warrant officer opened the door, and, at a sign from the Commandant, whispered a few words in his ear; the latter, after excusing himself to his guests, gave him an order in a low voice, and the officer retired as discreetly as he had come in.

"Señora," the Commandant said, leaning over to the young lady seated by his side; "are you afraid of the sea?"

"I?" she replied with a smile, "Why do you ask, Commandant?"

"Because," he answered, "unless you immediately leave my vessel, which, I confess, would greatly annoy me, you will be compelled to take a trip to sea for some hours."

"I am the daughter and cousin of sailors, Commandant; that is as good as saying that a trip to sea would be most pleasing to me under any circumstances; at this moment it would be a delightful interlude, and complete the graceful hospitality you have been kind to offer us."

"Very good," the Commandant said gaily; "you are a true heroine, Doña Mencia; you fear nothing."

"Or, at any rate, very little," she replied with an emphasis which escaped the notice of the Commandant.

"Will you permit me to ask, Commandant," said Don Serapio, "whether you are starting simply to afford us the pleasure of a trip, or whether a more serious motive obliges you to leave your anchorage?"

"I have no secrets from you," he said simply, "and a few words will explain the affair; for about a fortnight I have been playing a game of chess with a brig, whose appearance is most suspicious. Its rig, and fine lines, lead us to believe that it is a North-American privateer, trying to land arms, and possibly men, for the insurgents."

"Do you imagine," Don Cristoval objected, "that a privateer brig, knowing you to be in these parts, would venture to force a passage?"

"Yes, I do. These demons of privateers are afraid of nothing; and, besides, during the war of independence, I myself carried out more daring adventures than this."

"Then, we are about to witness a sea fight?" Doña Mencia asked timidly.

"Oh, do not feel alarmed, Señorita; it will not go so far as that, I hope; this brig, which I had lost out of sight for two days, has just reappeared, but this time with the apparent object of getting close enough to land to send a boat ashore. I will chase it vigorously, and do not doubt I shall compel it to put out to sea again, for it is impossible that it should attempt seriously to oppose us."

"Really, that is delightful!" Doña Mencia exclaimed with a laugh; "the fête will be complete: a trip to sea, a chase, and, perhaps, the capture of a vessel. You are really too kind, Commandant."

While the conversation became more and more friendly and lively in the state cabin, the corvette had started, and with all sail set, was pursuing Captain Johnson's brig.

"Halloh!" Don Cristoval suddenly asked, "What has become of our boat?"

"It was left fastened to a buoy," the Commandant said; "we will pick it up again when we return to our anchorage."

"Well," Don Serapio remarked laughingly, "if the privateer should feel inclined to fight, our sixteen men are quite at your disposal."

"I thank you, but do not think I shall requite their assistance."

"Who knows? No one can foresee events. Our sailors are brave, and, if it should come to fighting, be assured they will do their share."

Only one of the guests had remained silent during the breakfast, contenting himself with eating and drinking; while attentively listening to what was said around him. This guest was the lieutenant. So soon as the ship had started, he left the table, bowed to the company, and went on deck.

"Your lieutenant is no talker, Commandant," Doña Mencia observed; "he only opened his lips to eat and drink."

"That is true, Señorita; but pray excuse him, he is an old sailor, but little accustomed to society—he felt embarrassed and almost in his wrong place with you; but few men know their profession so well as he, or are so firm and intrepid in danger."

At this moment a loud detonation made the vessel quiver. "Ah!" said Doña Mencia with a cry of terror, "What does that mean?"

"Less than nothing, Señorita; we have merely hoisted our flag, and fired a blank shot, to oblige the brig to show her colours."

"Would there be any danger in going on deck?" Doña Mencia asked with curiosity.

"Not the least."

"In that case, with your permission, we will go up and see what is happening."

"I am at your orders, Señorita."

The breakfast was over; they left the table and went up on the quarterdeck. The ship offered to the sight of persons unacquainted with naval affairs, a most singular and attractive appearance. The powerful breeze had bellied the sails; the corvette bounded over the waves like a gazelle, but did not take in a drop of water over the catheads. On deck, the crew were standing silent and motionless by the standing rigging, the gunners at their pieces, and the topmen at their posts. On the forecastle Ramirez and his sixteen men were collected near the head, apparently indifferent, but actually watching the movements of the Mexican. At about a gunshot and a half distant, the brig could be seen, from whose peak haughtily floated a large American flag.

"I suspected it," said the Commandant, "it is a privateer, and has hoisted American colours to deceive us, but we are on our guard."

"Do you think, then, that ship is not American?" Don Serapio asked.

"No more than you are; it is an Argentine, or Brazilian privateer."

"Still, it appears American built,"

"That proves nothing; our ships, bought in different countries, have nothing that causes them to be recognized, for we have no docks."

"That is true; but look, she is going to tack."

"Yes, the sails are beginning to shiver."

The Mexicans fancied themselves so secure from an attack, that most of the crew had left their quarters to follow the manoeuvres of the brig; the sailors, perched on the yards, or leaning out of the ports, were curiously looking on, without dreaming of the danger such a breach of discipline might entail. In the meanwhile the brig came round, as Don Serapio had said. Suddenly, at the moment when it completed the manoeuvre, a detonation was heard, a shrill whistle cut through the air, and the corvette's bowsprit, pierced by a ball, fell into the sea, dragging with it the foremast.

This produced an extraordinary pause and confusion on board the corvette; the terrified sailors ran about in all directions, listening to nothing. At length the Commandant succeeded in overcoming the tumult; the crew recognized his voice, and at the order to fire, fifteen guns thundered at once, in reply to the unjustifiable aggression of the privateer.

CHAPTER XX
THE PRIZE

The damage sustained by the corvette was serious; the bowsprit is the key of the ship's rigging, its loss entailed that of the foremast, which the main-topmast, no longer stayed, speedily followed. The utmost disorder prevailed on board, when, as nearly always happens under such circumstances, the crew had suddenly passed from blind confidence to profound terror.

The deck was encumbered with fragments of every description, yards, spars, sails, stunsail-booms, and entangled rigging, in the midst of which the sailors ran about distractedly, abandoning their posts, deaf to the exhortations equally with the menaces of their officers, and having only one thought: to escape from the death they believed suspended over their heads.

Still, the officers did not at all conceal from themselves the gravity of their position, which the brig's manoeuvres rendered more complicated, and momentarily more precarious; they did all in their power, therefore, to restore a little courage to all these individuals, whom terror blinded, and induce them to sell their lives dearly.

A fresh incident occurred suddenly, which rendered the situation of the ship, if possible, more critical and desperate. Commandant Rodriguez had not left the quarterdeck; motionless at his post during the events we have described, he had continued to give his orders in a firm voice, apparently not noticing the symptoms of insubordination which, since the catastrophe had happened, were manifest amongst the crew. With pale face, frowning brow, and clenched teeth, the old sailor mechanically played with the hilt of his sword, taking every now and then a cold and resolute glance around him, while exerting his officers to redouble their efforts to do their duty bravely.

Doña Mencia and the two supposititious officers of the American navy were standing silent and attentive by his side, probably awaiting the moment for action. At the tumult which suddenly broke out on the forecastle, they all three started and drew nearer to the commandant When the brig had so skilfully carried away the bowsprit of the *Libertad*, Ramirez and his sailors were the first to sow and propagate terror among the crew by uttering cries of terror; and running in all directions. Their example was promptly followed. Then they changed their tactics, and began openly accusing the commandant by asserting that he was a traitor, who wished to ruin them, and surrender the corvette to the insurgents.

There is nothing, however stupid it may be, a thinker has said, which people may not be led to believe by a certain mode of treating them. This remark is strictly true, and this time again received perfect application. The sailors of the *Libertad* forgot in an instant all they owed to the Commandant, whose constant solicitude watched over them with paternal care, for they were urged on and excited by the perfidious insinuations of Ramirez and his comrades. The courage they lacked to defend themselves and do their duty as men of honour, they found again to accuse their chief of treachery, and seizing any arms they came across, they rushed tumultuously toward the quarterdeck, uttering menaces and cries of revolt.

The officers, justly alarmed, and not knowing what means to employ to bring these men back to their duty, collected round their Commandant, resolved to save themselves or perish with him. The old sailor was still apparently just as calm and stoical; nothing revealed on his stern face the agony that secretly crushed his heart. With his arms folded on his chest, his head erect, and a steady glance, he awaited the mutineers.

The latter soon invaded the after part of the vessel; but, after passing the mainmast, they stopped, through a remnant of that respect which is innate in sailors for their superiors. The quarterdeck is that portion of the deck which is exclusively reserved for the officers: the sailors, under no consideration, are allowed to tread it, except for the purpose of executing a manoeuvre.

On reaching the foot of the mainmast, then, the mutineers hesitated, for they no longer felt on their own ground, and at length stopped: for the mere fact of their invading this part of the deck constituted a grave infraction of naval discipline. We have said that they stopped; but they were like an angry sea which breaks against the foot of a dyke it cannot dash over; that is to say, yelling and gesticulating furiously, but yet without going an inch further. At the same time, however, they did not fall back.

But this hesitation and almost timid attitude of the mutineers did not at all suit the views of those who had urged them to insubordination. Collected in the rear of the sailors, they shouted and gesticulated louder than the rest, trying by all means to revive the fire which was already threatening to expire. The corvette's deck presented at this moment the most desolating, and yet at the same time imposing appearance. In the midst of the fragments piled up pell-mell on this fine ship so fatally decapitated by canister shot, these men, with their rude and fierce features, grouped in disorderly and menacing groups; and, scarce a few yards from them, a small band of calm and resolute officers, collected round the Commandant, who, standing on the quarterdeck, seemed to dominate over the men. Then, a little in the rear, Doña Mencia and the two American officers, apparently disinterested spectators of the events which chance compelled them to witness, but, in reality, following with anxious glance all the incidents of the drama that was being played before them. Assuredly a painter would have found a magnificent subject for a picture in the position of the different characters, and the expression that at times lit up their masculine faces.

And then, in the distance the lofty sails of the brig could be seen glistening, which was rapidly approaching, doubtless with the intention of coming, like the classic *Deus ex machina*, to unravel at the right time this situation, which every passing moment only tended to render the more complicated.

There was a momentary truce between the two parties, who, like practised duellists, had tried to discover their adversary's vulnerable point before crossing swords. A deep silence prevailed on the deck of this ship, where so many passions were fermenting in these hearts of bronze; no other sound was audible save the hollow and monotonous moaning of the sea, as it broke against the sides of the corvette, and the indistinct sound of weapons clutched by eager hands.

This hesitation had something sinister and startling about it, and the Commandant resolved to put an end to it at all hazards. He understood that he was the only person who could make an appeal to these misguided men, who might possibly not remain dumb to the voice of duty speaking through the lips of a man, whose noble character they had enjoyed many opportunities of appreciating, and whom they had been so long accustomed to respect and love.

Commandant Rodriguez looked slowly and sadly, but yet firmly, round him, and extending his arm in the direction of the brig, which was hugging the wind to be able to run alongside the corvette more easily, he said, in a loud and marked voice—

"My men, here comes the enemy. We have our revenge to take upon him: then why are you not at your quarters? What do you want of me? Are you afraid that I shall fail you when the hour for fighting arrives?"

At this direct and firm appeal a strange quiver ran along the ranks of the mutineers; some of them were even going to reply, when a voice was heard from the rear: "Who tells you that we regard that vessel as an enemy?"

Immediately hurrahs and shouts of joy, mingled with oaths and hisses, burst forth on all sides.

"The man who dares to speak so," the Commandant shouted, in a voice that for a moment quelled the tumult, "is a traitor and a coward. He does not form part of my ship's crew."

An indescribable tumult then broke out. The sailors, forgetting all respect and discipline, rushed toward the quarterdeck with frightful yells and vociferations. The Commandant, not at all disconcerted by this hostile manifestation, seized a pistol, which a faithful sailor handed him, coolly cocked it, and addressing the mutineers, said: "Take care. The first who advances one step further I will blow out his brains."

Some men are gifted with so great a magnetic power, and their influence over the lower classes is so real, that the two to three hundred mutineers, at the sight of this man, who alone withstood and threatened them with a pistol, hesitated, and finally stopped, with a vague movement of alarm. It was evident that this pistol was little to be feared, even under the hypothesis that the Commandant carried out his threat, since it would only kill or wound one man; still, we repeat, all these men stopped, surprised, perhaps terrified, but certainly not able to account for the feelings they experienced. A smile played round the Commandant's lips; he understood that these rough and rebellious natures had been subdued. He determined to make sure of his triumph.

"Every man to his quarters," he said; "the topmen will get the ship clear while the carpenters rig up a jury bowsprit."

And leaving the quarterdeck, the Commandant advanced resolutely toward the mutineers. The latter fell back as he advanced, without speaking or gesticulating, but only opposing that final resistance, the most dangerous of all, the force of inertia. It was all over with the mutiny, however; the crew, shaken by the firm and wise conduct of their chief, were on the point of returning to their duty, when an unexpected incident completely changed the aspect of affairs, and put the officers once more in the critical position from which the Commandant had extricated them with such ease.

We have said that Doña Mencia and her two companions attentively followed the incidents of this scene, in readiness to interfere, when the moment arrived. Commandant Rodriguez had scarcely left the quarterdeck ere the young woman, or young man, whichever it may please the reader to call this mysterious being, rushed forward, and seizing a telescope, fixed it on the brig, as if to feel certain of the privateer's position, and be assured of support if required. The brig was now only two cables' lengths from the corvette, and within a few minutes would be within hail.

Suddenly Doña Mencia, throwing off her feminine character, hurriedly tore off the dress that covered her, removed her bonnet, and appeared in the masculine attire El Alferez had worn at the pulqueria. This transformation had been so rapid that the officers and crew had not recovered front the astonishment this strange metamorphosis caused them, when the young man, drawing a pistol from his belt, cocked and pointed it at a number of cartridges the boys had brought on deck when the Captain beat to quarters, and which they had left lying pell-mell at the foot of the mizzenmast during the disorder that followed the fall of the spars.

"Surrender!" El Alferez shouted in a thundering voice; "Surrender, or you are dead men!"

Don Cristoval and Don Serapio were standing on the right and left of the young man, holding a pistol in either hand. Ramirez, for his part, had lost no time; by his care two of the bow carronades had been dragged from their ports and trailed on the stern, and two sailors, match in hand, were standing motionless by them, only awaiting the signal to fire. Ramirez and the fourteen men left him were aiming at the Mexican sailors. The crew was taken between two fires; two hundred and fifty men were at the mercy of twenty. The position was desperate, and the Commandant had not even the resource of falling honourably.

The events had occurred with such rapidity, this coup-de-main, prepared long beforehand, had been carried out with such coolness and skill, and all had been so thoroughly foreseen, that the Commandant, after taking a despairing glance along the deck, was obliged to allow that he had only one chance of escape—laying down his arms. Still he hesitated, however, and El Alferez understood the combat that was going on in the heart of the brave officer.

"We are not pirates," he said, "Commandant Rodriguez, we are Texans; you can lay down your arms without shame—not to save your life, to which the defeat you have just suffered causes you to attach but slight value, and which you would doubtless readily sacrifice to expiate your misfortunes— but you are responsible before Heaven for the two hundred and fifty men forming your crew. Why needlessly shed precious blood! For the last time I invite you to surrender."

At this moment a thick shadow covered the deck of the corvette; the brig, which everyone had forgotten, had continued to advance; it had come within pistol shot, and its lofty sails stretched out over the vessel and intercepted the sunshine.

"Halloo the ship!" a voice shouted from the stern of the cruiser; "Send a boat aboard us with your captain."

This voice sounded like a thunderclap in the ears of the Mexicans. The brig had shortened sail, and was now lying motionless to starboard of the corvette. There was a moment of intense silence, during which all eyes were instinctively turned on the privateer; her yards were lined with topmen armed with muskets and hand grenades, through the open ports the men could be seen standing by the guns, and it literally held the corvette under its fire.

"Well," El Alferez continued, stamping his foot impatiently, "have you made up your mind; yes or no?"

"Sir," the Commandant answered, "by an infamous act of treachery you have become master of my vessel; as any resistance is henceforth useless, I surrender."

And with a gesture full of dignity the old sailor drew his sword, snapped the blade asunder, and after throwing the pieces into the sea, retired to the stern with a calm and resigned step.

"Captain Johnston," El Alferez shouted, "your corvette is ours; send a boat's crew on board."

A whistle was heard from the brig's deck; a boat was let down, and a few minutes after, twenty privateer's men, armed to the teeth, and commanded by the Captain in person, stepped on the corvette's deck. The disarmament of the crew was effected without the slightest resistance, and Commandant Rodriguez and his staff were at once transferred to the brig, in order that the Mexican sailors, who were much more numerous than their visitors, might be without a leader in the event of their attempting to regain possession of the corvette by a desperate effort. But this precaution was unnecessary, for the Mexicans had not the slightest idea of rising; on the contrary, most of them were natives of Texas, who found among the sailors of the brig many of their old friends and acquaintances; in a few moments the two crews were on the most cordial terms, and mixed up together.

Captain Johnson resolved to profit by this fortunate circumstance; the privateer was in a very difficult position, and literally experienced at this moment an embarrassment of wealth; he had, without striking a blow, captured a first class corvette, but that corvette required a crew, and the sailors he could dispose of by taking them from his own ship to put them aboard the prize were insufficient; the good understanding that had almost suddenly sprung up between the two crews, therefore, supplied him with the means of escape from the difficulty.

Sailors, as a general rule, are men hardened to fatigue; faithful, but unscrupulous in politics, whose questions are much too abstract for their intellect, which is naturally limited on all affairs relating to land. Accustomed to be sternly governed and have all the actions of their life directed, from the gravest down to the most trivial, sailors are only full-grown children, who appreciate but one thing—strength. A resolute man can always do what he likes with them, if he succeed in proving his superiority over them.

Captain Johnson was too old a hand not to know how he should act under the present circumstances. So soon as the disarmament was effected he mounted the quarterdeck, took up the speaking trumpet, and making no distinction among the sailors scattered about the deck, he ordered a series of manoeuvres, intended to habituate the men to the sound of his voice, and prove to them that he was a thorough sailor, which all recognised in a few minutes.

The orders were then executed with such rapidity and eagerness that the corvette, almost unserviceable an hour previously, was soon under jury masts, and in a condition to sail for any port to which it pleased its new commander to take it. The deck had been completely cleared, the running rigging cut during the action spliced—in short, an hour before sunset any stranger whom accident brought aboard the *Libertad* could have formed no idea of what had really taken place.

When he had obtained this result, Captain Johnson smiled in his moustache, and ordered Master Lovel, who had followed him on board, to pipe all hands on deck. At this familiar signal the sailors, who were now quite submissive, gaily ranged themselves at the foot of the mainmast, and waited patiently for their new Captain's orders. The latter knew how to address rude fellows like these; after complimenting them on the intelligent way in which they had comprehended his orders, he told them that he had no intention of keeping them prisoners, for the majority of them were Texans like himself, and as such had a claim to his entire sympathy. Consequently, those sailors who did not wish to serve the Texan Republic would be landed at the first place on Mexican territory the corvette touched at; as for those who consented to remain aboard and serve their country, their pay would be raised to twenty-five piastres a month, and in order to prove to them the good intentions of the Texan Government towards them, a month's pay would be distributed on the spot in the shape of bounty.

This generous proposition was greeted with shouts of joy by those men who began at once to calculate how many glasses of tafia and measures of pulque they could consume for this fabulous sum of twenty-five dollars.

The poor fellows, ever since they had been in the Mexican service, had only been paid in promises, and for a long time past had considered this pay far too meagre. The Captain was aware of this circumstance, he saw the effect he had produced, and continued in the midst of a religious silence—

"Then, that is settled, my men. You are free not to remain on board, where I have no desire to retain you as prisoners. Still, reflect on the propositions I make you, in the name of the Government I have the honour of serving, for I consider them in every way advantageous for you. Now, let those who wish to enter on board the corvette pass to larboard, while those who wish to be put ashore can remain where they are. The purser will draw up the agreement, and pay the bounty at once."

The Captain had installed the purser at the foot of the mizenmast, with a table before him, and bags of dollars at his feet. This display met with the greatest success, nothing more was wanting, and the sight of the piastres decided even the most irresolute. At the command of "Go," given by the Captain, the sailors crowded round the purser, who ere long did not know whom to attend to first, so anxious were all to receive the bounty. The Captain smiled at the result of his eloquence, but he considered it advisable to go to the aid of the purser, and by his orders, the sailors displayed a little less precipitation in presenting themselves to him.

The enlistment lasted two hours. All the sailors entered all now joyously clinked in their horny hands the handsome piastres they had received; and assuredly, if a Mexican ship had come up at the moment, the new crew would have given it a rude reception, and infallibly captured it. The result obtained by Captain Johnson was easy to foresee: in every sailor there is something of the privateer, and ready money is the only available argument with him.

But Captain Johnson was a cool and methodical man, on whom enthusiasm had but a slight effect. He was not at all intoxicated by the success he had met with; he knew very well, that when the first effervescence had worn off, reflection would come, and with reflection that insubordination so natural to the sailor's character. Above all, he must avoid giving any pretext for mutiny; and for that purpose, it was urgent to break up the unanimity which a lengthened dwelling together had produced among them. The means to effect this were simple, and the Captain employed them. His own brig had a crew of one hundred and ninety men; of these he only retained fifty, while the others went aboard the corvette, one hundred and forty of her crew being transferred to the brig; in this way the two crews were fused, and were completely at the disposal of the Captain, who became their entire master.

The various events we have described, and the incidents that followed them, had occupied a considerable period; the whole day had slipped away, and the organisation was not completed till an hour before sunset. Captain Johnson gave the command of the corvette to Don Serapio, with Don Cristoval as first lieutenant, and Ramirez as master; while he himself retained the command of the brig. Then, when all was in order, the Captain had the Mexican flag hoisted at the peak of the corvette, which immediately started for Galveston.

The Captain returned on board his own vessel, taking with him El Alferez, to whose determination and coolness the Texan Revolutionary Government owed the possession of a naval force. The result was grand, and surpassed even the expectations of the insurgents. But that was not enough: on getting aboard his brig, the Captain ordered the Texan flag to be struck, turned upside down, and hoisted again with the Mexican colours above it. The brig set sail, and kept up with the corvette, being careful to keep under her guns, as if really captured by her.

The sailors did not at all comprehend this singular manoeuvre; but, as they had seen the Captain laugh, they suspected some stratagem, and, in spite of the shame they felt at seeing their colours beneath those of Mexico, they repressed their murmurs, in the hope of a speedy revenge.

In the meanwhile, the whole population of Galveston had since morning been plunged in the greatest anxiety. Assembled on the jetty, they had watched the obstinate pursuit until the vessels disappeared; the sound of cannon, repeated by the echo of the cliffs, had reached the city; a fight had, therefore, taken place, but what the result was everybody asked the other, and no one could answer.

The silence of the fort had also seemed inexplicable; they could not understand why it had not sunk the brig as it passed. Suddenly there was an outburst of shouts and cheers, for the brig and corvette reappeared at the entrance of the passage, with the Mexican colours proudly flying on the two ships over the Texan flag, which was disgracefully reversed. This delight knew no bounds when the ships were seen to anchor beneath the guns of the battery; the Mexicans were victors, and the Texan insurgents had suffered a defeat, from which they would not so easily recover.

CHAPTER XXI
A STRANGE LEGEND

We will now return to the Jaguar, whom we left departing from the pulqueria, and proceeding at the head of his bold companions toward the fort of the Point. But, before going further, in order to make the reader understand the almost insurmountable difficulties which the Jaguar would meet with on the audacious expedition he was attempting, we ask leave to tell him the legend current about this fortress, a legend which has survived to this day, in all its quaint simplicity.

The European traveller who visits for the first time Texas, and all the coasts of Southern America generally, experiences a feeling of indefinable sorrow at the sight of these gloomy and sinister shores, which have witnessed so many accidents, and against which the dark waves of the Pacific break with mysterious murmurs. All, in fact, disposes to reverie in these poetic countries: the sky, which resembles a plate of red-hot iron; the lofty denuded cliffs, whose capricious outline looks as if it had been cut out by some artistic giant of past ages, and bearing at times on their proud crests the still imposing ruins of an old palace of the Incas, or a teocali, whose massive walls are lost in the clouds—the ancient lurking places of those ferocious priests of the Sun, who made all tremble around them, and raised their bloody titles both afloat and ashore. Before the conquest, at the time when the descendants of Quetzalcoatl, or the Serpent covered with feathers, peacefully reigned in these countries, the thick walls of the teocalis stifled many a groan, concealed and authorised many a crime.

Of all the stories told us in our last journey through Texas, about these mournful abodes scattered over the country, we will only relate one, which has reference to the narrative we have undertaken to tell.

It was a short while after the daring expedition, during which Columbus, while seeking a new road to India, had found America again; the fever of discovery had affected every imagination; each, with his eyes fixed on the New World, which had sprung up as if by magic, rushed toward these unknown regions with all that feverish activity we have seen suddenly rekindled with reference to the Californian placers.

Among the adventurers who went to try their fortunes, some were only urged by the hope of making discoveries, while others, on the contrary, only obeyed the thirst for gold, and renewed, on another stage, the fabulous exploits of the Scandinavians—those bold kings of the sea, whose life was a continued combat. Among these men was one who had made, with the unfortunate De La Salle, that unlucky expedition, during which he crossed over the whole of Texas. This adventurer, however, Don Estevan de Sourdis by name, caring little for the unprofitable adventures the brave Frenchman undertook, secretly quitted his Chief with the vessel he commanded, and sailed quietly along the coasts of the new land so recently discovered.

The idea was excellent, and the profits were great: in a few months the adventurer's vessel was filled with riches, more or less honourably acquired. Still, for reasons best known to himself, Don Estevan felt no desire to return to France. He therefore resolved to seek a spot where it would be possible for him to build a fortress capable of protecting him, and serve him as a secure retreat against the pirates who traversed these seas in the same way as he did; he therefore began carefully exploring the Texan coast, in order to find a suitable spot to carry out his plans.

Accident led him to the mouth of the Rio Trinidad, a few miles from the spot where Galveston was built at a later date, in a wild and uninhabited country, whose appearance attracted him at the first glance. Like the old pirate he was, the Count admired the magnificent block of granite that commanded the entrance of the bay he had put into; and, seeing the importance of a citadel built on this rock, and the power it would eventually give his family, he resolved to form his nest there.

When his choice was made, the pirate had his vessel drawn ashore, camped with his men at the foot of the rock, and began reflecting on the means of carrying out his bold scheme. A good many things troubled him— in the first place, where should he procure the stones necessary for such an edifice; and if the stones were found, where should he get the masons to put them together.

Count Estevan de Sourdis and his comrades were excellent sailors— killing, pillaging, and ravishing conscientiously each time that the opportunity offered itself; but, as a general rule, they were very poor masons, and nothing of architects. And then again, supposing the stones were found, squared, and brought to the foot of the rock, how were they to be raised to the top? This was really the insurmountable difficulty; and any other than the bold pirate would have renounced the execution of a plan which he recognised as impossible.

But the Count was obstinate; he said to himself with a certain show of reason, that the greater the difficulties to overcome, the stronger and better protected from attack his castle would be.

In consequence, far from recoiling, he armed his people with iron crowbars, and began forming in the rock a path which wound round it and was to finish at the summit. This path, three feet wide at the most, was so steep and abrupt, that the slightest false step sufficed to hurl those who ventured on it down an abyss, at the bottom of which they were crushed to death. After a year of superhuman toil, the path was formed, and the count, scaling it on his horse, at the risk of breaking his neck one hundred times, planted his banner on the top of the rock, with a shout of pride and joy.

Another cry answered his, but it was so ironical and mocking that the old pirate, whose nerves were as hard as cords, and who had never trembled in his life, felt a shudder of terror run over all his limbs; his hair stood erect in horror, and an icy perspiration beaded on his temples.

The Count turned round; a man wrapped in a large black cloak, and with a red plumed hat on his head, was standing by his side. The man's face was ashy, his eyes glistened with a gloomy fire, and his parched up lips grimaced a mournful smile. The Count regarded him for a moment with surprise; but as, after all, he was a brave sailor who feared nothing in the world, he asked the stranger, in a firm voice, who he was, and how he happened to be at this spot. To these two questions the unknown answered politely that he had heard say that the Count de Sourdis was seeking an architect capable of building him a strong and handsome castle, and that he had come to treat with him. The chieftain bowed courteously, and the following dialogue took place between the speakers.

"Do you not think, master," the pirate said, "that this spot is excellently chosen for the place I meditate?"

"Excellency," the stranger replied, "you could not have found a better site all along the coast."

The pirate smiled proudly.

"Yes," he said, "and when my castle is built, no one will be able to assail it."

"Oh, of course."

"Look here," he continued, making the stranger a sign to follow him, "this is what I propose doing."

And walking round the plateau, he described the plan in its fullest details: the stranger approved of it by nodding his head and smiling his crafty smile. In the meanwhile time was passing: for about an hour day had given way to night, and gloom had gradually invaded the rock; the pirate, carried away by the irresistible attraction a man ever feels in ventilating his ideas, specially to a person who seems to approve of them, continued his demonstrations without noticing that the darkness had grown too dense for the person he was addressing to derive great profit from what he was saying; at length he turned to the stranger.

"Well," he asked him, "what do you think of it?"

"It is perfect," the other answered.

"Is it not?" the Chief asked, with an air of conviction.

"Yes, but—"

"Ah," said the pirate, "there is a but then?"

"There is always one," the stranger objected judiciously.

"That is true," the old pirate muttered.

"You are aware that I am an architect?"

"You told me so."

"Well, I have made a plan too."

"Indeed, indeed!"

"Yes, if you will permit me, Excellency, I shall have the honour of submitting it to you."

"Do so, my dear fellow, do so," the Chief said with a condescending smile, for he was convinced in his heart that his plan was the better of the two.

"Directly."

"But I have an idea."

"What is it?"

"Why, it is rather dark, and in order to judge of your plan—"

"A light would be necessary, I suppose you mean, Excellency."

"Why yes," the pirate replied, "I fancy it would prove useful."

"Pray do not put yourself out of the way," said the stranger, "I will procure one."

With the greatest possible coolness, he took off the feather that adorned his hat, and stuck it in the ground, when it suddenly burst into a flame, just as if it had been a torch. The Count was astounded at this marvel, but as, after all, he was a good Christian, and he was beginning to distrust his companion considerably, he mechanically prepared to cross himself. But the stranger eagerly caught hold of his arm.

"Let us lose no time, Excellency," he said.

And drawing a roll of parchment from under his cloak he unrolled and laid it before the pirate, who was in extasies at the magnificent plan he saw.

"What do you, think of that, Excellency?" the architect said, in a sweet, bitter voice.

"Sublime!" he exclaimed, transported with admiration.

"You are a judge," the other answered, "this is what I propose doing."

And in his turn he began entering into the most minute details, to which the old sailor listened with gaping mouth and flashing eyes, never leaving off looking at the splendid fortress drawn on the parchment. When the architect ceased speaking, the pirate was so confounded by all he had heard, that he remained for a moment stunned, and tried in vain to restore the regular flow of his thoughts.

"Well," he at last asked with a certain shade of incredulity, which involuntarily betrayed itself in his voice, "do you fancy yourself capable of carrying out such a masterpiece?"

"Nothing is easier."

"But we have no building stones."

"I will find them."

"I have no masons."

"I will procure them."

"But iron, wood—in a word, all the articles necessary for such a building, how to procure them?"

"I will take it on myself."

"But it will cost me a tremendous sum," said the Count, pressingly, for fear was more and more overpowering him.

"Pooh!" the stranger said, carelessly, and thrusting out his lower lip in disdain, "less than nothing, a trifle."

"And how long will you require to finish my fortress as it stands on the parchment?"

"Wait," the other said, calculating on his fingers, and scratching his forehead like a man who is seeking the solution of a difficult problem; "it is about nine o'clock, I think?"

"About," the Count said, not at all understanding the stranger's meaning.

"Well! By sunrise all will be ready, and you can take possession of your new residence."

"What, why, you must be the demon!" the Count exclaimed in utter stupefaction.

The stranger rose, bowed to the pirate courteously, and answered him with great politeness and a most gentlemanly manner.

"In person, Excellency. On my honour," he added, "I never could leave a worthy man in a difficulty. I was affected by your perplexity, and resolved to come to your aid."

"You are most kind," the old sailor muttered mechanically, not knowing what he was saying.

"That is my motive," said the other, with a modest bow.

"Thanks; and you ask me—"

"I have told you already—a mere trifle."

"Still——"

"We shall come to an agreement; besides, I am too much of the gentleman to treat you as a greenhorn. Still, to keep things straight, just sign this simple agreement."

"Pardon me; but I cannot read. I can sign nothing; besides, you can easily understand that I am not at all desirous to give you my soul."

"Come, Excellency," said Mephistopheles, "you can hardly suppose that I have any intention of taking you in?"

"What?

"Hang it all! Your soul has been mine for a long time, and I do not require your authorization to take it."

"Nonsense," said the worthy pirate, who was quite rebuffed, "do you think our Lord will not look twice before condemning a man of my sort?"

"Not the least in the world," the demon continued good-humouredly; "so reassure yourself. It is not that I intend to ask of you."

"Speak, then; and, on the word of a gentleman adventurer, I will grant it."

"Done!" said Satan, graciously stretching out his hand.

"Done!" the pirate replied.

"Come, that is settled. Well, you will surrender to me the first living creature you address in the morning when you wake. You see that I am not exigent, for I might have charged you much more dearly."

Don Stephen made a face, for the first person he was in the habit of addressing in the morning was his daughter.

"Do you hesitate?" the demon asked in a sub-acid voice.

The pirate sighed. The conditions seemed hard, still he must accept them.

"No, I don't," he said; "it is a bargain."

"Very good; now leave me to my work."

"As you please," the pirate answered, and prepared to go down; but, suddenly reflecting, he added, "Tell me, can you not do me a service?"

"With pleasure."

"During our conversation night has fallen; it is as black as in your domains, and I am frightfully afraid of breaking my neck in going down to the plain."

"Do you wish to rest?"

"Yes; the day has been fatiguing, and I am desirous of sleep."

"All right; nothing is easier."

"Then, I shall have my castle tomorrow?"

"At sunrise I promised it."

"Thanks; and now, if you will help me——"

"Certainly; hold on."

And the demon, seizing the tail of the horse on which the pirate was mounted, whirled the animal round his head, and then hurled it into space. The pirate, slightly stunned by the rapidity of his flight, fell without the slightest injury at the entrance of his tent; he immediately dismounted, and prepared for bed.

His boatswain's mate was waiting to help him in taking off his harness. The Count threw himself anxiously on his couch, but though he might close his eyes and turn and roll in every direction, sleep shunned him. The mate, who was lying in the doorway of the tent, was also awake, but through another motive; he fancied he saw strange lights running along the rock;

he heard the sound of hammers and crowbars, stone being sawn, and the creaking of pullies—in a word, those thousand rumours produced by masons, carpenters, and blacksmiths, when at work.

The poor sailor, not knowing to what he should attribute what he fancied he saw and heard, rubbed his eyes to assure himself that he was not asleep, and then thrust his fingers in his ears—fearing, for good reasons, that it must all be an illusion. At length, unable to doubt any longer, he resolved to inform his Captain, and entered his tent.

As we have said, the Count was not asleep. He rose in haste, and followed his boatswain's mate; then, as he placed the utmost confidence in this worthy man, who had served him for twenty years, he did not hesitate to tell him what had passed between him and the devil, and what he had himself promised, adding, in the most insinuating tone he could assume, that he counted on the mate's attachment to prevent his daughter entering the tent the next morning, as she was accustomed to do, and to find some means of getting him out of the scrape.

On hearing this avowal, and the proof of confidence that accompanied it, the boatswain's mate became anxious; he was very fond of his Chief, for he had risked his life twenty times for him; but the worthy sailor was a Breton and excellent Christian, and was not at all desirous of placing himself under the claws of Messire Satanas for an affair that did not at all concern him. Still, after a few moments' reflection, his face brightened and reassumed its ordinary look of careless gaiety, and he said with a laugh:

"Go and sleep, my Lord; tomorrow it will be day. After all, the demon may not be so crafty as he looks."

The pirate, comforted by the joyous air of his boatswain's mate, felt more tranquil; he returned to his couch, and speedily fell asleep. The sailor passed the whole night in prayer, and when the dawn began to suffuse the sky with white tints, he went to the kennel, fetched a poor mangy dog dying in a corner, thrust it into the tent, and letting fall the curtain, waited for what would happen. The poor brute was no sooner at liberty than it leaped into its master's bed and began licking his face.

"May the demon take thee, accursed animal!" the pirate shouted, awaking with a start, and furious at having been thus disturbed in his sleep.

A fearful blast shook the tent, a terrible yell was heard, and the dog disappeared. The demon fled, all abashed, with the scurvy booty he had secured. Messire Satanas had worked, however, conscientiously: a formidable fortress now rose haughtily on the crest of the rock which on the previous evening had been naked and deserted. The Count was delighted, and took possession of his castle the same day.

Still, what the demon had stated about his soul put a flea in the ear of the worthy seigneur; and hence, without loss of time, he occupied himself about his salvation. His first care was to establish a town near the fortress, to which he attracted, by promises, adventurers from all countries; then he sought a monk capable of liberating him from all his sins; and it is probable that he found one, added the worthy Franciscan who narrated this legend to us, in which he firmly believed, for Count Estevan de Sourdis died in a state of grace, after leaving the greater portion of his property to the clergy, founding two monasteries, and building three churches. In short, the ex-pirate made a fool of the demon to the end.

Without attaching to this legend the perfect belief of the man who told it us, still we were struck with admiration at the sight of the immense, perpendicular block of granite, on the crest of which the castle boldly stands, perched there like a vulture's nest, and we were compelled to allow that the means employed to build it seemed to us entirely incomprehensible.

It was this fortress that the Jaguar had resolved to carry by surprise. The task, if not impossible, was at the least very difficult, and it needed all the audacious rashness of the young Chief merely to conceive the thought of undertaking it.

The night was dark; heavy clouds laden with electricity coursed across the sky, and by intercepting the moonbeams rendered the gloom denser still. The conspirators passed silently through the deserted streets of the town like a legion of phantoms. They went on thus for a long time, with watchful eye and finger on the rifle trigger, ready to fire at the slightest suspicious sound; but nothing disturbed their march to the seashore, which they reached after making a thousand windings, in order to foil the spies who might have attempted to follow them in the darkness. The spot where they were was a small sandy creek, sheltered on all sides by tall cliffs; here, at a word from the Jaguar, they halted, for the difficulties of the expedition were about to begin. The young Chief assembled his comrades round him.

"Caballeros," he then said, in a low voice, "we are proceeding to the fort of the Point, which we must carry before sunrise; listen to me attentively, and remember my instructions, in order that during the expedition we may be exposed to no misunderstanding, which, in our present situation, would not only be mortal to us, but cause our comrades, who on their side are attempting a hazardous enterprise, to lose all the fruit of their labours."

The conspirators drew nearer in order to hear better. The swell died, at their feet with a hollow murmur, and out at sea could be seen the wares raised by the north-east wind, which would probably rise into a tempest within an hour. The Jaguar continued—

"The fort of the Point is impregnable, or, at least, passes as such; I have resolved to deprive it of the haughty boast, and for that purpose have counted on you, comrades. Owing to the opinion the Mexicans have of the strength of this citadel, they have considered it unnecessary to keep up a numerous garrison there, convinced as they are that its position will defend it, and that it is impossible to carry it, save by treachery. The garrison, therefore, is only composed of thirty soldiers, commanded by a lieutenant; it is small, and yet enormous; small, if we force them into a hand-to-hand fight; enormous, if we are compelled to remain at a distance. On the land side, the granite rock on which the fort is built is so perpendicular that we could not hope to ascend beyond one half of it; for, excepting the path cut in the rock, which is defended at regular distances by barricades, escalading is impracticable. We cannot, therefore, think of attacking it on that side. But the sea is left to us, if the land fails us; if we can succeed in landing on the narrow strip of earth which is left uncovered at low water for about an hour at the foot of the fortress, it is probable that we shall succeed in our enterprise; for it will never occur to the garrison that any attempt to attack them by sea will be made on such a night as this. That is not all—we must reach that strip of land, and speedily too; the sea is beginning to ebb, and the moment is favourable. This is what I propose doing."

The conspirators, collected round their Chief, paid the most earnest attention to his words. It was for them a question of life or death.

"Now, my companions," the Jaguar continued, "we have no boat in which to reach the base of the fort; the sound of oars striking against the thowls would give the alarm, excite the suspicion of the garrison, and reveal our presence; we must, therefore, cross by swimming; but it is nearly a league to go; the tide runs out fast, and we shall have to cross it at right angles; moreover, the night is dark, and the sea rough. I will only remind you of the sharks and tintoreras we run a risk of meeting on the way. You see, comrades, that it is a rude affair, and it is certain that we shall not all reach the sand strip. Some of us will remain on the road; but what matter, so long as we succeed? You are brave men, so I have preferred to speak openly with you, and allow you to see all the danger, than deceive you, for a peril if known is half overcome."

In spite of all their courage, the conspirators felt a spasm at their hearts; still not one of them hesitated, for they had freely offered their lives as a sacrifice; besides, they had now gone too far to recoil; they must proceed at all risks. We must say, in praise of the conspirators, that of all the perils enumerated by the Jaguar, only one really alarmed them. What they most feared was the meeting with the tintorera.

We will explain to the reader, who is probably ignorant of the fact, what this dangerous animal is, which possesses the privilege of producing goose flesh in the bravest man, on the mere mention of its name. The seas of Mexico, and especially the coasts, swarm with dangerous fish, among which the shark holds a very honourable place. But, though it be so dangerous, the Mexican pearl diver, who are mostly Indians, care little for it, and bravely fight it, when the opportunity offers. Still, there is a special sort they are extraordinarily afraid of, and that is the tintorera.

The tintorera is a shark of the largest size, and owes its name to a peculiarity that reveals its presence at a considerable distance. Holes placed near the snout of the fish distil a gluey matter, which spreads over its whole body, and renders it brilliant as fireflies. These phosphoric gleams are the most splendid on stormy nights, when the wind moans and the thunder growls. The same phenomenon is produced on dark nights; the denser the gloom, the more vivid is the furrow traced by the tintorera. This animal, fortunately, is nearly blind, and, consequently, cannot follow its prey by sight. They are also compelled to turn their belly completely up on seizing their prey. In the pearl islands of the Mexican coast there are several Indian and half-breed divers, who are not at all afraid of fighting them, and who frequently succeed in killing them.

"Now," the Jaguar continued, after allowing his comrades some minutes for reflection, "it is time for us to get ready. Listen to me. We are about to attempt a surprise, and must therefore act accordingly. Let us leave here our firearms, which would not only be useless, but might prove dangerous, if a shot were fired imprudently and revealed our presence; hence each will undress, only keeping on his trousers, and carrying his dagger between his teeth; that will be sufficient, as further clothing would only embarrass us in our long swim."

The night grew more and more dark; the sea moaned sadly, under the impulse of the *coromuel,* which was beginning to blow in gusts; the sea wolves howled in the darkness; the *gaviota* groaned sadly on the top of the rocks; and from time to time the lamantine, as if jealous to add its mournful moan to the sinister sounds of night, mingled with the sharp sighs of the wind its accents, melancholy and plaintive as those of a soul in pain;—all, is short, foreboded a tempest. The hour was well chosen for a deed of darkness.

The first emotion passed, the conspirators, galvanized, so to speak, by the firm and confident accent of their Chief, bravely made up their minds without observation or murmur. They threw down their weapons and arms, and silently ranged themselves on the beach, only awaiting the order to dash into the sea. The Jaguar, with fixed eye and frowning brow, remained motionless for some minutes, doubtless thinking of the immense responsibility he assumed in devoting to a probable death so many men who placed their hopes and confidence in him. At length he made a powerful effort over himself, a sigh escaped from his overladen breast, and, turning to his comrades, who were calmly awaiting the order to start, which would probably be a sentence of death to the majority, he said in a hollow voice —

"Brothers, let us pray!"

All knelt down, and the Jaguar offered up a prayer. His powerful voice was mingled with the howls of the wild beasts and the crash of the tempest; his companions repeated the sentences after him, with the faith of primitive souls, who regard the belief transmitted to them by their ancestors as the only true one.

It was at once a touching and terrible spectacle offered by these simple-minded, lion-hearted men, piously kneeling on this deserted shore in the black night, while the tempest raged around them, preparing themselves by prayer for the sacrifice of their life — alone in the gloom, without the dazzling prestige of a brilliant sun and thousands of spectators, but compelled to lay down their lives, and know no reward in this world.

When the prayer was ended, all rose to their feet. They felt stronger; as God would henceforth be on their side, what had they to fear? — they had made Him their accomplice. The Jaguar was the last to rise; his brow was serene, but a febrile ardour caused his eyes to flash; he believed in the success of his enterprise. After assuring himself that all his comrades were ready, he ordered —

"Take your daggers between your teeth: Heaven protects us. Forward, brothers, and long live liberty!"

"Long live liberty!" the conspirators shouted.

A dull sound was heard, as they dashed simultaneously into the sea.

CHAPTER XXII
THE SURPRISE

The Jaguar spoke truly when he said that the task the conspirators were about to undertake was rude. Swimming side by side, the Texans advanced in a straight line in the direction of the fort, which the obscurity prevented them seeing. The sea was rough and lumpy; heavy waves poured in, and rolled at every moment on their heads; the wind redoubled its violence; the terrible coromuel, the scourge of these coasts, where it causes so many shipwrecks, had risen; there was not a star in the sky to guide these determined men.

They swam on—not a cry, moan, or sigh revealing any fatigue or discouragement on their part. At the head of the gloomy line formed by the energetic heads of the conspirators, the Jaguar progressed alone. Three-quarters of an hour passed, during which all the strength and courage the human will possesses were expended in this struggle of giants by these men, whom nothing could quell. Not one had broken down; the line was still compact, and they advanced with the same vigour. Before them, at about a musket shot distance, a denser shadow was visible in the gloom, thrown out by the enormous mass of the fortress they were approaching!

Since the departure, the conspirators, with their eyes ardently fixed ahead, had not exchanged a syllable. What could they have said? They were perfectly aware of the probable consequences of their mad enterprise, and fully conscious of the danger they incurred. Besides, what was the good of speaking, when they could act? Hence they were silent, but they acted vigorously. Still, as all the men swam like otters, and were accustomed to the perfidious element in which they now were, they only expended the necessary amount of strength, and were very careful to keep the line regular.

At length, after superhuman efforts, they succeeded in cutting through the current that dashed with extreme rapidity and strength into the straits. The hardest work was over; from this moment they needed only to let themselves drift gently ashore, while careful to keep the right direction.

"Courage!" the Jaguar said.

This word, the first the young man had uttered since the start, restored the strength of his comrades and aroused their ardour again. The fortress stood out gloomy and imposing a short distance ahead, and the conspirators were already swimming in the shadow it cast. All at once a cry disturbed the silence.

"*Tintorera!*"

A brilliant mass came to meet the conspirators, leave a long phosphorescent trail behind it.

"Tintorera!" a second voice shouted.

In fact, another shark was advancing from the open sea and swimming straight towards the conspirators, leaving a line of fire.

"Tintorera!" a third voice said, with an indescribable accent of agony.

Three tintoreras beset the swimmers and momentarily contracted the circle in which they held them. The danger was serious.

"Forward, comrades," the Jaguar said, in his calm and sympathetic voice, "swim gently and noiselessly; you know that these monsters are almost blind, and more than half deaf, they have not seen us. John Davis?" he added.

"Here!" the American answered.

"Where are you?"

"I am the last but one on the right."

"Good! you will take the second tintorera and I the first. Lanzi!"

"Lanzi has just disappeared," a voice answered.

"Malediction!" said the Jaguar, "Can he be dead? who shall attack the third tintorera?"

"Do not trouble yourself, Jaguar," the well-known voice of the half-breed answered, "I am after it."

"Good! swim on, comrades, and leave us to cope with these monsters."

The conspirators continued to advance silently, although they redoubled their efforts. The Jaguar dived immediately and dashed toward the shark, which was swimming at a moderate depth. The Chief and the monster were soon so near that the brown fins of the tintorera grazed the shoulder of the daring Texan, who saw the glassy eye of the shark, half covered by a membrane, fixed upon him with an expression of cold malignity.

The Jaguar remounted to the surface of the water and clutched his dagger, at the same instant the monster's silvery belly was visible, as it opened its enormous mouth, armed with terrible teeth, close set as those of a harrow. The Jaguar drove in his dagger with all his strength, and ripped the belly for about one-third its length. The hideous tintorera, wounded to death, gave an enormous bound, while wildly beating the water, and then fell back stark dead.

The Jaguar, half blinded by the blood-stained water, and tossed about in the whirlpool it had caused in its flurry, did not regain his senses for more than a minute. At length, by a supreme effort, he returned to the surface, inhaled the fresh air, and stifled a cry of triumph on seeing near him the inanimate body of his foe the sport of the waves. Without stopping, he took an anxious glance around.

"It's all over," a voice said near him.

"Is that you, Lanzi?"

"It is," the half-bred answered, in a voice as tranquil as if he were on terra firma.

"Well?"

"The shark is dead."

"Now for the third, then. Where is John Davis? I do not see him."

"Let us go and see."

Not troubling themselves about their comrades, who were swimming towards land, the two lion-hearted men dashed to the American's help. But all was gloomy and silent around them; in vain did they cross-question the darkness, nothing appeared, neither man nor tintorera.

"Can he be dead?" the Jaguar muttered, in a hollow voice.

"Oh, I cannot think so," Lanzi answered, "he is so brave and clever."

"Suppose we hail him? He may be wounded."

"But we shall be heard from the fort."

"No, the wind is off shore."

"Help, help!" a voice shouted at the moment close by.

"That is he," said the Jaguar; "here we are, John, so have courage."

And redoubling their efforts they proceeded in the direction whence the cry for help had come.

"Help, help!" the voice repeated with such an expression of agony, that the two men felt themselves shudder, although they were so inaccessible to fears. There is in the parting cry of agony of a strong man conquered by necessity, so poignant and crushing an expression, that it stirs the hearer to the depths of the soul.

"Courage, courage!" the two men repeated, redoubling their already prodigious efforts.

All at once they saw a black mass swirling at about a yard from them and then sink. The Jaguar immediately plunged and brought it to the surface; this mass, which they had been unable to discover in the darkness, was the body of John Davis. It was high time for them to arrive; the American, finding himself conquered in the obstinate struggle he had so long sustained against death, was sinking. Still, he had not entirely lost his senses; being held above water, he inhaled the fresh air, and was soon in a condition to answer the questions his comrades asked him.

"Are you wounded?" said the Jaguar.

"Yes."

"What's the matter?"

"I fancy my shoulder bone is put out; the monster, in dying, dealt me a blow with his tail which all but made me faint. Had it not been for you, I was lost. But good bye, and thanks; lose no further time with a man who is half dead."

"We shall not abandon you if you do not abandon yourself, John. Lanzi and I, two powerful men, are ready to do everything to save you."

"We are too far from land."

"You are mistaken, we are almost touching it; a few more strokes and we shall find ground; let us act."

"Be it so, as you insist on it."

"Can you support yourself in the water by putting one hand on Lanzi's shoulder and the other on mine?"

"I will try, brother."

"Come on then."

John Davis, stifling the horrible sufferings he underwent, succeeded in doing what the Jaguar asked him, and all three then advanced towards the shore, which was, in truth, no great distance off, and, in spite of the darkness, its outline could be distinctly marked. But, in spite of all his courage, Davis's sufferings were so atrocious, that he felt his eyes grow dim and his strength all at once fail him.

"No," he said, "it is impossible and letting loose the support that had hitherto kept him up, he sunk.

"Cuerpo de Cristo!" the Jaguar exclaimed, with a sublime outburst of grief, "I will save him or perish with him."

He plunged boldly seized his friend by his black hair, and mounting again with him, held his head above water, while he swam gently with his right hand. Lanzi had in no way attempted to oppose the heroic action of the Chief of the Freebooters, but at the same time had not deserted him; he swam close to him, ready to come to his aid if needed.

Fortunately for the Jaguar, the enormous mass of rock on which the fort was built neutralized the effects of the wind, and produced a factitious calm which allowed the young man to reach with his precious burden the narrow tongue of land, where his comrades were already awaiting him; but on landing he fainted. Human strength has limits which it cannot surpass; so long as the danger endured, the Jaguar had struggled energetically, but, once it was over, and his friend saved, he had been, compelled to confess himself conquered, and rolled on the sand with terror.

The conspirators were terrified at the condition in which they saw their Chief, for what could they do without him—what would become of them? Lanzi reassured them by stating what had happened, and then all crowded round the young man and the American, whose condition was far more serious, since he had received an injury.

As we have said, only fatigue and moral over-excitement had caused the Jaguar's fainting fit. Thanks to the eager and intelligent attention of his comrades, he speedily regained his senses, and returned to full possession of his faculties. Time pressed, and they must act without delay, if they did not wish to be surprised by the return of the tide. So soon as the Jaguar had recovered, his first care was to count his comrades; nine were missing. These nine men had died without venting a cry or uttering a complaint; when fatigue crushed them, they had sunk sooner than claim assistance, which would probably have occasioned the loss of their comrades by compelling them to offer assistance, which would have exhausted their strength in a few moments. Great causes alone produce such acts of devotion.

The conspirators were at the very foot of the rock, at the top of which the fort was built. It was a great step made, but it was as nothing so long as the rock was not escaladed. But how to attempt that feat on a dark night and with a coromuel, which every moment blew with greater force, and threatened to hurl to destruction the man who was so rash as to venture to attempt such an ascent!

Still, they must act, and the Jaguar did not hesitate. He had not risked his own life and that of his comrades to be arrested by any obstacle, whatever its nature might be; impossibilities themselves must not stay him, for, although he might be killed, he would not recoil an inch. Still the means he had at his disposal were extremely limited; he had but a silken cord about a hundred fathoms in length rolled round his body, and his comrades had no other weapons than their daggers.

The persons who have read the early scenes of this story will doubtless remember the portrait we drew of the Jaguar. Although still very young, or at least appearing so, he joined exceptional strength to marvellous agility and skill; his adventurous character found delight in extraordinary things, and impossibilities alone offered any attraction to him. After reflecting for a few moments, he advised his comrades to lie down at the foot of the rock, lest they should be blown away by the coromuel, which was raging at the moment, passed two daggers through his belt, and began examining with the most scrupulous attention the rock he wished to attack.

This granitic mass, whose base was bathed in the sea and beaten by the waves, had never been seriously investigated by anyone, for who had any interest in such a thing? The Jaguar alone, since the thought had occurred to him of carrying the fort by surprise, had, on several occasions and for hours together, examined it with a telescope. Unluckily, through fear of exciting suspicions, he could only inspect it from a long distance, and hence many details escaped his notice, as he perceived at once when he began a serious investigation.

In fact, this rock, which at a distance seemed to form an almost perpendicular wall, was hollowed out at several points, and fissures had been opened by time—that great demolisher, which wears away the hardest granite. Though the ascent was still extremely difficult, it was not impossible; the Jaguar welcomed this certainty with a quick start of delight.

"It is all right, brothers," he said to his comrades, "so take courage; now, I entertain firm hopes of success."

And he prepared to mount. Lanzi followed him.

"Where are you going?" the Jaguar asked him.

"With you," the half-breed answered, laconically.

"For what good? One man is sufficient for what I am going to do."

"Yes," he answered; "but two are better."

"Well, come on, then." And then, turning to his attentive comrades, he added, "so soon as the rope falls, cling on to it without fear."

"Yes," the conspirators said.

The Jaguar then planted his dagger in a crevice above his head, and with the help of his hands and feet, raised himself sufficiently to thrust in a second dagger above the first. The first step was taken; from dagger to dagger the Jaguar reached, in a few minutes, a species of platform about two square yards in width, where it was possible to draw breath. Lanzi arrived almost with him.

"Well," said the latter, "this trip is rather amusing; it is only a pity that it is so dark."

"All the better; on the contrary," the Jaguar replied, "we need not fear a dizziness."

"By my faith, that is true," said the half-breed, who cared as little for a dizziness as he did for a grain of sand.

They examined the spot where they were. It was a species of hollow, probably excavated by time in the sides of the rock. Unfortunately, over this hollow the rock formed a projection, rendering any further ascent impossible. While the Jaguar was seeking on either side the means to continue his climb, the half-breed, thinking it useless to fatigue himself, sat down quietly in the crevice to shelter himself from the wind.

The end of the hollow was covered by a thick curtain of shrubs, against which Lanzi leaned with the confiding delight of a man who is glad to rest himself, if only for a moment, after his fatigue; but the shrubs gave way under his weight, and the half-breed fell down at his full length.

"Hilloa!" he said, with that magnificent coolness which never deserted him, "What's this?"

"Will you be quiet?" the Jaguar exclaimed, as he hurried up, "or we shall be found out. What has happened to you?"

"I do not know. Look for yourself."

The two men then advanced with outstretched arms, owing to the darkness.

"Why, it is a grotto. Viva Dios!" the Jaguar exclaimed a moment later.

"It looks to me very like one," said the half-breed, with his old coolness.

In fact, this excavation, which at a distance appeared a narrow fissure, concealed the entrance to a natural grotto, completely masked by the shrubs which accident had planted there, and which an equally great accident had enabled the half-breed to discover. What was this passage through? Did it go up and down? And was it known to the garrison? Such were the questions which the adventurers asked themselves, and they naturally could not answer them.

"What shall we do?" Lanzi asked.

"Por Dios! That is not difficult to guess," the Jaguar replied; "we will explore this cave."

"That is my opinion too; but I think there is a matter of inquiry to do before that."

"What is it?"

"Whatever this cave may be, and no matter where it ends, it is certain that it will, at any rate, offer us an excellent shelter. Supposing, at any rate, as is possible, that we cannot succeed in effecting the ascent of the rock this night, we will hide ourselves here during tomorrow, and be ready to finish on the following night what we shall not have time to effect during the present one."

"That is an excellent idea," the Jaguar remarked, "and we will immediately carry it into effect."

The young man unfastened the rope round his hips, and after securely attaching one end round a point of rock, and a stone to the other end, that the wind might not blow it about, he let it fall. In a few minutes the rope stiffened—the conspirators watching on the beach had seized it. Ere long a man made his appearance, then a second, and so on till all reached the platform. As they arrived, Lanzi sent them into the grotto.

"And John Davis?" the Jaguar asked reproachfully; "have you abandoned him?"

"Certainly not," the conspirator who mounted last answered. "Upon leaving I was careful to put the rope several times round his body, in spite of his objections. We only succeeded in overcoming his obstinacy by persuading him that the weight of his body would keep the rope taut, and facilitate my ascent."

"Thank you," said the Jaguar. "Now, lads, to work; we must not abandon our brother."

At the Chiefs order, or rather entreaty, eight or ten men seized the rope, and the American was soon hoisted on to the platform.

"What is the use of taking so much trouble about me?" he said. "I can be of no service to you: on the contrary, I shall only be in the way, and impede your operations. It would have been better to leave me to die; the rising tide would have formed my winding sheet."

The Jaguar made no answer, but had him conveyed into the grotto, where he was laid down on the ground. The young Chief then collected his comrades, and explained to them how, by a providential accident, Lanzi had discovered the entrance of the grotto. Still, it had not yet been explored, and it was of urgency to find out in what direction it ran. "Unfortunately," the young man added, "the darkness is dense, and we have no means of procuring fire."

"Listen, Jaguar," John Davis said, who had attentively followed the Chiefs remarks; "I will give you fire."

"You!" the young man said with a start of delight; "but no, that is impossible."

In spite of his sufferings the American attempted to smile.

"What! You a wood ranger," he said, "did not think of that! And yet it is very simple. Just feel in the right-hand pocket of my calzoneras, and take out a packet."

The Jaguar hastily obeyed; he drew out a small parcel about seven inches in length, carefully wrapped up in shagreen and tied with thread.

"What does this parcel contain?" he asked in some curiosity.

"A dozen *cabos*, which I brought with me on the chance," the American calmly replied.

"Candles! *Viva Dios!*" the young man exclaimed with delight; "that is a brilliant idea. You are an invaluable man, John. But," he added sadly a moment later, "of what use will they be?"

"To light us, of course."

"Unfortunately, all our matches are damped by the sea."

"Not mine. Do you imagine, Jaguar, that I am the man to neglect any precautions, and do things by halves? Feel in the left-hand pocket of my calzoneras, friend."

The Jaguar did not allow the intimation to be repeated. He found a second parcel smaller than the first, equally preserved from the wet, containing a gold mechero with its flint and steel.

"Oh," the young Chief said, "now we are saved!"

"I hope so," the American said, as he fell back on the ground, where he remained motionless, conquered by pain.

A few minutes later, four candles were lighted, and illumined the interior of the grotto. The conspirators restrained with difficulty a cry of terror, for, thanks to the precautions taken by John Davis, they were saved, but not in the sense meant by the Jaguar. This grotto extended a long distance; its walls were lofty, and it seemed to ascend; but in the centre was an opening, stretching across about two-thirds of its width, and whose depth appeared enormous: one step further into the interior of the cavern, and the conspirators would have disappeared in the abyss.

There are some dangers which go beyond the range of all human foresight, and which, through that very reason, render the most intrepid man frozen with terror. These men, who for some hours past had risked their lives twenty times in a mad struggle, and who only lived yet through a miracle, shuddered on thinking of the horrible danger they had escaped by a providential accident.

"Oh!" the Jaguar exclaimed with an expression impossible to render, "It is evident that Heaven is on our side, and we shall succeed. Follow me, brothers, for you must be as anxious as myself to hold the clue of this enigma."

All rushed after him. The cave took several windings, but, contrary to what is generally found in most natural grottos, it did not appear to have any other arteries save the one in which the conspirators found themselves.

The latter went on, following their leader step by step. The deeper they got into the cavern, the ruder became the ascent. The Jaguar advanced with extreme caution and doubt, for it seemed to him impossible that this passage should be unknown to the Commandant of the garrison. On reflection he supposed—and with some semblance of truth—that this cave had been excavated, in earlier times, by human hands, and that the abyss into which he and his comrades had all but fallen, was nought else than a well, intended to supply the garrison in the event of a siege.

He soon obtained a proof that his surmises were correct, for after marching for a few minutes longer, the conspirators were arrested by an iron-bound door, which barred their way. At a sign from the Jaguar, they remained motionless, with their hands on their dagger hilts. The moment for action had arrived: this door evidently opened into the fort.

The Jaguar examined the lock for an instant, and then ordered the lights to be put out, which was immediately obeyed, and the conspirators were again in darkness. This door, which was very old, and probably had not been opened for a long series of years, could not offer any serious resistance. The young Chieftain thrust the point of his dagger between the bolt and the staple, and pressed on it. The staple fell to the ground, but the door still resisted; it was fastened on the other side by strong bolts.

There was a moment of extreme anxiety and discouragement for the conspirators. How was the door to be opened? Must they turn back, and lose all the profit of such perils overcome, and difficulties incurred? The position was serious; but, as we have said, the Jaguar was a man who only took a delight in impossibilities. He lit a candle again, and examined the door with the most minute attention. The wood, acted upon by age and damp, fell off in scales, and melted into dust at the slightest effort.

When the candle had been again extinguished, the young man knelt down before the door, and began cutting it with his dagger, taking the greatest care to make no noise for fear of alarming the garrison; for though he was convinced that this door opened into the fort, he could not know to what point it led. After ten minutes of slow and continued toil, the whole lower part of the door was removed. The Jaguar crawled through the orifice, and, not trying to discover where he was, he got up, felt for the bolts, drew them one after the other, and quietly opened the door, through which his comrades silently slipped.

The conspirators then groped their way along the walls, not wishing to light a candle, for fear of giving an alarm, and trusting to chance to lead them in the right road. They were justified in doing so, for Lanzi reached a door, which he mechanically pushed, and which was ajar. This door opened into a long corridor lighted by a lamp, and the insurgents boldly entered the passage, after taking the precaution to take down the lamp and put it out.

It was now about half-past four in the morning, and day was beginning to break. At the end of the passage, the Jaguar perceived a motionless shadow leaning against the wall. At an order from his Chief, the half-breed glided like a serpent up to this shadow, which was nothing less than a sentry, who was quietly asleep, with his musket by his side, and on coming within reach, the half-breed bounded like a tiger at the throat of the sleeper, whom he threw down without giving him time to utter a cry. The poor fellow was bound and gagged, ere he was sufficiently awake to understand what was happening to him.

This sentry was stationed at the entrance of a guard-room, in which some fifteen soldiers were sleeping. The post was carried, without a blow, by the insurgents, who bound the soldiers, and took possession of their arms. The expedition was going on famously; but unluckily, while the scene we have referred to was taking place in the guard-room, the sentry in the passage, who had been neglected, succeeded in loosing his bonds and giving the alarm. The position had become serious.

"Come," the Jaguar said quickly, "it seems as if we shall have a fight of it. Well, several of you are now armed: comrades, remember my orders—no quarter!"

The insurgents, not at all anxious to be besieged in the guard-room, where it would have been easy to overpower them, then went out. At the moment when they appeared in the passage, they perceived some thirty soldiers, at the head of whom three officers in uniform marched, coming boldly to meet them.

"Fire!" the Jaguar thundered, "and then forward!"

Ten muskets were discharged, the three officers fell, and the Texans rushed ferociously on the soldiers. The latter, terrified by this furious attack, and seeing their leaders dead, offered but a weak resistance; after a few minutes of hand-to-hand fighting, sustained rather to save the military honour than in the hope of conquering the assailants, they asked leave to capitulate.

The Jaguar ordered a suspension of fighting, and ordered the garrison to lay down their arms, which they readily did. During the short fight, the Texans had lost eight men killed at the bayonet point. The fort of the Point, which was supposed to be impregnable, had been surprised by twenty-five men only armed with daggers. But these twenty-five fought for a holy and great idea—they were resolved to conquer or perish. The Jaguar had accomplished the task which had been allotted to him in the vast plan conceived by the Texan insurgents, and the capture of the fort must inevitably lead to the surrender of the town, if El Alferez succeeded in making himself master of the *Libertad* corvette.

We have seen how, on his side, that Chief had behaved, and what result he had achieved.

CHAPTER XXIII
EL SALTO DEL FRAYLE

The expeditious way in which the Jaguar had gained the capture of the castle, by firing, without any previous summons, on the Commandant of the garrison and his officers, was, perhaps, not strictly loyal, or recognized by the military code; but we must not forget that the Jaguar and his men were placed without the pale of the law by the Mexicans, that they were regarded as wild beasts, and a considerable reward offered for their heads.

Placed in such a position, the Texan insurgents must regard themselves as freed from any courteous obligation toward their enemies, and in fact were so. Until they were permitted to treat on equal terms with their old masters, they had only one thing to regard, namely, the object to be attained: under the present circumstances they had attained it, and no more could be asked of them.

The Jaguar's first care, so soon as he was in possession of the fortress, was to have John Davis installed in a comfortable and airy room; then he sent several men to the creek whence the expedition had started, to fetch the clothes and anything the conspirators had left there.

During the works necessitated by the new occupation and an exact inspection of the important fortress the Texans had succeeded in seizing, day had broke, and the sun risen. The Jaguar, after taking all the necessary precautions to prevent himself being surprised in his turn, took a telescope, and went up to the platform of the castle. From this point the eye surveyed an immense landscape, and a magnificent panorama was unrolled. On one side were the undulating Texan plains, which lofty mountains enclosed on the horizon; on the other, the sea with its grand and mysterious immensity.

The Jaguar first looked carelessly through the telescope at the town of Galveston, which was beginning to wake up, and whose streets were growing gradually peopled; next at the mainland, and the entrance of the Rio Trinidad, which was still plunged in a mournful solitude. Then, turning, he fixed the glass on the sea, and attentively examined the horizon. Lanzi, carelessly lounging on a gun carriage, was rolling a husk cigarette with all the serious attention he generally devoted to this important operation.

"Lanzi!" the Jaguar suddenly said, as he hurried to him.

"Well!" he answered, raising his head, but not otherwise disturbing himself.

"Do you know what has become of the Mexican flag we found in the commandant's room?"

"Indeed I do not."

"You must go and enquire at once, my good fellow. So soon as you have got it, bring it to me."

"Very good."

The half-breed rose and left the platform; in the meanwhile, the Jaguar, who was leaning over the parapet, seemed deeply interested. In fact, the chase of the privateer by the corvette was beginning at this moment! and the two vessels appeared under full sail.

"Oh, oh," the Jaguar muttered, "how will it end? The brig is very small to carry so large a vessel by storm! Nonsense," he added after a little reflection, "we have seized the fort, then why should they not capture the corvette?"

"I see nothing to prevent it," a voice said at his elbow.

The Jaguar turned and saw the half-breed standing by his side, with a roll of bunting under his arm.

"Well," he asked him, "where is the flag?"

"Here it is."

"Now, my friend, yon will hoist the flag on that staff; but, in order that our comrades may not mistake our meaning, mind and fasten a dagger to the top of the flag. The inhabitants of Galveston will not notice this addition, while our friends, who have an interest in carefully examining what goes on here, will immediately understand what it signifies."

Lanzi punctually carried out the order given him, and five minutes later, the Mexican banner, surmounted by a dagger, was majestically floating from the flagstaff. The Jaguar soon obtained the certainty that his signal was understood, for the brig, closely pursued by the corvette, waited till it had come within pistol shot of the fort ere it tacked, which it assuredly would not have done had there been any cause of fear.

During the greater part of the day, the Jaguar followed with the greatest interest the progress of the two ships, and witnessed the final incidents from his observatory. At about two in the afternoon, however, he went down into the interior of the fort, and, after recommending the greatest vigilance to his friends, he armed himself, threw a zarapé over his shoulders, and quitted the castle. By Lanzi's care, a horse had been prepared for him near the foot of the rock: the Jaguar bounded into the saddle, and after giving one glance at the fortress, he dug in the spurs, and started at a gallop. The Jaguar was proceeding to the Salto del Frayle, where, on the previous evening, he had appointed to meet Don Juan Melendez de Gongora.

The coasts of Mexico are probably the most varied of all those in the New World. The seaboard of Texas especially is so strangely broken up, that the mind loses itself in trying to discover what accident or antediluvian cataclysm could have been powerful enough to produce these bold gaps and sudden fissures in the tall cliffs that border it.

Not far from Galveston, on the seashore, there is a rather wide road, whose capricious windings follow for a considerable distance the crest of the cliffs. This road is usually followed by the muleteers and travellers of every description proceeding to Mexico. Being wide and convenient, it might justly pass as excellent in a country where the highways of communication are—or, at least, were—completely unknown, for at the present day, Texas possesses fine carriage roads, and long iron way. But at one spot, the road to which we allude suddenly breaks off: the cliff, cleft as if by a giant's sabre stroke, displays a yawning abyss, about ten feet wide, and some seven hundred feet deep. At the base of this fissure the sea constantly breaks in fury, producing a hollow and monotonous sound. On the other side of the gap the road begins again.

In Europe, where government is necessarily occupied in improving the means of communication, a remedy would easily have been found for this interruption by throwing a bridge across the fissure, but in America it is not so. The governments have something else to do than trouble themselves about the general welfare: in the first place, they have to raise as much money as they can by taxation; and next, defend themselves against *pronunciamentos* and ambitious men constantly on the watch to overthrow them. The result is, that all goes on as it best can, and each gets out of a hobble, in the best way he can contrive it.

Fortunately, the horses and mules, more intelligent than men, have produced a remedy for this neglect, thanks to that instinct of self-preservation which God has bestowed on them. Nothing is more curious than to see the passage of the fissure by a recua of mules. These animals come up gently, stretching over their necks, sounding the ground at each step, and sniffing all around with signs of the most lively alarm. On reaching the edge of the gap, they stiffen their front legs, bend the hind ones, and toss their heads; then all at once they take their spring, and fall on the other side upon all four feet, without ever making a mistake.

The Freebooters | 241

Still, it is necessary that the man who is astride them should completely lay aside his own will, and abandon them entirely to their infallible instinct. If he attempt to guide them, it is all over: man and steed roll to the bottom of the precipice, which both reach in small pieces.

As for the name of the Salto del Frayle or the Monk's Leap, which this spot bears, the following is the motive for it, according to the local chronicle. It is stated (we affirm nothing, and in no way guarantee the veracity of the legend)—it is stated, we say, that a few years after the settlement of the Spaniards in Texas, a Franciscan monk, the Pater Guardian, or Prior, of his monastery, being accused of insulting a maiden whose confessor he was, escaped from the hands of the alguazil sent to seize him, and fled across country. After a very long chase, and when closely pursued by the soldiers, who were furious at their inability to capture him, he reached the edge of this gap. Taking a glance at the abyss, the poor monk felt he was a lost man; recommending his soul to his patron saint, and calling Heaven to bear witness to his innocence, he leaped boldly across. The soldiers who arrived at this moment distinctly saw two angels supporting the monk under the arms, and they laid him in safety upon the other bank.

The soldiers naturally fell on their knees, and implored the blessing of the holy man, whose innocence was thus distinctly proved to them. The latter turned to them with a radiant face, blessed them with emotion, and then disappeared, to the sound of celestial music, in a cloud of purple and gold. Such was the story the soldiers told on returning from their expedition. Whether they spoke truly or falsely, no one ever knew; but one thing is certain, that from that moment nothing more was ever heard of the monk. The populace, who are always lovers of the marvellous, put the most entire faith in this story, and an annual procession was instituted, at which we had the honour of being present, and which, at each anniversary of the worthy prior's miraculous leap, is performed with great ceremony, in the presence of an immense crowd which has arrived from very part of Texas.

Whatever may be thought as to the authenticity of this story, it is certain that this spot is called the Monk's Leap, and it was here that the Jaguar had given the meeting to Colonel Don Juan Melendez. The sun had sunk almost level with the horizon when the young man reached the gap. He looked around him; the road was deserted, so he dismounted, hobbled his horse, lay down on the ground, and waited.

He had been there about a quarter of an hour, when the sound of a horse galloping reached his ear; he rose and looked round. He soon saw a horseman turning a corner of the road and recognized the Colonel. On reaching the Jaguar he bowed and leaped to the ground.

"Pardon me, my friend," he said, "for having kept you waiting, but it is a long distance from Galveston to this spot; and you and your comrades give us so much to do, that, Viva Dios! we have not an instant to ourselves."

The young man smiled.

"You are quite forgiven, Colonel," he said; "have you received any more bad news?"

"Neither good nor bad, but in truth very disagreeable; we learn that a corps of freebooters has been formed, of which you are strongly suspected to be the Chief, and which at this moment is ravaging the whole country."

"Have you heard no more than that?"

"Not up to the present."

"Well, before we part, I will give you some news, which, if I am not mistaken, will deeply annoy you."

"What do you mean, my friend? Explain yourself."

"Not at this moment. We have not come here to discuss politics, but our own affairs. Let us proceed regularly. We shall always have time enough to return to politics."

"That is true; but answer me one question first."

"What is it?"

"Is the news you have to tell me really serious?"

The Jaguar frowned and stamped his foot on the ground with suppressed violence.

"Extremely serious," he said.

There was a moment's silence; at length the young man walked up to the Colonel and laid his hand on his shoulder.

"Don Juan," he said to him in a kindly voice, "listen to me for a moment."

"Speak, my friend."

"Don Juan," he continued, "why do you so obstinately defend a lost cause? Why shed your generous blood in the service of tyranny? Texas wishes to be free, and will be so! Count the capable men who serve in your ranks; with the exception of two, perhaps three, there is not another you can mention: Mexico, exhausted by the revolutions which incessantly overthrow it, has at its disposal neither men nor money enough to assume a vigorous offensive: the very name of Mexican is odious to the Texans. On all sides the people are rebelling against you; it is a constantly rising tide, which breaks down every dyke. You are surrounded: within a month your army will be disgracefully expelled from our territory. Reflect, my friend, for there is yet time; return your sword to its scabbard, and leave fate to accomplish its task."

"Listen to me in your turn, friend," the Colonel answered, in a mournful voice. "What you have just said to me I knew as well as you do. I have felt for a long time past that the ground trembles beneath our feet, and that we shall ere long be swallowed up by the revolution; I therefore form no illusion to the fate that awaits us. But I am a soldier, my friend, I have taken an oath: that oath I must keep, at all risks. Moreover, I am a Mexican—do not forget that fact; I must, therefore, regard this question from a point of view diametrically opposed to yours. Besides," he added, with feigned gaiety, "we are not yet in the state you imagine. You have certainly taken from us a few pueblos, but we still have the towns, and hold the sea. You sing victory too soon; the Texan revolution is as yet only in the state of insurrection. At a later date, when it holds a strong town, and its government is constituted, we shall see what is to be done; but for the present there is no cause to despair, my friend, and you have not made the progress you fancy."

"Perhaps so," the Jaguar answered, with an equivocal accent that caused the Colonel to reflect. "I thought it my duty to speak to you as a friend, and give you some disinterested advice; if you will not take it, you are quite at liberty to neglect it."

"Do not feel annoyed; my remarks can have nothing to wound your feelings. I had no intention of vexing you when I spoke as I did. But put yourself for a moment in my place; if I had made you the same proposals you offered me, what would your answer have been?"

"I should have refused, by Heaven!" the young man exclaimed, impetuously.

The Colonel began laughing.

"Well, I acted as you would have done. What harm do you see in that?"

"That is true; you were right, and I am an ass! Forgive me, my friend. Besides, was it not agreed that political questions should never separate us? Let us, therefore, return to the object of our interview, which is of much greater importance to us, and temporarily leave the Mexicans and Texans to settle matters as they can."

For some minutes the Colonel's eyes had been fixed on the sea, and he had listened to his friend's remarks with a very absent air.

"Why," he suddenly said, "look there, my friend."

"What is it?"

"Do you not see?"

"What do *you* see, let me ask in return?"

"Hang it! I see the *Libertad* corvette, which has first anchored under the guns of the Point Fort, bringing with her a privateer brig, which she has, in all probability, captured off the coast."

"Do you think so?" the Jaguar asked, sarcastically.

"Look for yourself!"

"My friend, I am rather like St. Thomas."

"What do you mean?"

"That as long as I am not completely convinced, I shall attach but very slight faith to the testimony of my eyesight."

These words were uttered with such a singular intonation, that, in spite of himself, the Colonel felt ashamed. "What can you mean?" he asked.

"Nothing but what I say," the Jaguar answered.

"Still, I fancy I cannot be mistaken. I can very distinctly see the Mexican flag over the reversed Texan colours."

"It is true," the Jaguar said, coldly, "but what does that prove?"

"What do you say? — 'What does that prove?'"

"Yes."

"Are you so ignorant of naval matters, then, as not to know what takes place on board a vessel after an engagement?"

"I beg your pardon, friend, but I know all about it. But I know, too, that what we see may be the result of a stratagem, and that the brig, after capturing the corvette, may have an interest in concealing the fact."

"Come, come," the Colonel said, with a laugh, "that is carrying optimism a little too far. Let us leave the corvette and brig, and return to our own affairs."

"Well, I think you are in the right; for, judging from the turn the conversation has taken, we should presently be unable to understand one another at all."

During this conversation the sun had set, and night completely fallen. The two gentlemen passed their horses' bridles over their arm to prevent them straying, and then walked slowly, side by side, in the direction of the Rio Trinidad. The night was clear, the sky studded with a profusion of flashing stars, and the atmosphere of marvellous transparency; it was, in a word, one of those American nights that conduce to gentle reverie.

The young men yielded involuntarily to the intoxicating charm of this exquisite evening; yielding to their thoughts, neither dreamed of resuming a conversation suddenly broken off by a bitter remark. For a long time they walked on thus, till they reached an angle in the road, where the track they were following divided into several branches. Here they halted.

"We must separate here, Don Juan," the Jaguar said, "for we probably do not follow the same road."

"That is true, friend, and I regret it," the Colonel answered, sadly, "for I should be so happy if I had you constantly by my side."

"Thanks, friend, but you know that is impossible; let us, therefore, profit by the few moments left us to be together. Well, what have you done?"

"Nothing, alas! For a soldier is the slave of discipline; in a period of war, more especially, it is impossible for him to leave his corps. I have, therefore, been unable to obtain any information. Have you been more fortunate?"

"I can hardly say, yet; still, I hope. Tranquil has this very night to give me certain information, which will perfect that I have myself obtained."

"And is Tranquil here?"

"He arrived today, but I have not yet been able to see him."

"Then you imagine——?" the Colonel said, eagerly.

"This is what I have succeeded in finding out. Remark that I assert nothing; I am at this moment merely the echo of certain rumours, which may be well founded, but can also be false."

"No matter; speak, my friend, in Heaven's name."

"About six weeks ago, according to what my spies tell me, a strange man arrived in this country, bringing a girl with him. This man has purchased a rancho, of no great value, situated a few leagues from here, nearly on the seashore. He paid cash for it, shut himself up in the rancho with the girl, and since then no one has seen them. The man has immured himself in his property, to which nobody has admission; but whether this man be the White Scalper, and the maiden Carmela, no one is able to state positively, and I would not venture to affirm it. Several times I have prowled round the abode of this mysterious being, but have not succeeded in seeing him: windows and doors are constantly closed, nothing is heard of what takes place in this strange house, which, through its isolated position, is, to a certain extent, protected from indiscreet visitors. This is what I had to tell you, perhaps tomorrow I shall have learned more."

"No," Don Juan answered, pensively, "that man cannot be the White Scalper, or the maiden Carmela."

"What makes you think so?"

"The mystery with which the man surrounds himself. The White Scalper, you must not forget, is a man for whom the nomadic life of the desert possesses too great charms for him to be willing to shut himself up. And then, what would be his reason for doing so? To keep a young girl prisoner? But Doña Carmela is no frail and timid woman, weakened by the mephitic air of cities, without will or strength. She is a brave and courageous maiden, with a resolute heart and strong arm, who would never have consented thus to bow her head beneath the yoke. A man, however strong he may be, is very weak, believe me, when he finds himself in presence of a woman, who says to him boldly—No! Woman, through the mere fact that she has generally only one thought at a time, is greatly superior to us, and nearly always attains the object she desires. And then again, for what reason can the White Scalper, who had in his hands a thousand unknown desert hiding places to conceal his captive from sight, have retired without any plausible motive to the vicinity of a town, in a populous country, where he must expect to attract suspicion and arouse attention? No, it is evident to me that you are mistaken."

"Perhaps you are right; still, it is my duty to clear up the affair, and I will do so."

"Certainly, you will act prudently by doing so. I confess that, were it possible, I should be happy to accompany you on your expedition. For even supposing, as I believe, that this man is not the White Scalper, it is probable that the mystery with which he surrounds himself conceals a crime, and that if your expedition does not meet with the result you suppose, it will have, at any rate, served to liberate a maiden who is the victim of odious tyranny."

"Who knows?"

"Only one man, in my opinion, could put you on the trail of her we have so unfortunately lost, through the numerous relations he maintains with the Indians."

"Whom do you mean?"

"Loyal Heart—"

"That is true. He was brought up by the Indians, and one of their tribes has adopted him. He would be better able than anybody to supply us with information."

"Why have you not applied to him, then?"

"For the very simple reason that, on the day after the capture of the Larch-tree hacienda, Loyal Heart left us to return to his tribe, whither serious matters recalled him."

"That is annoying," the Colonel said thoughtfully.

"I know not why, but I feel convinced that this hunter, with whom I am but very slightly acquainted, as I only conversed with him once, and that but for ten minutes—I am convinced, I say, that this hunter may prove extremely useful to us in our search for the unfortunate Carmela."

"Perhaps you are right, Colonel. This night, as I told you, I am to see Tranquil, and shall have a serious explanation with him. He is as interested as we are, perhaps more so, in the success of our researches. He is a man of extreme prudence, and thoroughly conversant with the desert; I shall see what he says to me."

"Insist, I beg, friend, on establishing a friendly connection with Loyal Heart."

"I shall not fail; besides, Tranquil is sure to know where to find him."

"That is probable. Now, I can speak to you with open heart, my friend. Honour alone has hitherto kept me at my post; I desire to recover my liberty, and only await an honourable occasion to send in my resignation. I should not like to abandon my comrades in arms at a critical moment; but I swear to you on my honour, friend, that on the day when I am free, and that day is approaching I hope, I will join you, and then we shall find Carmela again, even at the risk of my life."

The Colonel uttered these words with a fire and animation which made his friend start involuntarily, and aroused in his heart a lively feeling of jealousy. Still, the Jaguar had sufficient power over himself to conceal the emotion he felt, and he replied in a calm voice:

"May Heaven grant that it may speedily be so, my friend. What could we two not do?"

"Then you intend to make the expedition you told me of this night?" the Colonel continued.

"It is not I, though I shall probably be present, but another person who will direct it."

"Why not you?"

"Tranquil desires it so; he is Carmela's father, and I must yield to his wishes."

"That is true. Now, when and how shall we meet again? I have the greatest desire to learn what may occur tonight; whatever be the result of the expedition, I trust to be informed of what you have done. Unfortunately, I fear it will be very difficult for us to meet again."

"Why so?"

"Why, my friend, you know as well as I do, the truce made between General Rubio and yourself expires tonight."

"Well?"

"I presume you do not intend returning to Galveston?"

"For the present, no; but I hope to do so shortly."

"Let us not trust to probabilities, for we run too great a risk of deceiving ourselves."

The Jaguar burst into a laugh.

"You are perfectly right," he said; "still, it is important that we should meet within the next twenty-four hours."

"Certainly."

"If I cannot enter Galveston, you can leave it, I suppose?"

"Oh, of course."

"Well then, the matter is easily arranged; I will tell you a spot where you will be certain of finding me."

"Take care, my friend, be prudent; I will not conceal from you that the General is furious at having fallen into the trap you so cleverly laid for him, and will do all in his power to seize your person."

"I expect so; but do not be alarmed, he will not succeed."

"I hope so, friend; but believe me, do not be too confident."

"I defy him to come and take me at the spot where I shall be within an hour, and where I shall be delighted to welcome you, if you are inclined to pay me a visit."

"And where is this privileged spot, my friend?"

"The Fort of the Point."

"What!" the Colonel said, suddenly stopping and looking him in the face; "Of course you are joking."

"Not the least in the world."

"What! You give me the meeting at the Fort of the Point?"

"Yes."

"Why, that is impossible."

"Why so?"

"Oh, you must be mad, my friend!"

"Remember that the fort has been in my hands for the past twelve hours," the Jaguar coldly interrupted him. "I surprised it last night."

"Ah!" the Colonel exclaimed, in stupor.

"Did I not tell you that I had serious news to impart to you?" the young man continued; "Would you like, now, to learn the second item?"

"The second!" the Colonel repeated, utterly astounded; "And what can the second item be? After what I have just heard, I can expect anything."

"The second item is this: the *Libertad* corvette has been boarded by the privateer brig, with which it and chored at sunset beneath the guns of the fort."

At this unexpected revelation the Colonel staggered like a drunken man; he turned pale as a corpse, and his limbs were agitated by a convulsive movement.

"Woe, woe!" he exclaimed in a choking voice.

The Jaguar felt moved with pity at the sight of this true and poignant grief.

"Alas! my friend," he said gently, "it is the fortune of war."

"Oh, Galveston, Galveston!" the Colonel said in despair, "that city which the General has sworn never to surrender!"

After a moment's silence, the Colonel mounted his horse.

"Let me go," he said; "I must immediately impart these frightful news to the Governor."

"Go, my friend," the Jaguar answered affectionately; "but, remember, that you will find me at the Fort of the Point."

"We are accursed!" the Colonel cried wildly, and burying his spurs in the sides of his horse, which snorted with pain, he started at full gallop.

"Poor friend!" the Jaguar muttered sadly, as he looked after him, "The news has quite upset him."

After this reflection, the young man mounted and went back to the fort, which he reached about half an hour later.

CHAPTER XXIV
THE LANDING

Immediately on reaching his anchorage, Captain Johnson, after conversing for a moment privately with El Alferez, gave orders that Commandant Rodriguez and his officers should be brought into his presence. The Commandant, despite the politeness with which he had been treated, and the kindness the privateer's men had shown him, could not forgive them the way in which they had seized his vessel; he was sad, and had hitherto only answered the questions asked him by disdainful silence, or insulting monosyllables. When the officers of the corvette were assembled in the cabin, Captain Johnson, turning politely to the Mexicans, said:

"Gentlemen, I am really most sorry for what has occurred. I should be glad to set you at liberty immediately, but your Commandant's formal refusal to pledge himself not to serve against us for a year and a day, obliges me, to my great regret, to keep you prisoners, at least temporarily. However, gentlemen, be assured that you will be treated as Caballeros, and everything done to alleviate the sorrow this temporary captivity must occasion you."

The officers, and even the Commandant, bowed their thanks, and the Captain continued:

"All your property has been placed in the boat I have ordered to be got ready, to convey you ashore. You will, therefore, lose nothing that belongs to you personally; if war has terrible claims, I have tried, as far as lay in my power, to spare you its bitterest conditions. If nothing retains you here, be kind enough to get ready to land."

"Would it be indiscreet, Captain, to ask you whither you have given orders to have us taken?" Commandant Rodriguez asked.

"Not at all, Commandant," the Captain replied; "you are about to be taken to the Port of the Point, whose walls will serve as your prison, until fresh orders."

"What!" the old sailor exclaimed in astonishment; "The Fort of the Point?"

"Yes," the Captain answered with a smile; "the fort which some of my friends seized, while I had the honour of boarding your fine corvette, Commandant."

The Captain could have gone on talking thus for some time: the old officer, confounded by what he had just heard, was incapable of connecting two ideas. At length, he let his head fall wearily on his chest, and making his officers a sign to follow him, went on deck. A boat, with a crew of ten men, was balancing at the starboard accommodation ladder, which the Commandant, still silent, entered, and his staff followed his example.

"Push off!" El Alferez ordered, who was holding the yoke lines.

The boat started and speedily disappeared. For some minutes the cadenced sound of the oars dipping in the water could be heard, and then all became silent again. The Captain had watched the departure of his prisoners; when the boat had disappeared in the gloom, he gave Master Lovel orders to weigh and stand out to sea, and then returned to his cabin, where a man was waiting for him. It was Tranquil, the old Tigrero.

"Well!" the hunter asked.

"They have gone, thank Heaven!" the Captain said, as he sat down.

"Then we are at liberty?"

"Quite."

"When shall we land?"

"This night; but is your information positive?"

"I believe so."

"Well, we shall soon know how matters stand."

"May Heaven grant that we succeed!"

"Let us hope it. Do you think the coast is guarded?"

"I fear it, for your vessel must have been signalled all along the shore."

"Do you know whether the Mexicans have other ships observing the ports, in addition to the corvette we have captured?"

"I think they have three more, but smaller than the *Libertad*."

"Hang it all! We must act prudently, then; however, whatever may happen, I will not desert so old a friend as yourself when unfortunate. We have still three hours before us, so try and sleep a little, for we shall have a tough job."

Tranquil smiled at this recommendation; but to please his friend, who had already laid himself down in his bunk, in the position of a man preparing to sleep, he wrapped himself in his zarapé, leant back in his chair, and closed his eyes.

The night, which at the beginning had been very bright and clear, had suddenly become dark and stormy; black clouds surcharged with electricity covered the whole of the sky; the breeze moaned sadly in the rigging, and mingled with the dash of the waves against the sides of the vessel. The brig was sailing slowly close to the wind, the only sails it carried being double-reefed topsails, the fore staysail, and the spanker.

At the moment when the helmsman struck the two double strokes on the bell, indicating ten o'clock, Captain Johnson and Tranquil appeared on deck. The Captain was dressed in a thick blue pilot coat, a leathern belt, through which were passed a cutlass, a pair of pistols and an axe, was fastened round his waist; a cloak was thrown over his shoulders, and a broad-brimmed felt hat completely concealed his features. The Canadian wore his hunter's garb, though, through the dangerous nature of the affair, he had added a brace of pistols to his ordinary armament.

The Captain's orders have been carried out with that minute consciousness which Master Lovel displayed in everything connected with duty. The boarding netting was braced up, and the running rigging secured as if for action. At the starboard ladder the longboat was tossing with its crew of thirty men, all armed to the teeth, and holding their oars aloft ready to dash into the water. They were, however, muffled, so as to stifle, as far as possible, the sound of rowing, and foil the vigilance of the Mexicans.

"That is well, lads," the Captain said, after giving a pleased glance at their preparations, "let us be off. Mind, father," he added, turning to Father Lovel, "that you keep a good watch. If we are not on board again by four in the morning, stand out to sea, and do not trouble yourself further about us; for it will be useless to wait for us longer, as we shall be prisoners of the Mexicans; and any lengthened stay in these waters might compromise the safety of the brig. Be of good cheer, though, for I have hopes of success."

And after kindly pressing the old sailor's hand, he went down to the boat, seated himself in the sternsheets by the side of the hunter, took up the yoke lines, and said, in a low voice, "Push, off!"

At this command the painter was cast off, the oars dashed together into the sea, and the boat started. When it had disappeared in the fog, Master Lovel ran at full speed to the stern of the brig, and leaned over the taffrail. "Are you there?" he said.

"Yes," a suppressed voice answered him.

"Get ready," the Master added, and then said to an old sailor, who had followed him: "You know what I recommended to you, Wells," he said; "I reckon on you, and intrust the lookout to you."

"All right, Master," the sailor answered, "you can cut your cable without fear, I will keep a bright lookout."

"All right; get in, men, and double-bank the oars."

Some forty sailors, who were well armed, like their predecessors, let themselves down, one after the other, by a rope that hung over the taffrail, and got into a second boat, which Master Lovel had ordered to be quietly got ready, and of which he took the command. He started at once, and steered after the Captain's pinnace, whose direction he was pretty well acquainted with, saying every now and then to the rowers, in order to increase their speed, "Give way, my lads, give way, all!" and he added, as he chewed his enormous quid, with a cunning smile, "It was very likely I should let my old fellow have his face scored by those brigands of Mexicans, who are all as crafty as caimans."

So soon as he had left the ship, the Captain, leaving on his right hand a small fishing village, whose lights he saw flashing through the darkness, steered for a jutting-out point, where he probably hoped to disembark in safety. After rowing for about three-quarters of an hour, a black line began to be vaguely designed on the horizon in front of the boat. The Captain gave his men a sign to rest on their oars for a moment, and taking up a long night glass, he carefully examined the coast. In two or three minutes he shut up the glass again, and ordered his men to give way.

All at once the keel of the pinnace grated on the sand: they had reached land. After hurriedly exploring the neighbourhood, the crew leaped ashore, leaving only one man as boat keeper, who at once pushed off, so as not to be captured by the enemy. All was calm, and a solemn silence reigned on the coast, which was apparently deserted. The Captain having assured himself that, for the present, at any rate, he had nothing to fear, concealed his men behind some rocks, and then addressed Tranquil.

"It is now your turn, old hunter," he said.

"Good!" the latter replied, not adding another word.

He left his hiding place, and walked forward, with a pistol in one hand, and a tomahawk in the other, stopping at intervals to look around him, and listen to those thousand sounds, without any known cause, which at night trouble the silence, though it is impossible to guess whence they come, or what produces them. On getting about one hundred yards from the spot where the landing was effected, the hunter stopped, and began gently whistling the first strains of a Canadian air. Another whistle answered his, and finished the tune he had purposely broken off. Footsteps were heard, and a man showed himself. It was Quoniam, the Negro.

"Here I am," he said. "Where are your men?"

"Hidden behind the rocks close by."

"Call them up, for we have not a moment to lose."

Tranquil clapped his hands twice, and a moment later the Captain and his men had rejoined him.

"Where is the person we have come to deliver concealed?" the Captain asked.

"At a rancho about two miles from here. I will lead you to it."

There was a moment's silence, during which the Captain studied the Negro's noble face, his black flashing eye, which glistened with boldness and honour; and he asked himself whether such a man could be a traitor? Quoniam seemed to read his thoughts, for he said to him, as he laid his hand on the Canadian's shoulder—

"If I had intended to betray; you, it would have been done ere now. Trust to me, Captain; I owe my life to Tranquil. I almost witnessed the birth of the maiden you wish to save. My friendship and gratitude answer to you for my fidelity. Let us start."

And without saying anything further, he placed himself at the head of the band, which followed him along a hollow way that ran between two hills.

While the incidents we have just described were taking place on the beach, two persons, male and female, seated in a room, modestly, though comfortably, furnished, were holding a conversation, which, judging from the angry expression of their faces, seemed to be most stormy. These two persons were Carmela and the White Scalper.

Carmela was half reclining in a hammock; she was pale and suffering, her features were worn, and her red eyes showed that she had been weeping. The White Scalper, dressed in the magnificent costume of a Mexican Campesino, was walking up and down the room, champing his grey moustaches, and angrily clanking his heavy silver spurs on the floor.

"Take care, Carmela!" he said, as he suddenly halted in front of the young woman, "you know that I crush all who resist me. For the last time I ask you: Will you tell me the reason of your constant refusals?"

"What good to tell you?" she answered, sadly, "for you would not understand me."

"Oh! This woman will drive me mad," he exclaimed, clenching his fists.

"What have I done, now?" Carmela asked with ironical surprise.

"Nothing, nothing," he answered, as he resumed his hurried walk. Then at the end of a moment, he returned to the maid and said, "You hate me then?"

Carmela replied by shrugging her shoulders, and turning away from him.

"Speak!" he said, seizing her arm, and squeezing it fiercely in his powerful hand.

Carmela liberated herself from his grasp, and said bitterly:

"I fancied that since you left the western prairies, you contented yourself with ordering your slaves to torture your victims, and did not descend to the part of hangman."

"Oh!" he said, furiously.

"Come," she continued, "this farce wearies me, so let us bring it to a finale. I know you too well now, not to be aware that you would not hesitate to proceed to odious extremities, if I would not submit to your wishes. Since you insist on it, I will explain my thoughts to you."

Drawing herself up to her full height, and fixing on him a bright and challenging glance, she continued in a firm and distinct voice—

"You ask me if I hate you? No, I do not hate you, I despise you!"

"Silence, wretched girl!"

"Yourself ordered me to speak, and I shall not be silent till I have told you all. Yes, I despise you, because, instead of respecting a poor girl whom you, coward as you are, carried off from her relations and friends you, torture her, and become her executioner. I despise you, because you are a man without a soul; an old man who might be my father, and yet you do not blush to ask me to love you, under some ignoble pretext of my resemblance with some woman I have no doubt you killed."

"Carmela!"

"Lastly, I despise you, because you are a furious brute, who only possess one human feeling, 'the love of murder!' because there is nothing sacred in your sight, and if I was weak enough to consent to your wishes, you would make me die of despair, by taking a delight in breaking my heart."

"Take care, Carmela!" he exclaimed furiously, as he advanced a step toward her.

"What, threats!" she continued in a loud voice. "Do I not know that all is ready prepared for my punishment. Summon your slaves, Master, and bid them torture me! But know this, I will never consent to obey you. I am not so abandoned as you may feel inclined to suppose; I have friends I love, and who love me in return. Make haste, for who knows whether I may not be liberated tomorrow, if you do not kill me to day?"

"Oh, this is too much," the White Scalper said in a low and inarticulate voice, "so much audacity shall not pass unpunished. Ah! you reckon, foolish child, on your friends! But they are far away," he said with a bitter laugh; "we are safe here, and I shall make you yield to my will."

"Never!" she exclaimed with exaltation, and rushing toward him, she stopped almost within grasp, adding,—

"I defy you, coward who threaten a woman!"

"Help!" the White Scalper exclaimed, with a tiger yell.

All at once the window was noisily burst open and Tranquil entered.

"I think you called, Señor?" he said, as he leaped into the room and advanced with a firm and measured step.

"My father! My father!" the poor girl shrieked, as she threw herself into his arms with delight; "you are come at last!"

The White Scalper, utterly astonished and startled by the unexpected appearance of the hunter, looked around him in alarm, and could not succeed in regaining his coolness. The Canadian, after lovingly replying to the maiden's warm greeting, laid her gently on the hammock, and then turned to the White Scalper, who was beginning to come to himself again.

"I ask your pardon, Señor," he said with perfect ease, "for not having advised you of my visit; but you are aware we are on delicate terms, and, as it is possible that if I had written, you would not have received me, I preferred bringing matters to the point."

"And pray what may you want with me, Señor?" the Scalper drily asked.

"You will permit me to remark, Señor," Tranquil replied still with the same placid air, "that the question appears to me singular at the least in your mouth. I simply wish to take back my daughter, whom you carried off."

"Your daughter?" the other said ironically.

"Yes, Señor, my daughter."

"Could you prove to me that this young person is really your daughter?"

"What do you mean by that remark?"

"I mean that Doña Carmela is no more your daughter than she is mine; that consequently our claims are equal, and that I am no more obliged to surrender her than you have a right to claim her."

"That is very vexatious," the hunter said mockingly.

"Is it not?" the White Scalper said.

Tranquil gave an ironical smile.

"I fancy you are strangely mistaken, Señor," he said with his old calmness.

"Ah!"

"Listen to me for a few moments. I will not encroach on your time, which no doubt is valuable. I am only a poor hunter, Señor, ignorant of worldly affairs, and the subtleties of civilization. Still, I believe that the man who adopts a child in the cradle, takes care of it, and brings it up with a tenderness and love that have never failed, is more truly its father than the man who, after giving it life, abandons it and pays no farther attention to it; such is my idea of paternity, Señor. Perhaps I am mistaken; but, in my idea, as I have no lessons or orders to receive from you, I shall act as I think proper, whether you like it or no. Come, my dear Carmela, we have remained here too long as it is."

The maiden bounded to her feet, and placed herself by the hunter's side.

"One moment, Señor," the Scalper exclaimed; "you have learned how to enter this house, but you do not yet know how to leave it."

And seizing two pistols lying on a table, he pointed them at the hunter, while shouting—"Help! help!"

Tranquil quietly raised his rifle to his shoulder.

"I should be delighted at your showing me the road," he said peaceably.

A dozen slaves and Mexican soldiers rushed tumultuously into the room.

"Ah, ah!" said the Scalper, "I fancy I have you at last, old Tiger-killer."

"Nonsense," a mocking voice replied; "not yet."

At this moment the Captain and his men dashed through the window which had afforded the Canadian a passage into the room, and uttered a fearful yell. An indescribable medley and confusion then began: the lights were extinguished, and the slaves, mostly unarmed, and not knowing with how many enemies they had to deal, fled in all directions. The Scalper was carried away by the stream of fugitives, and disappeared with them. The Texans took advantage of the stupor of their enemy to evacuate the rancho, and effect their retreat.

"Father," the maiden exclaimed, "I felt certain you would come."

"Oh!" the hunter said with ineffable delight, "you are at length restored to me."

"Make haste! Make haste!" the Captain shouted; "Who knows whether we may not be crushed by superior forces in an instant?"

At his orders, the sailors, taking the maiden in their midst, ran off in the direction of the seashore. In the distance, drums and bugles could be heard calling the soldiers under arms, and on the horizon the black outline of a large body of troops hurrying up, with the evident intention of cutting off the retreat of the Texans, could be distinguished. Panting and exhausted, the latter still ran on; they could see the coast; a few minutes more and they would reach it. All at once a band, commanded by the White Scalper, dashed upon them, shouting—

"Down with the Texans! kill them! kill them!"

"Oh, my God!" Carmela exclaimed, falling on her knees, and clasping her hands fervently; "will you abandon us?"

"Lads," the Captain said, addressing his sailors, "we cannot talk about conquering, but we will die."

"We will, Captain," the sailors answered unanimously, as they formed front against the Mexicans.

"Father," said Doña Carmela, "will you let me fall alive into the hands of that tiger?"

"No," said Tranquil, as he kissed her pale forehead; "here is my dagger, child?"

"Thanks!" she replied, as she seized it with eyes sparkling with joy. "Oh, now I am certain of dying free."

Lest they should be surrounded, the Texans leant their backs against a rock, and awaited with levelled bayonets the attack of the Texans.

"Surrender, dogs!" the Scalper shouted contemptuously.

"Nonsense!" the Captain answered; "you must be mad, Señor. Do men like us ever surrender?"

"Forward!" the Scalper shouted.

The Mexicans rushed on their enemies with indescribable rage. A heroic and gigantic struggle then began, a combat impossible to describe of three hundred men against thirty: a horrible and merciless carnage, in which none demanded quarter, while the Texans, certain of all falling, would not succumb till buried under a pile of hostile corpses. After twenty minutes, that lasted an age, only twelve Texans remained on their legs. The Captain, Tranquil, Quoniam, and nine sailors, remained alone, accomplishing prodigies of valour.

"At last!" the Scalper shouted, as he dashed forward to seize Doña Carmela.

"Not yet," Tranquil said, as he dealt a blow at him with his axe.

The Scalper avoided the blow by leaping on one side, and replied with his machete; Tranquil fell on his knee with a pierced thigh.

"Oh!" he said in despair; "She is lost! My God, lost!"

Carmela understood that no hope was left her; she therefore placed the dagger against her bosom, and said to the Scalper—"One step further, and I fall dead at your feet!"

In spite of himself, this savage man, terrified by the resolution he saw flashing in the maiden's eye, hesitated for a second, but, reassuming almost immediately his old ferocity, he shouted—"What do I care, so long as you belong to no one else!"

And he rushed toward her, uttering a fearful yell. Terrified at the immense danger to which his daughter was exposed, the hunter collected all his strength, and by a superhuman effort, once more stood menacingly before his enemy. The two men exchanged a terrible glance, and rushed on each other.

Carmela, almost dead with terror, lay stretched out between the two foes, forming with her person a barrier they did not dare to pass, but over which they crossed their machetes, whose blades met with an ill-omened clang. Unfortunately, Tranquil, weakened by his wound, could not, despite his indomitable courage, sustain this obstinate contest for any length of time, and consequently he only delayed for a few moments the fearful catastrophe he wished to prevent. He understood this; for, while wielding his machete with far from common dexterity, and not allowing his enemy time to breathe, he looked anxiously around him: Quoniam was fighting like a lion by his side.

"Friend!" he said in a heart-rending voice; "in the name of what you hold the dearest, save her—save Carmela!"

"But yourself?"

"Well," the hunter said nobly, "it is no matter what becomes of me, providing that she escapes this monster, and is happy."

Quoniam hesitated for a moment; a feeling of regret and pain rendered his face gloomy. But at a last glance from the hunter, a glance laden with an expression of despair impossible to describe, he at length decided on obeying him, and lowering his axe, which was dripping with blood, and red up to the wood, he stooped down to the maiden. But she suddenly started up, and bounding like a lioness, shrieked frenziedly—

"Leave me! leave me! He is dying for me, and I will not abandon him."

And she resolutely placed herself by her father's side. At this movement of the girl, for whom they were fighting so desperately, the two men fell back a step, and lowered the points of their machetes; but this truce was but of shout duration, for after a moment of respite, they rushed once more on each other. Then, Texans and Mexicans recommenced the fight with new fury, and the contest went on more terrible than before.

CHAPTER XXV
FORWARD!

In the meanwhile, Master Lovel made his men row vigorously, in order to reach land as soon as possible. But whatever desire he might have for haste, it was impossible for him to reach the shore so soon as he might have wished, for not knowing the coast, and steering, as it were, blindly, his boat ran several times upon submarine reefs, which caused him to lose a considerable amount of time by forcing him to change his course; hence, when he at last reached the shore, the Captain had landed long before.

The old sailor had his boat tied up to the Captain's, in order that they could be used if required, and then leaped ashore, followed by his men, and advanced cautiously inland. He had not proceeded many yards, however, ere a tremendous noise reached his ears, and he saw the sailors who accompanied the Captain debouch from the hollow way in disorder, and closely pursued by Mexican soldiers.

Master Lovel did not lose his heart under these critical circumstances: instead of rushing into the medley, he ambushed his men behind a clump of Peru and mahogany trees that stood a short distance off, and prepared with perfect coolness to make a diversion in favour of his comrades when the favourable moment arrived.

The Texans, with their backs to a rock, not ten yards from the sea, were fighting desperately against an immense number of enemies. A minute later, and all would have been over, but suddenly the cry of "Forward! *Texas y Libertad!*" was raised in the rear of the Mexicans, accompanied by a tremendous noise and a deadly discharge, almost at point-blank range, scattered terror and disorder through their ranks. It was Master Lovel effecting his diversion, in order to save his Captain, or his adopted son, as he called him in his simple devotion.

The Mexicans, who already believed themselves victors, were terrified at this unforeseen attack, which, owing to the vigour with which it was carried out, they supposed to be made by a considerable body of these terrible freebooters, commanded by the Jaguar, whose reputation was already immense in the ranks of the American army. Persuaded that the Texans had landed in force, and had only given way in order to make them fall more surely into the trap, they hesitated, fell back in their turn, and finally being seized with a panic terror which their officers could not succeed in mastering, they broke and fled in all directions, throwing their arms away.

The Texans, revived by the providential arrival of the old sailor, and excited by their Captain's voice, redoubled their efforts. Tranquil tied a handkerchief round his thigh, and supported by Quoniam, who, during the action, had not left him for an instant, he retreated to the boats, leading Carmela, and followed by the Captain and his brave sailors. The latter, like lions at bay, turned at each instant to dash with axes and bayonets at the few soldiers their officers had at length succeeded in rallying, but who did not venture to press too closely the terrible adversaries, whom, since the beginning of the action, they had learned to appreciate and consequently to fear.

Still fighting, the sailors at length reached the boats prepared for their reception. Captain Johnson ordered the wounded to be placed in the launch, and getting into the other boat with Tranquil, Quoniam, and the sound men, he put off from the shore, towing the boat that served as an ambulance. This daring retreat, effected under the enemy's fire, was carried out with admirable precision and skill. One part of the crew of the pinnace fired at the Mexicans who lined the beach, while the other portion pulled vigorously in the direction of the brig.

Ere long the coast disappeared in the fog, the shouts of the enemy became less distinct, the shots ceased, the lights flashing on the shore died out one after the other, and all grew silent again.

"Ah!" the Captain said with a sigh of relief, as he offered his hand to Master Lovel, "without you, father, we were lost."

"Aha!" the old sailor answered with a hearty grin, and rubbing his hands joyously, "I suspected that if you had a secret from me, it was because you meditated some act of folly, so that is why I came after you."

The Captain merely replied to his worthy mate's remark by a fresh squeeze of the hand. Carmela, with her hands clasped and eyes raised above, was praying fervently, while returning thanks to Heaven for her miraculous deliverance.

"This is the girl you have saved," Tranquil said; "it is to you I owe the recovery of my daughter, and I shall not forget it, Captain."

"Nonsense, old hunter," the Captain said, laughingly, "I only kept the promise I made you; did I not pledge myself to help you, even at the risk of my life?"

"And you were uncommonly near losing your stake," Master Lovel observed. "After all, though," he added gallantly, "though I am no connoisseur, I can perfectly understand a man risking his skin to board so neat a corvette."

This sally restored the gaiety of the sailors, which the grave events that had occurred had temporarily dissipated.

"Are we really out of danger, father?" the maiden asked with a shudder of fear, which she was unable to conceal.

"Yes, my child; keep your spirits up," the hunter answered, "we are now in safety."

At this very moment, the sailors, as if wishing to confirm the Canadian's assurance, or perhaps with the wish to mock the enemies they had so barely escaped, struck up one of those cadenced songs which serve to mark time, and the words of which each repeats as he lays out on his oars. Master Lovel, after turning and returning several times the enormous quid that swelled his right cheek, made a signal to the crew of the pinnace, and struck up in a rough voice a stanza, which all repeated in chorus after him. This song, which was as interminable as a sailor's yarn, would, in all probability, have lasted much longer, if the Captain had not suddenly ordered silence by an imperious gesture.

"Is a new danger threatening us?" Tranquil inquired anxiously.

"Perhaps so," the Captain replied, who had for some time been scanning the horizon with a frowning brow.

"What do you mean?" the hunter asked.

"Look!" the Captain said, extending his hand in the direction of the fishing Tillage, to which we before alluded.

Tranquil hastily took up the night glass: a dozen large boats, crowded with soldiers, were leaving a small creek, and pulling out to sea. The water was lumpy, the breeze blew strongly, and the over-crowded long boat advanced but slowly, as it was compelled to tow the pinnace. The peril which they fancied they had escaped, burst out again in a different shape, and this time assumed really terrific proportions, for the Mexicans were rapidly approaching, and would soon be within gunshot.

The brig, whose tall masts were visible, was, it is true, only two cables' length, at the most, from the Texan boats, but the few men left on board were not nearly sufficient to make the requisite manoeuvres to enable the brig to help its boats effectually. The position grew with each moment more critical, and the Captain sprang up.

"Lads," he said, "the ten best swimmers among you will jump into the sea, and go to the ship with me."

"Captain," the hunter exclaimed, "what do you propose doing?"

"To save you," he simply answered, as he prepared to carry out his design.

"Oh, oh," Master Lovel said hastily, "I will not allow such an act of madness."

"Silence, sir," the Captain interrupted him rudely. "I am the sole commander."

"But you are wounded!" the Master objected. In fact, Captain Johnson had received an axe stroke, which laid open his right shoulder.

"Silence! I tell you. I allow no remarks."

The old sailor bowed his head, and wiped away a tear. After squeezing the hunter's hand, the Captain and his ten sailors leaped boldly into the sea, and disappeared in the darkness. At the news of fresh danger, Carmela had fallen, completely overwhelmed, in the bottom of the boat. Master Lovel, leaning out, tried to discover his chief. Heavy tears coursed down his bronzed cheeks, and all his limbs were agitated by a convulsive quivering. The Mexicans approached nearer and nearer; they were already close enough for the number of their boats to be distinguished, and a schooner was already leaving the creek, and coming up under press canvas, to ensure the success of the attack.

At this moment a mournful cry, desperate as the last shriek of a dying man, came over the waters, and terrified all the men whom no danger could affect.

"Oh, the unhappy man!" Tranquil cried, as he rose and made a move to leap overboard. But Lovel seized him by the waist belt, and in spite of his resistance, compelled him to sit down again.

"What are you about?" he asked him.

"Well," Tranquil replied, "I want to pay my debt to your captain; he risked his life for me, and I am going in return to risk mine to save him."

"Good!" the Master exclaimed, "By heaven! You are a man. But keep quiet, that doesn't concern you; it is my business."

And ere Tranquil had time to answer him, he plunged into the waves. The Captain had presumed too much on his strength, he was hardly in the water ere his wound caused him intolerable suffering, and his arm was paralyzed. With that tenacity which formed the basis of his character, he tried to contend against the pain, and overcome it, but nature had proved more powerful than his will and energy, a dizziness had come over his sight, and he felt himself slowly sinking. At this moment he uttered that parting cry for help to which Lovel had responded by flying to his aid. Ten minutes passed, minutes of agony, during which the persons who remained in the boat scarce dared to breathe.

"Courage, my lads," the panting voice of Lovel was suddenly heard saying, "he is saved!"

The sailors burst into a shout of joy, and laying on their oars, redoubled their efforts. A frightful discharge answered them, and the balls flattened against the sides of the pinnace and dashed up the water around. The Mexicans, who had come within range, opened a terrible fire on the Texans, but the latter did not reply.

A dull noise was heard, followed by cries of despair and imprecations, and a black mass passed to windward of the long boat. It was the brig coming to the assistance of its crew, and in passing it sunk and dispersed the enemy's boats.

When she set foot on the deck of the brig, Carmela, at length succumbing to her emotions, lost her senses. Tranquil raised her in his arms, and, aided by Quoniam and the Captain, carried her hastily down to the cabin.

"Captain," a sailor shouted, as he rushed after him, "the Mexicans, the Mexicans!"

While the Texans were engaged in taking their wounded aboard, feeling convinced that the Mexican boats had been all, or at any rate the majority of them, sunk by the brig, they had not dreamed of watching an enemy they supposed crushed. The latter had cleverly profited by this negligence to rally, and collecting beneath the bows of the brig, had boldly boarded her, by climbing up the main chains, the spritsails, and any ropes' ends they had been able to seize. Fortunately, Master Lovel had the boarding nettings triced up on the previous evening, and through this wise precaution on the part of the old sailor, the desperate surprise of the Mexicans did not meet with the success they anticipated from it.

The Texans, obeying the voice of their Captain, took up their weapons again and rushed on the Mexicans, who were already all but masters of the forepart of the ship. Tranquil, Quoniam, Captain Johnson, and Lovel, armed with axes, had flown to the front rank, and by their example excited the crew to do their duty properly. There, on a limited space of ten square yards at the most, one of those fearful naval combats without order or tactics began, in which rage and brutal strength represent science. A horrible struggle, a fearful carnage, with pikes, axes, and cutlasses; a struggle in which each wound is mortal, and which recalls those hideous combats of the worst days of the middle ages, when brute strength alone was the law.

The White Scalper had never before fought with such obstinacy. Furious at the loss of the prey he had so audaciously carried off, half mad with rage, he seemed to multiply himself, rushing incessantly with savage yells into the densest part of the fight, seeking Carmela, and longing to kill the man who had so bravely torn her from him. Accident seemed for a moment to smile on him, by bringing him suddenly face to face with the Captain.

"Now for my turn," he exclaimed with a ferocious shout of joy.

The Captain wised his axe.

"No, no!" said Tranquil, as he threw himself hurriedly before him; "this victim is reserved for me; I must kill this human-faced tiger. Besides," he added, with a grin, "it is my profession to kill wild beasts, and this one will not escape me."

"Ah," the White Scalper said, "it is really fatality which brings you once more face to face with me. Well, be it so! I will settle with you first."

"It is you who will die, villain!" the Canadian replied. "Ah, you carried off my daughter and fancied yourself well concealed, did you? But I was on your trail; for the last three months I have been following you step by step, and watching for the favourable moment for vengeance."

On hearing these words the Scalper rushed furiously on his enemy. The latter did not make a movement to avoid him; on the contrary, he seized him in his powerful arms, and tried to throw him down, while stabbing him in the loins with his dagger. These two men, with flashing eyes and foaming lips, animated by an implacable hatred, intertwined breast to breast, face to face, each trying to kill his adversary, caring little to live provided that his enemy died, resembled two wild beasts determined to destroy each other.

Texans and Mexicans had ceased fighting as if by common accord, and remained horrified spectators of this atrocious combat. At length the Canadian, who had been severely wounded before, fell, dragging his enemy down with him. The latter uttered a yell of triumph, which was soon converted into a groan of despair: Quoniam rushed madly upon him, but, unfortunately, he had miscalculated his distance, and they both fell into the sea, which closed over them with a hollow and ill-omened sound.

The Mexicans, deprived of their Chief, now only thought of flight, and rushed in mad disorder to their boats; a moment later, they had all quitted the brig. Quoniam reappeared, the worthy Negro was dripping with water. He tottered a few paces and fell by the side of Tranquil, to whom Carmela and the Captain were paying the most assiduous attention, and who was beginning to recover his senses. A few minutes later the hunter felt strong enough to try and rise.

"Well!" he asked Quoniam, "Is he dead?"

"I believe so," the Negro replied; "look here," he added, as he offered him a small object he held in his hand.

"What is it?" the hunter asked.

Quoniam shook his head mournfully. "Look at it," he said.

After having attentively regarded the Negro for an instant, whose features expressed singular despondency, strange in a man of this stamp, he asked him in alarm:—

"Are you seriously wounded?"

The Negro shook his head.

"No," he said, "I am not wounded."

"What is the matter, then?"

"Take this," he said, stretching his arm out a second time, "take this and you will know."

Astonished at this singular persistence, Tranquil stretched out his arm, too.

"Give it here," he said.

Quoniam handed him an article which he seemed anxious to conceal from the persons present; the Canadian uttered a cry of surprise on seeing it.

"Where did you find this?" he asked anxiously.

"When I rushed on that man, I know not how it was, but this chain and the articles attached to it were placed, as it were, in my hand. When I fell into the sea, I clung to the chain; there it is, do what you please with it."

Tranquil, after again examining the mysterious object, concealed it in his chest, and gave vent to a profound sigh. All at once, Carmela started up in horror.

"Oh, look, look, father!" she shrieked, "Woe, woe, we are lost!"

The hunter started at the sound of the girl's voice, and his eyes filled with tears.

"What is the matter?" he asked in a weak voice

"The matter is," the Captain said rudely, "that unless a miracle take place, we are really lost this time, as Doña Carmela says."

And he pointed to some thirty armed boats, which were pulling up and converging round the brig, so as to enclose it in a circle, whence it would be impossible for it to escape.

"Oh! Fate is against us!" Carmela exclaimed in despair.

"No, it is impossible," Tranquil said quickly; "God will not abandon us thus!"

"We are saved!" Master Lovel shouted; "we are saved! Look, look! The boats are turning back!"

The crew burst into a shout of joy and triumph; in the beams of the rising sun, the *Libertad* corvette could be seen passing through Galveston straits, hardly two cannon shots' distance from the brig. The Mexican boats pulled at full speed in the direction of land, and soon all had disappeared. The brig drifted down to the corvette, and both returned to their old anchorage, which they reached an hour later.

The two ships had scarce let their anchor fall, ere a boat came alongside the brig, from the fort, containing; the Jaguar and El Alferez. The prisoners had been handed over to the Jaguar, who, while ordering them to be closely watched, thought it advisable to let them move freely about the fortress.

The success of the two hazardous expeditions attempted by the Texans, had given the cause they defended a great impulse. In a few hours the revolt had become a revolution, and the insurgent Chiefs men whose existence must henceforth be recognised. The Jaguar desired to push matters on actively, and wished to profit by the probable discouragement of the Mexicans to secure the surrender of the town without a blow, if it were possible.

In his conversation with Colonel Melendez, the young Chief had purposely startled him with the news of the success of the two expeditions, calculating for the success of future operations on the stupor General Rubio would experience on being told of them. But ere undertaking anything, the Jaguar desired a conference with his friends, in order to settle definitively the way in which he must behave under such serious circumstances, as he was not at all anxious to assume the responsibility of the undertaking that might be formed. This was acting not only with prudence, but also with perfect self-denial, especially after the way in which he had behaved since the commencement of hostilities, and the high position he had attained among his party.

But as the heart of even the purest and most honourable man is never exempt from those weaknesses inherent in human nature, the Jaguar, though perhaps not daring to avow it to himself had another motive that urged him to go aboard the brig so speedily. This motive, of a thoroughly private nature, was the desire to learn as soon as possible the result of the expedition attempted by Captain Johnson and Tranquil against the rancho of the White Scalper.

Hence, the young man had scarce reached the deck, ere, without returning the salutes of his friends who hurried to greet him at the ladder, he enquired after Tranquil, feeling justly surprised at not seeing him among the persons assembled. The Captain gave him no other answer than a sign to follow. The young man, not understanding this reserve, though feeling seriously alarmed, went below, where he saw Tranquil reclining in a berth, and a weeping female seated on a chair by his side. The Jaguar turned pale, for in the female he recognized Doña Carmela; his emotion was so extreme, that he was obliged to lean against the partition lest he should fall. At the sound of his approaching footsteps, the maiden raised her head.

"Oh!" she exclaimed, clasping her hands with joy, "It is you! You have come at last then!"

"Thanks, Carmela," he replied in a gasping voice; "thanks for this kindly greeting! It proves to me that you have not forgotten me."

"Forget you, to whom, next to my father, I owe everything! Oh, you know that was impossible."

"Thank you once again. You do not, you cannot know how happy you render me at this moment, Carmela. My whole life, employed in your service, would not suffice to repay the good you do me. You are free at last! Brave Tranquil, I felt sure that he would succeed!"

"Alas, my friend, this success costs him dear."

"What do you mean? I trust that he is not dangerously wounded?"

"I fear the contrary, my friend."

"Oh! We will save him."

"Come hither, Jaguar," the hunter then said in a feeble voice; "give me your hand, that I may press it in mine."

The young man walked quickly up to him.

"Oh, with all my heart!" he said, as he held out his hand.

"The affair was a tough one, my friend," the Canadian went on; "that man is a lion."

"Yes, yes, he is a rude adversary; but you got the better of him at last?"

"Thanks to Heaven, yes; but I shall keep his mark all my life, if God permit me to rise again."

"Canarios! I trust that will soon happen."

The hunter shook his head.

"No, no," he answered, "I am a connoisseur in wounds, through having inflicted a good many, and received more than my proper share: these are serious."

"Have you no hopes of recovery, then?"

"I do not say so, I merely repeat that many days will pass ere I can return to the desert," the hunter replied, with a stifled sigh.

"Nonsense, who knows? Any wound that does not kill is soon cured, the Indians say, and they are right. And what has become of that man?"

"In all probability he is dead," Tranquil said, in a hollow voice.

"That is all for the best."

At this moment Captain Johnson opened the door.

"A boat, bearing a flag of truce, is hailing the brig; what is to be done?" he asked.

"Receive it, Sangre de Dios! my dear Johnson. This boat, if I am not mistaken, is a bearer of good news."

"Our friends would like you to be present to hear the proposals which will doubtless be made."

"What do you say, Tranquil?" the young Chief asked, turning to the old hunter.

"Go, my boy, where duty calls you," the latter answered; "I feel that I need repose. However, you will not be away long."

"Certainly not, and so soon as I am at liberty again I will return to your side, but merely to have you carried ashore; your condition demands attention you cannot obtain here."

"I accept, my friend, the more so as I believe the land air will do me good."

"That is settled then," the Jaguar said, joyously; "I shall be back soon."

"All right," Tranquil replied, and fell back in his berth.

The young man, after bowing to Carmela, who returned the salute with a gentle and sad glance, left the cabin with the Captain and returned on deck.

[In our next volume, "THE WHITE SCALPER," we shall again come across all the characters of this long history, for the great stake is about to be played for: liberty and tyranny are at length face to face, and the destiny of a people will probably depend on the fate of a battle.]